Clive Ashman is an artist, writer, motor mechanic and qualified lawyer working in the Lake District.

'Mosaic' is his first complete book to be published. It is a work of fiction but based on research carried out in Yorkshire into real life events; some of it told to him by eye-witnesses, some found in the archives or museums, and the rest imagined on the basis of known archaeological and historical circumstances of the times.

'MOSAIC'

the novel

CLIVE ASHMAN

VOREDA BOOKS

VOREDA BOOKS
Sales address:
BCM Voreda Books, London WC1N 3XX
voredabooks@hotmail.co.uk

First published by Voreda Books 2008

A CIP Record for this book is available from the British Cataloguing in Publication Data Office

ISBN 978-0-9556398-0-7

Printed in Great Britain by Anthony Rowe Ltd, Chippenham, Wiltshire

Cover title illustration; 'MOSAIC' (The author)
Rear cover illustration and at p.420: Fragment of a dedication stone, Malton Museum, North Yorkshire (The author)

Front & rear cover design:
Julie Husband (Beverley) and David Bell,
Adkins Design (Market Weighton, E.Yorks). www.adkinsdesign.co.uk

FOR CHARLOTTE

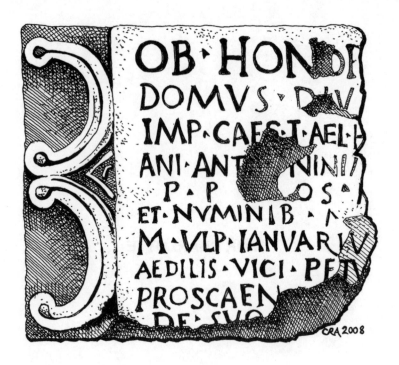

"DEDICATED TO THE HONOUR OF THE DIVINE HOUSEHOLD OF THE IMPERIAL CAESAR TITUS AELIUS HADRIANUS ANTONINUS AUGUSTUS PIUS: FATHER OF HIS COUNTRY, THREE TIMES CONSUL; AND TO THE DEITIES: MARCUS ULPIUS JANUARIUS, MAGISTRATE TO THE CIVIC SETTLEMENT AT PETUARIA, GAVE THIS PROSCAENIUM STAGE AT HIS OWN EXPENSE...."

Partial dedication stone dated to circa 140 A.D. found at Brough-on-Humber and now on display in the Hull & East Riding Museums, Kingston upon Hull
(Illustration, the author)

'MOSAIC': the map

KEY:

——	: Roman road	✈	: R.A.F. airfield
🏰	: Roman garrison	⊷⊦⊦⊦•⊸	: Railway line
Δ	: Roman villa	◍	: Modern town
DERVENTIO	: Roman place name	Malton	: Modern place name
PARISI	: Celtic tribal area	⚜	: Roman signal station

"He lives twice who also loves the past."

(Marcus Valerius Martial, Roman poet, c.40 -104 A.D)

I

There was a fear he had.

A private terror kept suppressed but so often coming along anyway – ever faithful but always unfriendly. The unwelcome guest at each and every attendance which his duties required of him; at the places and remains of those who'd died in dubious or mysterious circumstance. The people who kept him in work.

The taboos of modern life so often impose their natural aversion against the transactions of death. In his case at least, here was one taboo he could quite easily overcome, if only through so much exposure and weary familiarity. In that sense you could say it was something that almost ceased to trouble him. Except that there remained one fear so strong, a thought so much more compelling than all the rest, the one peculiar to him that came by night and never could be shed:

He was terrified on these occasions of finding a woman that resembled or evoked his wife.

An irrational fear, he would acknowledge. Morbid? Yes - of course. Unlikely and hard to justify? That's different - each time, he never knew. Whatever the chances, just the thought was powerful enough to dog his working hours and spoil his little leisure with its nagging dread. So when he got the call again, that characteristically brusque 'phone message from Superintendent Maister he'd collected at Inglemire Police Box, ordering his return as duty Inspector to the Central Police Station in Hull; in his mind's eye he could see it again – the unspoken horror that rose to occupy an empty back seat in the black Wolseley sent out by Maister for his deliverance.

The allocated driver of this dark and glossy motor car was, as ever, the dignified Sergeant Pickering. In his way as indispensable to the mournful ceremonials of joint investigation as his superior's morbid and inexpressible phobia.

Between them, this made up a team of three. He; then Pickering; and finally perhaps this imaginary figure to represent his fears - stalking them both like that extra companion which polar explorers on the edge of survival will consistently report as definite presence. Together they, and they alone, comprised that permanent and elite cadre - the Murder Squad of the Kingston-upon-Hull City Police.

Good men both, undoubtedly, but such grim work! (Angels of death?)

A violent town perhaps, but not a murderous city. Oh, no, not really. It was probably no more than two or three times this year that Maister had issued his summons and sent Sergeant Pickering over to collect him. But whenever and wherever the call went out, Detective Inspector Michael Tryton of the Criminal Investigation Department would obey at once. He knew its significance well enough and straightaway deferred to its urgency.

So they'd come tearing down Beverley Road together; Pickering serene and imperturbable at the wheel, carving a ruthless path through flocks of cyclists and overtaking trolley buses with that unlikely mix of consideration and outright speed which only a police-trained driver can manage.

In a town criss-crossed by railway lines, their level-crossings raised a conspiracy of obstruction to provoke the patient motorist - but this time they were lucky and found the majority unbarred.

The Central Police Station in Alfred Gelder Street was an Edwardian design fallen on hard times, its scabrous skin of rotting mortar and flaking paint ineffectively bandaged by flapping layers of expired public notices. Plans for its replacement by a bright modern building on a bomb site the other side of Queens Gardens were already drawn, so nobody gave a thought for the old place - its dignity draining away beneath slow cuts of neglect.

Tryton sprinted up its front steps under the blue lamp, his raincoat flapping open. He was still young and energetic enough to treat any staircase as challenge to a run, but beneath these remnants of exuberance lay a fatalistic feeling that once he stopped then middle-age would pounce.

In a large room facing out onto Alfred Gelder Street, Superintendent Maister of the Hull City C.I.D. sat four-square at a broad mahogany desk, hiding vainly from an advancing and for him quite purposeless retirement. The story was this monolithic slab of furniture was salvage from the bombed-out offices of a bankrupt shipping line, whose doomed vessels' fatal attraction to iceberg or U-Boat made the Luftwaffe's destruction of their commercial headquarters into merciful coup de grace.

There were common characteristics shared by all of these phenomena: iceberg low in the water; submarine hull-down with conning tower exposed; and Superintendent Maister cunningly dug-in behind his desk. Each of them the epitome of dangerous mass, partially-concealed. Qualities of structure, sensitivity, and humanity were equally shared between all these cold destroyers. All required respect on first meeting, and Superintendent Maister was no exception.

Tryton had removed his trilby hat before entering and now saluted. Since the war, Maister had become the only person he ever had to salute, regularly.

"Ah, there you are ....", his superior observed, as if he had been looking in his desk drawers for him all morning. Affecting the innocuous vagueness of some kindly grandfather was occasional pretence for Maister, his entertainment, but any rooky constable relaxing his guard upon its promise would soon hear a different roar.

There was a message for me at Inglemire, sir. I came at once."

"Good, good. Cigarette?"

Tryton declined. (He'd stopped smoking soon after the war). Maister took out a briar pipe from an inside pocket of his Norfolk jacket. He tapped it hard on the sole of one shoe and looked fiercely up at Tryton, who was still standing.

"Sit down then, Tryton, sit down. There's a chair behind you."

"Thank you, sir."

"Much on at the moment, eh, Tryton?" said Maister, smiling now and seemingly avuncular. The Superintendent took a tin of 'Old Holborn' out of his desk drawer and rammed a wad of tobacco into his pipe. The pipe was part of this kindly persona – all a trap, of course, but the time he took to light it gave Tryton time to consider what would be his safest response. The windows were shut and the Superintendent's stifling office began to fill with clouds of pipe smoke, so they both ended-up smoking anyway.

"Just the usual sort of thing."

Even as the answer was made, Tryton asked - why was he such a fool to himself?

Yet enough of the father-confessor hung around in Maister's lined and crumpled face to lure even those who well knew his crabbed and treacherous nature still to fall willingly into that simple trap. No wonder Maister's fame as a detective rested on his legendary ability to extract complete admissions from even the hardest case. But knowing all that, why shouldn't Tryton still admit to the kindly old duffer this one simple truth? That he was overrun with work and hard put to do a decent job of anything for want of time and help:

Like the case of the privation-crazed Polish jeweller reporting his squalid flat as burgled last weekend. Someone who could claim enough uncut stones - from those he claimed to have smuggled out of his country in 1939 - had gone missing as could pay off our National Debt - or what we owed the Americans.

The tedious nights spent watching a 'secure' compound at the docks where a tank of rationed fuel was being slowly drained over several weeks by a couple of well-known 'likely lads'.

The exhausting morning he'd just spent organising a search for a little girl gone missing near the drain bank at the back of Silverdale Road. Trying to sound reassuring to her desperate parents when his own head was still ringing with stock words of sad warning reserved by His Majesty's Coroner for the subject of unsupervised children playing on drain banks near deep water.

The armed raid planned for this afternoon on a derelict house off Hessle Road, where two deserters from Catterick Garrison were believed to be holed-up, complete with service rifles and the ammunition they'd thoughtfully-retained from military duty towards joining the rougher end of the Black Market. A worrying operation for Tryton who, with the end of the war, thought he'd never need be exposed to gunfire again.

No, there was no point in reciting this litany of routine. Maister would not be interested to listen and there was no desire to give him the malicious satisfaction any admission might allow. Everyone knew the Hull City Force were overworked and undermanned. That was why they were still recruiting ex-servicemen like him.

"Good, good. All fairly straightforward, run-of-the-mill jobs you can pass over to Inspector Witham for a while?"

"Well yes, I suppose I can, sir, yes. But what is it you want me to take on instead?"

4

"A suspicious death. A murder that may not be a murder, if you get my drift. I presume Pickering has told you the gist of it?"

"No, he's not, sir. Sergeant Pickering is not much given to unnecessary small-talk. Or confidences, either. But I've learnt from you that whenever Pickering appears as messenger then a death is announced. What's the deal on this one?"

"The deal is, Inspector, that I am placing considerable personal faith in you. I have to say that it goes against my own better instincts, Tryton, instincts I've long learnt to trust. I'm an old-fashioned copper but I know the world is changing. All the values which I took in with my mother's milk are being abandoned, one by one. No-one could learn policing in a year but the powers-that-be consider a whizz-kid like you to be the best thing since electric light."

"You don't like me, do you, sir?"

"It doesn't matter one jot who or what I like, Inspector! I'm just an old dog too tired for new tricks. You'll find me blunt in my speech. I'll say what I think even if some might think my bark's worse than my bite. As for you, Tryton, you're a Grammar School boy who's never walked the Hull beat alone or brought in six fighting-mad drunken dockers from the Old Town with only a truncheon, the authority of your uniform, and the gift of the gab as protection. But you had a 'Good War' and someone on the next floor likes you. So I've taken the hint and put my own department on the line by giving you Sergeant Pickering and a few murders."

"I haven't let you down, have I?"

"Not so far, no you certainly haven't, I'll admit that. But let me down on this one, this one above all others, and you'll be out on the streets with a torch and a rain cape, checking shop door handles down Whitefriargate for the rest of your career!"

"What's the job?"

"It's right up your street, Tryton. You're a military man, aren't you?"

"Not really, sir. Royal Air Force."

"Alright then. R.A.F. But part of our ex-service intake. A man like you.... just what we need for this enquiry. An officer and a gentleman..."

"I was a Sergeant Pilot nearly all my service. The people running our Armed Forces don't seem to like giving commissions to Grammar School boys."

By the set of Maister's jaw this appeared to be an outlook he would probably condone. Tryton wondered what he had done wrong in life to find himself at the beck and call of such a disagreeable overseer. Hadn't he had enough of such commanders under the discipline of wartime service?

"How long have you been with us, Tryton?"

"Two years, sir."

"Joined in nineteen forty-six?"

Tryton had to think for a moment. Yes, is that all it was?

At the end of the war, in May 1945, he'd found himself in Austria, high in an Alpine meadow scattered with edelweiss and abandoned Nazi jet fighters; Messerschmitt 262's - useless technology.

Suddenly he was converted overnight from valued combat pilot to redundant commodity. As his Squadron Leader of the time told him: "The R.A.F. has aircrew to cobble dogs..." It was a case of leaving the airforce on the spot, demobilised, demoralised and out on the streets in a cheap suit with no money and no prospects, or else doing something different for them. He'd opted to stay and so they'd put him in the Provost's Department, their equivalent of the military police. From that day to this he'd never flown an aircraft again and, in a curious sort of way, he was surprised to find he didn't really care, as if it was a chapter in his life which was now closed.

Tryton spent a rootless year in his new role, moving around various airbases in England and Wales, all of them winding down their facilities and activity. A year of locking-up drunken airmen, chasing stolen aviation fuel, and investigating kitchen stabbings in married quarters. A joyless, monochrome, exhausted country where thousands of men like him, demented by war, struggled to find a place to belong in a worn-out world they no longer understood.

Then, in the back of some Forces' news sheet, he'd seen the advertisement for ex-servicemen to join the Hull City Police at equivalent grade.

6

Unattractive backwater to many, for him it revived powerful sentiments. He'd been based outside Hull until 1941, at R.A.F. Leconfield where he was seconded to 485 (New Zealand) Squadron, flying Spitfires. Aside from familiarity with the area and dissatisfaction with the post-war airforce, there was another compelling reason to return...

"It hasn't taken long for us to make you an Inspector, has it Tryton?" said Maister, interrupting his reverie.

"I thought I'd be a sergeant all my life."

"That's an expectation we can still fulfill if you make a mess of this one! It's sensitive. I don't want people upsetting. You'll be treading on the toes of the military. 'Co-terminous jurisdiction' as the Chief calls it."

"Co-what, sir?"

"Military property. A death on the premises. One of their personnel in questionable circumstances. An unlawful killing; either manslaughter or even a murder, according to the initial report telegraphed to us. A squaddie on site is already implicated apparently, but there may be a contrary suggestion worth following up."

"Can't the Army investigate it for themselves, through the Military Police?"

"Up to a point, yes they can. But the fact is, we've been called in to 'assist'. More particularly, to act directly on behalf of H.M.Coroner in the investigation of a suspicious death for the purpose of Inquest. "Primacy of the civil power" as the Chief puts it. They don't want us in there, Tryton, but by golly they're obliged to have us! Very tricky. Very delicate. Just the job for you in fact – a young fella' with a career to make. So don't dare let me down, Tryton!"

"Where exactly is this military depot we're talking about?"

"What? Haven't I said? This is no depot, Tryton, it's a front-line posting. It's Bull Sand Fort, Tryton, Bull Sand Fort!"

"Right, sir! And where exactly is that?"

"Men generally are ungrateful, fickle, false and with you only as long as you succeed. When trouble approaches, they will turn against you."

(Nicholo Machiavelli, 1467 – 1527, Renaissance diplomat and political theorist)

II

It was the same black Wolseley which now took him through the city to Minerva Pier, where he and his sergeant boarded the Humber Ferry.

The "Tattershall Castle" was a traditional paddle-steamer, white-painted superstructure and varnished wood below decks but tatty and neglected when viewed in detail. Like so many things in life, it had not fully recovered from the war and the prospects for its restoration were bleak. The ferry nosed slowly out into the murky, grey waters of the Humber estuary, the distant Lincolnshire bank obscured today by low-lying mist. The ship embraced the great river as a veil for its shabbiness.

This estuary was wide and treacherous enough to offer all the traditional inventory of maritime hazards expected from the open sea. To this selection of perils its own local talent for constantly-shifting sand bars could often add an extra, fatal twist.

He was convinced that today's weather was even rougher than the usual offering. The ferry was all over the place and thoughtful, pale people retreated below - including his sergeant. The blunt bow of the steamer ploughed heavily into walls of water which streamed as spray across the broad observation bridge of the ferry. Looking at his watch, he found his assessment of sailing conditions supported when he realised the scheduled crossing time had already elapsed. A strong westerly wrestled against a rising tide and their vessel was caught in wild whirlpools of elemental combat, of winds colliding with water. As a result, it took well over two hours to reach the far bank.

On the other side, at New Holland, they moored beside a projecting jetty. Here, apparently one hundred yards out to sea, a rickety rail terminus shared space on the jetty, supported by the same spindly wooden pillars high above the waves. From its breezy platform they en-trained in old-fashioned 'clerestory-windowed' carriages. Despite their obvious age, these pre-war relics had been re-sprayed in the institutional maroon of the new but already-resented "British Railways", as if a coat of paint was all a worn-out network needed to bestow modernity and efficiency.

He allowed himself a moment's grieving for the former pre-nationalisation "London and North Eastern Railway" with its apple-green livery piped in yellow and black. The tinplate models of his childish teenage enthusiasms: "Sir Nigel Gresley" and "The Flying Scotsman". Basset Lowke and Hornby Dublo: a Golden Age of Innocence.

Tryton's mind returned to murder.

Sergeant Pickering: his driver, general factotum and designated assistant on this particular enquiry, was only now clearing his complexion of the yellow cadaverous hue brought on by the ferry crossing. A man of stolid land-bound virtues from a maritime city, already expressing concern that this ordeal by water was shortly to be resumed. He was not wrong. To that end, a black tank-engine spewing smoke pulled them to Grimsby in this almost empty train of soot-filled carriages.

Seated opposite, Pickering found yesterday's paper abandoned on an adjoining table and, with arms fully-extended, became hidden inside its wide pages. Victim of the fascination which other people's newspapers always hold, particularly on trains, his inspector scanned the front and back from a distance. If, on the world stage, 1948 was looking like an interesting year (what with Partition in India and creation of the state of Israel in Palestine) Tryton still found the front cover's reporting of Clement Attlee or Stafford Cripps's political puritanism on the home front just too dull for words. Reverting to reports on the back of Len Hutton's efforts in the Test Match against the Australians 'Down Under' offered much greater reader satisfaction.

The prospect of the London Olympics, first since the war, promised other cheering dispatches fit to balance dispiriting accounts of the Berlin Airlift on the front, as RAF aircraft flew 'round the clock' bringing supplies to raise the blockade made by the Russian Army against the western half of that desperate city. Depressed by Bad News from Abroad, Tryton's attention as promptly returned to studying the cricket on the back. (The classic Englishman's response to adversity).

"Would you like the paper, sir?" his sergeant enquired, unctuously. (There is nothing more irritating than holding a newspaper aloft for the benefit of someone else to read. Even if it happens to be a free newspaper).

"No, it's alright, Pickering."

He sighed and leaned back heavily in his seat to look around the compartment. A mesh luggage rack. Two broken light fittings. A pre-war photograph of Edinburgh Castle in sepia with chrome frame (glass missing). A reading lamp without a bulb. Bored, he turned and looked out of the window. The flat fields of Lincolnshire were giving way to the sprawling unsightly edges of Great Grimsby.

Bored again, he allowed himself another secret look at the front page of Pickering's paper - the 'Hull Daily Mail'. Apart from politics, local crime reports occupied a considerable portion of its densely-printed cover, reflecting the enduringly-prurient fascination of the British public with such matters. Daily doings in the Stipendiary Magistrate's Court in Hull. Even one or two cases he'd had some part in himself.

Tryton realised with surprise that the darkly-smudged photograph in the centre of the page was of two men beaming down fondly at a couple of skeletons in a trench. For a moment, as he looked at it, he thought someone must surely pull the communication cord and stop the train. A note from Superintendent Maister, summoning his new-made Murder Squad back to Hull, would be stuffed into his hand.

Happily, reading the copy with a little more care reassured him about that possibility: a local gardener at Brough-on-Humber had bounced the blade of his ex-Pioneer Corps shovel off the cranium of one of these characters while trying to turn over his vegetable patch. Assisted in more careful soil removal by Mr. Peter Slack, a keen local amateur archaeologist, both skeletons were revealed.

One bore some sort of silvered and embossed semi-circular armour on his upper arm, reported Mr. Slack, which prompted the newspaper copywriter to dub them both 'warriors' in his byline:

"In view of the fort at Brough and the finds recently made in this area, these are undoubtedly Roman", announced Mr.Slack.

"Roman, Roman? How does he know they're Roman?" demanded Tryton generally of the world around him, as they clambered out of the empty train and onto the deserted station platform at Grimsby: "If it was me, I'd have a pathologist and Scenes of Crime down there faster than you could say 'Unlawful Killing'!"

11

Having only read the sports pages, the 'small ads' and the shipping forecast, Pickering looked up at his superior with troubled incomprehension. He did not reply.

Brought from the station to Grimsby Docks by taxi, the last stage of their journey awaited them. Incongruous amongst the brightly-coloured 'side-winders' and stern trawlers were the dour grey and pugnacious lines of His Majesty's Motor Torpedo Boat "Interceptor".

"Hey, this is a bit of a lark! Eh, Pickering?"

It is awkward for a middle-aged man to have his junior in years senior over him in authority. It can sometimes lead to resentment but, to his credit, not so with Sergeant Pickering. That is not to say there were not times, as here, when he allowed himself some sign of irritation at the undergraduate enthusiasms of his new Inspector. Needless to say, it turned out to be no rational land-loving person's idea of a lark at all. While the M.T.B. "Interceptor" was certainly a fast patrol boat, its slab-like hull gave a truly sickening ride, crashing from one wave crest to the next with nauseating and random unpredictability.

They both reclined on deck in a canvas spray-shelter set behind the bridge and between the torpedo tubes, watching the boiling white water of their wake leaving a great, curving parabola across the estuary. If the grey of the broad river matched the grey paint of the boat's hull and superstructure, then the whipping and cracking White Ensign of the Royal Navy on the stern was as blanched as that foam. If the ferry crossing was rough, this one was worse. If its only virtue was that it was quick, there was still time for Pickering to be sick - twice.

There was a piratical tradition amongst the small gunboats and fast patrol vessels of the Royal Navy which went with their wartime role. Service dress was eccentric, tactics unconventional, beards irregular, signalling insolent, and more-minor naval regulations generally disregarded to the hilt. The flying of the Jolly Roger from the R/T mast could be considered commonest and most definitive of these conventional affectations, His Majesty's Motor Torpedo Boat "Interceptor" providing stereotypical example of this impudent breed in every respect.

Hardly surprising then that such a crew should view these two seasick 'coppers' cowering at the back of their vessel with a cold amusement; huddled where they could not see their approaching destination.

Out of the spray and mist, Bull Sand Fort was emerging like an iceberg of steel and concrete. Close up, it seemed immense.

Completed too late for the First War in 1919, but at enormous cost, and built upon extensive sand banks at the mouth of the Humber Estuary, its role during the Last War had been to prevent enemy shipping or submarines entering the river from the North Sea. It also had a significant anti-aircraft capability, but all these duties ceased on 6th January 1945. The two six-inch guns and the twin six-pounders which had been its wartime armament were, like the rest of the fort, now placed under a 'care and maintenance' regime. Responsibility for that in peacetime rested with soldiers of the newly-formed 422nd (East Riding) Coast Regiment, Royal Artillery.

One of their Maintenance Batteries (comprising a bombardier and up to a dozen gunners) was serving on the fort now and it was the fate of a member of the party, towards the end of a six-month tour, which was the reason for this queasy visit by two officers of the civil police.

Dragging themselves out of the torpedo boat and up the treacherous vertical ladders on the side of the fort's landing-stage was a desperate and frightening business. Adopting an upright posture in an effort to recover such dignity as attached to whatever authority they thought they had was the challenge that awaited them at the top of the jetty.

The wind which had tumbled their vessels of crossing now bullied them as pedestrians. A group of khaki-clad figures waited for them by the shelter of the fort, huddled under the searchlight sponsons. Any warmth in their greeting would clearly not extend to offering them a hand along the slimy planks of the jetty. This risky traverse they must make alone - towards receiving merely nominal encouragements at the finish:

"This way, Inspector ......that's right, up here! Good - welcome to Bull Sand Fort! Let's begin with some introductions - I am Captain Roskill, Military Police, and can I present you to Colonel Sir Martin Baynard of the Coast Artillery.."

His immediate assessment of Roskill was of a man he could deal with on equal terms. The limp handshake of Colonel Baynard straightaway belied his rank, an impression in no way bolstered when he spoke:

"Yes, Inspector, the Regiment is grateful to you for coming to our assistance at such short notice. Your colleague, Superintendent Maister, assured us that you were the men for the job."

Surprised at favourable references from such an unexpected quarter, he identified his own response as equally-feeble even whilst he made it:

"Well, my sergeant and I are very happy to offer whatever help we can to His Majesty's Army." (Carefully inching his way along a greasy gangway, Tryton instinctively realised that now was no time to mention Maister's "primacy of the civil power" idea).

At least these stilted pleasantries were adequate to get them off the jetty, out of the wind and into the relative comfort of the fort. This was a two-storey circular structure built out of steel plates and their cavities filled with concrete. Deposited on a sand bar in the middle of the Humber, its overall appearance reminiscent of some antique and portly Iron-clad, permanently run aground.

(Whilst Tryton had lapsed in recollection of its name, now he was here he could remember over-flying the fort many times in the early part of the war). They were taken to the Officers Mess on the first floor. Their overcoats were hung up to dry and they were offered tea. Even allowing for the steel chill of the fort, the hospitality was lukewarm.

"The pathologist won't be here for a couple of hours yet. We have left everything as found in the kitchen, with Captain Roskill's men guarding it. Are you ready to inspect the scene?"

Colonel Baynard was a mere reservist and no more familiar with death, one could assume, than any sheltered civilian. To a Regular or to these two policemen its prospect was sufficiently routine not to require the mental girding-up he obviously envisaged.

"Why not? Let's go!"

They crossed the fort by the central landing, beside the ammunition lift and the meat store.

Gunner Wykeham sat in a chair at a kitchen table, like a man taken by sleep at supper. His pallor confirmed this sleeper at least would never wake, not until the Last Trump. A steel knife was still held upright in an iron grip and his obviously-swollen face rested in a piece of bread on his plate. Over this macabre scene a 'Red-Cap' corporal stood guard with his rifle and bayonet at similar angle to the dead man's cutlery.

"Natural causes?"

"We think not ..."(for the first time, Colonel Baynard was showing some hint of drive or vigour)..."look at the colouring around his lips. This man has been strangled!"

"Really? What with? Where's the ligature?"

"We don't know that. We haven't found it yet. However, we do have the culprit and an admission."

"You mean you've solved it, already?"

Colonel Baynard's smirk showed a complacent self-satisfaction he could not trouble to hide.

"Well, that's how it looks, Inspector. Done and dusted. One of the gunners is in custody, although I've been asked to await your arrival before his formal arrest and charge. He admits it, you see ......do you really need to see him, yourself?"

They went down to the cellars, all four of them crammed together in the diesel-dank air. The Colonel led the way, followed by the two policemen and the Captain of Military Police bringinq up the rear. A peripheral glance at Roskill taken whilst hearing the Colonel's bland account of elementary deductions detected a slight bristling, as if he didn't think it was quite so simple, either. The suspect was being held in the Magazine. Since the end of the war, most of its ammunition had been removed and now it was as cold, damp and empty as the entrails of a hungry whale.

Gunner Rawcliffe sat down there in its dark, alone as Jonah.

Outside, two more 'Red Caps' armed with rifles stood with ostentatious vigilance before a bolted blast-door. Just in case the prisoner should spring up and force its bolts back, fight his way out of the cellars into the ammunition lift, then run out of the fort onto the jetty and from there swim over to Grimsby.

But not Gunner Rawcliffe. Oh, no. For here was a man of judgement:

A man who would rather stay under military armed guard in the leaking, sea-bound chambers of a half-empty ammunition store, facing a trumped-up murder charge; than ever find himself lost and alone in the gutters of Great Grimsby.

Captain Roskill had a brief word with his two sentries who then stood aside as the magazine door was released. Because of the chill of the cellars they'd all reverted to their overcoats and it was only then that Tryton noticed it. Colonel Baynard seemed to have an excess of rank upon one shoulder: an additional crown upon one epaulette. When this supernumerary moved, however, he could see that in fact it was no extra 'pip' but a black and shiny beetle. It fell wriggling into the shadows on the floor to be crushed under someone's heel. Unaware of his departing passenger, Baynard walked confidently into the Magazine.

Completely in the dark in all respects, Gunner Rawcliffe was only to be granted the gift of light (via an external switch) because of his visitors. He sat there blinking in the middle of the room and looked up with surprise as his two guards and these four VIP's came in at once. Altogether, they made the Magazine a little crowded.

In the same way that experienced police officers out on the streets will rarely run towards an exciting incident but rather stride briskly whilst the scene and its personalities unfold before them, so it was that Tryton would never interview the suspect first - however promptly caught. It was his settled method always thoroughly to study the 'locus in quo' - first of all. Only when the place of offence had given up all its secrets would he turn to the suspected actor to enquire whether it was they who'd wickedly strutted across the tainted boards. On this occasion, however, he realised why he was making an exception to his usual practice.

He was humouring the Colonel, Sir Martin Baynard, because in a way this over-promoted local gentleman was as much part of the scene to be studied as Gunner Wykeham's knife. He also knew that this Reservist gentry and his hard-nosed companion from the Military Police were testing him as much as investigating any crime. Well, let them. He still did not fully understand by what right he stood here inside this curious installation nor where his jurisdiction came from, but perhaps this was his first taster of whatever Maister's "primacy" theory might amount to.

16

Gunner Rawcliffe looked meekly up at them all as they stood sternly around him. He remained sitting, like the sad victim of some rare medical disorder paraded by an eminent but unfeeling consultant before a horde of indifferent medical students. His expression was pathetically hopeless as that same patient's, now notified by this collective opinion (with the callousness which only overworked medico's can muster) that he is not long for this world.

"Colonel, if I am to speak to this man then perhaps he can be left just to myself and my sergeant?"

Baynard took the point and cleared the Magazine. Sergeant Pickering slid a notebook out of his overcoat with commendable discretion and for once managed without licking his pencil.

"You are Gunner Cyril Rawcliffe?"

"Yes, how is he....?"

"Your colleague, Gunner Wykeham?"

"Wilf, yes, of course. How is he?"

"He's dead, Cyril. You must have known that."

"Dead! I knew it. I knew it. Then it must be me, it must be......"

"Must be?"

"I just hoped it wasn't...that it wasn't me...that I'd wake up and find it was all just a dream."

"A dream, Cyril?"

"A dream or a nightmare...."

Gunner Rawcliffe stared up at the ceiling, where violent shadows from the solitary bulb moved in exaggerated faithfulness to these three figures in the ammunition store. But some were not so faithful. There was a blackness which moved of its own accord and fragmented. More beetles fell on their backs on the table in front of them, tiny black legs waving in disgusting anguish. Rawcliffe abstractedly swept their writhing shells off and away with the khaki arm of his battledress tunic.

"It's the warm weather we've had. I don't know where they come from but there are masses of black beetles all over the fort. They get in everything. Even the food. We've had to get specialists in to kill them. To kill...."

"You mentioned a dream?"

"I don't know. I think it happened."

"What do you think happened, Cyril?"

17

"Well, you see, Wilf is in the same barrack room as me. He's the best footballer on the fort. We've got a team, you know, and it's my job to organise it. Once a fortnight or so, we get the supply-boat over to Grimsby and play some other regiment or a 'civvie' team perhaps. Wilf is our star centre-forward. The team is nothing without him. We'd been doing really well in the league as well - then suddenly he said he didn't feel like playing any more. I couldn't believe it. There was no good reason. He just said he wanted to go boozing instead. He said the football was using up all our shore-leave. A lot of the others would go to Grimsby, book in at the Salvation Army or a cheap guest house, then spend the rest of the day drinking. Back in the morning on the supply-boat. That was what he wanted to do. I couldn't believe it. Such a waste."

"What did you do?"

"I'm not sure. I know it was preying on my mind. It meant the end of the team, you see. I kept having these dreams, it must have been the funny weather - hot.

"I'd be arguing with him, violent arguments about him pulling the plug on the whole team. It was the same dream every time, one where we'd always end up fighting. I'd throw him off the fort apron into the sea, over and over again.

"But last night was different. Different and worse. I had actually, yes, I'd definitely gone through all the 'pros and cons' with him yet again in the Mess before 'lights out' but, no, he was adamant. No more football! It must have been at the front of my mind when I went to bed because I dreamt - or thought I dreamt - about strangling him. Holding him by the throat. Bashing his head against an iron frame somewhere. A bunk bed. It was so vivid - I even got out of bed and tiptoed over to his bunk to check he was alright, because I'd convinced myself he would be badly hurt. But, no, he seemed to be breathing alright, or at least he was then. Yes, I'm sure he was. So I thought he must be O.K. - I told myself it must have been a dream. Or did I dream the bit where I checked on him? I don't know anymore....."

"Later on, I'm pretty sure I heard him get up in the night and leave the room. By then I was stuck in that half-world between half-awake and half-asleep...."

He paused and wiped his eyes before continuing:

18

"I pictured him going downstairs covered in blood and bruises – perhaps to get help - but it was as if there was nothing I could have done to help him myself. Like I was paralysed. I wanted to get up and warn him but it seemed I couldn't move. At first, when I woke up this morning at reveille, I thought I'd imagined the whole thing. Then people came into the room and told me. I just couldn't believe the news. So I told Colonel Baynard what had happened. He listened ever so patiently to what I had to say - he really is a good officer, you know, even if he isn't a Regular. I'd trust him with my life."

"I think you just have done, Cyril. What exactly did you tell Colonel Baynard?"

"That I must have killed Wilf Wykeham......................"

He considered Gunner Rawcliffe carefully. Only nineteen and football mad. Condemned to see out his compulsory National Service with the Royal Artillery in this offshore concrete hulk. Condemned by a nation inured by Hitler to living on a permanent war-footing and now resigned to further conflict, this time with Joe Stalin's Soviet Russia. (What a place to wait for Armageddon!) And, if his present commanding officer had his way, condemned for the murder of a comrade-in-arms on the basis of a dream and a half-baked confession. The lad could hang for this.

"Did you give Wilf anything to eat or drink, Cyril?"

"Me? No, why should I? He'd had his tea in the Mess. He could always pop down to the kitchen for a snack if he really wanted. Why are you asking me that?"

"Your chum wasn't strangled or bashed around the head at all, Cyril. It looks to me like he was poisoned!"

"Poisoned? Oh, no! I didn't do that! Hey, if you're right, where does this leave me?"

"Stuck in the Magazine for a few more hours yet, I'm afraid, Cyril. At least until we can convince your Colonel, which is not going to be a happy task, I fear. Come on, Pickering, let's go and have another look at the kitchens."

Their interviewee called after them as they made for the door: "Hey, will this get me out of the Army before we end up fighting the Russians?"

"Don't bet on it, Cyril. Sit tight!"

19

As the blast-door was secured again behind them, Baynard was hovering anxiously nearby. They barely acknowledged him as they headed for the stairs.

"How did you get on?" he trailed after them.

To walk away from someone when they are speaking to you is of course the height of rudeness, but he now felt so much more confident of their position that this is exactly what they did to Baynard. 'Primacy of the civil power' thought Tryton to himself:

"Very useful indeed. Just off to the kitchens..." is what he actually said.

Like a King in State, guarded by silent sentries, Wykeham lay. Not in his cups but in his plates. The two 'Red Caps' in the kitchen jerked upright like scandalised priests as these policemen burst into the room, breathless from the stairs.

"Ere, steady on there, sir! Colonel's Orders! Nobody's to touch 'im till the 'ologist gets 'ere.... Sirrrr.... please ....not anybody, 'e said!"

The protest was too late but would have been ignored whenever given. Tryton had taken the late-lamented Wilfred by the hair and notwithstanding the rigours of death been able to pull his face away from the plate. Whatever sweetmeat had been the final, fatal, gastronomic attraction was shared equally between the plate and his frozen features. A slice of bread. A ration book-exceeding and a quarter master-defying generosity of spread. And one flat, shiny beetle, as dead as the gunner.

"Take a look at this, Pickering."

Baynard and his entourage were next into the kitchen, as Colonel the only one of his party to be silenced for a moment by the effort of the stairs. In this calm before the storm the more articulate sentry knew he would have to get his excuses in fast:

"Sir, I told 'im! I told 'im not to touch 'im! 'E took no notice of us, sir! We tried to stop 'im..."

Oxygen combined with venom to give their commander speech again: "Shut up, you stupid soldier! Get out of here, the pair of you!"

Needing no further encouragement, both 'Red Caps' scuttled out of the room, dragging their still-bayoneted rifles behind them. Baynard turned angrily to those still holding Wykeham's head: "What's going on here? What do you think you are playing at?"

20

"Come and see for yourself."

Baynard advanced but Roskill was right behind him, obviously still seething at the treatment of his military policemen by these civilians, whether the uniformed reservist or these two flatfeet. Despite his clear resentment, an overriding professional curiosity forced him to ask:

"What's that stuff around his face?"

Inured as everyone was become to wartime deprivation continuing in post-war rationing, those reconstituted substitutes or indigestible alternatives passing for a balanced diet, it was still hard to accept this dietary horror before them could approach anything you might call food. Smeared on both the bread and over the deceased's mouth was a pale yellow, semi-transparent material with the consistency of old butter.

"Well, it could be margarine...." offered Baynard, apparently keen to divert the obvious conclusion.

"Is it hell!" swore Tryton, slamming a large plain tin which he'd snatched from a nearby shelf down onto the table, hard. He was angry with himself as much as anyone, for letting these fatheads provoke him through their blind resistance to an inconvenient and embarrassing explanation. If that was how they wanted to play it then let them suffer the backwash.

There was a label on the tin:

"THE CONSOLIDATED CHEMICAL CO.
PATENT INSECT KILLER
'ONE SLUG KILLS ALL BUGS'
Instructions: Simply spread on affected area."

They watched him in unwilling fascination as he attacked the lid with an Army tin-opener taken from the standard mess-kit. With frantic energy he levered the jagged tinplate away:

"Look!" There it was. A tubful of the same, apparently-identical, buttery material.

"This whole fort is suddenly infested by a plague of black beetles. They're everywhere, getting into everything, even the rations. Driving the troops mad. Some bright spark from Public Health is brought in and he recommends this stuff. Just the ticket. Bound to wipe them out in a matter of days. So the bombardier gets his gunners to spread it all over the walls and ceilings. Everywhere, in fact. Casements, barracks, kitchens, the lot!"

21

"That doesn't mean people have been eating it...." stabbed Baynard, beginning to retreat.

"One way or another, this man did! Only the pathologist can give us final endorsement but, a pound to a penny, Gunner Wykeham died for one of two reasons: Either he came downstairs for a midnight feast and found a tin of this stuff, mistaking it for butter or margarine with the consequence you see. Rationing makes people a bit greedy for the chance of a little extra, particularly if it's free, doesn't it, Colonel? Or else the pale commodity spread across his face really is what His Majesty's Army offers its conscripts as 'ersatz' butter and what actually killed this young lad was one or more tainted beetles, spewing poison, falling in agony on his illicit snack."

To this theory Captain Roskill offered unexpected support:

"You know, you might just be right, Tryton. After all, if he crept in here at night, with only the low-level lighting on, it would be quite dark and he might well not have read the tin or else seen the creature. Those things are falling dead off the ceiling all the time."

Good! At least he had the Military Police on his side - for now. But Baynard was still quibbling: "This is mere speculation, Inspector. We will just have to wait and see what the pathologist has to say about the cause of death, I think."

"I'm no forensic scientist, Colonel, but I'm still certain about it. As you say, we must await confirmation from those learned gentlemen who can tell us more exactly what did for Gunner Wykeham, either way."

He could have saved his breath. Taking a conciliatory tone with the Colonel was in practical terms a complete waste of time.

The scene and the body were secured again and there was a long embarrassing wait, pending the arrival of a pathologist whose verdict could settle this struggle between the authority of civilian and military police, once and for all.

Tryton and Pickering dragged a pair of bentwood chairs up from the Officers Mess into one of the now-empty six-inch gun positions and spent a couple of hours writing up their notebooks and looking out to sea. Colonel Baynard had retreated to the Observation & Control Post, where he seemed to be encountering great difficulty persuading an Army telephone operator to put him through to a more senior officer.

Eventually, the supply boat brought the Home Office Pathologist, Professor Edgar. A large jolly chap in morning suit and bowler hat for whom the precise estimation of Time of Death had become his vocation's Holy Grail.

For a man whose entire working day was spent carefully dismembering other people's loved ones, with or without the assistance of power tools, his sunny disposition came as something of a revelation. If tea-time questions from a devoted wife about 'Nice day at work, dear?' seemed feasible part of his domestic routine; when the time came for him to tell the trial judge what he thought about cause of death, men hung upon his every word.

Different again in his formal professional capacity, where he became quiet and intense, on Bull Sand Fort he reverted to his natural jovial mood only once a complete examination of the scene was over. However, any offer of opinion upon the issue of the moment – the only reason for this strange gathering in the middle of Humber Roads, after all – seemed unlikely to be forthcoming immediately afterwards. Instead, warming themselves over tea and toast in the Officers' Mess, he regaled his reluctant audience with well-rehearsed stories of some celebrated cases in which he'd played important part: - the 'Bridlington Brown Paper Murders' or the 'Barnsley Body in a Barrel'.

It was as if he needed time to think and this was how his mind won him the chance.

After some time had passed in this vein, and clearly satisfied he had done his bit to lighten the mood of the party, Professor Edgar suddenly became sombre again.

He was ready to announce some preliminary findings, which he launched into without any further nicety of introduction: "There is no doubt in my mind that this unfortunate young man died from the effects of poisoning. There is no sign of any forcible application to him of the powerful insecticide which must be the culprit. It does therefore seem likely that, in tragic error, the material was self-administered, exactly as the good Inspector suggests. If not spread on bread, just one beetle-full would have given adequate dose."

23

So that was that. Any final answer could only come from a proper autopsy and arrangements were therefore made at once for urgent transfer of the body to the mortuary in Hull. The careful and reverential loading of a coffin onto the supply vessel which waited at the jetty was followed with another tedious sea-crossing. Their leave-taking of the fort was as brusque and cold as its walls.

Sergeant Pickering had been designated Coroner's Officer. By the time their ship docked at Hull, his 'mal de mer' had returned with a vengeance. One of his duties would be to accompany the body to the city mortuary but the difference in corporeal health between himself and his charge looked marginal. Professor Edgar stowed a large fob-watch in his waistcoat pocket and gave Pickering an enormous blow between the shoulder blades with an outstretched palm: "Make sure they don't slide you into the drawer next to him, eh, Sergeant?"

Pickering slumped into the passenger seat of the waiting hearse, which was followed by a taxi filled by the pathologist and Captain Roskill. As surly on their departure as their arrival, Baynard had stayed on the fort. Tryton knew that, however satisfactory in its conclusion the enquiry had been, this was not how Colonel Baynard wished it to end. Having presumably already trumpeted his detection of an 'Army Strangler', Tryton's alternative analysis must have made Baynard look a fool to his bosses in the General staff. If he was the instrument of that loss of face, then Tryton knew he'd made a powerful enemy for himself in this part-time, regimental gentleman. Since he did not plan ever to find himself upon Bull Sand Fort in his lifetime again; to join the 422nd (East Riding) Coast Regiment Royal Artillery; or ever to apply for membership of the Holderness Hunt, this acquiring of ill-will was not something he expected to cause him major difficulty. After all, in his line of work, it was occupational hazard to incur resentment.

And it had always been like this. Every case he'd ever investigated seemed to leave at least someone with a sense of burning injustice, even if just the victims of crime raging at inadequate punishments imposed.

In about eighty per cent of cases, it was of course the defendant found guilty by a court and sentenced who felt so badly done by – product of the criminal mind's ability to rationalise and excuse intolerable acts, even to blank out its own memory. One of the first discoveries of his new profession.

These prejudices born of experience did not mean he'd identified Baynard as criminal. Of course not - just stupid. Tryton would classify the Colonel in his 'Other Interested Parties' category; along with those retired obsessives who write to newspapers or parish vigilantes. Once classified, he forgot him as quickly. Life moves on.

Left alone on the dockside, Tryton faced a fifteen-minute walk to the place where they had left the Police Wolseley. He was glad of the chance for thought this promenade gave him.

The cobbled roadways were busy with canvas-sided lorries driving from the unloading ships to the warehouses of fruit importers. Squadrons of dock workers cycling home at the end of their shift weaved in and out of traffic and the random stacks of crates or pallets. Without exception, every one carried a gas mask case on a strap diagonally across the chest, although there would be nothing more warlike inside than a sandwich tin and a flask of cold tea. Tryton remembered how, during the war, every man, woman and child had been required religiously to carry their gas mask in all conditions. Ironically, considering all the atrocities they did endure, a gas attack was amongst the few which never came.

From the river, ship's hooters sounded as attentive tugs drew a freighter into the main, deep-water navigation channel. Behind the docks, the clash of shunted railway wagons jostling in the marshalling yards appealed to his schoolboy sense of drama. After the poisoned insanity of that offshore concrete hulk, he was glad to be in this busy place, full of life and activity.

There remained one melancholy duty left him before he could slough-off the morbidity of this gloomy day: Gunner Wykeham's parents. When he got to the Wolseley it seemed to be as reluctant to make this journey as he was. Riverside damp had permeated its ignition and it took aggressive use of the starting handle to persuade it into life.

The Wykehams' 1930's Tudor detached was the end one in a row of eight on Anlaby Road, where a straight tree-lined boulevard sped from the urban margins of the city into the beginnings of open country. Its structure was neat and well-maintained; the exterior paintwork smooth and shiny in white and black. It was a house for persons who require an ordered life and the front garden, in its linear formality, conformed to this ideal. Except that the standard rose trees, lashed tightly to posts, served in their vertical only to satirise the posture of the house.

All four-square and not a crack to be seen in its brickwork, Balmoral Villa rested at some four degrees out of true. It was apparent that three out of the seven adjoining properties had been bombed flat in a line during the war. They now amounted to no more than piles of rubble behind privet hedges, whose garden gates still swung aimlessly on rusty hinges as token memorial to the ruins. In the three years since the end of hostilities, no-one had yet got round to clearing the sites and filling the bomb-craters. Either the blast from the explosions or (more probably) changes to the fractured water table, through the deep craters, had caused Balmoral Villa its genteel lean. The whole building carried an air of dignified embarrassment in its inclination, like an old lady unexpectedly affected by an excess of Christmas sherry and slowly tippling over.

As he approached the rhomboid front door, Tryton was mentally revising his demeanour and attitude. For those who enquire about and deal daily with death, a little black humour 'off camera' gives balancing antidote to grief or shock. Perhaps they'd not treated the remains of this young conscript with proper reverence at every stage of their enquiry. Now it was different. To these aged parents, the policeman was not reporting the inglorious demise of a pale and lanky youth, in ill-fitting uniform of coarse khaki and heavy boots. This National Serviceman killed in peacetime by a freak catering accident would remain to them their first-born, their golden-haired and entrancing infant, sacrificed for his country. Here was the true measure of their awful loss, his to announce.

Hardly had he knocked once on the glossy door, using a brass knocker in the grotesque shape of the 'Lincoln Imp', than it was pulled violently open. A tall, stooping gentleman in his late fifties. The father of the man.

26

"Are you the police?"

"Yes, I ...."

"Very impressive, very impressive, officer. I have only just telephoned the police station. Didn't expect a response as prompt as this, though! By Jove, no!"

"Well, I came as soon as I could..."

"Very good, constable. Well, you'd better come straight through and have a look for yourself. Although I fear the blackguards responsible are clean away."

Unable to protest, he was led through the canted doorframe into the tilting hall of Balmoral Villa. He was able to make polite greeting to Mrs. Wykeham as she stood nervously in the entrance to the front sitting-room. (Obviously not expected in there, then). Instead he found himself brought into the kitchen at the back of the house and drawn up to inspect a broken window.

"There it is! 'Smash and Grab', I expect you chaps call it. An off-ration joint of meat, fresh from my brother-in-law's farm at Riplingham, waiting there beside the sink for Mrs.Wykeham to cook it. But 'No!' - a couple of adolescents, trespassing, garden-hopping. Looking out for an opportunity to take for nothing what their elders and betters have laboured for."

"I'll take the details..."

"Yes, you might as well. For all the good it'll do us, eh, constable? Little chance of catching them, as you well know! And if they were caught, what then? Put them before the magistrates. And what can we expect from them, eh? I'll tell you what. Nothing! How do I know? I'll tell you how. I play golf with a magistrate - Mr. Burton. You probably know him. Off the record and on the Q.T. - he told me: Hardly any powers and hardly any inclination. 'No moral courage', he says!"

"I'm afraid it's not really my place to..." Tryton's attempt to either disassociate himself from this line of argument or in someway speed up its conclusion was futile. His role as audience was inescapable.

"No, constable. You will know as well as me. All the burglaries around here are committed by juveniles. No sooner are they caught and let off than some do-gooder lets them have another chance for more of the same. Old ladies frightened in their beds. Domestic terror. And our meat!"

27

"They are children in the eyes of the law, Mr. Wykeham..." he managed to put in, anxious in some charitable way to mitigate and spare the father's passion in view of what he was about to impart. It was no good.

"Children! Children, constable?" Wykeham Senior almost roared in reply "How can you call them children? Sixteen years-old. Six foot tall. I can remember being sixteen. My idea of right and wrong was as clear then as it is now. Children, my foot! They're fully grown and offending apace against a society that's too mealy-mouthed to do anything practical about it."

Mrs.Wykeham bobbed apprehensively at the kitchen door. He was grateful for her intercession on his behalf: "Now steady on, dear. Don't take it out on this young constable. He won't want to stay in the police force if every householder takes it out on him, personally, every time he attends the scene of a burglary."

"Yes, alright, Dora. Of course I'm not blaming this young man here. Especially not when he's been so prompt to respond. But we are parents. We know a thing or two about children. I blame the parents of these thieves and hooligans. If they're brought up properly by parents who take an interest, then none of this sort of thing need happen. Never had anything like this with our Wilfred, did we dear?"

"No, dear. A lovely boy! Our son, Wilfred. He's in the Army, you know. The Artillery. Not a Regular, of course, oh no - National Service. He wants to study to be an accountant when he comes out..."

Mrs.Wykeham caught the blank, miserable look in the policeman's eyes even before he spoke: "You didn't come about the burglary, did you?" she said softly. He shook his head silently.

Through a side window they saw a uniformed 'bobby' cycling in through the open garden gate. ("Come about the break-in"). After a short word with the Inspector, he waited tactfully outside.

The Wykehams waiting in agonising silence in their own front sitting room, hugging each other. He tried so hard to be positive in the way he broke the news, but it was hardly 'Our Glorious Dead On The Field Of Battle'.

Whoever decorated their front room had lined its floral wallpaper up on a true vertical, presumably through using a plumb line. Tryton studied its contradictions with elaborate care, as though they might restore him to a world of order and normality he'd somehow lost touch with. However hard he tried, their effect inside this subsiding house was deeply troubling. One vertical fought with another, leaving no certainty of where the real truth lay.

Gerald Wykeham had been a man of strong opinions, but the news of his son silenced him. Parents expect their children to outlive them. A neighbour came round to comfort Mrs.Wykeham whilst her husband went with the Inspector in a black police car to the public mortuary on Spring Street. Sergeant Pickering, the normal colour back in his face by now, was waiting there for them as Coroner's Officer for the wretched task of identifying the body.

"You're a young man, Inspector," the father observed afterwards, as he struggled for self-control. "Such a young man to be an Inspector. Too young to know what it is like to be bereaved."

"Not too young, Mr.Wykeham," he cut in bitterly. "Death is no respecter of Youth. Not when War is its servant."

"Forgive me, Inspector. We all suffered in the war - who did you lose?"

Tryton was completely taken by surprise. His job was to escort the victims through their ordeal. He did his duty and then went away. The grief was their problem which he left behind, with them. He did not expect them to shine a black-edged mirror straight back at him, as if to catch him out. The answer he blurted out was unintentionally frank:

"Many good friends ......and my wife!"

(Jenny Wren....)

29

"If they attack our cities, we will simply erase theirs!"

(Adolf Hitler at the Sportspalast, Berlin, 4th September 1940)

30

III

"A North-East Coast Town..." the radio would call it.

"A north-east coast town was subject of further attacks by German aircraft last night..." was all the announcer on the BBC Home Service would say. Those who adjusted the bakelite dials on their 'Bush' valve radios could imagine him, sitting in the cellars of Broadcasting House in London before a huge microphone. His oiled hair was slicked back flat to his scalp and he adjusted dark, horn-rimmed glasses to read the tea-time news.

Every now and then, plaster would fall as dust from the ceiling. It danced in the lights to settle on the shoulders of his black dinner suit, like granular dandruff. In the streets above him, buildings burned and children died. Fastidiously he brushed the white powder from the suit which the Director General, Lord Reith, required of his staff. (London was burning).

"A town on the north-east coast...."

The censor would not allow the agony of this other city to receive the dignity of its name. Why not? *"Useful intelligence to the Enemy."* Even the weather was censored.

The Germans knew anyway. They had looked in Mr. Baedeker's helpful little pre-war travel guide, under 'K' for Kingston-upon-Hull: England's third-rate, third port. The place where the English Civil War had started, two hundred and ninety-nine years ago: the very first act of defiance entered against the Royal Authority of Charles I, when the city garrison under Sir John Hotham at the Beverley Gate denied him entry into his town and access to his ammunition stores. The Kingstown that refused its king. Could its population be driven into insurrection again?

In briefing rooms at airfields all the way from Norway and down into the Reich itself, Luftwaffe navigators scored crisp and confident lines with compass and protractor straight across the sea - to the town on the North East Coast. Upon those projections they flew in waves; Staffel after Staffel; Jagdgeschwader after Jagdgeschwader. In Heinkel One-Elevens; Dornier Seventeens; and Junkers Eighty-eights - green masterpieces of aeronautical engineering and precision manufacture, their tail fins adorned with that apotheosis of wickedness; the swastika. Emblem of evil, badge of the Hun.

31

Night after night, these were the airborne machines that delivered the agonies of Hull. Even in daylight.

Small boys in 'Fair Isle' arm-less jumpers, grey shorts and sagging socks stood on heaps of rubble gazing up at the vapour trails. In the sky above them, Gods fought.

Mobile flak batteries, manned almost entirely by women, rotated their Bofors guns at the same heavens, spewing lines of molten tracer up at flying devils.

Only six thousand out of ninety-three thousand houses left undamaged after one thousand hours of air raids. One hundred and fifty-two thousand people left homeless, albeit alive. One thousand, two hundred and fifty-eight civilians killed and three times that number left injured, maimed and wounded. Five years of destruction left enough scars to last a generation and beyond.

The worst night of the whole war: 8th May 1941:

In the heart of the city, Victoria Square was devastated in a rain of explosives and incendiaries whilst that Monarch of Happy Memory looked down upon the barbaric work of Hitler's Luftwaffe with haughty, bronze disdain. The Hammonds' department store was completely wrecked and W.H. Smith's newsagents gutted by fire; as parachute-born land-mines blasted through the Metropolitan Dance Hall, through Jameson Street and many other areas. In one night's fell work, four hundred and fifty people were killed outright and many more left maimed and injured.

The crowning tragedy of that single night was the destruction of the Prudential Tower. This Gothic monument to the commercial ambitions of an Insurance company stood at the apex of an important, central business area, where King Edward Street met Paragon Street in Queen Victoria Square. Beneath it, an underground cafe provided bomb shelters and refreshments not only for the professionals of commerce but also to Admiralty staff working in adjoining offices.

At least eighty people, many of them girls from the `Women's Royal Naval Service', or "Wrens" as they were affectionately known, were immolated in the firestorm unleashed upon those buildings. (Their indecipherable remains still rest irrecoverable to this day, under the charred and compressed rubble of the basement).

For Flight Sergeant Michael Tryton, serving with the RNZAF Spitfire squadron based at RAF Leconfield, most of that memorable night was spent high in the air above the flaming city. "Bandits high…"

In a hellish sky streaming with parabolic arcs of tracer and criss-crossed by his own sides' searchlights, he and the other scattered aircraft of his Flight separately hunt the dark bombers of their enemy. He knows the German aircraft are no match for his Supermarine Spitfire, an already-famous fighter whose Rolls-Royce Merlin engine and remarkable manoeuvrability mean it can see off most of the Luftwaffe's fighters, let alone these twin-engined bombers.

Far from home, harassed by searchlights and "ack-ack"; weighed down with bombs, their frightened crews fear the Spitfire more than any other British aircraft. Yet these craven fears do not make it into a 'chicken shoot'. Even a Spitfire could be brought down by too open and unwise an angle of attack upon a bomber whose rear-gunner stood wide-eyed and alert amongst his coiling ammunition belts. Which is why, with the fires of burning Hull cartwheeling beneath him, Tryton must pull back violently on the joystick to bring his aircraft up in a yammering climb; right up close beneath the unprotected belly of the lumbering, twin-engined aircraft silhouetted above him, whose bombardier is still holding his pilot steady over the distinctive silver basin of King Edward Dock, hanging on the signal to let go their deadly load.

In the momentary flash of a bomb burst he satisfies his conscience that this huge black shape is indeed a Junkers 88, before plunging a gloved thumb deep into the firing button. His guns claim vicious retribution for the fires below in a livid line of ammunition that tears into the German fuselage, severing control wires, airframe spars and petrol pipes, until the entire machine staggers and ignites under this lacerating salvo into one enormous chrysanthemum of boiling flame.

Still in the climb, his own aircraft would have flown straight into the fireball and itself succumbed, but he flicks it over onto its back and rolls away. This textbook manoeuvre, so deftly accomplished, should have saved him from being brought down by his own target but, in a skyful of flying metal, the statistical chances of escaping unmarked considerably reduce.

He hears with dismay a loud 'bang' as some solid object smashes through the engine cover in front of the cockpit. Either a piece of the disintegrating Junkers has got him or else he's been hit by friendly fire from his own ground batteries, attracted by the flaming debris in that part of the sky.

Within seconds a thin, white streamer of dense vapour began to show at a new hole in the engine cowling to form a trail behind the diving aircraft. The plane was obviously losing coolant and he scanned oil temperature and pressure gauges, grimly expecting the worst. It was re-assuring to see that for the moment they remained healthy, but he could see the altimeter spinning remorselessly as they lost height. Even so, he still kept the nose of the aircraft resolutely down, determined to quit the dogfight continuing about him, above the burning city where his Kiwi comrades scattered the ragged German formations all over the North Country.

He'd done his bit.

Turning north for the short flight to their base at Leconfield, he realised that, in addition to the external vapour trail, hot 'Glycol' was spraying internally under pressure through the bulkhead and into the cockpit, mainly onto his legs. So highly-pressurised the cooling system, he knew the plane and its engine could not last long with any breach. Despite thick, service trousers, his thighs were already stinging under this scalding shower and he tore with gloved hands at the deflated 'Mae West' life jacket, pulling it from his chest onto his knees to act as a crude deflector. With bleak resignation, he noted how the needle of the temperature gauge had made its first discernible movement beyond the normal running position. As the engine lost coolant, the hotter it would get, but he still hoped to have landed safely before this ever had mechanical effect.

For all his youth he had been well trained as a pilot; determined and methodical in his temperament. Think positive! It was not far to Leconfield, say fifteen miles from Hull, and he'd made up his mind he would bring his machine back in one piece.

Whilst the temperature gauge rose, so oil pressure imperceptibly began to drop and it was these instruments which became obsessive focus of his attentions.

Airspeed and height reducing all the time under a controlled descent, he slid back the centre section of the perspex canopy to dissipate a scalding cloud of coolant still invading the cockpit. He ducked lower in his seat behind the windscreen as the slipstream clawed at helmet and goggles. Carefully he lowered the undercarriage in readiness for landing and only now did he break radio silence, to make his first contact with Leconfield Control.

Their rebuff was so unexpected an addition to his accumulating woes that, even when challenging it, he could not imagine their second refusal:

Leconfield would not have him!

A maverick German - medium-bomber or long-range night-fighter - had either deliberately avoided the hell over Hull or else been driven off from there and, despite the black-out, found the nearby market town of Beverley as minor recompense. The pair of bombs it dropped on the paint-brush factory of Messrs. Leak and Co. in Hengate should wreak some serious havoc on the British War Effort, in the interior decorative field at least, gratifying to the Austrian housepainter if no-one else.

That achieved, its exuberant crew looked around for more and latched onto an RAF Anson of a liaison flight, bumbling home. Emulating that aircraft's slow approach to landing lights lit briefly for its assistance on arrival at Leconfield, the following German crew had with brass nerve switched on all their own green and red navigation lights. Having waggled its wings in ostensibly-friendly fashion, the raider was allowed unhindered to make an apparent approach for landing which was really just a low pass. This equally low ruse enabled it to drop some sticks of bombs down the centre of the runway and put several dozen cannon shells into the hangers and an adjoining administration block.

The Avro Anson which had unwittingly given access to this pathological gate-crasher was also set ablaze as it taxied on the apron. Fortunately its crew all managed to get out and run across the grass to safety, just before their machine blew up.

This then was the chaotic scene which greeted Sergeant Pilot Tryton as he flew into Leconfield at hangar-roof height. The runway was illuminated in the red glow of the burning transport plane and he could see figures running around near the Tower.

Now he could understand the reason for his controller's harassed diversion of him on to RAF Driffield, the next station.

Understanding the decision was one thing but coping with it was another. For the first time that night it occurred to him the odds were amassing against his ever making it.

He'd lost a considerable amount of height in the disappointed expectation of landing and his airspeed was as dangerously low as his altitude. The drag caused by the lowered undercarriage was a further clog on forward movement and the aircraft was at risk of stalling. Unhooking his oxygen mask, he pulled back on the stick again and delicately raised the rev's with the throttle, in an effort to gain height and speed.

The white plume still emitting from the engine cowling spat back globules of hot oil which spattered the armoured windscreen with rainbow stains and turned the white cloud into a filthy grey. Oil temperature was now well above normal running and nudging critical, whilst pressure was falling away steadily. Such a high-pressure system and the powerful engine it was meant to protect could not stand up to this sort of treatment for long. As the coolant slipped away, engine lubrication was suffering as rising operating temperatures thinned the oil and burst the seals.

Terminal failure loomed. As airspeed and altitude fell, so the supportive effects of air-cooling were lost, all these problems conspiring until the point arrived where the engine would seize solid and the plane fall out of the sky.

These were the facts and likely consequences his analytical mind rapidly reviewed, even as he struggled to pull the aircraft up. Driffield was only another ten miles on, just minutes away in normal flying. But this was not normal flying.

The original determination had been to bring his machine back in one piece; an optimistic expectation as it now seemed. High, but not high enough for safety, he was still too low to bale out. Gaining any more height looked most unlikely with an engine audibly beginning to labour. If he jumped out now his parachute would never have opened before he hit the ground anyway. Pulling his life-jacket over his legs to protect them from the hot coolant meant he'd had to undo some of the straps for the parachute harness. If he jumped out now, there was no certainty he'd even stay attached to the 'chute.

There was no choice but to stick with it. The die was cast.

36

If only one card was left in his favour, then it was shown to him now. The first faint glimmerings of dawn. This weak blessing was enough to show him the tall outlines of trees his aircraft could barely clear. He sawed at the joystick to swerve around rather than over them, whilst dairy cattle stampeded before the stricken Spitfire as it hedge-hopped from field to field. Fortunate he was indeed that open countryside was what he crossed, for even a church tower would have been enough to bring him down.

Engine temperature was off the clock, oil pressure zero.

He dared not retract the undercarriage for fear that when he needed it again on final landing it would not operate. Left down, it was adding appreciably to his difficulties in the velocity department.

At least Driffield Control were willing to clear him for approach and he warned them of the likely tidiness of his arrival. He requested fire appliances as if he was ordering from a menu, even though he well knew they would be waiting there for him anyway, as a matter of course. Like any wartime airman, there was many a time when he'd stood by the wind-sock himself, sick at heart, watching a doomed aircraft staggering back, only for its crew of young men to die in flames within sight of home, on friendly tarmac in front of their friends. Now it was his turn.

The Rolls Royce engine was running really rough, spewing black smoke to obscure the view ahead. Oil was pouring onto the hot exhaust manifolds then igniting and leaping up as bright yellow flames. He side-slipped into wind and adjusted the ailerons and trim so that the plane was set up for its designated runway, just visible in the dawn light.

Something like a quarter of a mile out, Fate administered to him her wickedest gift, as if she had been savouring his struggle, waiting to strike. It was at this most critical and dangerous moment, at the immediate point of landing, that his tormented engine blew. Overheated metal welded where once it had smoothly slid. He struggled with the controls to keep her straight and level but now found himself master of an overweight burning glider.

Landing wheels skimming the airfield perimeter hedge, he knew he was coming in much too low and much too fast.

She touched down on grassland even before reaching the beginning of the concrete runway but, such was her speed, launched into the air again. Horrified spectators realised that this first impact on rough ground had broken the starboard oleo leg of the undercarriage, which collapsed back into the wing well. Useless.

When the plane came down for the second time onto the concrete, only one wheel was in position and the aircraft now tipped onto its starboard wing, sliding along the runway sideways in a shower of sparks. Instantaneously, the effect of this one-sided braking was to spin the Spitfire violently around at right angles, so that she left the runway at once, taking to the grass again and traveling faster. He was no longer its pilot. He was just a frightened man strapped to a metal seat inside a burning bobsleigh, watching death rushing towards him at terrifying speed.

It was at this point that the remaining undercarriage leg had the belated good grace to collapse in sympathy with its weaker brother. Flung completely down onto its belly, this abrasion was good for scrubbing-off a few more unwanted miles per hour, but the battering to her underside as she continued to slide like an out-of-control sledge now ruptured twin fuel tanks under the wings.

Chased by two fire engines and a khaki ambulance with enormous red crosses on the side, the Spitfire swerved aimlessly towards a row of Hurricanes neatly parked at Dispersal, out on the airfield perimeter. He thought of his young wife and the life they would have lived together, as he braced himself for the suffocating agony of fire.

Covering those last few hundred yards of ground, the still-sliding plane hit a broad stretch of sand which had the effect of quite sudden deceleration. To the surprise of everybody watching, her mangled propellor blades dug unexpectedly into this soft ground, barely feet from parked Hurricanes whose ground crews had already fled the scene. The Spitfire flipped violently up onto her nose, almost as if she were going to go right over and onto her back, throwing the unfortunate pilot hard into his belts before falling back to earth.

Notwithstanding the force of this impact and its momentary stunning, he retained sufficient presence of mind and instinct for self-preservation to release his belts and scramble out of the already-open cockpit, down onto the wing and away from the wreck as fast as he possibly could.

The fact that he had landed with the cockpit canopy already slid open was one of the few things to have operated in his favour that dreadful night. The whole aircraft was swimming with aircraft fuel and he realised all his flying kit was soaked in it. He found himself seized bodily and carried swiftly to the ambulance, even as the brave fire crews began to hose his aircraft (more for the protection of the nearby Hurricanes than the salvage of his own).

If any of his rescuers had lit a cigarette, Tryton in his flight suit and the whole aircraft would have gone up like a Roman Candle. They had more sense but there were plenty more sources of flame and ignition. Since the engine was already burning as he came down, it seemed that the only things to have prevented an explosion were (firstly) that the quantity of fuel being shed was too much to ignite; and (secondly) that the best chance for its flammable vapour to put on a show had been ruined by his random nose-dive into a natural sand-pit.

"I think that must be the worst landing I've ever, ever seen," commented the first aid orderly, admiringly, as their khaki Austin K2 ambulance bounced slowly across the grass on its way back to the control tower.

"It's been one hell of a night!" agreed Tryton, ruefully. His vagueness explaining such a spectacular accident made him sound like some drunken baronet found in his wrecked sports car by a disapproving policeman - one of the 'Bentley Boys' wrapped around a tree in Berkeley Square. Whatever the explanation, it was good to be alive.

He was checked over by the squadron medical officer; showered; given an early breakfast, and then debriefed. He claimed his "kill" - one Junkers 88. (His first ever). He felt quite proud of himself… at first …and his squadron was duly notified by telephone of his landing, although they clearly had other preoccupations.

Everyone at Driffield was really jumpy because of what had just happened at Leconfield. It was not long since Driffield 'field' had itself lost twelve men and numerous aircraft on the ground in a surprise German daylight raid, so it was not hard to blame them if they feared for repetition now. Nevertheless, he was warmly congratulated by the resident aircrew, many of whom he already knew through inter-squadron socialising.

After an enormous breakfast in the officers mess (where what clearly mattered was that he was a pilot, not a mere sergeant pilot) and simultaneous de-briefing by a middle-aged intelligence officer who waited patiently between mouthfuls of bacon, he went to bed.

Stripped of his petrol-soaked flying kit and blessed only with a pair of borrowed, stripey pyjamas, he still slept the sleep of the just in a draughty Nissen Hut; on a bed whose owner - for all he knew - might have been posted 'missing' that same morning.

He had been in the air with little intervening sleep for what had been two sequential nights of heavy German raids over Hull. Physical and emotional exhaustion gave him deep rest.

If he slept well, he woke badly. The rising warmth of a fine May afternoon permeated the pre-fabricated barracks where he lay and filled his pre-waking imaginings with nightmarish scenes on board the exploding Junkers he'd riven with gunfire. In the overheated confusion of half-asleep and half-awake he was acknowledging the reality denied in euphoric wakefulness.

This 'kill' was not the simple downing of an impersonal machine, a Junkers 88; Reichmarshal Goering's "Wonder Bomber". He had killed five men at one stroke and, as a man fresh from the terrors of a burning aircraft himself, could easily imagine just how they died. He had never harmed anyone in his life before, apart from the occasional school yard fisticuffs, but now for the first time he had surely killed. In quantity. Five men: Sons, husbands, fathers all; for aught he knew. The ripples of grief spread outwards into the world from his single act.

Getting up quickly, he put on the ragbag of ill-fitting service clothes he had been lent. He had not seen his wife of three months for nearly three days.

Jenny was the well-brought up daughter of a local ships' - broker but she'd volunteered for the 'Women's Royal Naval Service' before ever he met her. Of all the armed services, this glorified Girl's Public school in naval uniform was the only one that remained truly voluntary. She really could leave whenever she wanted, not that there was much likelihood of that with Jenny. He teased her about it and called it "The Chalet School" but she would point to all the girls in overalls 'degaussing' minesweepers in dry-docks up the Old Town, or posted 'missing' on Atlantic crossings, and tell him to "button his lip".

He first met her at a dance at the American 'Red Cross' in Whitefriargate in Hull and couldn't believe his luck. Later, he'd repeatedly phoned her at home and (after getting past mother) persuaded her to come to the cinema with him. He could remember it was the 'Monica Cinema' on Newland Avenue but had no idea what picture they'd gone to see. He was too busy looking at her.

In the middle of the film there was an air raid. A notice was projected onto the screen by the management, announcing that an air raid was on and that those people who wished to should leave the cinema now. Most people did as they did and stayed to watch the end of the film. He thought it was an American gangster movie because there was a lot of shooting on the soundtrack which masked the noise of the raid. When they came out they saw that a terraced house nearby, which had been intact when they all went in, had suffered a direct hit. It had been as near as that, but then wartime was so often like this.

She looked wonderful in her uniform and he loved walking down the street with her on his arm. If there was one thing he liked better than a pretty girl in uniform, it was a brunette in black stockings. In the sober smartness of navy blue, the vivacity of her youth and personality shone through her brown eyes under a mop of dark hair held in check by a peaked cap. Everyone warmed to her, everyone liked her.

Of course the acronym for the 'W.R.N.S.' became "wrens", and that tiny but courageous British riverine bird was the obvious mascot for the ladies of the Royal Navy. In English folklore, that same creature had acquired the affectionate epithet of 'Jenny wren' and it was an irresistible joke to anyone who discovered his own 'wren' was indeed a Jenny.

"Better than spinning....." was her standard retort. Nevertheless, he knew she shared many of the indomitable qualities of that little, bright-eyed bird in its instinct for survival and he loved her truly for it.

Her parents lived out at Swanland, one of those comfortable villages to the west of Hull where the professional and trading classes were migrating in search of a northern equivalent to Surrey's 'Metroland' - commuting from the country. If she was on duty in Hull and he was on leave then he would spend many hours playing snooker with her father in a large room over the garage. He was usually careful to let him win. He helped her mother with the washing-up and she called him 'a gentleman'. This did not make their approval absolute.

Jenny was married at nineteen. Her parents were aghast. They might have found him charming but, when all was said and done, he was barely twenty-one; just another wartime flier with no life-expectancy.

What her parents failed to understand was that this was precisely the reason which caused all the rush. Neither of them were prepared to risk his chances of survival through a long drawn-out engagement before they went to bed together, but Jenny at least was determined that the proper social niceties should still be observed. (The influence of the Church?)

So be it. But, in wartime, people's priorities and plans became so much more short-term. Neither of them really knew enough about each other to envisage an entire span together. It was right for the moment – what the future would bring, no-one could say or guess. He told her not to stay a widow for the rest of her life; if anything happened to him and the letter of farewell all aircrew had sitting on their personal file in the adjutant's office ever needed to be delivered. She said nothing, just shook her head and her brown eyes welled over. They did love each other.

He got a lift in a Bedford truck which was taking some aircraft parts over to Leconfield. When he got there, they were still clearing-up after the previous night's raid. All his flight, 'B' flight, were in the air again. There were no spare aircraft for him to use and his own remained at Driffield with its back broken. It was a write-off.

The Ground C.O. gave him a twenty-four hour leave pass, to give him "a breather". A salvage squad had found most of his Junkers 88 on Welton Wold and was apparently bringing the tail-fin back as a trophy to decorate the stand-by hut. (By now he didn't really want to know anymore and perhaps it showed).

He took a bicycle from a pile near the sandbagged guardroom and rode off to the farm just outside Beverley on the Malton Road, where he was billeted. At weekends Jenny would drive out in her father's car, petrol ration permitting, and they would have frantic sex. The love came afterwards.

It didn't take long on the bike to get from Leconfield to the farm. There was nobody in the yard as he rode in and crossed to the row of farm workers' cottages. Theirs was the far end one. The others were occupied by Canadian airmen or New Zealanders. Loyal friends from across the world, come to the aid of the Mother Country, ready to die with us against the Nazi tyranny.

He leant the cycle against the garden fence by the gate and looked up at the house. The curtains were still drawn, as they had been when he had left it three days ago. Pity. He allowed himself this one small admission of disappointment. Through the obligations of their respective Services, he knew he was not likely to see her again until Friday or Saturday next. Nevertheless, there had been just a hope that she might have come home for some reason, a small hope he knew. He desperately wanted to see her, to tell her of his ordeal of survival, to hold her.

It was an odd war like that. One minute you were fighting for your life in the air, the next having a pint with your mates in the pub or taking your wife or girlfriend out to a dance.

He unlocked the front door, its green paint bleached, cracked and faded by the sun. Inside, the cottage was penetrated by muslin filtered shafts of late afternoon sunlight through drawn drapery. He flung these leaking dams to sight aside and daylight deluged the familiar room. On the window ledge, mantelpiece and piano top, fieldflowers like poppy, ox-eye daisy and buttercup sagged in milk bottle; vase and jam jar, slowly dying. It must be nearly a fortnight gone since she first picked and placed them.

He lifted up their wedding photograph in its silver frame from the piano and looked at it. He knew he must see her today - he could not wait for the end of the week and, this time, it was not just for the sex. She would want reassurance, too.

Upstairs, in their bedroom, the sheets were as crumpled as when they left them - first she, then a few hours later he too. He opened the wardrobe and took out a sports jacket and his best cavalry twill trousers. Transport was going to be a problem and he mentally debated wearing his spare RAF uniform; if only because the goodwill attaching to it should improve his chances of a lift in whatever motor vehicle was passing. On the basis that she might be at her parents, he opted for the civilian version. He put on his best check shirt and a silk cravat. The only concession to the service was a miniature gold RAF badge pinned on his jacket lapel.

He walked across the yard to the farmhouse. Mrs. Andrew was busy, sliding a large tray of meat pies into the oven for the farm workers' lunch tomorrow. She readily gave him permission to use the telephone in the hall, but the operator at the other end was unable to put him through to the Admiralty offices in Paragon Street. Most city centre lines were down after last night's raid, she told him, it was not unusual. Instead, he tried the 'in-laws' out at Swanland. Their line was still working but it rang and rang without answer. Either they were away at some Golf Club dinner or helping in the Swanland Forces canteen, one of their contributions to the War Effort.

He would go anyway. With a raid like last night's going on, she would know he was involved. Somewhere high above her in the darkness, in danger of his life, defending his country, fighting for her. Privately, she would be worried sick and the very best thing he could do was to let her know as soon as possible that he was OK. Turn up outside the office and wait to meet her as she was coming down the steps after work. Joyful reunion in the street. Take her out somewhere for a surprise dinner - if they could find a restaurant that hadn't been bombed - a surprise celebration just to celebrate the simple pleasure of still being alive and still being together.

He cycled into Beverley and went straight to the railway station.

More problems. Apparently no trains were running right into Hull because of last night's raid on the city. According to the angry old man in the ticket office, the Leeds train had arrived five minutes late, only to see the Hull station platform where punctuality would have placed it receive a direct hit from a German bomb, right before the driver and fireman's horrified eyes.

If he could not get in all the way, then at least he was taken as far as Cottingham on an overcrowded train where there were as many standing as sitting. Arriving there, and in the confusion of leaving the carriage, he found someone else had already removed his cycle from the guards van and made off.

Standing outside Cottingham Station, he knew he was still some miles from the city and now a pedestrian. As he set off grimly towards Hull Road, he was growing more concerned yet for Jenny's safety and for how much raid damage she would have to negotiate if she was to get safely out of the city. At this rate, it was looking like he would not arrive at her office until after she'd left and he did not want her walking around in the blackout on her own.

Passing the driveway of a large house set behind a screen of mature trees, the black bonnet of an old-fashioned Austin 10 saloon nosed in front of him. Its elderly driver let him cross the footway in front of him before pulling out onto the main road and then drawing up alongside. He was in luck:

"Do you want a lift?"

His "Oh, yes!" was prompt and appreciative: "I didn't think I'd get there in time!"

The driver smiled: "It says in the newspapers we can't all go around on our own by car, not when petrol's so short and so many go without. Just a case of getting over our ingrained English reserve, eh?"

His rescuer was a retired 'Weights and Measures' officer of the City Council, called away from the enjoyment of his pension by his erstwhile employers to replace younger colleagues now in the Forces. Someone was still needed to make sure the pubs don't try and serve short measures under cover of wartime. He, too, was travelling into the city but remained sanguine about their chances of getting right into the centre:

"I've spent the last two nights in the air raid shelter we've got in our cellar. It's been really bad – a lot of damage. The Hun has given us a real pasting and no mistake. Probably the worst we've had in nineteen months of war. If it's like this out here in Cottingham, then I fear for some serious casualties in the town – and I'm not talking a few cuts from flying glass."

This gloomy prophesy began to acquire greater credence the nearer they drove to that place. The roads were increasingly busy with army lorries, ambulances and vehicles of the salvage corps, soldiers hanging off the sides. If there was a surprising number of private cars moving about, mudguards painted white and headlamps blanked off for the blackout, the one thing strangely absent was sight of any of the city's buses.

Their first real obstacle came on Spring Bank, where this main thoroughfare was blocked by temporary wooden railings hung with ominous signs: "ROAD CLOSED. DANGER. UNEXPLODED BOMB". Nearby, policemen in dark blue-painted steel helmets stood about, keen to reinforce the authority of this blockade. The Austin turned off, speeding instead through shabby back streets where children with dirty faces still played amongst the ruins of bombed-out housing. A pall of smoke hung over the city from hundreds of fires, many of which no-one had yet made any attempt to extinguish.

The old Weights & Measure man tut-tutted and, only now noticing his passenger's small lapel badge, tried to draw him into conversation and out of silence, on the subject of 'The War In The Air'. Unfortunately, his previously grateful hitch-hiker had become monosyllabic. Worry was eating him up.

On Ferensway, they found themselves at the gates of devastation. Black smoke still rose from the Paragon Railway Station and the City Bus Station, both of which had taken direct hits. Large pieces of building lay prone in the roadway in front of them and an Air Raid Protection Warden in another steel helmet stepped out to prevent them travelling on any further.

Tryton thanked the old man for the lift but the latter was too preoccupied with struggling to reverse his car out of the danger area under the stern supervision of the ARP warden to acknowledge his mumbled words of thanks.

Tryton stepped out onto the pavement, to find another sign lying flat in the road in front of him, knocked over either by blast or by passing vehicles. "DANGER OF FALLING BUILDINGS" it said. Flickering paraffin lamps with blue glass marked the edge of every bomb site, like candles to the dead. Broken glass crunched underfoot as he walked, blown into glittering grit by the explosions.

As well as conventional explosives, the German aircraft had brought hundreds of parachute mines which drifted slowly in with flapping canvas like butterfly wings, before exploding. Thousands of incendiary devices had been dropped onto the city and the air was thick with the taste of their flowering.

As he walked past the shattered Railway Station and entered Paragon Square by the Cenotaph, an old-fashioned, open-top, MG sports car, hand-painted red, came tearing up. It was filled with junior Army officers and at first he thought they were going to stop him from going any further. In fact, it was an Army Bomb Disposal Squad and he realized they had rather more important things to worry about than one errant pedestrian.

When he entered Paragon Street he gasped and broke into a run. Already horrified by what he'd just seen in the square – the state of Hammond's Department store on his left, reduced to no more than five floors of open concrete shelving supported on blackened and twisted pillars - what now met his eyes ahead was still incredible. He had a view straight down Paragon Street into Victoria Square, the natural focus of the city, and instantly marked the huge gap visible in the building line.

"Jenny!" he implored, and ran.

True, the Prudential Tower still stood. But only just. Like a veteran boxer in his last fight, struck immobile under a welter of hammer blows from a younger, stronger opponent, it lingered still. Not quite upright.

The Prudential Tower, for the moment, still stood. But the Prudential Buildings, to which this tower had been no more than a fanciful Gothic finial, an endpiece, were gone. Entirely vapourised by blast and devoured by the ensuing firestorm as they were, he struggled to accept the totality of their destruction. Exhausted men of the Auxiliary Fire Service played their hoses on the smouldering plain of rubble.

47

Their office had been on the first floor. Her job was to plot the constantly shifting patterns of the minefields, laid by the Kriegsmarine and swept by the Royal Navy, onto Admiralty charts. It was an office joke that another girl, Margaret, whose brother was on destroyers, would always slightly exaggerate the scale of those minefields in the interests of his safety.

Now there was no office.

If there was warning of a raid, as there usually was, then she and her colleagues would go down onto the basement and while away the time in a large cellar which also doubled as a popular café. Now he could not even say where the basement had been.

He stepped nearer in the desperate fantastical hope that somehow those inside that cellar might have survived and merely be sealed in by rubble, like trapped miners, awaiting the arrival of their rescuers with cups of tea. A weary fireman, his helmet, face and overalls all whitened by dust and ash, must have read these thoughts as he walked across: "Move away from there, please, it's not safe. If you've come for someone, I've got to tell you – no-one got out alive!"

"My wife's in there…." he sobbed.

The fireman took his arm: "Look, I'm sorry, pal. They wouldn't have known what hit them!"

He staggered away aimlessly in his grief. In the same square, the bulky Edwardian rectangle of the City Hall, the Victorian pomp of the Town Docks Offices, and the classical simplicity of the Ferens Art Gallery had all – by a miracle – survived intact. But the building which stored his greatest treasure was burnt to cinders. Tears ran down his face at this unbearably cruel throw of fate.

The square streamed with water from broken hydrants, shattered mains and leaking firehoses. The tears of the city.

Army lorries stood at various angles, blocking the square wherever they'd slewed to a halt, whilst khaki figures clambered miserably over the ruins, struggling for purpose. Tram and telephone lines hung down, snapped like so many threads of life. Above this melancholy scene, the Prudential Tower, wreathed in smoke, stood as a dark lighthouse hijacked by wreckers.

A painted sign, newly-erected, referred enquirers to the 'Casualty Information Bureau' at 3, Ferensway Arcade.

Driven by the hope of information, the chance that someone could show him she had not been in the office last night, he retraced his steps to find the stairway and waiting room of these premises jammed with people, all as desperate as he. He heard a thick-set, ugly man with an East Hull accent shout: "Bloody RAF! Where the hell was the air force? Bloody fly-boys!"

In the throng, it was hard to tell whether this was directed specifically at him but, in any case, he resolved to keep his head down. The latest casualty bulletins were pinned to the yellow walls and he skimmed them feverishly.

"Bloody Brylcreem Boys!"

He was next in the queue. A middle-aged spinster with greying hair gripped in an angry bun and black rings around her eyes stood defiantly at a desk with the bundle of casualty lists in her hands:

No, the final casualty figures had not been issued. No, there was no list at all for Paragon Street or King Edward Street. No, she could not - and would not - confirm that there had even been Admiralty offices in Paragon Street, let alone that such offices might have been hit or casualties taken there. She could at least confirm that some naval personnel were amongst the overall casualties in the city last night. (In a maritime town like Hull, this concession was hardly surprising). However, these casualties (whoever and wherever they were - and she was not saying) had not yet been recovered or identified. No, it was not known at present whether - or when - any of last night's casualties could or would be recovered. Next!

He fell back, his eyes stinging, and the queue shuffled forward past him, anxious for news of its bereavement. He retreated to the stairwell, stumbling blindly. A brown hand from a tweed sleeve seized his arm firmly and a man spoke in his ear:

"There's a Wren in the Infirmary!"

He ran out into Ferensway where, behind twin lanterned gates, there was a hospital – the Hull Royal Infirmary, or so he thought. This place of care revealed more scenes from Dante: White overalls splashed with red. Casualties lying in scorched and shredded clothes, their faces and hair still blackened by fire and soot. The cries of the injured and shell-shocked. Trollies pushing quickly through the crowded corridors to the operating theatre, their passengers insensible.

49

This building too, just up the road from the railway station and on the same side, had itself been hit. Desperate efforts to shore up and repair the structure or to salvage equipment went on amongst the cool determination of the medical staff. The entire hospital had become one big accident and emergency department. Except that none of this was through any accident but the wicked designs of men. Barbarians!

Information as to names and places was even more elusive amongst all this scurrying and distress. He roamed the corridors unchallenged, looking closely at everyone he could see but, drawn into this terrible institution, they all looked like patients, not people.

He found a Staff Nurse who thought she could remember - although she could not be entirely certain, having been at work for twenty four hours continuously without a proper sleep and now uncertain of even what day it was. But, yes, she thought she could remember a girl in Wren's uniform being brought in; in the early hours of the morning following the raid the night before. She was not here now though and she thought – if it was the patient she was thinking of – that it was because she had been transferred to the other hospital, to the one on Prospect Street, because of the shortage of beds and space caused by the bomb damage. He took her hand and thanked her warmly before tearing off outside.

It was getting dark again. The air raid sirens began to howl once more, a dirge for a dusk that always brought bombers, but he ignored them, crossing the debris-strewn roadway of Ferensway yet again, this time heading east. On the other side, he became confused in the dark, cobbled streets and stopped an exhausted-looking woman pushing a pram with a rolled-up mattress tied on top, asking her for directions.

Eventually he did find the hospital on Prospect Street. It was not so far away from where he'd first started, from the railway station. The awful scenes within were much the same as he'd observed over the way, but at least they seemed to have more of a system for booking people in and more idea of their intake.

Yes, they had a Wren. No, they did not know her name and – no, prepare yourself - she is too badly hurt and too far from consciousness to tell them. This way.

His fingers dug into the bony wrist of the motherly nurse that led him like a child straight into the relevant ward.

Amongst a chaos of screens and wires, of drips and bandages, there was an iron bedstead with a navy-blue uniform jacket, filthy with ash and brickdust, hung over the progress chart at its end. Beyond these tell-tale entries of decline, a young woman's head rested deathly-pale on a whiter pillow.

He turned away in complete despair. It was Margaret, the map-drawer whose brother was in destroyers. Lucky Margaret.

At the age of twenty-one, he became a widower.

"There's no need for archaeology in Hull - it's all in the history books!"

(Reported remark of a Kingston-upon-Hull city councillor)

In the last week of September 1941, as the thousands of German troops engaged in 'Operation Barbarossa' entered Kiev and prepared for their attack on Moscow (in fatal emulation of Napoleon Bonaparte's own, most-disastrous throw), everyday life in Little England continued.

Despite the bombing of the nearby city of Hull, the aircraft factory at Brough-on-Humber continued with its vital production for the war effort; output pretty-much unabated. The sixth annual general meeting of Blackburn Aircraft Limited, reporting an annual profit of £212,969, was held there at its registered offices in obedience to the Companies Act. While self-congratulatory applause from directors, shareholders, and employees still rang through the airfield hanger converted for their meeting, a fall of stones in a mile-distant quarry would have done well for echo. If the plaudits of profit are soon forgotten, this shimmering report of stone on stone rang long through the centuries - beyond the reach of any auditor:

Workmen operating a mechanical shovel in the limestone quarry known locally as the "Cockle Pits", on the west side of the main Hull-to-Leeds road, were busy removing top soil in order to get at valuable yellow stone beneath. The more of Hull was bombed, the more of this stone would be needed for its eventual reconstruction. Removing this layer of soil over stone, the overburden, today revealed something rather more than the geological prize expected.

"Hey, George, come and have a look at this!" shouted the driver's mate to his colleague operating the levers on the mechanical excavator. The mighty cast iron jaws of the digger's bucket dangled aloft and ajar, like some fossilised tyrannosaurus, as its operator abandoned his seat. Together, they stood looking down into the pit created in the rich, alluvial loam. They were old men, too old to be called up for service in His Majesty's Armed Forces, but hardened by a lifetime of working outside in all weathers. Grizzled as they were, these two knew they'd found something rather special. Perhaps the most memorable moment of their hard lives had just occurred.

Beneath the topsoil was a layer of blown sand, perhaps three feet thick. It was probably this, nature's gentlest packing, which preserved a decorated pavement, some fourteen feet square. Even these rude mechanicals bore an innate sense and simple understanding of their local history. They guessed at once it was Roman.

George dropped down into the hole, sweeping more sand away with his cap and soon exposing more of the pavement. Their excavator had removed nearly every trace of whatever building once covered the pavement, but at least it left the floor itself intact and in good condition. What few remnants of robbed wall remained were substantial in their footings, not surprisingly made from limestone.

George was joined in the hole by his mate. In the centre of the pavement they saw a fluted medallion pattern, like an open umbrella viewed from above. This was flanked by rectangular panels patterned in either chequers or ropework. At one end of the pavement there was a hole where it had collapsed into a void beneath. The two men studied this using a torch and realised how the floor was supported on many small pillars, constructed from brick tiles. It would be established that this was a hypocaust - the Roman way of centrally-heating a room: not only under its floor but also up the walls, through hollow clay pipes.

"I think we'd better tell Mr. Watts about this...." said George who was always the strong-minded one. He stumped off to the shed by the quarry entrance serving as a site office. After a few words with the foreman, who came over to look, it was agreed that he could get his bicycle and ride to Brantingham Post Office to use the telephone there.

Mr. W. Clifford Watts was the proprietor of the quarry and his men could well imagine his displeasure if notified of their discovery any later than immediately.

Whilst Mr. Watts was the operator of the quarry, the site itself was actually owned by his landlord, Mr. Arnold Reckitt of Brantinghamthorpe Hall. Mr Reckitt was industrialist turned landed-gentry, the managing director of the Reckitt's household chemical company; famously making its commercial name and fortune with an eponymous blue dye.

He and Watts for their part called on Mr. Tom Sheppard, the Director of Hull Museums, whom they asked to supervise the proper excavation of this first pavement as well as a second one found shortly after. These gentlemen in turn enlisted the assistance of Mr. A. Heslop Antrum, a local architect who, with the help of their enthusiastic workmen and between them together uncovered both of these pavements and another four rooms from a much larger Roman Villa.

It was the Roman writer Cato who described the ideal place for the establishment of a villa and its estate as not far from a main road (to take its produce to market) with ready access to a town (where the produce would be sold). So it was here. The builders of Brantingham Villa must have borne that dictum closely in mind, for it was only a mile or so to the Civitas of Petuaria (the county town of the local Parisii tribe) or the adjoining military and naval base of Brough-on-Humber. Here too was landfall for the regular ferries plying the grey-brown waters of the Humber, linking the main road up from Lindum Coloniae (Lincoln) with its continuation to the garrison town of Derventio (Malton) to the north; a millennia-and-a-half before the Hull steamers that take their place in wartime Britain.

If we hear a lot about Roman roads, it's easy to forget how important water-borne transport was to them - for transporting heavy goods and troops in quantity. A surviving piece of Roman price-fixing, the Edict of Diocletian, confirms the point. Transporting goods by water was seven times less expensive than moving goods by road then, and the Humber gave access to half of England this side of the Pennines. In particular, to the north-east, its estuary gives access to the broad mouth of the sinuous Ouse, that river upon whose banks stood Roman Britain's second city – Eboracum: "the place of the boar". York - headquarters of the military zone.

Aside from these strategic considerations, the villa site was an admirable one in itself; standing on the brow of a hill forming the last rise of the land before its southerly descent into the Humber itself.

Further north, behind the villa, the escarpment of the high ground we know as the Wolds rises rapidly to dominate the horizon. These are the final most northerly extensions of those chalk uplands which have their beginnings in the rolling downland of the South Coast. For the length of England, this type of terrain and the agricultural-cum-social patterns of the Roman villas that go with it are inextricably linked. As Mr. Sheppard was quick to explain to Mr and Mrs. Reckitt, when they visited the excavation site.

It was a happy discovery for everyone. Something they all took the more pleasure in announcing at a time when Britain stood alone against the Nazi threat and newspapers or radio only brought bad news. They were pleased to have their picture taken together by a photographer from the Hull 'Daily Mail'; contemplating the new-found pavement in stiff-backed poses like the three Edwardians they really were. On Saturday, 27th September 1941, they even made the front page of the 'City Final' edition, this story and their picture being rushed to newsagents' shops across the county in a fleet of red and black 'Daily Mail' vans run on scarce rationed petrol.

As their own chauffeur drove them in a little more comfort back to Brantinghamthorpe Hall in the Rolls-Royce, Arnold Reckitt acknowledged for the first time in his life the significant directness of that familiar lane known locally as Brantingham Outgang. Running straight from what they now knew to be the site of a Roman villa, across the main road and into Brantingham village, at the foot of the Wolds escarpment, it then joined up with the Wolds road emerging from that narrow defile; Brantingham Dale.

He pointed to the road ahead. "Straight as a legionary javelin!" he exclaimed to his wife, and she laughed. (As she said later: "Arnold is getting quite carried away with all this Roman business!") But once through the village, past the church and up through the dale, the modern road becomes too hemmed in by dark trees and high ground to resemble the sort of road the Roman army would engineer for its use. Rather the high-level route, with long views and sparse vegetation. That's the one they would have favoured, he was sure of that.

For his own part, Mr. Sheppard's more learned money was on the desperate incline of nearby Spout Hill. Its stern directness and unsympathetic gradient appears the obvious design of an infantry-minded engineer. Sheppard was reinforced in this view by its noticeable width. Those broad margins and its subsequent continuation - at the top of Spout Hill - as a bumpy green lane, still with generous verges and that certainty of alignment, were all characteristic of every Roman road he knew of in England which had survived undeveloped.

Having dutifully waved the Reckitts 'goodbye' from the quarry gate, Tom Sheppard was released by the landowner's departure to resume his lonely study of what they'd unearthed over the last few days. This appearance of sadness was more than figurative. At the end of the week he would retire from his post as Curator of Hull Museums, a role in which he'd acquired an international reputation before the war. Yet here he was - at the final end of that career - gazing down at what could prove his most spectacular find of all.

The second mosaic they'd found was smaller, simpler and squarer. Nine foot by nine. Outer contrasting blue bands in the pattern led into a square border of red, white, and blue fish scales. Within that border, a frame of solid triangles, grey on white. The central square bearing the characteristic 'running pelta' design as it's known, in blue on white. The patterns and the colours were given by the *tesserae*; small cubes less than half-an-inch square cut from blue limestone, or red brick, white chalk, or orange sandstone by the unknown craftsmen who made these pavements.

Despite the miracle of their survival, Tom Sheppard was seriously worried about how these relics could survive much beyond their discovery. As he'd said, at this time when newspapers and radio could offer little beyond bad news of world war, their reporting of this find had excited enormous interest over the last few days. There'd been a constant stream of visitors to the site ever since these discoveries were first announced in the Yorkshire Post and the Hull Daily Mail's report would only add to that.

Despite their enthusiasm, many of these visitors had proved themselves thoughtless, actually stepping onto the pavement and scattering or loosening the *tesserae* with their feet.

Sheppard wondered whether Mr. Watts would allow the pavements to remain in position but protected by a lock-up wooden shed. The combination of a small admission charge and the sale of an illustrated handbook he had in mind could well be enough to finance such a modest structure, if Watts was agreeable.

He looked up as a warm, westerly breeze soughed through the high wood bounding the quarry on its east side. Those melancholy lines of A. E. Houseman, penned in the ruins of the old Roman city at Wroexeter in Shropshire, came at once into his mind: "The gale it plies the sapling double, But the Roman and his trouble are ashes beneath Uricon..."

Sheppard wondered how this great house and the country estate which undoubtedly went with it had met their end. With a bang or a whimper? Fire and storm, or just fading away?

In the soil, upon and around the pavements, he and his colleagues found countless fragments of Roman pottery, painted wall plaster, and pantile roof tiles. Every single piece a true reminder and real evidence of real lives lived in this place, so long ago. Some of the pottery he recognized as made locally in the Thorlam Kilns, near Holme-on-Spalding Moor; a Roman factory he'd excavated himself before the war and written a learned paper about. Looking at the position of the debris and the burnt layers which went with them, there seemed little doubt to him it must have been a sudden end, not any gradual slide into dereliction.

On the evidence of a couple of coins found there, these two rooms could not have been built any earlier than the reign of the Emperor Constantine the Great, he decided. This was a late flowering of prosperity in the history of Roman Britain, fostered perhaps by wealthy refugees fleeing barbarian attacks on the north European provinces of the Empire; Germania and Gaul. Even then, Pictish raiding boats from Scotland and Saxon longships from across the North Sea had already been making their greedy and destructive forays against the coasts of Roman Britannia for at least a century. Were they the people who'd destroyed the villa?

What was certain now was how, in September 1941, it was the self-same coastal regions of continental Europe which spawned today's raiders, albeit by a means and on a scale unimaginable to the Romans or their enemies.

(History repeating itself?)

Sheppard pondered the irony of a group of English quarrymen unveiling this local monument to the triumph of barbarism over civilisation; ancient parallel to the destruction being wrought every night by the Luftwaffe upon the Kingstown of Hull only a dozen miles away. If Sheppard and his friends couldn't save Hull, at least they could save what was left of this villa – a job which turned out harder than expected. It wasn't long before the limitations of wartime and the depredations of visitors persuaded them that the best way to preserve these pavements would be carefully recovering them with the gentle earth that had already guarded them so well these sixteen hundred years past. Finally, the industrialist landlord and his quarryman tenant agreed between them that the site of the villa should remain protected as an elevated 'island' even if commercial quarrying operations must continue around it. Apart from these arrangements, that was an end to it. Nothing else could be done because of the war and, not for the first time in its history, the villa waited for peace.

Which is not to say it was forgotten about. Neither is it entirely right to say nothing else could be done because of the war. In fact it was only a short report of the discovery which was written up in the 'Yorkshire Archaeological Journal' for that year, entered as part of a wider review headed: "Roman Yorkshire 1941".

And there was one further thing, something which was arguably only achieved thanks to the war.

Mr. Sydney Coverdale, a keen local subscriber to the Journal and a well-known member of the 'Society for the Promotion of Roman Studies' had recently enlisted in the RAF under a sense of patriotic duty. The science of aerial photography of archaeological sites was then a novelty still in its infancy but, by sheer force of personality, Aircraftsman Coverdale was able to persuade his RAF superiors and a pilot to allow the diversion of a practice photographic flight over Brantingham just to put a few extra frames in the camera.

Coverdale had high hopes for what they might show.

Unfortunately, when developed his proof prints didn't show any signs of the villa itself, at all. In view of its total destruction by old quarry workings perhaps attracted there (long ago) by the ruins of the villa in the first place, this was not so surprising. No more need be said about it here, either, but for two salient points left to mention:

One is that, if these aerial photos didn't show the villa house itself, they did at least reveal clear traces of some other Roman buildings across the road, in an adjacent field associated with the villa, so confirming the history and wider extent of the site.

The other point is that, whilst this determined effort didn't add an awful lot to contemporary archaeological knowledge of the site, it is still worth mentioning here because the high-speed De Haviland Mosquito PRU ('photo-reconnaissance unit') aircraft used for this important flight was actually flown by another personality important to our history.

Life being full of coincidences (and as the Squadron's flight records in the Hendon archive disclose), it just so happened to be Flight Sergeant Michael Tryton whom his superiors asked and who so cheerfully agreed (as personal favour for Aircraftsman Coverdale) to take the young lad up. Tryton could himself remember taking his sky-blue Mosquito high up over the Humber before diving it steeply-down fast and low onto Brantingham fields – just to get a few extra frames into the 'can' on this, his last-ever training flight in this particular machine.

Though he did not know it then, a good many years were to go by before Michael Tryton would ever see the green fields of East Yorkshire again; what with his posting to North Africa coming through so soon after; at the end of the same month.

After all that wretched business about losing his wife in the 'Blitz', the Adjutant thought it might do him good, cheer him up a bit. Get some of that grief out of his system in the chance of strafing German transport columns in the Western Desert, or bombing panzers in the Wadi. Give their General, that Erwin Rommel fellow, something to think about in the process.

About time the 'Desert Fox' was brought down a peg or two.

"How much sleep, I ask you, can one get in lodgings here? Unbroken nights (and this is the root of the problem...) are a rich man's privilege"

Juvenal (Roman poet and Stoic) 60 -140 A.D.

V

Leaning on the rail of the ferry boat that brought him across the great river, he felt it stagger as it hit the rolling wake of the warship which crossed their bows, heading with obvious urgency for the open sea - battened-down on some affair of state.

Some of the other passengers joined him to admire the sleek lines of this ship of the line, this first-rater, as it creamed through a boiling foam of its own making ahead of them, madly pursued by gulls.

White ash oars rose and fell in rhythmic obedience to the hortator's drum beat as the gilded stern, adorned with the personal flag of the Praefectus Reliquationis Classis, slid across their sight. His new-found companion at the rail, the sort of stranger who speaks to you when you rather hope they'll latch on to someone else, took off his greasy Phrygian cap and waved it at the passing trireme, concerned lest his fellow travellers might somehow overlook this piece of marine magnificence sweeping by.

The 'Defensor' of the Abus Squadron..." he announced helpfully, as if his listeners could not read the carved lettering on a plaque so clearly picked out in red and set above the traditional 'eye' on each side of the prow.

"Not often you'll see a vessel of that quality so far north in this day and age", continued their lecturer, smoothing lank hair down before re-glueing his hat in situ.

Now entering calmer waters, their rotund and bobbing ferry boat approached the muddy creek leading into the haven where other warships or patrol vessels of the Classis Britannica, great and small, were usually berthed when off-duty. At low tide they either rested on the dark-brown, stinking mud or were pulled up into a large, walled enclosure intended to protect them against attack from the landward side. The tide was ebbing fast and already some of the bigger merchant ships lolled idly against the rotting jetties as the waters withdrew. Seabirds rose into the sky and wheeled about, yelling with greed as the retreating tide exposed their favourite diet of lugworms on the mudbanks.

"Welcome to Petuaria!" said Phrygian cap through stained teeth: "Travelled far?"

"Far enough," his new friend thought to himself, as he trawled his sparse repertoire of small-talk for a suitably non-committal reply: "From Lindum Coloniae."

That was giving nothing away, since the Lindum road ended abruptly on the southern side of the great river - on that ramshackle wooden pier where he and the other travellers had taken this ferry together, sharing the cost. Where else would he have come from, for goodness sake?

"Travelling on to Derventio, are we, or perhaps cutting across to Eboracum in pursuit of some pressing matter at the Court of the Praeses?"

"No, no, I'm hoping to stay on here in Petuaria for a few days." (Why so specific a question about the Praeses?)

"There you go! I was marking you down as a serious man of business, but no harm done. It's just my little entertainment when travelling, you know, but no offence intended. However short the journey, I always like to place my fellow travellers. Ports and harbours: "All these people!" I say. "Rushing about! Where are they all going, Felix, what do they do for their living?" Just my little game, you see."

"No, well if it's business, it's only family business - a death in the family."

Perhaps he could have said something more titillating to Phrygian Cap's overweening curiosity, his blatant nosiness. Something like: "How kind of you to be so interested in my private business. Let me satisfy your indecent interest in other people's private affairs by announcing myself: I am Flavius Candidus, a beneficarius consularis appointed by the civil governor. As an officer of the provincial government, I am sent on the personal directions of the Vicarius himself to make discreet enquiries into certain suspected irregularities in the local government of Petuaria".

As if that type of frank indiscretion would not have got his unctuous enquirer all agog. It would as likely also guarantee a fatal "accident" for one or both of them within the very next trajectory of the Unconquered Sun God. Which is precisely what made any idea of such mischievous frankness so easy to resist.

"I'm so sorry, friend. The Gods of the Shades await us all…"

Happily, his questioner seemed sufficiently diverted by the melancholy attractions of funeral ritual to be satisfied with this first answer, if only for a moment. The governor's enquiry agent took this ideal opportunity to counterattack with questions of his own: "Ha! Now if there's one thing I've learnt only too well, it's the sheer fragility of human existence. Today, it's someone-else's turn and the ancestral duties are mine to perform – because I'm their executor. Tomorrow may be different! But enough of this gloomy talk! What about yourself? Come a long way?"

"Left Aquae Arnemetiae three days ago. Perhaps I should introduce myself, friend: Cicerius Felix of the Parisii tribe."

"A homecoming for you, is it then?"

"Well, yes and no! Of course you're quite right - as the 'Civitas Parisii' this old place truly is my home town but, no, I've not lived around here since I was a lad. So, the answer's 'yes' - you do find me here on business too - but I'm afraid it's company business, not family affairs."

By the look of him, with his greasy hat, stained leather jerkin and bad teeth, it could only be dirty business. Nevertheless, like all good investigators you have to be a good listener and Candidus affected his interest well:

"So, Felix, let me be the curious enquirer now. What line of work brings a busy man like you to a quiet place like this, even if it is company business?"

"I'm a mining engineer. I manage one of the lead mines near Arnemetiae – up in the hills behind the spa town."

Felix looked the type – as if he most naturally belonged underground, spending his life that much closer to Hades. Candidus could imagine him in that nightmare world of lost souls; amongst the manacled slaves and dangerous convicts; the constant darkness and sudden flooding; the bad air and daily 'accidents'. It took an effort to sound interested:

"A responsible job, then?"

Flattery had the desired effect. Felix summoned up the requisite phlegm into his mouth and spat it with great force into the foaming waters, as if to emphasise his deep approval of the facile respect conveyed in this question:

"You're telling me! Never a moment's peace! If it's not the workforce getting stroppy or some idiot falling down a shaft, there's an argument with the metalworkers over pricing the concession they have for reworking slag. Is it me or are people getting more greedy these days? Everyone wants their cut, that's for sure! Of course, the government's always interfering too, what with the tax inspectors snooping round and all the legislation we get. A new law for every day of the week. If you ask me, there's too much of that. Laws can't fix everything, you know. Needlessly stifling the spirit of free enterprise, it's my belief. Regulations about how you treat the slaves; regulations about where you can dig your shafts, how close to water courses, and so on. Frankly, it's getting well nigh impossible to run any sort of business successfully with all that bureaucracy breathing down your neck."

"I didn't know there were lead mines around Petuaria....?"

"No, you're right - there aren't. But I'm employed by the "Societas Lutudarensis", a private mining company. Like I said, we operate out of the hill country near Arnemetiae. Do you know it – Lutudarum? No, I didn't think you would. Around Navio? No, not been there either? Well, it's a good way from here, but we do transport quite a lot of product over to Petuaria on these big barges you'll see, before shipping it out to Gaul, Germania and the Rhine from our big new warehouse on the wharfside here."

"You've come to have a look over that part of the operation?"

"Well, I suppose so. Errr.. not exactly. Look, I'll be quite honest with you – after all, you might pick up some useful information for me yourself, while you're here. You look a bright sort of fellow, so let me know if you do. I'll make it worth your while…"

There was a pause while Felix looked sidelong at his fellow-passenger as if weighing up how much to tell him, before continuing, obviously encouraged:

"What happened is my company lost a whole consignment of lead ingots. 'Pigs' as we call them in the trade. A complete cart-load disappears in broad daylight, not far from this port. Stolen probably but, as you can guess, there's hell to pay! One of our bosses, a director of the company, lives just outside Petuaria in a big smart villa. There's quite a few of them live around here - another co-director, a man called Protius, he lives in that massive place you saw just where we got onto this ferry." (He paused again).

"...But the one I'm going to see has his country estate on the opposite side. This side, where we're going. He's the one in charge of import-export for our company. The top man. A busy person with big responsibilities. Imperial interests to answer for, too, if the profit line drops. So, an important fellow and – more to the point – someone particularly powerful hereabouts, I'm told. The power of 'life and death' too, I've heard it said. Problem is, he's the very one I've got to go and see. Face-to-face. *"Invited over to make my report and my explanations, if you please"*. I don't mind telling you - I'm not much looking forward to it....." (His voice trailed away at the prospect).

"You mean Marcus Ulpius Januarius, don't you?"

Felix stiffened markedly at the name: "You know him? I thought you said you'd never been to Petuaria?"

"No, but of course I've heard of him. Everyone has – no-one planning on coming to Petuaria can avoid doing so. So, yes, I do know – or I've heard – that he's the most important man locally, just as his ancestors were for generations before him. But, no, I've never been to Petuaria myself, not till now."

Felix nodded, realising that perhaps that he'd talked too much on the most interesting topic (himself) and would do well to retake the initiative on the questioning front: "I don't think I caught your name, friend..?"

"No, you didn't! I'm Sextus Valens. I'll be getting lodgings in the town, but perhaps we can meet up for a drink, sometime, if you're here for a few days too..."

Distasteful as Felix was, Candidus realized he could prove a lucky break as a contact in the Januarius retinue. For that reason alone he would have to be cultivated - even if he could not be trusted with his new friend's real identity.

"Yes, thank you. I'd like that," said Felix faintly and doubtfully, already diverted by imagining the likely course of this imminent meeting with his eminent employer.

The sails on their small ferry had been rolled-up and stowed, so it could be rowed up the creek. Now it was being moored at a jetty in the lee of the town walls.

Since the tidal waters were presently so low, its passengers all found themselves required to scramble up a tall rickety ladder, set against a dockside treacherous with green slime. Fortunately they all managed this ugly obstacle without serious harm in time to receive their personal luggage at the top, thrown carelessly up to them by the surly ferryboat men.

Certainly the haven was busy enough. Ponderous merchant ships, broad in the beam, were tied up at the wharves for loading and unloading, lesser vessels bobbing around them.

Candidus had done his homework. He always did – a habit going back to his army days. The more pre-planning for the 'operation' they did, the luckier they were – as the Painted People well knew to their cost. Even without its benefit, he could describe the local trade well enough: Luxury goods came in from the Continent: those fine wines, the pottery, glassware and big amphorae of olive oil. To pay for them, out went the bulk grain of the Parisii in enough quantity even to feed the Rhine garrisons; the black iron work; the British tweeds; the carved trinkets of Whitby jet; the hunting dogs and, of course, the company lead.

Smaller, flat-bottomed boats continued this lucrative trade where the bigger vessels couldn't go: deeper into the estuary's extensive network of creeks and inland waterways; all the way up to Eboracum, military headquarters of the north, and across all the great rivers that fed the Abus.

Transporting goods by water in this way had been proven to be many times cheaper than their delivery by road. As a method, it probably predated the first road – hard to imagine, now, what those cruel and primitive days must have been like. A time before Rome – all those dread centuries of barbarism and darkness, waiting for her civilising light. A light that suddenly flickered.

These were troubling times.

If - as a port - Petuaria seemed to be thriving, it was a different story as a town. As he made his way up the short rutted road from the Haven, whistling tunelessly for company; up through the south gate and into the civilian settlement; he suddenly remembered how its entry in the Official List was shown.

The List was a document he'd first consulted in the Record Office at the Governor's Palace in Londinium. To give its full title, the *"Notitia Dignitatum tam Civilium quam Militarium in Partibus Orientis et in Partibus Occidentis"* was a list of officials of the Civil Service; of army officers' postings and all military units, with their respective places of station.

Since, as the elaborate title makes clear, this comprehensive digest tries to cover both Eastern and Western Empires, it's hardly the thing for light reading at bedtime. Nevertheless, at a time when still only planning this expedition of enquiry to which Candidus was by now inextricably committed, it seemed an essential part of his preparations to unroll a dog-eared copy of the 'Notitia' and see what it might say about the lovely town and idyllic environs of Petuaria Civitas Parisiorum.

His friends would say that Flavius Candidus was a literate if not a literary man. He had always enjoyed his reading and took some personal pleasure in research. (Less common in a soldier nowadays than it might once have been). In an age when the standards and prevalence of literacy amongst the public were undoubtedly slipping, like so many other aspects of civil society, his known facility with the written word was undoubtedly another reason for his master's choice of agent for this mission.

It is also the reason why, before ever reaching 'P' for 'Petuaria' in the manuscript, Candidus allowed himself an indulgent diversion along the way, into 'L' for 'Londinium Caesariensis', just to see what entry his new employer's establishment might deserve. Self-esteem still swollen from official confirmation of his recent appointment, Candidus had given a little whoop of triumph to find his own name and job title now added in fresh ink to the scroll by a meticulous archivist, even if it only came after some thirty others. The longer-serving members of the civil governor's staff in the capital were duly itemised first in that older faded ink which goes with seniority. Even so, the shrivelled clerk sitting at the desk opposite him in the hushed gloom of the State Record Office had given a basilisk's glare at his gleeful chortle, placing a bony finger of disapproval against bloodless, pursed lips. Candidus just grinned back, and gave him the sign of the horned one.

He reflected gratefully on what turmoil had produced a pressing need for men like himself in public government.

Say what you like about that miserable old pagan, the Emperor Diocletian, he did his bit for the bureaucrats. Rightly perceiving on his accession that something had to be done to stop the Empire destroying itself, in a recurrent spiral of provincial governors removing their soldiers from the frontier to engage in suicidal civil wars in order to claim the purple, Diocletian decided that the answer was to split everything.

How ironic then that, immediately after he'd done that, the old man went straight off to his own sunset home for retired emperors at a place they actually call Split, on the Adriatic coast. (Alright, 'Spalato' if we're going to be formal). Diocletian was terrified of any one man having enough power to challenge the Emperor concentrated in his hands. He was also wise enough to realise that the Empire had become too much for one man to run on his own. Accordingly it was divided between west and east, and his chum Maximianus was named as joint 'Augustus' with him. Job done.

Each of them appointed a bright lad as his 'Caesar', their designated heir. What could go wrong? The idea was that, for the first time and without a descent into civil war, the succession should run more smoothly in future through abdication of the Augustus in favour of the younger chap, once the whole thing got as tiring as Diocletian obviously thought it was. Early retirement beckoned.

Over a century ago, that ruthless but clever man, the Emperor Septimius Severus, had already had the same idea when he'd carved the province of Britain into two – so doubling the administration. (Pity his sons were such wasters – well, one was a fratricide, which by definition means the other one never got chance to prove his worth, poor lad). So 'Britannia Superior' was born, with its capital at Londinium, while 'Britannia Inferior's capital was established at the present-and-most-revered Emperor Constantine`s favourite city, Eboracum. No wonder he favoured the place. The city he'd first set out from after his father's loyal British legions declared him Caesar there, to march on Rome and a date with Destiny at the Milvian Bridge. "Eboracum the Blessed".

Add to this effect the reforms made by Diocletian and you have layer upon layer of civil servants. Men like Candidus.

The end result is that more people are working for the state now than for themselves. Production evaporates whilst taxation blooms. Each province has its governor and each governor has his own staff. The long-running joke about the receivers and the collectors of public money outnumbering the tax-paying classes soon loses its humour. But Candidus knew he shouldn't be laughing anyway – after all, he was a beneficiary of the system himself, whatever he thought about it.

Everyone knows to their cost how Diocletian's Edicts affected every individual in the Empire. They probably still do for that matter, especially those making your father's job hereditary for you.

There's no way getting round it - serfdom has come to match slavery as the way of life for so much of our population. Perhaps it's not your problem, so long as it's the next guy who you see dragging a crude wooden plough across a field or hauling charcoal into a heated stack. These are sights you can see everywhere. That and the dying – after all, life is cheap and human labour even cheaper.

Usually it doesn't even register. You can't let it, can you, not unless you're one of these Christians with their overactive conscience?

After all, there are much more important things to worry about, aren't there? Like the economy or the increasing number of barbarian raids; the growing threat to the towns from raiders, outlaws, or the roaming bands of unemployed. The brutal, bloody mindless crimes of the disaffected and disinherited. No wonder some folk look forward more to the Kingdom of God when life on this earth is so short for them and so wretched. How can we expect them to stand up and defend a greedy society that seems to care so little about them?

What's the solution? Well, it probably depends on what you think is the biggest problem. Is it a military problem, a social problem, or an economic problem? Diocletian had thought it was an economic problem.

The economy? Now there's a mess! He certainly bit off rather more than he could chew when he attempted to fix prices by law with such a permanence they could literally be carved in stone.

Did it work? Well, what do you think?

70

Executing a few merchants for breaching the retail price index certainly got tongues in the marketplaces going, but it didn't exactly cure inflation. Their peers thought they knew better than the Emperor: "Let the market decide" they said. Unfortunately, Diocletian's casting vote on that suggestion was to outlaw it as too brutal a mechanism.

After all, let's not forget there were soldiers literally starving to death in their frontier forts for want of supplies, for goodness sake! What else could he do?

The old misanthrope, if he was still alive, would inevitably insist that what he did was necessary to save the Empire from disintegration, and probably rightly too. But the only really lasting effect of it all was to increase already-excessive levels of centralisation and control from a hard-nosed bunch of professional corridor-stalkers and committee fixers, obsessed as they were with obtaining micro-control of every aspect of our state. Initiative and problem-solving withered – at least till modern times, it must be added.

Happily, the Blessed and Most Magnificent Emperor Constantine is of course become the Divine Face of Enlightened Rule. His Own administration, naturally, is beyond any reproach. After all, He it is who has given this Island of Empire one of the longest periods of peace in all its recorded history and, if anyone's listening (the frumentarii are everywhere), I think we would all be quick to agree that his achievement has been reflected in the unparalleled levels of prosperity and economic growth seen on all sides. (For officials of the public administration, at the very least).

But no-one who cares about their nation and their native province can avoid mention of how the British 'diocese' as it is now called has recently been further divided – giving us more bureaucracy yet. That much must be admitted.

Official control of the military and civil administrations has been split between the 'Dux Britannarium' and the 'Vicarius' respectively. There are now four (yes, four!) separate land provinces instead of the original one; Maxima Caesariensis; Flavia Caesariensis; Britannia Prima; and Britannia Secunda.

I know what you're thinking, but we can be sure there were good reasons for this division.

71

Each province now has a man of equestrian rank as governor - the 'Praeses' that our new friend, Phrygian cap, was referring to. That is except for Maxima, which has a proconsular governor in Londininium rubbing shoulders with his senior colleague, the Vicarius, as "Primus inter pares".

Whilst the military are separated off. Their structures are quite outside the control of the civil governors altogether and include their military excellencies the Duke of Britain and the Count of the Saxon Shore. (Have you got it – does that make it clear? I'll draw a diagram, if it helps….).

So, you ask, why are we Romans always re-organising and restructuring?

Apart from that the fact it seems inherent part of human nature, the main answer is simple enough. It's all about preventing too much power being concentrated into the hands of one man.

Particularly military power. If no-one has the means to bid for the purple - as the Glorious Constantine himself admittedly once did, albeit for all the right reasons – the down side of this policy is that no one commander is left with sufficient military resources or individual authority to do anything useful when a real crisis blows up. (Like a big barbarian raid, for instance).

It goes without saying that all these important people need the administrative support of numerous other civil servants - four times as much bureaucracy as was ever necessary before is needed to run what was once one single province.

No wonder there's an economic revival going on in Britain, what with all these official stipends sloshing about looking for something to be spent on, even if it's only bribes, booze and back-scratching. Houses and silverware. None of it is actually producing anything of value but pity the poor taxpayer who has to pay for all this bureaucratic self-indulgence.

The old-style colonial administrators of the early Empire; those senior soldiers like Agricola who once ran our new provinces economically; balanced between ruthless ferocity and a military restraint tinged with charming whiffs of amateurism, they are all long gone. In their place a basilica full of clerks has grown up.

Rome has discovered a new type of empire-building, conquered at the point of a quill.

72

This then is that great quivering hierarchical heap of civil administration and taxation which gives our Flavius Candidus and so many others like him gainful employment in a dangerously insecure world.

It was this same state of affairs which required him to spend a couple of lazy afternoons in the Governor's Library and Public Record Office in Londinium. The same reason why, when first going on official business, he would always have a look in the 'Notitia Dignitatum' - to see 'Who's Who, and What's What'.

Under 'P' for 'Petuaria' it was good to see that the obvious information was readily available. The Notitia records its status as one of the four County towns of the Parisii tribe, its honourable title of 'Civitas' signifying this pre-eminence in the canton. The fort and its (two) units of garrison are listed, along with its official function as designated fleet-base for the Abus Squadron of the Classis Britannica, the British fleet.

The Notitia also serves as a form of itinerary or route-planner. That was his second reason for studying it that warm afternoon in the Record Office at Londinium. In that context, it soberly confirms how Petuaria is one of the officially-designated ports of arrival and departure for Imperial Officials coming from the continent of Europe, which gives it an extra importance out of all proportion to its size. Presumably it was just such an urbane and sophisticated visitor who'd made his own unofficial entry in the Londinium copy. In a stylish round hand and a rather decadent green ink, someone had carefully and neatly written next to the "Petuaria" heading this terse endorsement:

"HELL- HOLE".

Walking up the main street of Petuaria Civitas Parisiorum, away from the haven, the first inklings of truth in that anonymously scathing graffito about this tiny, walled town started to become apparent.

The acutely-cambered street was considerably higher than the original ground-level frontages of the shops, houses, and workshops which abutted onto it; no doubt due to generations of re-surfacing work and dumped rubbish, rotting-down. Many of the frontagers had needed to cut steps up through this accumulating silt in order to recover access directly back onto the roadway from their colonnaded verandahs below.

Stumps of so many sacrificial altars stuck out of the rubbish; past offerings in thankful stone to the twin Gods Oceanus and Neptune from grateful travellers - pleased to scramble out onto a landfall the Northern Ocean made many doubt they'd ever see again.

It was disappointing to see the mean character of so many of these frontages; deliberately-built of narrow face to avoid the most expensive multipliers in the property market, whether of rent, taxation or purchase. As a result, behind the shop front, they would extend a long way back from the street instead, to recoup this space at lesser cost.

They were not well-made buildings. Generally only the foundations or ground floor at most were built of stone. As for the rest, any further height was gained through half-timbered constructions whose panelled infill was mere wattle and daub. Roofs usually tiled in local yellow stone faded to grey, although sometimes an expanse of orange pantiles provided the occasional splash of colour and welcome hint of quality.

If most windows were filled by wooden shutters with few instances of proper glazing to be seen, behind the front street too many other windows gaped open to the elements altogether, crowned by roofless eaves.

Dereliction was everywhere.

Nevertheless, it still looked as if most staples of a comfortable life could be purchased locally, either on the spot or made to order. Candidus saw wine shops; butchers; numerous fishmongers' stalls; cutlers; several potters and weavers shops.

Over the fish, he was glad to smell the seductive aroma of new-baked loaves. Judging by the buxom bonny girl calmly smiling down at him from her watchful place at an upstairs bakery window, these were not the only softly seductive commodities readily to be had in Petuaria.

Unfortunately he heard an angry reproach from another within as she was pulled quickly away, out of sight of the whistling stranger passing by below.

Not such an outpost of civilization after all!

He even saw a wooden-shuttered workshop purporting to advertise itself as the premises of a mosaicist. Their only reason for existence must be that somewhere around here were enough people with sufficient taste, enough sophistication, and a big enough income to require and afford such skills.

If there were, few other signs of their influence were detectable. The new bread had been a momentary posy, a brief bouquet in an otherwise less-pleasing assault on the nostrils, where the overwhelming tang was that of salt marshes, spiced with the whiff from the fish landings.

It soon became apparent that Petuaria had a problem with drainage, as well as fish.

Whilst the Empire had suffered terribly at the hands of deranged Emperors, greedy financiers, over-ambitious Generals and invading barbarians, the one thing you could never accuse it of falling foul of was drains.

The Divine Augustus may have found Rome brick and left it marble, but he and all his successors were first driven by the priority of ensuring that all things distasteful (including, it must be acknowledged, a few political rivals) were flushed unseen down the Cloaca Maxima (the Great Drain) and into the Tiber. The importance of public health meant that the water you drank, that you washed in, or even that playing lightly in the atrium fountain, had to be aqueduct-fresh.

At Lindum Coloniae, fifty miles south of the opposite riverbank, it is loudly claimed to this day, with swelling civic pride, that their sewers are so tall you can march an infantry cohort straight through without even ducking their helmeted heads. (Assuming their command by a particularly brutal centurion, that is....).

In Petuaria, by contrast, the smell of stagnant water comes not just from the adjoining salt marshes. After the few days' dry weather they'd just had, there still seemed to be plenty of pools of standing water about. Neither had the big culvert covered in flagstones beside the main street achieved anything useful towards dispersing it. The water lingered, adding to the omnipresent smell of drains - Candidus thought it unhealthy.

In his first stroll along the principal thoroughfare, he was similarly struck by the significant absence of imposing public buildings.

There were no obvious statements of civic pride to be found on this, his first-but-perfunctory reconnaissance of the town. It was true that many similar towns had suffered the complete destruction of such structures, particularly during repeated barbarian inroads in the last century.

It was also true that the Edicts of Diocletian and the tax system had done just as much as the barbarians to inhibit repair or replacement. Prosperous merchants, pompous councillors, or famous sons of a town would at one time have felt moved to enhance both their community at large and their personal standing within it; through the application of their accumulated riches towards some prestigious public building programme.

Whether it was the provision of a paved market place or the improvement of an existing Forum with flanking colonnades; the addition of a Basilica for use as law courts and council chamber; or the construction of Public Baths, or even just latrines, there had always been men prepared to spend considerable sums to the benefit of their fellow citizens.

Not anymore.

"Reform? Reform? Aren't things bad enough as they are?" were the apocryphal words of some aged Senator or Italian civic leader said to have come from this era of legislation, when Diocletian even purported to fix the price of a haircut by law for ever. If these price-fixing measures failed embarrassingly completely, his swingeing taxes and the drastic step of making all employment hereditary from one generation to the next knocked on the head forever both the entrepreneurs themselves and also the means or impulse for that sort of local largesse.

Civic office ceased to be an object of desire and ambition and became an intolerable burden. Failure to collect sufficient local taxes from his countrymen left the reluctant office-holder with personal liability to the state; inevitable personal ruin leading to disaffection, outlawry or death.

Increasing enemy inroads into the Empire had seemed to be leading towards the population being obliged to pay more and more to a state that seemed less and less able to protect them.

The only public works being made now were crenellated ramparts, built crudely and quickly in times of civil emergency.

There was a smell of corruption and decay in the air at Petuaria whose pungency quite shocked him. Even in its sharp acuity were the first hints of a warning that he might not find the execution of his commission such an easy task in a place like this.

However, the problem of the moment was simply where to stay. By reason of his occupation, Candidus was fully entitled to the convenient privilege of staying at the mansio reserved for Imperial officials and the despatch riders of the Imperial Post. In view of his journey here incognito, and the discretion needed for his enquiry, that luxury would have to be resisted. He did not want to draw attention to himself and a common lodging-house was the obvious alternative.

He found one back down by the harbour; another two-storey longhouse. It smelt strongly of boiled fish but the lady of the house seemed attentive enough. In the hallway, a group of sailors from one of the merchant ships loading in the haven were loudly playing the board game of 'Ludus Latrunculorum' with glass counters and two bone dice, shaken in a cup carved like a tower. They seemed unduly irritated by the brief interruption as he passed through with the slave who showed him up to his room. They had had drink and large piles of coin were obviously at stake in their game of 'Little Pirates'. Candidus decided he would do well to steer clear of this little lot, who looked like a bunch of off-duty brigands themselves

His 'room' was more of a glorified cubicle. He'd seen better barracks in the army but they were free and this was only cheap. Still, you get what you pay for. The slate bed had gone flaky through lack of polish and he cut his leg on it, climbing onto the sagging, straw-filled mattress. As he cursed this unexpected wound the house-slave came in, bringing a bowl of tepid water to wash the journey away, but he sent him packing in irritation at its temperature. He would rather wash off the dust and soak away his aches in a proper bath, if he could find one.

There was drunken shouting audible from the hallway and the prospect of a nap before finding himself something to eat for the evening receded.

He changed out of his dusty travelling gear and unrolled a woollen 'Gallic coat' to change into. His dirty clothes and other bulky items of little value, such as a cloak and a travel rug, were bundled together and put into a wooden locker beside the bed. His valuables, namely money; an old 'crossbow' brooch to fasten his military cloak; a letter of introduction and authority from the Vicarius rolled inside a leather document tube; and his little silver badge of office as 'beneficarius consularis' were all tightly packed into a leather purse strapped to his chest.

He'd no sooner slid the woollen coat over his head to restore decency and dignity than there was a scratching sound. He paused and listened - the usual mice in the eaves, perhaps? It became a 'tapping' around the door. The shouting had stopped and it was quiet in the room, which was so very dark because the one tiny window had its wooden shutter nearly pulled to.

There was another 'tap', clearly coming from the door. The sailors downstairs could be heard arguing violently over the board game and their reckless wagers. Perhaps he would have done better to have booked into the mansio after all. If it had blown his 'cover' it would at least have offered him some degree of official protection – and a bath.

"Who is it?" he said, quietly.

The door opened but the landing beyond was in total darkness, leaving whoever was silently pushing from behind in complete shadow. This was no mouse. He would have appreciated the reassurance of a weapon directly to hand.

Indeed, in view of the nature of his mission, it's true he'd seriously thought about so equipping himself. Unfortunately, Roman Law viewed any idea of a personal right to bear arms most sternly - the thin end of an anarchic wedge. Possession of an offensive weapon in a public place, other than for hunting or military use, would soon see you up before the magistrates. A town like Petuaria would be sure to have two, each appointed by the Ordo (the town council) and in an incestuous community like this you could be sure that the one sitting - if he found himself arraigned - would be the worthy Marcus Ulpius Januarius himself.

The only solid object available which he could readily lay his hands on as the door slowly creaked further open was a leaden oil-lamp holder. He grasped it deliberately, as if it was a club.

78

"Who is it?" he asked again, more loudly. The door creaked further open.

"It's only me....................." cooed an alarmed female voice. (His landlady). "I was just checking you were alright; that you didn't need anything..." she hushed, emerging into the pencil-thin beam of light that the closed shutter allowed.

A woman of middle-years, a property-owner in her own right, trapped by that unsaleable possession in this terminus of Empire. She was like an opulent pink and white rose in September, gone to seed and spilling over. Literally. He looked slowly and reluctantly away from the artlessly-loose chiffon at her deep but lowering cleavage. After a week on the road and in this light, it was a comforting sight.

"I thought you were asleep," she said.

"No, I was just going to have a nap."

"Oh! Well, sorry to disturb you! Anything you want. Anything. Just let me know."

He knew she meant exactly what she said. For a brief instant he was tempted by this apparently-unconditional opportunity but then discretion, questions of personal health, and the thought of her regular accommodation of the mariners that came and went with the tides, dissolved his reckless impulse.

"Yes....I mean, no! Thank you.....but, yes, there is still one thing."

She stopped and turned her head in a girlish way that just looked ridiculous: "Yes. Of course. What is it?."

"Is there a public bath house in the town?"

Her smile distorted into something closer to a snarl: "There's one behind the High Street. Nearer to the fort. You'll probably be able to get a meal there too. I'll see you in the morning, you can settle up then."

With that she turned in the hallway, on what he was still interested enough to note was a dainty heel, and went tripping down the stairs as if some critical domestic emergency had suddenly arisen. Soon she could be heard pouring bitter bile and ridicule on one of the slaves in the kitchen. He had made the right decision. Unwilling to offend his hostess further, he made sure he slipped out of the house quietly. The hallway was empty when he went down the stairs.

If he had to bathe, then clothes were going to be a problem. Or rather the lack of them. Obviously, there were no inhibitions for him or in this society about communal bathing. After all, even the latrines were public places, for both sexes. Most bodily functions could take place in public – including dying, which - in the form of gladiatorial combat at least – was only recently supposed to have been banned as a spectator sport, in this northern Province of theirs. No, the only self-consciousness he would feel would be at the leather purse so obviously strapped to his torso and the unwelcome interest it might attract. In any event, the water and steam would ruin its valuable contents. The purse would have to be hidden before he entered the bath-house, rather than entrusted to the non-existent security of the individual wall niches usually provided for bathers' clothes.

The bathhouse was near the barracks. It had probably been built originally for military use only, but the decline in the garrison and subsequent growth of the town seemed to have led to its take-over for the civic good. It was a rambling establishment of concrete-lined rooms which had gradually been added to over the years as required.

Next to it was the first monumental building he had found in the town. The theatre. An embanked semi-circle of stone seats faced a proscenium stage of ornamental classical pillars and doorways. It was entirely deserted and grass was forcing its silently-violent way through the paving whilst a lagoon of yet-more stinking and stagnant water filled the area between the lonely stage and its empty seats. It looked as if the flanking walls at the sides had already received the attentions of stone-robbers, removing the dressed limestone for other more menial projects. It was a long time since any actor had declaimed in this melancholy place.

Under a carved stone in the shape of a sightless theatrical mask, this one being 'Tragedy' and so easily remembered, he found a loose flagstone. He looked around carefully to ensure no-one had followed him into this ruin or was observing him and then quickly lifted the stone to hide the purse that contained his identity within.

80

As he walked back across the side-alley and into the adjoining bathhouse he heard the sound of trumpets from the compound as the sentries changed watch. A familiar and reassuring ritual, heard with some nostalgia. He knew that the public baths were the place to find what in Petuaria equated to 'society', where he could rid himself of the grime of his long journey up from Londinium, get himself a meal, and begin the process of finding the contacts and gathering the information he needed to fulfill his mission.

He was sitting naked and half-asleep in a wicker chair within the tepidarium, the warm room, while a slave applied oil to his back as preliminary to his entry into the caldarium, the hot room, when somebody called his name. In fact he did not respond at first, partly because his wits were numbed by the soporific effect of the warmth, but also because – to be fair - it wasn't actually his name:

"Greetings to you, Sextus Valens! We meet again!"

Fortunately he had enough about him to remember this was the persona he had resolved to adopt as his 'cover' and was left sufficiently alert to recollect that, so far, he had only been required to offer this fiction on one occasion, and that was on the Abus ferry to the egregious mining engineer, Cicerius Felix. Squinting his eyes to peer through the steam he could see it was indeed Felix, even more unsightly unclothed. He noted how heavily tattooed he was over most of his body with elaborate curling, Celtic designs, which was hardly surprising since the man was obviously at least half-native.

"Ah, Felix. I knew we'd meet up again, soon. Greetings!" he responded, with feigned enthusiasm.

"Sextus Valens, can I introduce you to my old friend Marcus Rufinus, gubernator of the Sixth Victorious Legion."

The man with him was older and uglier, with brown leathery skin that hung in folds. His eyes were almost hidden under beetling, bushy brows that were mere precursor to the black and silver body hair sprouting in unusual quantity from every orifice and all over the rest of his frame. This 'gubernator' was a river pilot for the Army but looked more like an escaped wild boar.

This was a treacherous and complex estuary with shifting sand bars and countless tidal creeks. It gave access to half of Britain and was also the main line of supply for the enormous and insatiable requirements of the military garrison at Eboracum. Accordingly, the Army had its own barges, lighters and coastal traders to bring grain, leather, foodstuffs and equipment to its troops. If those vessels and their valuable cargoes were not to be lost to natural hazards, then river pilots like Marcus Rufinus were constantly needed to guide them to safety.

By contrast, for man-made hazards (read 'enemy raiders') the warships of the Classis Britannica were deployed, patrolling the shipping lanes in constant readiness.

Rufinus was studying him through the steam with the same frank suspicion he probably reserved for an emerging sand bar at low tide. His conversation showed that same, innate sense of tact and charm one would expect from the social peers of Cicerius Felix:

"That's a nasty scar!" he observed in what was apparently his most amiable tone, almost straight away.

"Yes, I suppose it is…" Candidus was forced to admit, taken aback at the brutal directness of this extremely personal inspection. The wound had become an accepted part of himself, its occasional ache like a meeting with an old but fractious friend. He rarely thought about it anymore. The blunt remark on it from this inscrutable river-pilot embarrassed him. Momentarily wrong-footed, he felt himself obliged to explain the livid pink gash that ran right across his chest: as if he should.

"Got it in the Army. On the Northern Frontier. Hunting spear in the chest."

He could remember it as if it had just happened twenty minutes ago. The blank surprise at its impact, then falling down into the heather. Trying to sit up and noting with irritation the white heron feather decorating this smooth wooden shaft that suddenly sprouted from the riveted mail shirt he'd worn that day. At the time he couldn't feel anything. Shocked as he was, he'd thought it would just be a case of pulling the bloody thing out and getting on with whatever they were doing at the time - some sort of incursion patrol. Bandit country.

But then came the pain. A mighty wall of it that crushed his torso, squeezed the moisture out of his body and robbed him of speech and reason. He was told later that his men had refused to leave him behind. Ripping two saplings out of the dark moor and lashing them onto a pair of inter-locked shields, they fashioned a kind of litter on which they bore him all through the dangerous borderlands. Their journey back to the Wall took several days and he was somehow kept alive (if not fully conscious) by herbal potions mixed along the way by the 'arcani', the native frontier scouts whom 'Fortuna' and a wise commanding officer had sent out to guide his unit safely back within the gates.

A little Greek doctor at the main military hospital in Luguvallium town had re-ordered his breathing gear and carefully stitched the gaping wound with painful precision. The agony and loss of blood should properly have done for him but, thanks to the efforts of this tiny disciple of Aesculapius and the obstinacy of his own soldiers, his life was saved. He was equally as fortunate to survive the ravages of the ensuing and inevitable infection, a grim period whose only saving mercy had been the cloud of red-tinged oblivion in which he'd floated, insensate, for over a fortnight.

Nevertheless, "For you, the campaign is over!" his miniature physician had soberly announced to him when returned to the world, and he was soon invalided out of the Army on a half-pension. Leaving the Army was like leaving his family, like a bereavement. He reluctantly entered the alien world of civilians and left behind him the certainties of that all-enveloping institution which – for all its manifold cruelties – had in its own rough way looked after him for so many years.

It was only after a long period of convalescence with relatives in the south, and the contacts obtained through his chance-meeting with an old mess-mate under the bronze, triumphal statue of the Emperor Hadrian, right in the middle of Thamesis bridge, that he was lucky enough to find himself taken on in the office of the civil Governor at Londinium Caesarensis. As a beneficarius consularis.

It was obvious this Rufinus (as an Army man himself) viewed his wound and his story of its provenance with some approval, as further questions showed: "So what was your unit then?"

"A Cohors Equitata. One of the old-style, part-mounted, part-infantry units you'll still find up there on the Wall garrison."

"Yes, the Army has changed its thinking a lot these days..." sighed Rufinus, with obvious regret ".....but not on the Wall."

"No. So how are things with the Sixth then?" (Get the old salt talking and see what he has to say).

"Don't ask! I'm not the right person to ask, anyway! Hardly feel I belong. Called back to regimental headquarters once a year to get paid, if I'm lucky, that's how much the Sixth Victorious Legion means to me. I know the Fleet is supposed to be part of the Army, but we all know that in practice it operates as a separate service. Yet they're still the people I belong with; the ones I drink with; think with .." (He lowered his voice here). "Of course, since the bad old days of Admiral Carausius, the Emperor cannot trust the Classis Britannica and an Army River Pilot should stick to his own troop-transports or supply ships....."

He paused ominously, before resuming: "But the Sixth, well, let me tell you it's not the Legion it once was. Hundreds of years of honourable service and now there it is, sitting in its depot - understrength, under-equipped, and under-employed. State secret of course, but they'd be stuck to put fifteen hundred properly-trained men into action."

"Really? A quarter of its traditional strength? Why's that?" Candidus pressed him further. (In any other social situation this man would be a bore, but there was useful information to be had here, if the conversation was properly directed).

"Money! If the people who pay the taxes only knew, there'd be a public outcry. There's a fortune being spent on payments to the northern tribes. 'Clients' they call them. Money to go away – protection money. Always a mistake. You'll know all about that, if you've served on the frontier. Paying them off: "Don't come a-raiding anymore." And another fortune spent on tablet-scratchers and bean-counters warming their backsides in cosy offices all over the Province. Blooming bureaucrats everywhere. But none of it on the army, on the people who could make a difference and give us real security. No wonder the only alternative is to buy the enemy off!"

Candidus coughed and adjusted the bath sandals worn to protect from the scalding floor. Just as well he'd not disclosed his official status.

Rufinus ignored this phlegm-clearance and continued his monologue: "A fortune is being wasted yet there isn't the funding to support it coming into the Province from the centre anymore. Partly because we're so self-reliant here now. There isn't the equipment, either - swords and armour from the state armouries just isn't being made or imported in the quantities needed to replace what we're losing through fair wear and tear. These endless military expeditions into the east will be the death of us! When will government ever learn? We are losing entire Legions in the deserts of the Eastern Empire; sending them out to capture oceans of useless sand dressed up in cheap helmets, no body-armour and big, daft, round shields you could serve a five-course dinner on. No matter how many troops; send them out into the heat and equipped like that against heavily-armoured Sassanid horse archers and none will come back to tell the tale!"

"Well that's their problem, isn't it?" put in Cicerius Felix, unhelpfully, conscious that by now he was hardly contributing to the conversation.

Rufinus turned on him: "No, because it's the same here. The Sixth has been run down for years in just the same way, purely to save money. We kid ourselves the legions are what they were but, instead of restoring a system that works, they tinker about, desperately looking elsewhere for answers in novelty. The latest bright idea is the 'Mobile Field Army'. A completely-new regiment with no history, no traditions, no sense of allegiance, no base and no equipment. A load of barbarian mercenaries in thin trousers and tin helmets, billeted on some unlucky town to bleed the populace white with their requisitioning for food while they impregnate all our daughters!"

He turned back to his first listener: "You and I are alike, Sextus Valens. Men who live everyday with the knowledge that - not much more than one-hundred-and-fifty miles north of here - there are filthy little people with pointed beards; people who live in tunnels under the ground and hate Rome so much yet still covet the wealth of our cities; evil little people who loath our whole way of life but still salivate at its richness."

"The Picti" said Candidus - as if it was necessary to name them when everyone in the room knew perfectly well who and what he meant.

This unexpected passion in the aged legionary's response was verging on the overpowering but he continued in full flow regardless: "Yes, of course! And these are the quality of troops that stand between us and the Painted People. Understrength, because of these plagues that keep coming in from the East, yet unable to recruit because of the Laws of Heredity. The Blessed Constantine has given us peace for many years but with it come the sort of troops who have forgotten how to fight."

For such an angry old combatant, this hot room was about the worst place he could be. His leathery features were red beneath and beaded in sweat. Concerned for his welfare, they carried him and his rage through into the cold room for a pore-closing dash in the cold bath. This stopped his diatribe for a while, as they were dried off and dressed by slaves. It was over wine and a meal taken reclining on couches in the dining room when Candidus, still sub-nomen 'Sextus Valens', set him going again:

"Tell me, soldier, what's the quality of garrison here in Petuaria?"

Rufinus carefully removed a fish bone from between his teeth as if he was considering the point, and then for the first time in their discussions looked directly at his interrogator. It was a hard look, as if to say "Why is this fellow asking so many questions?" but was gone in a flicker with his reply:

"Rubbish, if you ask me," he said scornfully. His fingers explored the crooked gaps in his brown teeth again, before he enlarged on this dismissal: "There was a fort here in Petuaria before ever there was a town. Hundreds of years ago. Then the army pulled out and the civilians took over. Regional capital. The people around here are growers and farmers - all they want a town for is as a market, a centre. Not a place to live, just a place to sell their produce and livestock. Isn't that right, Felix?" He turned towards the engineer, as if to invite him in.

"Well, yes, it is, Rufinus, my old friend. The Parisii don't want to live in towns. Remember we were once the chariot people, the proud horse-breeders of the grasslands. But we've grown used to it and been glad of the trade and the port. That's brought us quite a lot of prosperity we'd never have had otherwise", he remarked, glad to be brought back into the conversation, before returning to his drink for another swig.

Rufinus nodded: "And then the maritime trade brought us something else. The 'sea-wolves': Saxons, Frisians, Angles and Jutes. Murdering thieves in their black longships. Criminals sneaking ashore on the coast or up the estuary. Killing and robbing, then quickly rowing off."

"Is that when the town was first walled?" asked Candidus, looking again at Felix for an answer.

"Well, yes, I suppose so. Too long ago to be sure. It must be a good hundred and fifty years ago that these raids first started and it was only later that Saxons could reach up here. In a small way at first, more of a nuisance. People probably thought it was just a temporary problem; 'The army will sort it'. Special measures - security will be restored. The bad people sent away. So, first of all the earth rampart of the original fort was adapted for the town, but I would think we probably didn't get proper stone defences until my grandfather's day, say about fifty years ago."

"Has your family ever actually lived inside the town, Felix?" replied Candidus.

"Funny you should ask that. My uncle does but, no, not the rest of us. Since he's clerk to the town council he has to live here, of course........ got no choice. But not us. No, we're country folk. Get a bit edgy inside the walls, you know. Need the wide open spaces."

(What an incestuous little community it is, Candidus thought again, everybody knowing everybody else and their business. Kick one and expect them all to limp). But he continued to direct their discussion, regardless:

"What's so bad about the garrison here?"

Rufinus was glad of this chance to resume his favoured theme. He spoke swiftly, before his tattooed friend could offer his own observations:

"No proper fort, not now. Just a crenellated compound left in the corner of the town, so they're all mixed-up and mixed-in with the civilians. As a military man, a veteran, you don't need me to tell you about the effect of that. Entirely prejudicial to the maintenance of military discipline and good order. Fights over girls. Distractions. Tradesmen banging on the gates with unpaid bills. Fathers or mothers wanting to see the commander – "Have you seen what your soldier has done to my daughter?"…

Rufinus smiled at him: "You were a soldier. You know the score. Have a look at the layout for yourself tomorrow, or when you leave the baths tonight. You'll get the picture..."

"Yes, and tell him about the quality of our guardians," whispered Felix, already drunk and leaning across from his couch as if to emphasise the need for elaborate discretion. They all looked around, but in fact the three of them were alone in the dining room, apart from the slaves that were serving. In the absence of any army uniforms, Rufinus was clearly encouraged to offer his professional assessment unencumbered:

"Two units. Brigaded together in the one compound. Elementary bad practice, of course. Always leads to trouble, as I said. You'll remember a similar arrangement back in the Wall-depot up at Corstopitum, I expect. Fights every pay-day. Lads even getting killed. Didn't they put a partition-wall up between them there, just to stop them scrapping?"

Candidus winced at the recollection but had to laugh: "Yes, I remember it well. A rough old place - Corstopitum in its day. Sometimes it was hard to say who we'd been sent up there to fight - the Painted People or the Fourth Cohort of Most Loyal Gauls!"

Rufinus laughed a hollow grim laugh that came up from his stomach: "Now I'm a river man. I'm no infantryman although I can tell a good cohort when I see one. As a navigator I know what goes on, out on the eight rivers, and I've worked every one of the big forts of the Saxon Shore, all the way up the east coast. That means I can see a role for my old mate Sabinus and his lads in 'Numerus Barcariorum Tigrisiensium'. A funny unit, I know. Started out in their grandfather's day doing a job not too different to my own - bargemen for the army. Asiatics all, I expect, used to handling wide flat-bottomed transports in the reeds of the Tigris River, out in the Far East. A bunch of irregulars brought over here by the commissariat to run grain barges, lighters, up from the corn-growing areas of the Iceni via the Foss Dyke, past Lindum Coloniae, and eventually into our own Abus River... Then a couple of generations go by, and suddenly the Army is finding Saxon raiders are getting up the estuary and terrorising its lines of supply. The lighter-men are issued with swords and helmets, suddenly a nice quiet job is getting a bit serious, and what have you got?"

88

"Cut-price marines is what you've got and that's what they remain. Post them to Petuaria, boy meets girl, and in a short space of time the lads you're recruiting for their father's jobs in the Tigris Boatmen are as Persian as woad. Add a local C.O. who persuades them into the long, shallow-draughted craft the traders round here run up the hundreds of creeks that line the estuary and you've got a rapid-reaction force that has done for many a longship out of Frisia, never to return."

"Well, they sound pretty useful to me - if not in the most obvious traditions of the Roman Army. What's the problem then?" Candidus pursued the point, finding that he was genuinely interested despite himself.

"It's the mix. Inside one camp. Too volatile." Rufinus paused to throw his apple core into the charcoal brazier that warmed the room. It flared at the offering. The serving men took this opportunity to refill their pottery tankards with red wine, and not for the first time.

Having taken another considerable swallow from the contents of his, Rufinus explained: "These Numerii, these irregular units, they're no better than the barbarians we are trying to hold back. Now, I know what you're going to say. I know that the military history of Rome is littered with examples of barbarians recruited to fight other barbarians, whose success even leads as a matter of military fashion to the adoption of some of their methods or equipment. I accept that. But with the Petuaria garrison you are seeing the absolute bottom rung of that ladder."

It was obvious that Rufinus was a man who found it difficult to come to a conclusion and surprisingly garrulous for someone of such craggy appearance. No doubt the wine had oiled the willing deliverance of his lengthy opinions. Candidus pressed him again: "So what is the other unit here actually called?"

"Numerus Supervenientium Petuariensium", said Rufinus in a slow, sarcastic way.

"Sounds good," said Candidus. "The 'Petuaria Interceptors'. What's wrong with that lot, then?"

Rufinus glanced first at Felix and clearly derived re-assurance from the comatose appearance of the engineer on his couch, mouth ajar like the yawning entry to a Pennine drift-mine.

"A bunch of local plough boys with about as much grasp of battlefield methods as a Reds-against-Blues faction fight after a chariot race. Dear old Felix would kill me if he heard me, but the sad fact is that the Parisii never were a warrior tribe. When the Legions first came through here like a dose of salts, two and a half centuries ago, all his ancestors ever wanted was to keep to the quiet life that is the only charm of this little backwater."

"Well, if the Tigris Boatmen are locally recruited now, as you say, why are they so different to the Petuaria Interceptors?"

"I think it's the ethnic mix. There's still that Eastern strain running through the boatmen. That taste for the cloak-and-dagger stuff. A hand over the mouth and blade to the throat. That's their style and very effective they are too, with their little quick patrol boats. They've got the amphibious capability - makes them quick and useful. But the 'Interceptors' are just a bunch of red-faced, blonde youths looking for someone to bash over the head with something heavy. Not at all sophisticated."

Candidus laughed out loud, so loudly that Felix woke with a snore in his throat. He had warmed to the lugubrious pilot for his forthright views and, taking another mouthful of the red, Rhineland wine which attentive slaves constantly replenished, he now thought himself amongst Good Companions. These two he had thought brutish and crude now turned out to have sparkling wit, biting insight, and a strongly developed sense of the public good.

Candidus gestured with his arm as a preliminary to the making of such an approving and extravagant statement, but he caught his beaker and in error swept it from the bronze tripod which supported it. The vessel smashed on the floor and the red wine flooded across a mosaic picture of a mythical sea-creature with the head and forequarters of a bull and the body of a serpent. Instinctively, he tried to rise to recover the item, but realised that his legs did not consider themselves included in the party, whilst his head now weighed twice as much as the rest of his body. It had been a good night and he'd learned much, but enough was enough.

Felix was insensible but Rufinus received his apologies and farewells with good grace. It was obvious he was just getting into his stride so far as the wine was concerned.

The shock of the cold night air restored Candidus to some extent.

The little town was in darkness, apart from the occasional gleam at the window of some upper room. Candidus crossed the narrow, cobbled lane between the bath-house and the derelict theatre and entered through an archway amongst the tiered stone seats, whose backs he used to steady himself.

As for many, the face of Tragedy was easier to find than expected.

His fingers sought the loose flag, guided by the illumination of a harvest moon which threw the carved features of the scowling theatrical mask above into sharp relief. The stone lifted. The document tube that held his personal and professional identity was lifted out, still wrapped in the leather purse.

Safe.

He turned to walk away and suddenly the entire world exploded in a blinding flash which filled his head with straight lines of white light, criss-crossing the night sky, as he saw himself cartwheeling across the fleeting image of a burning city far below.

On the second blow he fell unconscious to the ground.

"Only the dead have seen the end of War"

(Plato, Greek philosopher and teacher, 427 – 347 B.C.)

VI

Having finally retired from the museum in September 1941, Tom Sheppard never saw peacetime or lived to see the pavements of Brantingham unearthed again. His spirit was broken by the total destruction in June 1943, during an air raid, of the Hull Museum in Albion Street which had been his life's work; the keystone of his international reputation; his pride and his joy. This and retirement took away his sense of purpose, the physiological props of routine, and with them his health.

By February 1945 Sheppard was dead, with three months still to go before the final German surrender. For Britain and its soon-to-unravel Empire, the beginnings of a slow process of healing, reconstruction and re-assessment were needed as soon as the War ended. What happened today continued to be frozen like a snapshot as "History" tomorrow. As it was then, so it always will be. Despite these difficult post-war years, people retained a strong pride about their older past, even as the events of the present unfolded apace.

In 1948, Arnold Reckitt and a gentleman of Elloughton, Mr. J. Taylor, thought again about the Roman mosaics buried at the Cocklepits. They agreed that now was the time for them to be lifted and presented to the Hull Museums. Tom Sheppard's successor as Director, Mr. J.B. Fay, was enthusiastic about the project. He understood the symbolism. For a city like Hull, still a wasteland of bomb sites as politicians and planners wrangled interminably in public enquiry and smoke-filled room over mere outlines for re-building, such a scheme would be a morale-lifter. The gilded equestrian statue of King William III, entitled "Our Great Redeemer", had recently been returned on a low-loader to its traditional resting place in Market Place, brought back from wartime evacuation in a Sancton apple orchard. A symbolic homecoming. Inspired by its past, exhausted by the present, all of Britain needed a better future.

In Hull, the city was recovering its identity, seeking acceptance of a more recent ordeal through its re-classification with past vicissitudes.

A therapeutic process.

The two sieges of the English Civil War; the typhoid and cholera epidemics of Victorian times; the comprehensive bereavement of whole communities when local 'Pals' battalions were slaughtered in the poppy fields of Flanders, gave a litany of suffering only added to by the 'Blitz'. But there was real comfort to be had from the popular belief these large scale tragedies only strengthened and in no way dimmed the spirit of place or the continuity of community.

All in all, Fay saw an opportune moment to present the Roman pavements from Brantingham in exhibition, so that his fellow Hullensians could compare their current plight with "The Roman and His Trouble". Perhaps we will think ourselves the more fortunate, he thought, despite the bleak regime of post-war austerity and rationing that clung on after and into the peace.

He would take charge of the whole thing, Fay decided and, his bold assumption of authority meeting the acquiescence of Reckitt and Taylor, the next move was to enlist specialist help.

'O.Toffolo & Son Limited' were a reputable Hull firm with authentic Latin pedigree who were natural experts in marble, inlays, and most important to this assignment, mosaics. Their commission was to remove the two pavements so far found to Hull. One technique used involved applying resin to the face of the fragile Roman floors which, once strengthened with a fabric backing, enabled the entire item to be rolled up like a latter-day carpet and taken away. Unrolled at the other end of the journey, in the place of display, it could be consolidated and the resin removed.

In late September 1948, a group of tradesmen's vans and busy figures were assembled in Mr. Clifford Watts quarry, around the bastion-like 'island' of the villa remains, safely preserved in the middle of the site since 1941. Mr. Peter Slack, amateur archaeologist of Brough, was the man entrusted with the disinterment of the pavements and their record by drawing. To his excavator's skills and fine draughtsmanship, the photographs taken by Mr. Ian Sanderson (who'd travelled through from Scarborough for the purpose) would add the irrefutable corroboration of the lens.

The team mood was buoyant. This was no mere 'rescue' dig. Something tangible and valuable was to be brought away for preservation. The uncertainty and insecurity inevitable in the first excavation during wartime was now absent. In the room resting on hypocaust pillars was Floor I, its fluted central medallion surrounded by panels of alternate chequers or stylised ropework. This mosaic was selected as the first to be uncovered, photographed and treated. With this work completed over a period of days, it was decided that the delicate task of its removal was best left to another day, for the sake of fresh wits and renewed co-ordination. This was not a job to be rushed at the end of a tiring day.

The weather was mild and rain unlikely. "One night in the open won't harm it, not after sixteen hundred years below ground" observed Fay, cheerfully. Weary figures in 'demob' trench coats or blue overalls embarked in little Morris vans to make a convoy through the quarry gate; out to Brough, home, and tea. Happy in their work, satisfied with their progress, they knew they'd made a good start and drove away content.

It was a warm evening but what kept the rain off was the wind, driving the clouds along before they could unload their burden of water like bombers over a city. In the great wood that bounded the quarry mighty trees moved in unison, the wind roaring through their branches. Countless thousands of leaves rustled and whispered in dessicated conference. No-one who stood in this place amongst the raging trees, viewing the blue banks of Lincolnshire beyond the silver river, could resist a thought for those who'd lived here or for how these residents of the villa came to leave it, and why. Only someone utterly lacking in imagination could fail to ask themself how it had all ended; what became of the building or those who'd once lived here?

As it happens, not far away and on that same afternoon, Inspector Michael Tryton of the Hull City Criminal Investigation Department was meeting people who, if pressed to offer a charitable opinion in polite company, he might have called 'lacking in imagination'.

En route to Beverley with Pickering as his driver, for a liaison meeting with the East Riding force, they had made a short cut through a housing estate on the northern edge of the city.

Driving down a broad tree-lined avenue between rows of pre-war council houses, a man suddenly ran straight across the road in front of them. Pickering braked hard in an emergency stop and they were just able to avoid running him down, the drum brakes squealing. Pickering sounded the horn loudly, more to register retrospective protest than any warning of approach. With that gratitude commonly shown by other road users spared death or mutilation by an alert motorist, the runner made a short, stabbing gesture implying imminent violence and sexual insult in equal measure, before jumping a fence into a garden. As the two plain-clothes detectives watched the retreating figure with hurt puzzlement, he was followed across the road by a uniformed but helmet-less policeman.

"It's Bob Kexby", said Pickering.

"Come on, lets get after him", shouted Tryton, "Something's going on."

The Wolsley was left in the middle of the road with its doors open, but Pickering was professional enough to stop the engine and remove the keys before sprinting after Tryton. For all his mature years he was a fit man. The same, unfortunately, could not be said of Police Constable Kexby, who was fading fast, the back of his neck and close-cropped head glowing red under the strains of physical effort and a constricting uniform collar. He was yet to realise that reinforcements had arrived and in his own mind was no doubt preparing himself for tackling this man without support. It was only when Tryton went steaming past that he realised he was not alone. Falling back, he was still able to offer words of warning to his overtaker, as he went by: "Watch out, sir! He's got a knife!"

Tryton followed the runner through an arched passageway and found himself in a 'ten foot', as the unmade lanes between back gardens were known locally. In a confusion of overgrown hedges, ramshackle garden sheds, and prefabricated asbestos garages, their quarry had momentarily disappeared. As Tryton paused to spot him again, he was joined by Pickering, who'd just fallen over a bin. The struggling local bobby was not far behind.

"There he is!"

The runner, a heavily-built man stripped to the waist, was at the back door of an adjoining house, shoulder-charging it open.

A woman with dyed blonde hair showing dark at the roots, wearing the unusual combination of a paisley dressing-gown with black wellingtons on her feet, appeared in the garden next to them. She spoke in strongest North Hull but her fear and desperation needed no interpreter.

"Oh my God, you've got to stop him! My bairns are in there."

"Who is he?" asked Tryton.

"It's my boyfriend. We had a few drinks and a bit of a row – he got a knife and I ran to my sister's house over the road. A neighbour called you lot and he's run back here. This one is our house."

"Where are the kids now?"

"Upstairs. But you don't know what he's like with drink inside him. A different person. He could do anything. He's got a knife and only one of them is his own bairn, anyway. I can't trust him with them. You've got to help me"

"Pickering, you go round and cover the front. Kexby, you come with me."

"Yes, sir."

They advanced up the garden path, the frame of the back door sagging where the door had been smashed open like matchwood. There was shouting upstairs.

"Draw your staff, please, Kexby."

"Sir!"

Tryton was first into the kitchen. He found himself face to face with the gentleman of the house, a shirtless fellow showing a dragon tattooed across his chest. Similar engravings on his left upper arm included the distinctive shape of a blood-red heart, recorded filial devotion to "Mother" This first hint at kindness was strengthened by the letters "LO-V-E", decorating the individual fingers of his left hand; an encouraging sign of sentiment soon neutralised by "H-A-T-E" decorating the individual fingers of his right hand.

As if to deny, conclusively, any promise in his more affectionate body-markings, this maliciously-inscribed right hand proved its mettle with a tightly-held carving knife. Probably only a kitchen knife, but long and sharp enough for all that. Its shaped black handle was gripped with hate, literally:

"Get out of my fucking house, copper!"

97

Police Constable Kexby joined them in the kitchen, but Tryton never took his eyes off the wild and ever-so-slightly unfocussed pupils of the knifeman opposite:

"Alright, son. Just calm down. Nobody wants any trouble. The missus giving you grief? Listen, I know the feeling. We've all had it. Why don't you just put the knife down then we can have a talk about the problem, man to man..."

"Get out of my fucking house, copper!"

He made a waving motion with the blade, describing throat severance. They could all hear children crying upstairs.

"Look," said Tryton, "let's be reasonable. We just want the kids safely out of here. Nobody hurt. That's all."

"The first to touch my fucking bairns gets this. Fuck off out of here!" He made a stabbing motion at Tryton. Kexby stepped forward with his drawn truncheon and the knife man turned on him.

"Get out of my fucking house, you black bastard! Back off copper!" (Kexby backed off).

Here was a local peculiarity Tryton had long observed. If, in any other part of the country, they were known as the 'boys in blue', the 'thin blue line', or even 'bluebottles'; then here in Hull they were always 'black bastards'. Odd really. It was not as if their uniform serge was any darker than elsewhere, unless the overcast gloom of East Coast weather too often made it so. Either way, Tryton knew Bob Kexby well as a settled family man of impeccable provenance. His parentage couldn't be in doubt, so it wasn't personal. Nevertheless, the knifeman had now fixed on this dishonourable aspersion, because he repeated it:

"Put that thing away, you black bastard, or you'll all get this!" (Waving knife).

Tryton glanced up at the ceiling to the sound of crying infants. In that same moment their parent was gone. Tryton and Kexby jammed in the door frame together for a second as they tried to follow him up.

"Get out of my way, you bloody fool, Kexby!" he snapped.

"Sorry, sir! After you."

The door from the kitchen led directly into a living room in complete disarray. Armchairs and a sofa were overturned. A stoneware cider jar rolled, stopper-less, across a cold hearth.

Another door led into the hallway, to the front door and staircase. Kexby opened the front door to admit Sergeant Pickering in from the front garden, while Tryton made straight for the stairway. Kexby was happy to defer to his superior in approaching the man upstairs. He didn't want to be accused of getting in the way a second time but was at least second man up the narrow stairs. Pickering brought up the rear, his view of the landing blocked out by Kexby's labouring bulk.

Tryton and the master of the house renewed their acquaintance at the head of the stairs. Rage at this perceived invasion of privacy now knew no bounds. He tore a full-length door from an airing cupboard and hurled it bodily at the three officers with enough force to send them all staggering back down the stairs again. He was more agitated now. The knife-waving circles became short stabbing movements; backwards and forwards, backwards and forwards.

Tryton could see into the front bedroom where the children were. Their hysterical distress was pressurising everybody, including the knifeman. He could see a little girl of about four with large dark eyes and a smudged face ramming a dirty towel into her mouth, screaming all the while. A little boy of similar age clutched his sister in mute terror, whilst a babe in arms rolled in the cot, rattling the wooden bars repeatedly. This adult who, if not by blood at least by arrangement, filled the role of parent appeared immune to their well-being and the risks this confront-ation posed to their future equilibrium. (Was his own childhood crazed by similar dramas?) The police regrouped. All three of them. With one truncheon between them.

"Just put the knife down!"

"Back off the lot of you, you fucking black bastards!"

In the stand-off, Tryton had time to reflect momentarily on the sheer violence of language. It was as if the monstrous frustrations borne out of strong liquor, starved hope, sparse intellect, strangled vocabulary and no other outlet for passion could find their only satisfaction in these incoherent threats.

Tryton remembered seeing good old Inspector Arnott standing up in the Magistrates Court after the event, prosecuting just such a case for the police before a bench of shopkeepers', solicitors' and landowners' wives.

To protect their middle-class sensibilities (real or imagined) the kindly Inspector usually veiled his account with reference to "the usual Anglo-Saxon obscenities". Whether this convention of the courtroom really spared their blushes, or simply represented his collusion in their joint hypocrisy, could only be guessed at: "Four letter words …effing and blinding…"

Let's face it, everyone knew these terms in all their glory, however genteel their background, even if not everyone used them. As for the breed of horsey Tory matron that disproportionately made up the Hull Bench, they were hardly averse to language of this colour. Even if it was only unleashed in the privacy of their stables or whilst flying over the jumps with the Holderness Hunt.

Tryton wondered idly about the real nature of the Anglo-Saxons. The sea people who arrived suddenly then quickly took over England. We know what they're like now - what were they really like then? In the whole Matter of Britain, why ever did Inspector Arnott (a Border Scot) have to choose them to pick on? What manner of men, what kind of culture, could become so synonymous with such emblematic crudity of thought and poverty of language? Should we be sad for them, if this is become their epitaph and their legacy? The next question was, would they even care?

While they waited there, he amused himself with the idea of this drunken Hullensian blade-runner as true inheritor to all those who'd founded the English; to the people whose craftsmen wrought the metal treasures of Sutton Hoo; the Gospels of Lindisfarne; the poetry of 'Beowulf' or the chronicles of Bede. Such an idea seemed almost as ridiculous as it was surely likely (whatever Inspector Arnott told the Hull Bench). On the other hand, that the people of Anglo-Saxon England would have been positively proud to paint their warrior culture as a society constructed at sword-point represented a probability he must allow - in this private debate he was having with himself – at least until the smashing sound of a chair going through the front bedroom window signalled a sudden end to any further discussion of The Anglo-Saxon Bequest.

Tryton's thoughts returned to action: "Come on men, we're going in!"

The airing-cupboard door offered a useful siege weapon. Tryton and Pickering held it by its handles like a giant shield, with Kexby advancing alongside under its protection. The knife man met this six-legged siege engine head-on, striking with his blade around the edges of the panel as it battered him back across the landing.

"Stick him, Kexby"

As a war machine, Police Constable Kexby was heavily armoured and slow-moving, but he could still deliver a powerful blow nonetheless. His truncheon caught their opponent full on the back of the head while he was attempting to stab Pickering in the neck over the airing-cupboard door. It put 'me laddo' straight out onto the floor, like a golfer struck by lightning. All three of them grabbed him immediately. Between them they dragged him roughly down the stairs and then out to the car, insensible. The mother of some of his children was waiting for them there at the garden gate, still lovely in wrap and wellingtons. They braced themselves for her gratitude:

"Where are you taking him?"

"To the police station. He's under arrest," said Pickering patiently.

"No, you fucking well aren't! Bloody Gestapo, the lot of you! He's done no-one no real harm. Let him go!" She barred their way, her early appreciation ebbing fast.

"Stand aside, madam. Can I suggest you see to your children?"

"Fuck off, copper! They've had worse. They're O.K. You're not taking away my fella."

She tried to pull their arms from the comatose prisoner and was joined by members of the crowd, who'd till now seemed content with their role as onlookers. One stone flew through the air and then another.

As they got to the Wolseley, a brick destroyed its windscreen. Luckily they hadn't got into it yet at this point. Pickering fastidiously removed the offending slab from his driver's seat, carefully placing it beside the handbrake for retention as evidence while Tryton and Kexby slid into the back seat with the arrested man squashed between them.

"Bastards!"

The mob were pulling laths off garden fences to arm themselves. Pickering gunned the engine as the Wolseley pulled away sluggishly, its rear doors flapping open. There was a hail of missiles landing on its roof and the hostile crowd, mainly women and children, beat the car with sticks torn from gardens as it drove off.

The women here were the worst, shrieking threats and insults, and it was considerable relief to leave their barrage of words, sticks and stones far behind. On departure, the mob naturally dispersed, inwardly satisfied it had played its allotted part and fulfilled its traditional function.

By the time they arrived at Inglemire Police Box, their prisoner was fully conscious and showing signs of being difficult again, so he was handcuffed tightly. Tryton telephoned for a police surgeon and a police van to attend at the Box, leaving him there with Kexby and another officer to keep him quiet pending the arrival of the 'Black Maria'. He and Pickering taped a sheet of cellophane across the front of the Wolseley as temporary windscreen then set off again for Beverley. On a slow journey through low-lying countryside they soon saw the shape of Beverley Minster rising ship-like above the flat fields, so reminiscent in its landscape-setting of those great cathedrals of Northern France; Chartres and Rouen. The picturesque and comfortable old market town of Beverley, where nothing much dramatic disturbs its quiet complacency of centuries, promised the type of peace they were looking for.

They made their way through the late afternoon traffic, heading up Toll Gavel and then from bustling Saturday Market into North Bar Within. Queuing at the town gate of North Bar, where a hand-painted sign announces its mediaeval construction in 1410 (from tiny brown bricks too small for anyone to throw) at a cost of ninety six pounds, they waited while a dark-blue and cream double-decker bus negotiated the low archway. It was clearly especially designed for this one route, with its coachbuilt upper-deck uniquely-shaped to pass through the Bar's narrow arch.

Their own unusual coachwork was attracting rather more public attention.

Idling strollers and home-going school children stared open-mouthed at the battered police Wolseley with its missing windscreen. Tryton waved slowly from the back seat like the president of some tin-pot republic on a State Visit but his audience looked back unimpressed, licking their ice-creams blankly.

Out through the gatehouse and along the elegant parade of North Bar Without, leading into leafy New Walk where the Sessions House could be found. Adjoining the eighteenth century court house was the Victorian Police Station in yellow brick, screened by ancient trees from the period houses opposite.

Their little diversion in North Hull had made them an hour late for their joint meeting with the East Riding police. Tryton could see Superintendent Maister's new Jowett Javelin already parked in front of the classical pillared portico. A gilded statue of blind Justice, complete with sword and scales, looked down approvingly on the shiny black scarab which was Maisters' pride and joy.

"Nice car," said Pickering as they pulled in alongside.

"Nice salary, if you're a Superintendent" added Tryton dourly, with an unattractive whiff of envy.

It was whilst they were standing there, briefly admiring the aerodynamic lines and sweeping tail of their superior's Bradford-built motor car, that its owner emerged from the police station. He strode angry and red-faced towards them, raincoat flapping over uniform jacket and silver braid:

"Where the hell have you been Tryton?"

"I'm sorry, sir, I got involved in a bit of a domestic…"

"Your private life is your own affair, Tryton, but this was an important meeting and you've let me down."

There was no point in explaining. Maister continued his diatribe: "Anyway it's over now. I would have liked to present you to the Chief Constable. Well I have done in practical terms…."

"I beg your pardon, sir?"

"I remember you once told me you'd served in the RAF police, guarding airfields and so on."

"Well I did, sir, but what's that got to do with this meeting?"

"Liaison with our friends in the East Riding Force. Modern policing, fit for purpose in a new age. Civil contingencies and major incidents. Reorganising for mutual aid against new threats. Co-operative arrangements. Strategic responses. Protecting the aviation industry and our national security. Specialists wanted in a time of danger."

"Very interesting, sir, but what's all that fancy talk got to do with me?"

"You're our tame specialist. That's why we're lending you out to the County force."

"I thought we were your murder squad."

"You are, Tryton, you are. But since it appears no-one's being murdered at the moment, it seems a terrible waste of rate-payers' money to have you kicking your heels at Central, checking the Stolen Cycle Register."

"What's the job?"

"An aircraft factory. Complete with runways. A commercial undertaking, yes, but also a facility of national and strategic importance. Military aircraft. Secret prototypes. The Chief is getting worried about their security, what with the growing Russian menace and all that jazz. So are the company. Exceptional threats call for exceptional measures, Tryton. He wants a man who knows how to police an airfield, the best way to guard the gaps in miles of fence."

"Why can't the board of directors sort it out for themselves?"

"They can, Tryton, they can - up to a point. But you're needed as an adviser - both for the company gatemen and to local 'plod' – the East Yorkshire Constabulary, I mean."

"All right, sir, where is it?"

"Blackburn Aircraft Company Limited. Brough-on-Humber. Report to the local nick at 0800 hours tomorrow and make yourself known to the beat bobby on duty. He'll take you up to the factory, where you'll be given a tour by their security."

"Yes, sir."

Maister turned towards his car, absently lifting a fleck of dust from its gleaming black coachwork with his finger.

Something must have clicked in his mind as he did so because he turned back to look at their Wolseley, parked in irritating proximity to his new Jowett. It was as if he hadn't noticed it before. He slowly scanned the broken headlamps, cellophane windscreen, dimpled roofline and scarred bodywork with growing disgust.

"What the hell have you done to your vehicle, Tryton?"

"Oh, er...yes! I'm sorry about that! We ... er ... we met some people who don't like black cars... sir!"

Maister looked back at his beloved Jowett and its immaculate paintwork. The inward shudder at the thought of his own car suffering such treatment was almost visible. He got in and started the engine before winding the window down:

"We haven't got police cars to waste on stock-car racing, Tryton! They're not free you know, but paid for by the taxpayer! I want that bloody car down the repair shops and fixed, first thing in the morning. You will do that for me, Pickering. As for you, Tryton, the best thing you can do is use the London train tomorrow to get yourself over to Blackburn's. You'll find its first stop is at Brough. It's not far from there to the police station. Someone will meet you there and take you across to their factory. The walk will do you good!"

They stood there miserably and watched him go, pulling out onto New Walk straight into the path of a little old Austin Seven tootling past. There was an angry blare of twin horns from the Jowett and then he was gone.

Tryton looked up at the gilded figure atop the Sessions House and sighed heavily: "There's no justice!"

"He isn't a nice person is he, our Superintendent Maister?" observed Pickering.

Tryton shook his head: "He doesn't have to be. He's a senior police officer, Pickering. That's what it does to them. Some folk think the service should run on bullying and that people like him help it along. Either way, let's pray that you or I don't end up the same way!"

"Prudent men are wont to say - and this not rashly nor without good ground – that he who would foresee what has to be should reflect on what has been, for everything that happens in the world at any time has a genuine resemblance to what happened in ancient times".

(Niccolo Machiavelli, Discourse on the 1st decade of Livy)

VII

The following day came much as his Superintendent had predicted it would. (One of the hardest adjustments for Tryton after the war was the idea of planning ahead, when for years he'd lived each day for itself with little expectation of another).

Having reported in at Central around half-past six that morning, he crossed the waking town on foot to catch the seven o'clock London train, the 'Yorkshire Pullman'. This route inevitably took him down Paragon Street and by the bomb site where Prudential Buildings once stood. Hoardings papered with fly-posters advertising all manner of jolly product or public entertainment provided a shabby screen for what still remained in practical terms a War Grave. As a police officer based in the city it was a place he might often pass several times a day, but he never went by without a thought for Jenny. In fact it was less of a thought and more of a prayer.

Sometimes he would wonder what he was doing in this place, in this job. Sometimes he would believe that he came back to Hull and the East Riding, not because he was an ex-RAF Provost answering an advertisement from an undermanned local police force, but because he was a combat flier who'd lost his nerve; returned to haunt old airfields, old bomb sites, old memorials.

But there was no visible memorial for Jenny or for any of her colleagues who'd died together on that fine May night in Paragon Street, seven short years ago. Michael Tryton was neither sentimental nor self-pitying, but the fact remained that all he had of his wife lay under all this compacted rubble, hidden behind those ugly wooden hoardings. He would never admit to his colleagues in the police but there were times when he stood there in the pouring rain, on the site of the Prudential Tower, with tears streaming down his face. Thinking of Jenny.

They'd noticed this at Leconfield from the beginning, of course – a fighter pilot losing the 'edge' that could keep him alive in the air. His superiors were older men not unsympathetic to this young widower, but good people were dying everywhere all the time and they couldn't look after everyone. A change of scene was what he needed – a different theatre would do.

107

Four months went by, then they posted him to North Africa, into a ferocious campaign which by 1943 took him right across the Med' and into Italy. The end of the war in 1945 found him in Austria. It was only then that he realised he'd completely lost touch with her parents. He tried to find them when he came back to Hull but they'd moved clean away. He knew they were broken by the loss of their sparkling only daughter and his war-service had taken from them a son-in-law who might have provided some compensation. In cutting themselves off from each other, they had all cut themselves off from Jenny.

Today it was the merest pause, the slightest genuflection he gave as he went past the place of her rest.

He crossed the broad open tarmac of Ferensway by the South African War Memorial, where two pith-helmeted infantrymen in white stone clutched bronze rifles, caught in frozen alarm forever. At least their unmarked graves in the red earth of the Veldt had some expression in the world, albeit thousands of miles away and fifty years on, but his preoccupation with this idea of memorial nearly brought forward the order for his own. A cream and red bus swinging around in front of the railway station narrowly missed catching him as he leapt onto the pavement, its driver cursing him out of a side window. (More Anglo Saxon).

The London train pulled out five minutes late, which is probably what got him aboard. Its passengers were an odd mix of business types settling down for the long run to the capital and aircraft workers fidgeting with newspaper and lunch-box for their ten-minute trip to Brough. When the train made its first stop, he joined the melee for the doors and gave as good as he got, finding himself deposited upon the desolate platforms of this main-line halt. Weary of further combat, he let the mob of blue-overalled technicians barge off the platform and over the foot bridge before he thought it safe to follow them at a more considered pace.

In Station Road he bought a newspaper from a tiny shop so ill-lit that, even in daytime, two paraffin lamps burned in its furthermost recesses to illuminate items held in stock from before the war. A customer in this establishment was a rare event to be savoured. He was served slowly and deliberately by a little old lady, bowed in back but not in spirit, who demanded to know if he'd come from the railway station.

108

She insisted on recounting to him (upon this flimsiest pretext) her lengthy memories of when, as a young girl, she regularly saw King Edward the Seventh en route from the Royal Train at the railway station to visit Mr Christopher Sykes M.P. at Brantinghamthorpe Hall, or off to join high society gatherings at nearby Tranby Croft.

Despite Edward's reputation for an almost unwholesome interest in young women, Tryton detected disappointment in her role as mere wayside spectator to historic events. Only an oblique reference to 'a kiss' hinted at one possible reason. It certainly coloured her references to the more well-known scandals his visits always brought in their wake. One was the notorious defamation case resulting from cheating allegations made after an illegal baccarat game held at Tranby Croft. On 2nd June 1891, this required Edward (still at that time the Prince of Wales) to enter a witness-box in the High Court in London. Unprecedently for an heir to the throne, he'd been called there to testify for the plaintiff, Sir William Gordon-Cuming, in an unwisely-brought case of slander. It didn't do either of them any good. After seven full days of evidence, the claimant's case was peremptorily thrown out by the jury in just ten minutes. Gordon-Cuming's reputation went with it, while the Prince's was hardly enhanced by his proximity to another scandal. High stakes indeed.

Another example was the notorious ill-treatment of his host at nearby Brantinghamthorpe Hall. Weaker son of the formidable Sir Tatton Sykes of Sledmere, the late Christopher Sykes was an ailing toady driven by a disastrous combination of natural obsequiousness, social snobbery and a sincere sense of fealty and duty to the Crown, to tolerate both the consumption of his entire fortune and the destruction of his self-respect in the cause of hospitality to the Prince who eventually became his King. As the old lady well knew, not since the time of Elizabeth I had a courtier been so comprehensively ruined by their future Monarch.

Once doused in brandy by this perpetual Prince, she told of how "dear old xtopher" had merely bowed his head and dutifully observed: "As Your Royal Highness pleases."

Admirable, devoted loyalty or contemptible, craven weakness? Hard to say.

Driven perhaps by a comparable sense of unquestioning duty to that self-indulgent King-Emperor, it was the same private British soldiers commemorated in the Ferensway Cenotaph who'd fought and died for him, from Africa to Afghanistan.

If his newspaper-seller-cum-sybil couldn't resist drawing modern parallels for her mesmerised customer, it was one final throw-away reference to her period in service at Brantinghamthorpe Hall that provided closest clue to her ancient passions - before Tryton could snatch the change she held as ransom for his attentions and fled. As glad of fresh air as escape from the gloom of her newsagents, his hard-won paper stuffed into his raincoat, he wondered why anyone nowadays should care one jot about these weary events of sixty years ago, retold in 'Ancient Mariner' fashion by such a lonely old soul.

Anyway, he had far more important things to worry about than the past. Like, where to go now? (There was no question of nipping back in there to ask!) He headed back down the street towards the oddly-named "Ferry Inn" - odd because the only Humber ferry he knew of nowadays ran straight from the Minerva Pier in Hull while this one seemed nowhere near the river. Clearly, this pub's name must hark back to earlier days, like every thing else in Brough did (including the residents).

When he found them, the police station and courthouse proved to be right next to the pub, but set back in an unexpectedly ornamental garden at the end of a gravel drive. Open fields unrolled beyond and behind it, with the masts of yachts to reveal the narrow creek at Brough Haven.

If the aircraft factory on the far side of the railway by the river seemed like a small town, the little town of Brough that named it seemed no more than a village. It was difficult to understand why this undistinguished miniature settlement deserved a main-line station and all the machinery for the administration of justice. A pub named after a ferry that did not exist and a miniature mud-bound harbour with a few beached yachts only served to compound the puzzle. Why would anyone want to come here? (Apart from a King, up for a country house weekend with the ladies).

Having crunched down the gravel drive, he found the tiny one-roomed police office empty.

Letting himself in with a standard 'police box' key through the front door, beneath the traditional blue lamp, he was disappointed to discover no-one waiting for him. The courthouse next door was empty too.

With time to kill, he made a short tour of inspection. There were three grim cells, all decorated with cream and green ceramic tiles for lavatorial effect and equipped with doors of a thickness fit to have satisfied the Medicis. A police sergeants' office (locked), two bakelite telephones (one black, one red) and an air-raid siren on a shelf, still in wooden packing stamped "G.O.C. Northern Region, Imphal Barracks, York". Chipped enamel mugs, some acetylene cycle lamps and a broken truncheon completed this eclectic collection of artefacts. He spent some time studying an Ordnance Survey wall-map of the Brough area before sitting down to read his paper.

Becoming immersed in an entertaining account of developments in the "Alderman Stark affair" - a senior Councillor brought to book by his peers in the Police Committee for allegedly commandeering a police car to take him from the city's bus station all the way to Blackpool (Hull continuing to enjoy its traditions of municipal misconduct) - left him slow to register a vehicle pulling up outside. When he did so, he saw it was a small truck. The sign-written side-panel read "TOFFO..." so far as he could see from the window, which made him assume it belonged to a confectioner. Presumably its driver was the person banging on the police station door, obviously impatient to make some rationed sweet deliveries once the right address was found.

"Alright, alright!" shouted Tryton from his comfortable newspaper-reading chair, taking his feet off the desk. He went reluctantly to the door and released the latch. A tall, gaunt-faced young man with jet black hair, dressed in the interesting sartorial combination of brown leather motor-cycle jacket and muddy white tennis shoes was waiting there for him:

"You've got to come at once! There's been a terrible tragedy!"

"Hey, now steady on! I don't actually work here, you know ....

"What? Well, are you a policeman or not?"

"Well, yes, I am. But..................."

"Then you've got to come at once. A tragedy! An-atrocity-in-the-night!"

111

There was just the hint of Italian in the way octaves rose towards the end of a sentence. Absent anyone else, Tryton had to accept that - for the moment - he had become 'ex officio' the Brough Police so far as this anxious messenger was concerned.

"But I've got no transport."

"Please get in my van. It's not far."

He looked across. It was a maroon Morris three-hundredweight pick-up, sign-written in cream cursive lettering on the door: "O. Toffolo and Son, Ltd. - Specialists in Terrazzo and Mosaics, Temple Street, Hull" he read.

The visitor was right - it wasn't far. Two minutes jammed together in the pick-up's tiny cab but still insufficient time for his excitable driver to give any more sensible explanation. As they swept in through the open gates of Brantingham Quarry, Tryton was hopeful of meeting someone more lucid.

A group of grim-faced men stood in a semi-circle around what looked like a small spoil heap in the centre of an otherwise clear area amongst the workings. Tryton was introduced to Mr. Fay, the Director of Hull Museums; Mr. Slack, the archaeologist; and Mr. Sanderson, the photographer. He found these gentlemen and their helpers incandescent with self-righteous rage and disbelief.

Their complaint, put simply, was that an ancient Roman floor from a great house or palace once existing in this place had, from its discovery in 1941, been preserved on top the small earth mound around which they were gathered. These learned gentlemen had last night left it intact after a day's work preparing it for removal with resins and netting. On their return to the site this morning they'd discovered the incredible. The pavement had been stolen!

Their incomprehension made them impatient of routine questioning to establish the problem. No, they had no idea who could have done such a thing! The quarry operators had carefully left it intact for seven years, throughout the war, and were hardly likely to destroy the thing they'd cared for so long on the night before its planned removal, were they? It weighed tons. Whoever had done this thing must have had access to heavy mobile lifting-equipment to achieve its disappearance so quickly. To have managed it during the hours of darkness made their criminal feat all the more astonishing.

112

"You are dealing with one out of two types of animal...." thundered Fay, the Museums Director. "This is the work of either a pathological vandal or else a well-organised collector, possibly someone based abroad. I do fear a country policeman like you couldn't track down either type..."

Tryton was stung by this implied slur on his personal capabilities but it was that same professionalism which prevented him biting back. "I think I'll just have a look around," he said quietly, instead, and set off on a tour of the quarry perimeter. The group by the mound scowled at him as he trudged away.

The quarry was a featureless spot. Piles of yellow stone provided the only points of interest. Any fragments of square, coloured stone of the type described to him as making up the pavement would have been immediately apparent in this whitened wasteland of chalky mud. They were quite right. There really was no trace that he could find. A neat and tidy 'job' indeed. Professionals?

His route around the perimeter soon brought him back facing the high wood which forms the eastern boundary to the site. A public footpath crossed the quarry from the southern edge of the wood heading west to a sunken, sandy, farm lane which provides the western boundary of the quarry. Tryton left the quarry and instead followed this footpath, heading east. It was heavily overgrown and clearly rarely used, compressed as it was between the clawing branches of the wild wood and a rusty barbed wire fence adorned with strongly worded "Keep Out" notices on the quarry edge. The width of the wood at this, its southerly margin, was perhaps no more than one or two hundred yards. (He was never any good at putting a figure on distance). The path curved slightly around the copse-end, so it was not possible to see right along but - about a quarter of the way down - Tryton suddenly became aware of a figure crouched in the undergrowth at the periphery of the trees. This person was sitting just inside the wood, just off the path.

"Hey, you!"

He wasn't sure whether his voice would carry that far above the roaring and swaying of the mighty trees but there seemed no response anyway.

He shouted again. At this the figure stood up, stepped onto the path some forty to fifty feet ahead of Tryton, and started to run away - really fast by anyone's standards. Tryton began to run, too, but it was difficult going on the overgrown footway. Obstacles hidden amongst nettles and brambles threatened to bring him down several times. As if the trees opposed him.

The youth ahead covered this treacherous ground adroitly and so much more rapidly. Like a deer through the woods. When he got to a stile, where the path joined another farm track marking the eastern edge of the wood, Tryton was already falling further behind than when the race began. He wasn't a big lad in either height or build but what was distinctive was the flying jacket, which Tryton recognised immediately as the issue-type worn by the American air-force during the war, identifiable by a large, embroidered squadron badge on the back.

"Hoi, sonny! Police, stop!"

The youth was already in the lane ahead when Tryton tripped on a trailing root and fell hard and sideways against the barbed-wire, slashing his raincoat sleeve open on its vicious strands. He had tumbled amongst nettles but soon realised that the stinging in his right arm where the cuff had ripped apart was from something sharper than nature's barbs. Struggling to his feet he found blood running fast down his hand but, clutching his injured arm with his good left hand, he still dashed to the stile and looked up the track.

There was a green truck parked in the lane which ran to the main road. The small youth already had its door open and sprang from the running-board into the cab. Tryton recognised the vehicle type. During the war he had seen hundreds. It was what he used to know as a 'Dodge Weapons Carrier' although no doubt its official, military nomenclature was something more staccato: "Truck, 4 ton, 4x4, Weapons Carrier, Dodge, USA." Whatever you call it, or however it was described by the commissariat, these had once provided commonplace transport for the Allied Armies. That did not mean this example was an official army vehicle nowadays.

Its driver was frantically trying to start the engine while Tryton jumped the stile and sprinted towards them.

No doubt these lorries were widely-available to the general public secondhand; as surplus to the modern army. That seemed the likely status of this one. The matt green paint of its war service was faded almost to dark grey but it still defiantly bore the white Allied Star stencilled onto its bonnet like a veteran his campaign medal.

Even as he stumbled down the lane to within feet of the mighty bumper and armoured headlights, Tryton was acknowledging its familiarity with the unspoken affection and respect of one superannuated ex-combatant for another. Its headlamps flared as the engine caught. Such nostalgic goodwill was not likely to be offered its driver, whose guilty flight caused Tryton's painful fall onto barbed wire. For a brief moment, as the engine coughed into life and the gears snatched into reverse, Tryton's eyes met their eyes.

The American flying jacket matched their transport in weary vintage and drab utility. So too did their khaki peaked cap which, until the effort of forcing a recalcitrant gearlever into reverse dislodged it, successfully hid the wearer's face. Everyone wore army surplus these days.

But just for the briefest of moments, in seconds recordable only upon one hand's fingers, Tryton caught and mapped the facial features of his fugitive with total clarity.

Cross-examined at Quarter Sessions by hostile defence Counsel with their standard question: "Do you really expect this court to believe it, when you say you'd know this person again?" he would have rejoined with the most insistent and passionate of affirmatives. Even though he already knew His Honour would never let the case go to the jury, not on the basis of one fleeting identification from a mere policeman.

Tryton's brain had recorded that face with a totality of definition perfectly equal to the big lenses of those wing-mounted cameras in his old PRU Mosquito. Already the image was permanently hanging in the darkroom of his mind. He could have sat down and drawn it beautifully. As the driver's cap slid back, a veil of shining auburn hair was released to slide forward over delicate eyebrows arching with stress. Brown eyes like almonds shone above discreetly-carved cheekbones, parted lips hinting at intoxicating combinations of sensitivity and sensuality.

"Stop!" he shouted desperately, but she took no notice, the Weapons Carrier skidding violently in a screaming arc of mechanical protest: Out onto the main road she went at a reckless angle with no notion of whatever speeding traffic she might strike – lorry or car. Tryton ran out onto the Leeds Road after her, drops of blood falling from his finger-tips like a votive sacrifice.

"Stop! Police! Stop! ....I'll know you again!"

Of course she took no notice. He heard the straight-cut gears whining as the Dodge accelerated away. Sluggishly, yes, but still faster than he could ever run. West it went, out towards South Cave and then, who knows?

Standing exhausted in the roadway, a red hand-print stark on his pale raincoat like a heraldic badge, he watched the humped canvas tilt of the old Dodge disappear from sight. There was no civil registration plate to record. Only the register of her face, framed in the iron surround of the windscreen.

Tryton meant it. He'd know her again.

"The watchmen that go about the city found me; they smote me; they wounded me"

('Song of Songs', Solomon - 974-937 B.C.)

VIII

"Two gentlemen to see you."

He groaned, the announcement bringing him into painful wakefulness. The pain in his chest which had become a constant friend at morning these two years past was there as ever. But the violent ache in his neck and from the back of his head, where the hair was matted with dried blood, was novel addition.

"Two gentlemen to see you."

The messenger was insistent. She stood in the doorway looking down at him - obviously uninterested in his condition. No doubt the 'Pink Rose of Petuaria' had long ago exhausted her dew of human kindness so far as drunken bloody men, returning from a night's drinking, whoring and fighting, were concerned.

Candidus had no recollection of how he'd managed to drag himself back from the derelict theatre, across the darkened little town, let alone find his lodgings. He did remember banging on the studded doors until eventually some grumbling slave came to fumble with bolts and bars to let him in. No doubt he'd woken the entire household. This lady's indifference to his injuries was first instalment of their thanks for it. He was unable to sit upright but rather rolled onto his chest, face down on the side, so that he came onto the floor by kneeling beside the bed. Struggling to his feet, he saw there was blood on the hairy striped blanket in which he'd been wrapped.

"See what you've done to my bedding!" shrieked the roseate harpy that was his hostess.

"I'm sorry…" mumbled Candidus, "…..don't worry, I'll pay you for it."

"You certainly will", affirmed the lady, her eyes glittering at the prospect of a lodger that paid, and paid extra at that.

"Tell them I'll be down in a minute." Mollified at the thought of money, she turned on her dainty ankle and set off to pass this message to the visitors.

He would have been leaving anyway that morning, so he gathered together what remained of his possessions and went downstairs.

Since he knew no-one else in the narrow world of this tiny 'urbs', he assumed - in his semi-concussed state - that if he had two visitors then it would be his drinking companions of the night before - Felix, the mining engineer and Rufinus the river pilot. Which is why it came as such a shock to see what manner of men waited on his company.

To be concise, he could best describe the pair as looking like a couple of out-of-work gladiators. Since certain provincial legislators had only recently sought to ingratiate themselves with Blessed Emperor Constantine's long-standing Christian faith by purporting to deny our northern folk (at least) those bloody entertainments which had amused the population so well these hundreds of years past, 'unemployed' would be just what his two visitors must be. Hard men in dangerous need of a good living.

If it was gratifying for Candidus to know that, in his own small way, he was helping provide purpose and occupation for redundant fighters, for men otherwise still reeling at their loss of income, status and self-esteem through these Edicts made in Constantine's name, he must still wonder at who might have sent them.

The larger of the pair lumbered towards him and, if their size is compared, it is only in the difference between a six and an eight-decker war-galley. Candidus flinched but this bear of a man extended his arm only to open a fist, not to clench it, revealing a small parchment roll crumpled flat by its illiterate bearer. He dared not take his eyes off either of them to study this squashed gift.

The bigger one was middle-aged with the bulk of a strongman turning to fat through lack of exercise. Whether by way of sentimental reminder or because he could afford no replacement, he still wore the red training shirt of some defunct gladiators' school, its yellow trident badge woven across his chest in saffron hemp.

His smaller, younger friend with the shaven head wore a lighter shift with German trousers belted at the waist and tied with thongs at the ankle. His forearms were bare to the shoulder but for curious armoured shoulder pieces trimmed with silver and embossed with crude figures of a native Mars, clutching spear and oval shield.

These men had never been soldiers but were obviously accomplished killers for all that. Which was why Candidus decided that the only safe course was to be very, very polite indeed:

"Can I help you, gentlemen? I understand you wanted to see me?"

The eight-decker just grunted and pointed to the paper now in Candidus' hand.

He unrolled it carefully, re-assembling where it had become torn through rough-handling, then reading it out aloud as he was obviously required to do: "Marcus Ulpius Januarius, Aedile of the Civitas of Petuaria, presents His Compliments and requests the favour of Your attendance upon him this day in the Basilica upon the sitting of the Law Courts."

Such kind invitation into the distinguished company of the very man who was focus of all his enquiries could not possibly be turned down. Nor would it be resisted. Candidus nodded kindly, smiled broadly and spoke slowly, as if to difficult children:

"Thank you. Please tell your master I shall be more than happy to attend on him. I will be right along, just as soon as I have settled a few small points of business here…"

His feet, as they do say, never touched the ground. Grabbed by each arm, he found himself outside in the street before breath could be drawn, as he was frog-marched away at high speed. Only the 'Pink Rose' watched him go and seemed to care. He could hear her shrieking from some upper room:

"Hey! Where are you going? Where are you taking him? What about my bill? Where's the money he promised me? Hey! Bring him back."

Fearful for his own safety at the hands of enormous thugs; on his way to the tender mercies of the most powerful man in Petuaria, but without enough money to pay anyone's bill; Candidus could still admit these gentry had saved him from more embarrassing scenes yet. It did not take them long to drag him roughly through the back lanes and side alleys; up to the market place and into the mouldering town hall. Dignified in Petuaria by the title of 'Basilica', Candidus had seen bigger cart-sheds in his own country. Compared with the famous Basilica on the hill in the centre of Londinium Caesariensis itself, this was frankly pathetic.

They pulled him into the Basilica through a small door off a colonnaded walkway. Expecting to be dragged in front of the court now sitting, Candidus found himself speculating with genuine interest about what he might be charged with. Instead he found himself propelled into the public seats at the very back of the court, where his new friends plonked him down - hard - onto a long empty wooden bench before sitting down themselves, jamming him tightly in between. It was like being squashed between two smelly old cart-horses, each one stinking of sweat and leather traces.

The Court was indeed in session. At the other end of the hall was a raised tribunal with table and chairs set upon it. Two men in white togas were each seated behind the table on folding campaign chairs with no backs. Clerks sat below the tribunal at wooden desks where they recorded the proceedings in shorthand on wax tablets. To one side sat an officer of the local garrison, legs outstretched, whilst four of his soldiers in chain shirts and bronze helmets stood by to guard the dignity of the court. No-one in Britain wore the toga these days, other than on official occasions. An awkward draughty handicap of a garment it is, but retaining its potent symbolism of office even now. So it was, when local aristocracy or the well-to-do fulfilled their civic duties in the function of magistrate, then they would always take on the toga and leave their 'British Cloaks' at home.

Unusual to see two magistrates sitting together - obviously a busy day.

Candidus studied them as well he could at the length of the hall. The younger of the two he took to be Januarius but this was not the displaced patrician he'd expected, the sophisticated schemer he'd been warned about before setting off from Londinium. He looked more like a red-faced farmer, although there was no doubt this was the man in charge.

His colleague on the bench was elderly and stricken with the first idiosyncracies of senility. Whilst the man who must be the source of his forceful invitation watched and listened to the proceedings with a sharp eye and an inscrutable half-smile that could as well be mockery as approval, his elder on the bench wrote constantly with a feverish hand, even when naught occurred.

Before them stood, manacled, a desperate filthy man. Hobbled by chain-linked clamps welded shut over ulcerated legs, his head stayed bowed in silence. Yet it was clear he still had some friend in court, some country jurist who would plead for him. This homespun fellow stood before the tribunal, in front of the sagging prisoner, and postured like Cicero. He spoke of fairness - of "aequitas" – solemnly invoking the long-dead ghosts of Julianus, of Papinian and Ulpian.

Januarius nodded so sagely at these impeccable legal authorities and with such a smile of pleasure that might persuade the less-experienced advocate of some success with their passionate mitigation. Still smiling, he leaned across and whispered in the ear of the still-scribbling colleague beside him on the Bench, who nodded only the once, over his curling parchments. Whether deafness was listed amongst the latter's afflictions could only be cause for speculation but it was the briefest of discussions before the old man returned to his writing and Januarius' stern eye to the prisoner. He knew his law and this closing speech in judgement was delivered immediately, just as clearly, concisely and confidently as his manner suggested it might be, its purity of syntax unexpected in this backwater of Empire:

"This was a despicable offence. Your friend must have told you how the law could deal with it by immediate execution, and the law would have been right. You are truly fortunate that he has succeeded today and persuaded us to mercy. The sentence of this Court will send you to the mines, instead. Take him away!"

Abandoned by his advocate, the unfortunate prisoner babbled of innocence and origin; that he was a 'transmarinus' and - as a Roman citizen from beyond Britain – must deserve better. He was wasting his breath. Two soldiers stepped forward and wrestled him to the floor before dragging him out regardless.

In the pause before the next case was called on, Candidus considered the likelihood that it might just be the lead mines in the hills above Navio where this prisoner would find himself. Starved, beaten and frozen out of existence, lying on his side in the filthy water of a pitch-dark seam while trying to wield a pick axe against the rock-fall. Life in the mines assured an early death as surely as consignment to the cell under Rome's Capitoline meant strangulation in the morning.

On the other hand, and in the spirit of fairness clearly suffusing the whole ethos of the court, it had to be admitted what few sentencing options were actually available for the magistrates to choose from. Between flogging followed by death and flogging simpliciter, only hard-labour or fines provided light relief. Yet as the day's business unfolded (the disposal of a month's worth of wrong-doers at least), Candidus could not help noticing what a high proportion of them seemed to end up in the mines. With manpower in such short supply these days, whether for industry, agriculture or soldiering, how fortunate were the Societas Argentorium Lutudarensis in the part-time judicial duties of their shipping partner. (Who says you can't get staff?)

Precluded as he was by tight escort from wandering-off and able by detention to give the proceedings closer than usual attention, Candidus reached another interesting conclusion: This was a court frightened of its jurisdiction, a tribunal scared of its town, a magistracy a-feared of its public. Or so it could be thought.

The first case described, Candidus had only seen halfway through. But the accused was not only a citizen, as all the inhabitants of the Empire had become - this century gone - he was, as he'd pointed out himself, a 'transmarinus'. Here was someone entitled to expect rather greater indulgence than a mere Briton but, even if Candidus arrived after details of his offence were given out, the cold indifference of Januarius to his special status as foreigner was something to behold.

Men from the town appeared on serious charges - two for breaking the public peace and one for carrying a weapon in public, the precise offence Candidus (at some risk to his own personal safety) had been so careful to avoid committing. To them, Januarius spoke softly like a disappointed father and then he just fined them. This was the majority of cases; the balance being the wayfarers and runaways; the outcasts and mariners who, as already explained, so often went straight to the mines. (What a happy band Cicerius Felix would have, trailing behind him on his return journey to Aquae Arnemetiae or Navio).

Even a stranger could guess at once when a local man was called up and arraigned.

Whilst the bench at the back of the hall where Candidus and his two chums waited remained quite empty, cleared by their palpable menace and the unique reek of the amphitheatre, all the other public seats were packed. In a town on the way to nowhere, where the intellectual pleasures of the theatre had been abandoned a generation gone and the preferred pleasures of the circus were now denied by more recent legislation, then this was one of the few free entertainments left.

When, aside from drinking, gambling and whoring, the only pastimes available to those few that knew leisure were watching big ships come and go on the great river or waiting for the next Saxon raid, then this was entertainment with a capital 'E'.

What could be better than seeing strangers; these foreigners and "comers-in"; all sent to the mines? That'll teach them, with their funny accents and their strange clothes. They won't come here again! But when it's a local lad - there is a ripple that goes through the public benches, a buzz of excitement, a nudge of the elbow. Each one of them had his own supporters club rooting for him at the back, like a famous charioteer or (dare it still be said?) a gladiator killing his way through to survival in one of those ten-day shows we used to enjoy in the good old days.

For these prisoners, the whistles and calls of the mob gave them a cocky confidence almost daring to outface the court. That said, there was no doubt Januarius retained considerable control of his public, displaying a common touch to rival that of the legendary Gracchi brothers in the days of the Republic. Clearly there was a mutual respect here, his authority deriving from something more than inherited wealth or status. Having four soldiers and the commander of the garrison present at his beck and call must surely help as well. Now there was something to include in his report, assuming he ever lived to make it.

Eventually the last miscreant was admonished or dragged away, his grumbling relatives or hangers-on gathering together their effects for departure. An outdoor cloak here, a sack of apples there. One woman was so anxious properly to secure a brace of tied game birds that she nearly left the basilica without the tightly-swaddled infant dozing in a basket on the floor at her side.

The court rose.

Candidus found his mouth dry and tried to swallow. What was to happen to him now? The soldiers saluted the tribunal under the direction of their officer and withdrew. The two gladiators stood to attention from their seats in the shadows at the back of the hall then advanced. Since he was still pinioned so tightly between them Candidus found himself emulating their actions, albeit involuntarily. His legs had lost all sensation through inaction and the head wound from last night remained painful.

They brought him straight to the front, where Januarius was in earnest conversation with the old man who shared his jurisdiction and the military officer. As they approached Januarius turned pleasantly towards him, as if greeting a friend at a dinner party. The unsocial proximity of the two warhorses delivering him up was seemingly no matter for remark. Obviously, it was not the done thing to pass complaint on his host's over-physical enforcement of a kind invitation.

"Ah, Flavius Candidus!" said Januarius. "What a pleasure it is to meet you at last, especially after I've heard so much about you..." (Well that was that! Not much mileage in the 'Sextus Valens' story, then).....Can I introduce you to an old friend, my neighbour and fellow magistrate, Marcus Senilis."

Candidus bowed and made inarticulate mumblings of greeting to them both. The gladiators suddenly let go and left him wobbly on his unsupported pins but he was still bright enough to appreciate the joke in the elder magistrate's patronym. With a few more platitudes, Januarius sent this same worthy tottering off to the litter waiting outside to take him back to his villa. That left Candidus alone with Januarius, the local commander, and the brains trust presenting him. Fortunately the latter two were told to wait in the cross-hall whilst Candidus and the soldier withdrew at the magistrate's behest to a small ante-room his host used as his office, when in town.

Januarius looked him coolly up and down. He was a tall man and this advantage gave him the need to stoop slightly to address others, which he did with a fixed stare. This posture of looking down slightly and an indeterminate smile meant his manner seemed constantly to flit between sincere interest and patronising condescension.

In returning this steady gaze, there was momentary opportunity for Candidus to study the exact facial map of the man he'd been sent to investigate for the Imperial Governor. Age? Late thirties, early forties, he would guess. The outdoor complexion and illusion of a smile is already noted. To these could be added features and a colouring still more Celt than Latin. Give longer hair, take that toga away, place him yelling on a wicker-sided chariot with a spear in his hand, and his ancestor of centuries past is recreated, offering defiance to the Legions of Vespasianus. (Except that the easy-going Parisii had never offered much real defiance to anyone).

Yet this veneer of Romanitas; of sophistication, was not so thin. His forebears had generations of its accumulation to change them from chieftains to provincial senators, from mere collaborators to powerful local instruments of delegated Imperial authority.

These thoughts took seconds. His study spoke: "Sit down, Flavius, sit down! You must still be exhausted after your long journey up from Londinium."

Reassured by this genial tone and becoming more confident that, whatever was in store for him, it did not include indictment before the court or dispatch to the mines, Candidus was keen to cut the small talk and answer the burning issue: "How did you know I was here? How did you know who I was?"

"Flavius, can I first introduce you to my dear friend Claudius Sabinus, commander of that magnificent body of men, the Numerii Barcariorum Tigrisiensium. He will explain."

Januarius turned to his companion. The Praefectus whose long shanks had been stretched out awkwardly from his uncomfortable stool all through the court hearing was a lean-looking bearded man of middle years. His gaunt cheekbones were still marked where the hinged flaps of his helmet tightly fastened over them. A prominent nose completed the overall appearance of a hungry sparrow hawk, hovering for prey.

As he shifted in his chair, chain mail in need of oiling chinked and rustled:

126

"Someone was attacked in the old theatre last night. The Town Watch say they heard a commotion but found no-one. At first light, one of my own men found a trail of blood spots which led from the theatre to a common lodging house in the lower town, near to the haven. I understand they are the premises where you have been staying."

Januarius leaned forward: "Flavius, my dear fellow, Sabinus is always very thorough. It's a small town. Everyone knows everyone else and their business, before they even do themselves. We never have so many travellers here that we do not know what they are and where they are. Sabinus will explain:"

The commander resumed his report, unmoved by praise: "My men searched the old theatre and found this amongst the stalls."

There was a package on the table between them, rolled in cloth. The soldier unrolled it. Inside was a leather purse with a long strap which Candidus recognised as his own. Januarius leaned forward again and undid the purse then gently tipped it upside down over the table. Its contents, each of which the magistrate took in his fingers and carefully held up for wordless inspection, were revealed to be almost complete. Only the money was missing - hardly surprising.

Piece by piece, Januarius silently held up an old, bronze, crossbow brooch; a leather document tube (on which Candidus noticed the wax seals were now broken - again hardly surprising) and the silver badge of office for a Governor's Beneficarius Consularis. There was a little stone statuette of the goddess Fortuna decorating a small shelf on the back wall of the office. To her, Candidus offered up short but fervent prayers. He really did not know which way this interview was going – apart from the mines perhaps.

Again without comment, Januarius undid the broken seals and removed the endpiece of the document tube. On balance, Candidus felt relieved to see the general letter of authority and introduction from the Vicarius of Britain was still there. Januarius withdrew it from the tube and sat quietly for no more than a few seconds as he quickly read its contents. He looked up again, his florid features perhaps a little more so than before. He extended an arm over the table and indicated the objects which he had so neatly and precisely arranged upon its surface.

"Are these yours?"

Candidus had no option but to face it out. Twenty-four hours into his enquiry and already it would seem he was exposed.

"Sir, they are. And glad I am to get them back. I really am most grateful to you all..."

"Flavius, my dear fellow, whatever are you up to, here in Petuaria? Wandering into a ruined building in the middle of the night. Getting beaten-up. Falling into the hands of robbers and lucky to escape with your life. Roughing it in a seaside boarding-house, full of sailors and goodness knows what other low-life. A man of your status is perfectly entitled to the comfort and security to be found in a Mansio of the Imperial Post, somewhere on the better side of town. Whatever are you doing here, living like this?"

Candidus swallowed imperceptibly: "Just passing through. On my way up North. Can't really say much more than that. Government business. I'm sure you understand. You need not concern yourselves. I am just in transit."

This stiff response clearly found no favour with his questioners. Now it was Sabinus that spoke: "So why did you tell Cicerius Felix that your name was Sextus Valens?"

Januarius nodded thoughtfully as if that was an interesting question which had been exercising him, too. Candidus moved uneasily in his own chair, making its loose joints squeak. A more honest reply was going to be needed for this one:

"Yes, I'm sorry about that...   "

No doubt he was. Genuinely sorry. Sorry that he'd been caught out. Suddenly he felt as if he was about eight again. His mother had always told him that if he lied it would inevitably catch him out and here he was. Somewhere amongst the Shades of the Underworld, she would be pointing her disapproving finger at him.

"He seemed to be asking a lot of questions. I'd never met him before and didn't think it necessary to tell him all about myself. Discretion is a requirement of my employment, after all."

A fair point, one that seemed to satisfy them to an extent, but Sabinus could not resist the temptation of asking the obvious question: "A man like you is the 'eyes and ears' of the Vicarius. You've not come here to check up on us, have you?"

128

Here then was the 'hundred thousand sesterces' question. Girding himself up ready for the vital denial, surprise and relief were equal as he heard the magistrate intervene to his aid: "Don't be so silly! Of course he hasn't, Sabinus, you old cynic! Everyone knows that the Vicarius is my father-in-law. He wouldn't need to do that, and he wouldn't want to, either. I hope I've always willingly and deservedly fulfilled the obligations placed upon me. Both as dutiful son-in-law and through my civic office. I'm always conscientious in making sure I provide regular reports to the governor. Besides, our friend here is Beneficarius Consularis, a respected officer of the Civil Service. After all, it's not as if we're dealing with some dog from the frumentarii, is it?"

Sabinus sat back in his chair, trying not to show dissatisfaction at an unanswered question headed off in this way, but this reference to the secret police was an unwelcome note. Indirectly, it somehow flawed this otherwise-sweeping reassurance. Either way, Candidus still considered himself rescued and it was probably wiser to add nothing more than Januarius had said already. Perhaps sensing the chill he'd evoked, Januarius stood upright and turned his hands outwards like a man well-versed in the signals that close meetings:

"Good. Well, that's that! What I suggest now, is that you come home with me. Indeed I insist on it. I can't have a senior member of my dear father-in-law's staff slumming it in lodgings, not when I can offer the hospitality of my own household nearby. However, I do have a couple more things to do, first. People to see. While we're still in town this afternoon, perhaps I can show you around, give you a quick tour of the old place. It might be instructive. Then you can give a proper report to dear old Longinus on just how things were in the Civitas of Petuaria before you head north and get on with whatever affairs of state concern him up there. A couple of days at my villa should set you up nicely for the next leg of your journey."

It would have been churlish to refuse such a generous offer of accomodation, let alone find fault with incidental overstatements of Candidus' real seniority on the governor's staff. (Fact is, the Vicarius wouldn't recognise his outdoor clerk even if he fell over him; perish the thought of such a distinguished accident).

Candidus accepted the invitation with effusive thanks - and rightly so. His original aim of getting into the Januarius retinue was proving far easier than he'd dare to hope.

They left the Basilica and walked briskly across the forum, a gravelled open space bounded on all sides by colonnaded walkways. Since it was Saturday, there was a busy market going on, stalls selling all manner of local produce alongside imported items like pottery or oil. It was a mild day once out of the estuarine breeze and Januarius had discarded his toga in the room where they'd interviewed the Beneficarius Consularis. Now clad in just a tunic of simple cut but expensive weave, he strode confidently through the crowd with Candidus and Sabinus hurrying to keep up. Two surly and thick-set figures followed the three of them at a discreet distance.

Januarius gestured vaguely at these sinister shadows: "Don't mind my two German friends, Flavius. Their grasp of courtesy is as weak as their Latin, I'm afraid, but they are bound to me for ever and love me as a father. It is three years since I rescued them from the Altar of Nemesis in the City of the Legion, but I believe their flame of gratitude still burns as strongly as ever. I can rely on their loyalty to do whatever I bid. A man of my standing, living out in the countryside beyond the urban limits, he needs people like that immediately around him, because dear old Sabinus and his men must owe their first duty to the protection of this town and its citizens. Isn't that right, eh, Sabinus?"

Sabinus grunted his dour agreement to this brief assessment of military priorities prevailing in the tactical defence plan for Petuaria and district.

Crossing the market place, Candidus saw symptoms of that same sympathy between magistrate and population he'd noted earlier in the court room. In an era of severe division between rich and poor, this fellow-feeling was all the more remarkable. Stall-holders and townsfolk alike called out to him as he swept past at the head of his small entourage. To each and everyone of them he would give cheery reply, identifying his well-wisher by name and invoking the blessings of Fortuna, his hand spread aloft in a magnanimous gesture that was almost imperial...

130

Here and there the speed of their progress was thwarted by some client petitioner or confidante who would anxiously draw their patron aside: whether to crave his support in a land dispute; entreat intervention against oppression in the taxation authorities; or perhaps seek advice in the affairs of their council. To every supplicant Januarius was attentive and courteous, yet wise enough to avoid unrealistic promises and still retain a degree of detachment; his dignity and his safety. If the complex web of mutual obligation woven by patronage was conventional to the organisation of Roman society, here at Petuaria there were already occasional worrying signs emerging that it was being concentrated towards another level of ambition altogether...

"Each of them comes to me, Flavius, and on their neck they bear a monkey which clings to them with vicious little hands. They tell me of their clinging monkey of woe and, if I did let them, they would walk away with it left on my own neck. Whatever I can do for them, it's essential I hand back to them their monkey when they go."

Having cleared the open space of the market, they were quitting the Forum proper through a tall, brick-built, triumphal archway onto the main street, when something leapt from the shadows and seized the magistrate tightly by the arm. It was a hunched, wizened and ragged figure which ambushed him in the cool gloom of the arch and, for one fleeting second, Candidus believed it was that figurative monkey which held his host, brought to literal life by this last remark.

The gladiators sprang from their place in the rearguard before even hawk-eyed Sabinus had unsheathed his Army long-sword. The two Germans violently attacked their patron's assailant with bare hands but, for all their brutal thuggery, could not detach its clawing grip. In this thudding melee of punches and swearing, a shrill and querulous voice was heard above it all: "Marcus Ulpius Januarius, Aedile of Petuaria, may the Goddess Fortuna, the Seven Planets and the Twelve Constellations, all bless you and the Spirits of Your Ancestors!"

Januarius screamed at his companions: "Take your hands off her! Have respect for the Sibyl".

So that was it.

This crone was the local seer and here she was on her knees before the momentarily-rattled magistrate. Astrology was a superstition so universal in its adherence as to amount to a religion but Candidus (for his own part and quite against his times) believed himself a modern rationalist, proof against the rag-bag of half-informed logic and outright fantasy found in this creed of stars and fateful forces. In a society crippled by the horrendous fatalism so-often engendered by such beliefs, there was no doubting the power which could become available to those purporting to be its announcers. Candidus was left wondering just what might be the true spiritual promptings of Januarius, as the hag intoned:

"Marcus Ulpius Januarius, your forebears were chief among the Parisi tribe and in the foundation of the Civitas. Generations of the Januarii have been pre-eminent in this place. Now there is fear. The sea drives you to the barbarians. The barbarians drive you to the sea. I see floods and swords. Strange creatures have been observed in the great river and fiery portents in the sky. In the entrails of sacrifice I have seen clear confirmation of my dreams and visions. Through the clouds of years, for a millenium on - and then half a millenium on again - my dreams have flown ahead of us like speeding arrows. I hold your arm so tightly, Marcus Ulpius Januarius, because you must take courage from augury and because I alone can tell you the future".

"Be of good spirit! Fifteen hundred years from now, the town of Petuaria Civitas Parisi still clings to the northern bank of the mighty Abus river just as it always did; its haven still full of sails; its old perimeter standing witness to the bold expansion of its new; the inheritance of the Januarii well-recorded and their law courts still intact; far throughout the murk of centuries. And an Imperator whose Imperium extends beyond even the furthest expedition of Alexander is come in fire and steam here to Petuaria; all the way from his great palace in Londinium Caesariensis. Fear not for the future, O Januarii, for your greatest days are yet to come!"

She held him quite still in her brown and bony grip, beady black eyes locked onto his; once-proud Januarius weak captive at her hands. Forced to bend the knee before a magic more ancient than even its messenger.

For the first time, Candidus saw this local magnate and politician as he could be, his defences breached. If the old trout that did this to him was no wall-painting, Januarius must surely have seen her before. No, it was not her scrawny appearance or rancid breath which upset but the prophecy itself, whose content went to the root of his deepest concerns and finest fixations: "Your greatest days are yet to come."

The man was distinctly shaken but, as the shock abated, Candidus could see elation flowing in to take its place. Januarius was not just transparently superstitious but also ambitious. This aspect made him doubly-dangerous. It only reinforced the urgency of Candidus reporting back to Londinium as soon as he was able.

Reverentially, the Magistrate eased himself gently free of her persistent grip, divesting his elegant tunic of those claw-like hands. He fumbled in a pocket: "Good woman, I thank you for your inspiring words of comfort. Your wisdom is rightly valued in our community. Please take these coins to honour the Temple of the Sibyl and for her own comfort..."

There was a faint glint of silver and then the old bat was gone, scampering away up a side alley. Candidus saw Januarius breathe out heavily and then run long fingers over his forehead to rearrange dark, thinning hair flopping awry during this strange confrontation. There was sweat on his forehead but, in a moment, the confident assurance of a leader of men, a landowner and patron, was completely restored.

"Come!" he said. "I promised you a guided tour of our little vicus and you shall have one. The best place to survey our civic attainments is from the walls."

In a modest settlement the size of Petuaria, you were never far from its boundary, here marked by masonry defences. Claudius Sabinus seemed embarassed by the incident in the Forum tunnel, made an excuse of seeing a man about a horse, and left before they got to the walls.

As Januarius sprinted up some rather worn and treacherous steps to the rampart walk, Candidus swore inwardly at the unwelcome exertion this would require of him. His rib-cage ached and gripped him tight but the unease bordering on fear imposed by the two Germans close behind inspired him to a respectable trot, if only to maintain the distance.

Breathless at the fighting-top, Candidus was almost pathetically grateful for the breeze off the river where it came through gaps in the battlements. To his right, Januarius could be seen jogging sedately along the walkway towards the first-floor doorway of an intervallum tower, waving for him to follow. The heavies behind had obviously not let physical training lapse with the closure of their gladiators' school for they were right on him.

Candidus pursued Januarius to the bastion as quickly as his wave suggested he ought. When he did, he found the door ajar and, inside the turret, an unreliable ladder with the unexpectedly-agile Januarius swarming straight up it.

Candidus set himself similarly to its rungs with a will but the whole business gave painful reminder of his condition as an Army veteran out on invalidity gratuity and still bearing (untreated) a nasty knock on the back of his head from the night before. Hunger hardly improved his overall health. In short, he felt quite unwell and could cheerfully have slid back down the pigeon-dropping encrusted ladder into the hostile clutches of the two Germans again.

Fortunately he was spared the ignominy of such descent by Januarius himself, who seized him strongly on the forearms with a vigour surprising in a man of middle age and public office, dragging him up through the wooden trapdoor and depositing him onto the roof of the tower. Here, stone crenellations gave protection against vertigo as well as the pointy missiles of the outlawed or unjust. Encouraged to have made it, even with help, Candidus scrambled up from an undignified all-fours and looked out over the wall across the rooftops of Petuaria.

If Januarius looked like a farmer, his investigator had from the outset recorded in him the manners and habits of a patrician. It was with such unconscious disdain that he watched his reluctant guest assuming a standing position, but it was also only as Candidus dipped his head to rise that the magistrate spotted the dark and matted blood disfiguring his scalp:

"My dear fellow, that really is a nasty wound! How ever did you get it? Is this your souvenir of last night's adventure and source to Sabinus's trail of blood spots?"

Candidus nodded glumly. To be honest, he was getting quite fed-up with the Petuarensian tendency to comment on other people's bodily disfigurement.

What a good thing last night's resistance to temptation denied the 'Pink Rose' her own chance of private survey; such coquettish announcements would have made those of others' even more irritating. If that northern frankness was this time coupled with a certain aristocratic condescension, then at least the magistrate was also offering him some practical help:

"Flavius, my dear fellow, I cannot have a guest of mine wandering about the place with an injury like that left untreated. By the time we get back to the house I shall make sure my private physician, Nicomedes of Epidaurus, is there to treat you. This man is not your ordinary 'medico', either, but ordained priest in the cult of Aesculapius. He will do very well by you, as you shall find, I promise you."

So saying, he leaned through the battlements and shouted instructions to the matched pair dawdling below, outside the turret door down on the rampart walk. Obediently, they set off for the House of Nicomedes.

The doctor would doubtless find his delivery to the Villa of the Januarii similar in courtesy and speed to that of Candidus to the law courts. Prompt to obey, they still showed a loyal reluctance to leave their master alone with this suspicious stranger, like dogs that distrust a visitor, but their patron shooed them away. At least he had no such misgivings: "I brought you up here, friend Flavius, to give you instant overview on the current situation at Petuaria." Januarius spoke easily to him as if they'd known each other for years:

"Now your worthy master - dear old Longinus, father to my lovely wife - he may not have been expecting us to figure in that report on more northerly matters he's obviously commissioned you in. Yet I can't imagine him failing to reward your professional initiative if you take the opportunity to do so. For myself, I'd be failing in my own duty to him (and through him to the Blessed and Most Merciful Emperor Himself), if his devoted and obedient son-in-law, as aedile in ordo, did not make opportunities for fact-finding available to you, his humble instrument. Honoured as I am in his affection and trust with delegated powers of the Vicarius within this Canton."

Redundant horse-soldier he may be, but his brief career as 'legman' for the political establishment had already taught Flavius Candidus how to recognise cant when he heard it.

This pretty speech of Januarius was cant with a capital 'C'; cant in aspic with larks tongues; cant delivered up on a solid silver service impressed in relief with dancing bacchantes.

However, they do say that presentation is everything. Since Candidus felt obliged to receive this message with affectations of credence and warm approval for a number of compelling reasons, none of them admirable, he swallowed any sarcastic response. As if the speaker's power and wealth were not good enough reason already for biting his tongue and nodding wisely in all the right places, Candidus knew that accepting these politically-correct protestations would not only spare him a trip to the mines but also bring a luxurious roof; a square meal; and some half-competent medical attention.

(From these weak priorities of the flesh, some might think Flavius Candidus was letting the wider public and patriotic interest in the outcome of his covert mission slide. Starving as he was; suffering the remains of a hangover and the sting of an unclean head wound, perhaps some passing diminution of purpose could be forgiven. After all, he was still heading in the right direction).

So it was that the Beneficarius Consularis stood attentively with his rescuer on the tower, together inspecting the buildings and panorama laid out before them; a scene in which this Januarius - for all his worldly air - obviously took some little local pride.

Beyond the circuit of walls and grey roof tiles, a limitless sky above took the sheen of the bronze river for its lower lintel below. Spars of tide-stranded ships clustered like dead trees in the haven, some never to leave. The once-lethal length of a trireme rested oar-less and impotent; rotting in its fortified galley-pen on Petuaria Hard, stripped bare by navy shipwrights for a refit which never came. To the north of the town, beyond the walls, a still-prosperous suburb accumulated under its protective lee. Uninhibited by the mean and narrow plots available inside the gates, seemingly oblivious to the industrial long-houses and fish-smoking sheds scattered outside amongst them, here and there the architectural pretensions of a middle-class had been allowed free rein. Comfortable colonnaded views of tree-crowned downland rearing up from the alluvial plain gave them private reward for the provincial peace of Pax Romana.

To the rolling west the Eboracum road traversed that plain. Across the defensive ditches beside the walls it ran, through the citizens' allotments of cabbages and beans, lined with the melancholy but eternal tenure of wayside tombs; until a mile away it skirted a large square plantation of tall and ancient trees. Still sparse of leaf on this chilly April day, the transparency of a thousand, thousand branches offered a distant glimpse of whitewashed walls and long roofs of terracotta red. A great house that lay beyond it - the Villa Januarii.

To be fair, when viewed from the height of its bastions, the miniature town of Petuaria did not look such a bad place after all – as long as you did not draw breath and scent its whiff.

A strong breeze off the river took the tangs of salt and fish from his nostrils, whose only successor was the scent of burning applewood smoke, emerging through the hole in the roof of a half timbered longhouse beside the earthern rampart-backing. Its bad drains and flooding were obscured amongst the buildings; its charmless population hidden in their small insulae of lanes and alleyways. All was well.

"This place means a lot to me." (Here at last was Januarius speaking truth in simple words. The mask must slip). "My ancestors made this town, salvaged the beginnings of a settlement, hundreds of years ago, from the abandoned barracks of what was, briefly, a frontier fort, founded by the Ninth Legion under the governorship of Petilius Cerealis. Here is no pretty Calleva, no smart Corinium, but a survivor. A town that has come through wars, invasion, famine and pestilence. Emperors come and Emperors go, but Petuaria remains and, I am ever more encouraged to believe, will always remain. Long after you and I are gone."

"You take comfort from the seer?"

"Flavius, my dear fellow, I would not offend you but surely there is no man that can deny the influence of the Fates. I do hope you are not one of these followers of the Christus, this God of slaves and women?"

"Sir, I am not. But let's be realistic. I hope no offence is taken from my reminder that 'this God of slaves and women' as you call it is the preferred cult of the Imperial Household and our Blessed Emperor Himself – and looking ever more likely to become the established ritual of the Roman State."

High on his tower, Januarius waved his hand airily at this unnecessary statement of the obvious: "Yes, yes! I know, I know! Do not get me wrong. I count the Bishop of Eboracum close amongst my friends, even if we beg to differ in our creeds. Why, I even contributed in subscription to an emergency fund to bring the fellow back from Gaul, where he and some other British Christians of rank got stranded without cash after some half-baked conference for their cult. Silly, really. The man's from a good family too - renounces his own wealth and then looks to others still with means to pay the cost of his ferry back. Where's the sense in a religion like that, eh?"

"I make no criticism, sir. There is no obligation. But I take it your beliefs rest with those of the Army and you remain unconverted?

"Yes. And to a man who still carries himself like a soldier, I think I find myself in good company..."

"Perhaps you are right. But was it not that same British Army which first proclaimed the Great Constantinus in the garrison at Eboracum? The same army that brought him across the Alps to his final confrontation with damned Maxentius at the Battle of the Milvian Bridge? And did not the fiery sign of the Christus on eve of battle encourage him to victory?"

"Oh, yes. And in his deep gratitude did not our Great Emperor remove the Birds of Jupiter, great Zeus's harbingers of Victory, from the standards of our Legions? With their ensigns stripped of the Eagles, is it any coincidence that the fortunes of our armies fall with them? We are lucky, over here. Across Germania and Gaul, the barbarians stream unchecked whilst our soldiers stumble under ironic banners labelled: "In This Sign Conquer". You speak of a fiery sign but I would not underrate the influence of a domineering mother....."

"You are not impressed by the miracles then?"

Januarius raised his arm again, as if to signal impatience at any attempt to impose more than lip-service to the government line in matters spiritual. The question obviously annoyed him.

He moved angrily away from the battlements to the centre of the fighting platform where a large object of irregular outline rested under a faded, green tarpaulin in the middle of the turret roof. Upon this item he made a stand and his reply:

"Bah! We had miracles a-plenty with the old Gods! How many of those were really moving under the laws of hydraulics or the pressure of steam, applied by a technically-minded High Priest?"

"Then where will we find truth and answer for the questions of our lives?"

Januarius shook his head: "The old certainties are failing us, Flavius Candidus. The things we believed in and set our courses by, as new people come along - bearing new orthodoxies with which to hunt down and persecute the old ones. Religion and belief, state and law, the discipline of the army. The bricks of social order. We take our way of life for granted - unchanging from generation to generation, father to son – but nothing is sacred. Yes, I must concede how things that once were need not always stay the same, however long they might have endured before, but when things we once were told represented greatest wrong are now held up to us as utmost virtue, what are we to think? It just gets more and more difficult for a simple man of honest belief - either to keep up or else to change his credo fast enough - before the police are at his door!"

"We think the institutions and foundations of our state look much the same from the outside – their facades reassuringly-similar from one generation to the next. But the constant meddling of idiots, their reckless experimentation with tried and trusted method, the lethargy of the civil service, together they undermine and destroy what was so carefully built-up out of the wisdom and experience of centuries. Take the legions as a prime example! Eventually the outer shell becomes just a façade, preserved only to conceal what new incompetence or decay is willfully fostered from within". (He paused again).

"There was a Marcus Ulpius Januarius before me, friend. I am not the first in my line to bear all those three names together. If we do not stand firm in this place, in this island, even in this Empire; then I fear I may be the last!"

"When was your namesake?"

139

"Why, you walked in his ruins, friend! He's the man who built the old theatre, the miserable ruin where you were attacked last night. Most of the market place – our Forum - was his work originally. A benefactor of his community. Would I could come anywhere close! A great man for whose cultured and literate neighbours the gift of a proscaenium stage was a matter for gratitude. What's more, they used it, too. In his day, in the reign of the ancient Emperor Antoninus Pius – a good and pious man if ever there was one - there were the plays of Secundus; the comedies of Plautus; and "The Frogs" of Aristophanes, all performed in a little trading-station on the north bank of the mighty Abus river, in the Island at the End of the World."

"But now it's derelict."

"Yes, it is, and more's the pity! My grandfather served as Tribunum Militum in the Twentieth Valeria Victrix. A legion to fear and admire in the finest traditions of the Roman army. He told me once that in those days there was not a man in the Legion who could not read and write. When he came home on leave to Petuaria there were shows and plays to see at the theatre. Now, barely one-in-three of our citizens can even manage their alphabet. Written Latin is a closed book, dog-latin the height of learning, whilst our garrison is a ragged peasant militia whose commander stands as stranger to the indispensable military wisdoms of Julius Frontinus and his 'Stratagemata'. We learn nothing and are fast forgetting whatever we knew. Small wonder then that the theatre founded by my great ancestor lies abandoned, sinking slowly under floods and stone robbers. Young people today would rather spend two days travelling to Eboracum to see a decrepit 'net-and-trident' man go through the illegal motions with some arthritic swordsman in an alehouse yard, than stay in their own town to see travelling actors present "The Trojan War" abridged for simpletons."

The tide was rising already. Candidus watched a heavily-laden grain ship let go the lines that held it to the dockside and point its carved swan's head away from the moorings, ready to negotiate the harbour bar and head for the Rhineland. There must be someone on board who understood the essentials of navigation, of latitude if not longitude; who knew their night sky and the heavenly constellations. There would be skilled craftsmen down in those low sheds where all the banging and fumes came from.

140

It was not all bad, not all despair. Surely not.

The lively activity in the ships' haven, the traders in the market place, the noise of iron workers' hammers in their workshops, they all seemed to belie that decline in learning of which Januarius spoke and even those symptoms which Candidus himself detected. His glance back at the town must have signalled scepticism for any more negative theme because it was renewed by Januarius with fresh feeling:

"I've asked you up here because we are in serious need of help. Look at that corner of the walls, where they meet the haven."

Candidus looked. There was a break in the high ramparts where a landslip had undermined the walls. The whole south-west bastion had gone completely, slid away, but its place was crudely shored-up in half-hearted manner with piled rubble and nailed planking. This might have kept out sheep but no longer presented effective military obstacle to any more serious attacker.

The 'V' ditches which might once have broken up a charge were choked with dead dogs and domestic ordure. Januarius was right. You could see how maintenance had either failed altogether or was at best inadequate. Nothing worked properly anymore – not even the self-respect of citizens.

"These are our problems – floods and raids. And it's not just the ships of the sea-wolves which prey upon us. Even the sea itself, even the Great God Neptune has turned against us. The tides are higher than they have ever been in living memory. Sometimes it rains for days. Sea levels are rising all along the coast – nobody knows why. Is it something we have done? Are the Gods angry? What sacrifice can we make to appease them? What pleasure should we forgo? The Seer says nothing will do - it is their punishment for us. Whatever the reason, Neptune has seen fit to take our south-western bastion from us. The defences stand exposed. There is flooding in the town and the quaysides fall into dereliction because they are too low."

"Yes, I'd seen the standing water....."

"Our defences are undermined and our garrison down here on the bottom edge of the military zone is a gang of illiterate peasants. Look at this!"

So saying, Januarius tugged at the greasy tarpaulin which sheeted a mysterious structure on the roof of the tower. As the cords and canvas fell away, it was revealed. A catapult. Or, to be more accurate, a ballista.

Candidus was impressed: "So the defensive installations of Petuaria are not so mean, after all?"

Januarius scowled: "Bah! It is not as good as it looks. What do you think this is?"

Candidus knew full well. (Or thought he did). He knew his catapults. From the heavy-duty stone-throwers emplaced on the static defences of the Northern Frontier or the mighty blockhouses of the Saxon Shore, right through to the smaller, cart-mounted, bolt-firing machines used on the battlefield in close support to the infantry; he'd seen them all.

Januarius caught his complacency of experience and threw it back at him: "Take a closer look, friend. You may be surprised…."

He did and he was. It was not like any machine he'd ever seen before. Candidus was no engineer but could guess how it worked. This was not the usual one-shot weapon. Instead, arrows or bolts could be fed - one at a time but under their own weight - from a hopper into a firing tray as each engaged in turn upon a metal 'finger'. This was repeatedly drawn back and then released by an automatic trigger, powered and synchronised (like all these movements) by a flat-linked iron chain running off pentagonal gears for the length of the catapult. With the benefit of a reciprocating action on the winch, here was a devastating weapon which could automatically maintain a steady stream of iron-tipped missiles in a narrow arc until its magazine was exhausted. On a tightly-packed body of men or a distinct entity such as a raiding boat, the destructive power must be immense.

"It's incredible."

"Yes, of course it is. Or rather, it could be. But look at the state of it now."

Candidus looked again. He realised that the metal parts were oxidising, despite a thin layer of grease. Its ropework was powdered with mildew, its tension lost.

"My Magister Ballistae lies on his sick bed in the town, dying of a typhus or some disease brought in from the east. He is the only man in the province who can operate and maintain these weapons. In his head, he carries the designs of that legendary engineer to the ancients, Dionysius of Alexandria. From the arsenal at Rhodes he brought to us here, in our little northern Civitas, the finest secrets of the Greeks in the construction of ordnance. But the technology is dying with him and with it the strength of our unique defences. There are few left in this town to do calculus and none at all to grapple with the mathematical concepts giving life to these machines. Our kingdom of iron turns to rust."

They descended the tower to walk the full circuit of the walls, silent for a 'Master of Catapults' who lay dying somewhere to the centre of their solemn circumference.

Others of his bastions made emplacement for ballistae but these at least were the more conventional one-shot type and stood presently in better repair. Upon a corresponding turret on the opposite side of town, the western prospect, they saw where the second of the repeating catapults was mounted. It, too, bore early blooms of damp and neglect.

Candidus bent down and idly sighted along the firing-tray. He did so in relaxed mood until the sudden and shocking realisation it was set to fire straight down the Eboracum road made the blood burn in his face. He did not know what to say but dare not comment on this astonishing discovery, striving as he was in his own head for more charitable interpretation of what strategies this alignment suggested. (Surely the only body of men likely to approach from the west was the Legion itself?) Instead he busied himself with the mechanism, adopting the rare attention for these times of the scientifically-intrigued. It gave him time to think.

"You said you needed help. What can a humble Beneficarius Consularis do?"

"Supportive representations. Strategic observations in your report to the Vicarius."

"But you are Aedile of Petuaria and son-in-law to the Vicarius. How can my influence remotely match your own?"

Januarius looked away: "You may or may not know, but there are difficulties.....

"What do you mean?"

143

The half-smile came and went again, but there was no direct answer. "We in Petuaria need our friends at court. I wonder whether you may turn out to be amongst them! Don't be alarmed - our hopes are entirely patriotic. Men and money. Expertise and equipment. In one way we might seem well-protected, buffered by the military zone from the Northern tribes, but in another we find ourselves a crumbling bulwark of Empire on the frontline ourselves; limitanei exposed to the most violent raids of the sea-wolves. Someone must hear the prayers of the Parisii....."

Candidus understood this simple message but had long ago reached the cynical realisation that few things in life are as they seem. Januarius was a professional politician and - in classic style - entirely avoided further explanation of what "difficulties" might hamper the relationship of father and son-in-law. Candidus was in no way dismayed. This he would find out for himself.

"I will do what I can. Of course, I will."

Januarius gripped his arm tightly in a gesture of appreciation.

They both climbed down from the ramparts and took his horse-litter home through the twin-towered east gate, as the late-afternoon light began to fade and the houses beyond the walls put out their dogs and watchmen. Two grey-beards in antique helmets fastened the metal-plated doors of the old gatehouse behind them as they set out on the compacted gravel of the Eboracum road.

The curfew trumpet sounded its nightly lament across dusk-fallen fields as the town battened down for the night.

Passing the wayside tombs of the late and the good in the gathering gloom, Candidus peered out through the gold-tasseled curtains of the swaying litter for his first glimpse of the Villa Januarii.

"Police are the first and greatest blessing of a people"

(Menes, Pharaoh of all Egypt - First Dynasty)

IX

The office girl upstairs, visible through plate glass at her desk in the garage showroom above, crossed her legs. A navy-blue pleated skirt rode up to offer pleasing glimpses of well-toned thigh, the merest hint of stocking-top. The two policemen stood there goggling. Tryton gave a guilty start when he realised how preoccupied he and his sergeant had become – each one mesmerised by this lovely vision of flesh and sinew. Meanwhile, the workshop foreman stood patiently at the counter before them, watching and waiting for these Constabulary Lotharios to add their official signature to the proffered invoice.

"She has that effect on everyone", he said, wearily. (After all, as he commented later, this was a garage he was trying to run, not a knocking shop for coppers).

The Inspector elbowed his elder subordinate gently in the ribs: "Pickering, you old rogue! And you a married man with children." For all the bravado, old-fashioned church-bound moralities still dogged them both.

His sergeant laughed: 'Now, come on, sir! Just 'cos I've already ordered doesn't mean I can't still look at the menu!"

If Pickering was a man of humble origin he retained a high degree in courtesy notwithstanding. Taking that jokey rebuke for a wandering eye in a man of family responsibilities, Pickering would never dream of returning the crack. Not against the loyalties of a young widower. That was too cruel – a personal dilemma he would quietly leave for his youthful superior to settle for himself, in his own time.

Fact was, Tryton couldn't settle it. Not while the young wife he'd lost seven years ago still lacked Christian burial barely a mile away. It was as if he was stuck grieving. Killing Germans hadn't worked as a cure, either. But, for all that, he'd become a very different man to the one he was when Jenny died. Colder and more solitary. Four more years of war had seen to that. He wondered how they would have developed together if they'd both survived. What they would have become together. Children. A family. A household. Summer holidays on the beach at Scarborough. Joyful Christmas mornings. The wasted possibilities killed his humorous mood at once.

"When you've finished admiring the new models in the showroom, perhaps one of you gents could initial the job sheet to authorise payment," said the elderly foreman.

Every garage workshop had one of these; a mournful "gaffer" in brown overall coat, loose tie, pencil behind the ear, and drooping white moustache; his lugubrious manner providing impervious cushion between outraged customer and inept mechanic. His role of honest broker belied by the bosses' rich satisfaction with his billing record.

They'd had the car a full three weeks since the incident in North Hull. The damage was beyond the capabilities of any Police workshop so the Wolseley was taken to this main dealers on Anlaby Road; their pre-war building a confident statement of automobile empire in brown brick, ribbed concrete, and curved glass. Its chromed and mirrored split-level interior seemed deliberately designed by some fevered architect expressly to show off the legs of directors' secretaries to best advantage.

Their car was in the yard at the back, behind the bodyshop. New black coach paint gleamed in the sun. There had been a thorough mechanical overhaul, too. Brakes bled, grease nipples greased, valves ground. The two policemen made a short inspection of what they'd come to see as their personal transport. Dents in the roof had been filled or beaten out, new headlamps and windscreen fitted, and the paintwork refinished. A good job, well done. But wait! There was more:

"Pickering, what the hell is that?" (A shiny, silver monstrosity was mounted on the bumper).

"It's a bell, sir."

"And what on earth is that thing on top for?" (The translucent box, newly-screwed to the roof).

"It's a light sir. You press a switch on the dash and it lights up, sir. It says "Police".

As if to avoid any lingering doubt for the hard of hearing, pressed aluminium signs announcing "POLICE" had been screwed to both front and rear bumpers.

"Who on earth told these clowns to put all this gubbins on the car? I thought they were just going to repair it?"

"It's Mr Maister's idea, sir. It's part of his 'More-Visible-Policing-Presence' policy."

147

"But hell's bells, Pickering! We're the C.I.D! Being "more visible" hardly helps in our line of work. Discretion counts, and its gone right out the window if we drive around Hull lit up like a blooming Christmas tree, all gongs and whistles going!"

There was nothing to be done. After a fortnight's work on foot, they were still glad to have transport again. The motor car creates dependency in all those who use it but this one had suddenly become an embarrassment, a liability in effective police work.

Pickering had an informant to see in the Old Town and so they'd requisitioned from petty cash the approved amount for a beer fund: "Informant's Expenses" it would say in the ledger, but most of it still went down policemen's throats. They went to the Pier Head and placed the Wolseley as unobtrusively as its new accessories would allow, parallel to the kerb in a line of canvas-backed, fruiterers and fish merchants' lorries.

Due to meet Pickering's informant in the front bar of the "Minerva" public house, they took up position by the front door at a round table in the window overlooking Minerva Pier, where the Humber ferry docked. Outside, the estuary was raging away to itself; sky and water and Lincolnshire conjoined in a violent meeting of grey horizontals.

Tryton bought the first round; two pints of best bitter at ratepayers' expense. Since the new Chief Constable was paying, it was only right and proper his name should be toasted. He raised his pint glass and touched that of Pickering.

"Sydney Lawrence!" they both said together, laughing.

The informant never turned up. No wonder. Tryton expected he'd been put off by the obvious proximity of a fully-equipped police car parked so close to the pub. Informants tend to be nervous people who don't like fuss. It was dark outside now and he looked along the line of lorries on the other side of the road, anxious no one should use the inadequate lighting of infrequent street lamps as cloak for malicious damage to the newly-refurbished Wolseley. Hull folk were more than capable.

By this time they were each on their second pint. Outside it was raining even harder. Tryton scanned this stationary convoy of canvas-sided trucks and there was their Wolseley; still where they'd left it and apparently in good order. Reassured, his eyes ran back down the column one last time .

148

It was then that he saw it. Fourth lorry down from the police car, tightly parked between two fishmongers' sign-written wagons: a Dodge 'Weapons Carrier' in faded olive drab. White star on the bonnet, US Air Force serial stencilled on the bumper.

Tryton slammed his beer glass down hard onto the table and pressed his face against the pub window, wiping condensation away with his sleeve. Pickering looked up at him in disbelief but soon understood his inspector's terse explanation. They left their beers unfinished and first checked the pub, looking in every smoke-filled public room for a young woman with auburn hair wearing an American flying jacket. She was certainly not in here, not amongst a crowd of serious male drinkers, mostly dockers and warehousemen, settled in for the duration.

They went into the dark streets outside. Apart from nocturnal activity in some fruit importers' warehouses, the area was practically deserted. They checked the Dodge. Tryton looked across the canvas weather screen and into the cab. There was no-one inside. Pickering felt the bonnet and put his hand through the armoured grille to feel the radiator: "It's cold," he said. "Not been driven for hours."

Where was she then?

The only thought that occurred was that she could have taken the ferry, coming back tonight. Its return-crossing was due in about three-quarters of an hour. Watching and waiting is the most familiar component of police work and that was what they would do. Pickering moved the Wolseley into an adjoining street and then returned on foot to take up position beside the ferry booking office, where he could safely observe all disembarking passengers without himself being seen.

Tryton clambered over the tailgate, up through the canvas shroud and into the back of the Dodge. In between the seats and rifle racks he found himself falling over piled-up wooden trays. Their contents, which seemed no more than small rocks and stones, showered onto the floor as he squeezed past to sit behind the left-hand, drivers seat. Here he would await the return of its mysterious owner.

It was a chilly night, what with the wind off the estuary and the time of year. After an hour on a metal seat with only flapping canvas to insulate him, Tryton was losing the feeling in his toes.

149

The ferry from New Holland was running late. When it did arrive, there was quite a flood of people off it, some with cars and taxis to meet them. As this rush of activity died away almost as quickly as it began, Tryton wondered if they'd been wrong in their guesswork and faced a longer wait.

No sooner had this doubt entered his mind than the sound of light footsteps beside the truck dispelled it. Tryton held his breath. The cab door opened and someone slight of build in a woollen hat climbed softly into the driver's seat. Before the engine could be started, Tryton kneeled around the side of the seat and seized a slim arm tightly from behind. The driver gasped at this detainer, as Tryton shouted into a concealing woollen hat near where an ear might be expected:

"Inspector Michael Tryton, Hull City C.I.D. There's no need to be afraid - but don't try and start the vehicle, whatever you do!"

His request went unheeded for he heard the engine churn. In a moment Sergeant Pickering appeared at the driver's door and joined in the struggle. Clearly there was strong reluctance for any form of detention. As Tryton and the victim of their ambush fell sideways across the cab onto the passenger seat, he banged his nose hard on the steering wheel.

Her woollen hat came off and his face was brushed with auburn hair last seen in the lane at Brantingham a fortnight ago. Its fragrance was released with it, tantalising his nostrils and all his senses.

"Let-me-go!" she screeched. The motor was running and he felt the lorry jolt suddenly forward.

"I'm sorry, miss, but I can't do that - not 'till you sit nice and still and switch off the engine. We are Police Officers!"

He showed her his warrant card but it was quite unreadable in the dark. No-one could have blamed her for fearing the worst.

Pickering reached over and killed the engine whilst Tryton held her tight. Too tight, to his uncharacteristic and great discredit.

Hugged her, almost.

His heart pounded in his temples and the adrenalin released was more than that of any conventionally-difficult arrest. He felt like a small boy on a hot summer's afternoon who stalks and captures some exotic butterfly in his hands, feeling its delicate but implacable determination to escape from the prison of his will.

Except that this was Hull on a wet Tuesday night and this moth was biting both his wrists with sharp little teeth:

"Miss, I am arresting you on suspicion of theft. You do not have to say anything but I must warn you that anything you say may be written down and ..."

At least she stopped biting his wrists (particularly welcome since the one slashed on the barbed wire at Brantingham still pained him) and looked up: "Theft! What are you talking about, what theft?"

"The theft of a valuable antiquity from a quarry just outside Brough."

"The Roman mosaic, the pavement?"

"Yes, that's it, miss."

"You limeys have got to be joking!" (She laughed and became very still).

Pickering at least had had the foresight to anticipate the niceties in such an arrest. He'd already phoned ahead from the pub for a policewoman to help receive their prisoner. Upon her arrival they made the short journey to Central together in the Wolseley without difficulty.

As they drove through the evening streets, Tryton studied her features out of the side of his eye, as they were alternately side-lit by passing lamps then plunged into a darkness from which only the white orbs of her frightened eyes could emerge. The almond shaped eyes, those arching eyebrows reflecting the sculpted cheekbones. Those lips.

He'd meant it. He would know her again. And here she was. His prisoner! Improper and intoxicating sensations of power confused his judgement. It was only when Pickering pointed out to him that his nose was bleeding from where he'd hit it on the steering wheel that some semblance of professional sense returned.

"Put her in an interview room."

Pickering was uneasy. He was sensible but sensitive enough to detect an extra edge to his superior's mood, beyond the understandable excitement of any policeman at a serious crime detected through an observant arrest: "What are you going to do with her, sir?"

"What do you think I am going to do, Pickering? I'm going to interview her, of course!"

"For what? For an offence committed outside the city jurisdiction, for which you've no more evidence than driving away too quickly from a quarry where a dodgy old man in a raincoat has just chased her down a footpath? Think carefully about it, sir! Wouldn't it be safer to hand her over to the wooden-tops of the East Yorkshire force?"

Few receive good advice with good grace. Tryton was furious: "I don't need you to tell me my job, sergeant! I'll do as I think fit! Meanwhile you can do something more useful than bleating to me, by getting on the blower to your garage friend with his tank-recovery Scammel and arranging for this woman's transport to be towed in here to Central. At once! I want that vehicle searching stem to stern, and immediately. See to it!"

He'd never, ever spoken to Pickering like this before and no sooner had he uttered his tirade than he deeply regretted it, but the sergeant was gone in an instant without another word and the right moment for an apology gone with him. Tryton stormed down to the interview room, pausing only to count to ten before opening the door where she sat so quietly at a table, this woman who (did she but know it) had already made such an impact in his life. Thank goodness he had a policewoman standing nearby – even if it was grimfaced WPC Horncastle, planted firmly on her tree-like legs, with arms folded across a broad front and showing a scowl fit to scare horses.

"Right, miss. Perhaps, first of all, we can establish your name?"

"I want to see the American Consul."

"I take it you are an American national, then?"

"I want to see the American Consul. And I want to see a lawyer. Now!"

Tryton was not used to having terms dictated to him by someone he had just arrested. ("Even less by a woman" - as he was to tell Pickering in the canteen, later on). The first inklings of a determination to match his own began to dawn, nevertheless, and with them the almost dormant recognition of a familiar temperament he'd once known long ago in another, long-lost beauty. Disturbed by resurrected emotions such as these, he showed himself as rattled: "Look lady! This is not one of your Jimmy Cagney movies! This is England and you're being held on suspicion of a serious criminal offence…"

"Don't give me that crap, Lieutenant! I want a lawyer and I'm entitled to a lawyer. Get me one and we'll chat. Till then I'm saying nothing!"

Baffled and infuriated, Tryton stormed out again, the interrogator as petulant child. In his heart of hearts he knew he had bitten off more than he could chew but no woman was going to do this to him. If she wanted a lawyer, by gum, he would get her a lawyer.

Tryton's revenge took half an hour to arrive from his usual place holding up the bar of 'The George' Public house in that narrow lane they call "Land of Green Ginger". Even if it was only a three-minute walk from there to the Police Station in Alfred Gelder Street, Meredydd Parry-Jones, Solicitor & Commissioner for Oaths, always took the full half-hour to arrive. He had his priorities and here was a man who never left his pint unfinished; whatever the call, whoever the prisoner. "They're not going anywhere are they, after all?" he would scoff to his friend, the landlord, polishing glasses behind the bar.

If Parry-Jones was handicapped by a nervous high-pitched laugh and a question mark over his client account, he was still the only brief who would turn out at this time of night for anyone. Tryton watched him take her 'client instructions' with exaggerated attentiveness and detected her disgust with inward satisfaction. The lawyer stank of beer and moved with the deliberate instability of the serious drunk.

That evened the score, then: 'One-all'.

Whilst her delicately-flared nostrils filtered the bar-room stench of her new friend-at-law, Tryton made his way back down to the station yard in time to see the Dodge rolling in on the end of a recovery truck tow-hook. It was set down under powerful outdoor arc-lights to enable the thorough search Tryton had ordered.

Pickering stood nearby, talking to the driver of the Scammel, who could be overheard asking him about the well-being of his 17 year-old son, just back from the Holy Land, a divided place where the Army had held a thankless ring between two emerging and implacably-opposed nationalisms, each of them bitterly blaming the British for their plight. Still not old enough to vote, his first introduction to death had been the shocking sight of a bombed hotel and some of his own officers blown to bits.

The lad hadn't been back in Hull a fortnight for his leave before being sent straight off to the jungle to fight Chinese communists in Malaya, a troubling development which for some reason Tryton had not yet got round to mentioning, only doubling his admitted sense of guilt. Pickering's first-born was hardly out of childhood yet Tryton had to date barely managed to offer his colleague, the father, even a fraction of that sincere interest which prompted the garage-owner's concerned enquiry.

Tryton waved him over to the side of the captured Dodge: "Look," he said. "I'm sorry for bawling you out like that. I know you've got a lot on your plate just at the moment..." That oblique reference to Pickering's soldier-son seemed the best apology he could muster, but it was accepted with typical good grace.

"That's O.K. but thanks for mentioning it, anyway. I know he'll be alright. He knows what he's doing. Never mind, sir, I think you've got worries of your own right now" said Pickering quietly.

They searched her truck, an iron-clad for a butterfly. Under the lights with the canvas 'tilt' pulled back, they found the wooden trays Tryton had fallen over when first entering it: Stacks of them. Market gardeners and fishmongers trays, filthy with loose earth and filled with material. Old bones. Pot shards. Fragments of red brick and unidentifiable ferric objects, deformed by ancient swellings of orange rust. They had all been carefully sorted and stored according to category. Many were individually labelled with cryptic and speculative descriptions in a neat feminine hand: "Samian mortarium fragment (Gaulish, mid. 1st Cent. A.D.?)."

Pickering took off his trilby and smoothed back his hair. Tryton suddenly thought how old and tired he looked in the harsh white glare of the floodlights.

"What's all this junk, sir?"

Tryton was no classicist but he knew, all the same: "The owner of this truck is an archaeologist, Pickering. That means she digs old things out of the ground to put them in museums. And that means it's no coincidence she just happened to be driving away from Brantingham Quarry on the morning that a Roman floor is stolen."

There were shovels and trowels in the rifle racks, their blades still fresh with earth.

In a brown envelope on top of the dashboard there was a letter which Tryton took out and read, from a man called Ian Richmond at the University of Oxford. (Someone else to pull in for questioning?) It was addressed to "Miss Z.Macsen, 38 North Bar Without, Beverley". The content was no more than academic's blather but it referred to her pursuing research in Romano-British studies. The link was obvious. Case solved?

"Get this little lot photographed, please, Pickering."

Tryton re-entered the building and ran up the stairs two-at-a-time as he always did, invigorated in his purpose by what they had found in the Dodge. Back to his old self. She waited on his whim, still in the interview room, but Tryton was bouncy with confidence, the letter in his hand.

" What does the 'Z' stand for, Miss Macsen?"

"Zuleika!" said Meredydd Parry-Jones, stepping forward from the shadows: "My client is an American citizen here in this country for academic research. But what a privilege it is for a Man of Wales to be called out on this dark and stormy night to assist a lady - one not only of such dazzling beauty but also bearing such a famous name."

"Famous?" said Tryton, puzzled. "Do you mean Zuleika - as in "Pygmalion" by George Bernard Shaw?"

"No, you English clod!" hissed Parry-Jones. "...Macsen!"

"What's famous about that?"

"Prince Macsen Wledig, a Hero of Wales."

"Never heard of him."

"No? Well a flat-foot like you, Tryton, wouldn't have, would you - spending all your time looking through upstairs windows and rifling through dustbins for other peoples' business as you do."

Bolstered in his enquiry as he was and feeling there was little in the ethics and practice of Parry-Jones' approach to his own profession to bear superior comparison with his, Tryton was content not to rise to this sneer.

In his book, he would rather treat this exchange as part of the lively repartee natural between 'Those who Defend Society' and 'Those who Defend Its Enemies'. This left him happy to humour the solicitor for the moment.

"I think you've been spending too long in 'The George', Meredith. So who was this Prince Macsen then? What did he ever do for Wales?"

Anxious to show off both his knowledge and his instinct for folklore, Parry-Jones had become diverted from his still-silent client: "Yes, that is his name in Welsh, in the tales. But his real name was…"

Before he could even finish, it was done for him from an unexpected quarter: "Magnus Maximus! The last British usurper. He removed the entire garrison of Britain in three-eight-three A.D. to take onto the continent in support of his claim to the Imperial throne!"

Both Tryton and Parry-Jones turned as one to look in frank surprise at the table where the young American woman sat. So she had a tongue, after all. Tryton turned on her:

"Listen to me, Miss! You, me, this police lady and 'Merlin' over there haven't gathered here in this police station for a cosy talk over tea and scones about ancient history. You're not in your Oxford college now! You're in an ex-army truck full of artefacts, posing as an archaeologist. You're a foreign national – an American - from the country that bled us white with 'Lend-Lease' and 60 year's worth of War Debt for the privilege of fighting Hitler alone before you lot ever got involved. You also come from a country where there are thousands of collectors wealthy enough and greedy enough to pay someone to ship out the stolen antiquities of other lands to decorate their Californian beach-homes. Your people have still got operational airfields all over Lincolnshire and you personally have got the American Air force literally written all over you – your jacket and your transport! I'm investigating the theft of a Roman mosaic and it seems to me that you've got both the motive and the necessary knowledge. And quite probably the necessary contacts. So how am I to know that you weren't directly involved in getting that mosaic out of that field and into an empty bomb-bay in the very next B17 'Flying Fortress' flying out of this country and back home to the U.S.A? "

"Because I wasn't. Because I didn't take the pavement", she stated calmly: "How could I?" (He still noticed how she'd flinched when he mentioned the aircraft).

"Well talk to me then. Let's start with that morning, exactly a fortnight ago. What was an American at Oxford doing up here in Yorkshire, hiding out in the wood next to Brantingham quarry on the morning it was taken?"

"You're right. I am an archaeologist. That's true. It's not how I originally came to be over here but it is something I got into. I'm following a course of research at your University of Oxford with a view to a doctorate"

"And your research is in Romano-British Studies?"

"Yes, of course it is. Don't worry, I have documentary evidence of this."

"That's alright. We believe you on that much. But what were you doing in the wood?"

"The specific title of my PhD. Study is "The Roman Villa System in the North"

"So?"

"The 'villa' in Britain covers everything from a native farmstead, modernised with rectangular buildings, up to the sort of large country estates which were not seen again until the wealthy English gentlemen of the eighteenth and nineteenth centuries."

"Yes, yes, very interesting. But why Brantingham?"

"Because there is a line of villas running along the southern edge of the Wolds, associated with the Roman town at Brough, which are the most northerly villas so far found in Roman Britain. Between here and Hadrian's Wall there are only a few more that have been found."

"Yes, Miss. Absolutely fascinating. But please answer my question. Why you? Why in that wood? And why on that morning of all mornings?"

"Because there is a villa at Brantingham. As you well know, now. And because the villa at Brantingham seems the most important. It was nearer to the town. There are others nearby, at Sancton and Newbald. They liked the sandy soil – easy to cultivate and turn with the primitive ploughshares they had in those days. Handy for the York road, too. But the villa at Brantingham seems to have been the most elaborate. Decorated pavements and painted walls. That's why I've been making it the focus of my research."

"And what have you found out?"

"That the quarry men found two pavements there in 1941 during 'The Blitz'. They were covered over until now, when a bunch of local amateurs started to take steps towards getting them removed for display."

"Yes, that's right. And were you involved in that process at all?"

"No, I damn-well wasn't."

"Why not? Surely it was a golden opportunity for your research?"

She bit her lip and looked at Parry-Jones. His cheering leer offered her little encouragement.

It was then that Tryton had his flashback. To a damp September's morning on an RAF airfield in East Yorkshire where low-lying mist clung to the runways and deformed the silhouettes of aircraft parked out at dispersal. One of the last warm days of the year was about to begin, a day of golden sunlight before the insidious gradual onset of winter; a winter which would kill thousands of German soldiers who had penetrated deep into the heart of Mother Russia dressed only in summer uniforms.

On this dog-day at the end of summer, Sergeant Pilot MIchael Tryton went out to his aircraft for a practice flight. A photo-reconnaissance De Haviland Mosquito, the "Wooden Wonder", was his transport of delights; a plane so fast it need not bear armament. There was no German aircraft could catch this twin-engined sportster of the skies as it flew in, took vital photographs of railway marshalling yards; of gun emplacements or the damage done in last night's raid; before returning to the nearest friendly darkroom.

But today there was no risk, no need for weaponry. No enemy territory to cross. No flak. Just a practice run with some new cameras fitted to try them out. He'd taken a young aircraftsman along with him in the jeep, out to dispersal. (Couldn't remember his name now - enthusiastic chap. Keen on photography. And history, of course). Took the lad up - his job to operate the cameras and make sure they worked all right. Quite obviously never been up in an aircraft much before - ground crew really. He was sick into one of his gloves almost straightaway after they took off; probably that bit when Tryton peeled away from straight and level, putting the plane onto its side then dropping the nose to take a closer look at merchant shipping in the Humber.

That was it! Bull Sand Fort. Funny how unrelated things in life come to tie up after a few years.

He remembered how they'd got a few shots 'in the can' of the anti-aircraft fort down there. From a safe altitude of course – didn't want the gunners to get the wrong impression and think he's Jerry! Didn't want them opening up with the 'ack-ack'.

But there was something else - something working away in the back of his mind. Drawers in the filing cabinet of memory sliding open for the first time in years.

Yes. He remembered it now. They'd come in fast and low off the estuary and the lad said there were still a couple of shots left on the film. Keen on history, he said. "Archaeological digs" he called them. Explained to Tryton how there'd been a big Roman house right below them, near to where the Blackburn aircraft factory is now, at Brough. Could he take a couple of exposures of the fields down there, just in case something showed up as marks in the crop?

Pleased to oblige. He'd rolled their light-blue painted machine over on the moment and brought it around again in a couple of slow passes. Virtually stood the Mossie on its bloody wingtip. Below them the green fields of England spreading out to a blue horizon, the England they would willingly die for if it were needed to protect the land and the values this timeless countryside represented for them all.

The young technician in his left hand seat had pressed the camera button and shouted "Bingo!" just as the plane came roaring over a tall wood by the river, its engines screaming. Then he was sick again, now into his other glove.

When they got back to Leconfield, the Squadron C.O. was waiting for them with an official complaint from the factory manager at Brough – his precious barrage balloons buzzed by some idiot in a Mosquito. Yes, he remembered it now. Seemed like only yesterday...

Suddenly Tryton realised everyone was staring at him; Parry-Jones, the American woman, and W.P.C. Horncastle. "I'm sorry. I was just thinking. Far away. You were telling me why you didn't get involved in the operation to remove the pavements?"

"Gee! How can I put this? You can't imagine what it's like for a single woman on her own in a foreign country"

"No, I can't, Miss … but this is England!"

"Amazing! So it is…. I never realised. Look, Lieutenant, the thing is that, from my point of view, I didn't even want them to lift that pavement in the first place. I didn't want any part of it. Where I come from, anything over one hundred years old and people get really excited. But over here, you've got antiques falling out of your attics. In fact sometimes I look around and everything appears old and worn. Then I get a reaction – I feel like I want to see something new just for a change; something clean and shiny and loud! Probably covered in chrome, like a Buick!"

"So you didn't approve of the recovery operation?"

"No I guess I didn't, if I'm honest about it. I suppose I wanted it to stay where it was, where it belonged; where it had lain in the earth for the past sixteen hundred years. Where it was made. The rightness of place."

"Did you do anything to stop them – the archaeologists?"

"No, of course not. How could I? No, all I did was to hide in the wood and watch them. That's not a crime over here is it, yet?"

"Of course it isn't. If that's all you did. So, were you there when it was stolen?"

"No. You must believe me, Lieutenant. I was only there in daylight. On that morning when you chased me, I'd only just arrived in the wood."

"And you'd been observing their preparation work all the time it went on?"

"Yes."

"Do you have any idea who could have carried out this night-time removal?"

Again she paused. She knew better than to look at Parry--Jones but he was staring fixedly at her, his bar-room pallor flooded from the power of the moment. Tryton was looking at her too, well aware that a hiatus like this from an interviewee meant there was something she knew but feared to impart. The tiny pink tip of her tongue ran along an already moist lip in a way that made him burn up inside. Eventually she spoke: "I think I can help you."

Tryton could not do otherwise than keep her in overnight. She might do a flit.

160

Back at his lodgings the thought of her in the cell tormented his imaginings. He dare not let her go, in every sense, although he was yet to properly acknowledge this fact. He ordered she be provided with the necessary comforts but she had still been distressed at the prospect. (Claustrophobic?) His hope was that keeping her in would not lose him her co-operation but he dare not release her on police bail for fear she simply fled abroad. He slept fitfully, waking to find himself engaged in long imaginary conversations with her where she fixed him with those eyes whilst combing long auburn tresses out. He realised she was standing alone on a high, dark tower surrounded by besieging soldiers equipped with ladders and engines of war. He found himself flying over the tower where she stood and, circling, identified its gothic finials as those of the Prudential Tower itself before he woke in a hot sweat, screaming:

"Jenny!"

The following day was fine and clear after a light frost, one of the last of spring. He and Pickering took the American woman with W.P.C. Horncastle as chaperone, out in the Wolseley to the gates of Brantingham Quarry. From there she directed them via Brantingham Outgang and the village itself up through the enfolding Dale, past the church and onto the desolate tops of the Wolds.

"Where are you taking us?"

"I don't know what it is called but I do know the route. I once followed a construction worker's truck, way out here. It came from the quarry where the guys in it had been looking at the pavement after the people that were working on it had gone home."

"What sort of truck? Did you get the registration?"

"No, but it belonged to a firm called – now, wait a minute. I know, it was something Imperial...no, er, was it "Consolidated Gypsum Products Inc."? Something like that. It was a big, yellow dump-truck covered in white dust. I didn't check out the registration plate."

"And where did it go?"

"To what I guess is a big mansion somewhere out here, out in the backwoods. I'll know the entrance to it when I see it."

161

If the local term 'Wolds' - an ancient word - had once meant 'woods', her description of 'backwoods' was nowadays inapt. After a thousand years' deforestation and hundreds of years' more intensive farming, woodland was a generally rare commodity up here, out in these big chalk fields bounded by sparse hawthorn hedging. Centuries of sheep had seen to that. As they journeyed through its empty landscape of rolling downland, they passed a wide green field full of hundreds more sheep - all grazing with their bodies facing in the same direction. In the centre of these woolly flocks a circular tower of dark red brick rose sinister from the turf - surreal and inexplicable structure in open countryside. As they passed, a sudden spurt of billowing smoke and steam issued from the top of the tower, before subsiding.

The romantically-inclined might have fancied this to be some dragon's lair but Tryton knew its reality was more mundane. This was a tunnel ventilation shaft for the Hull to Barnsley railway line with the smoke of the 9.30 a.m. express rushing-by below. Nevertheless, as an allegorical vision, the image of this dark and smoking tower in that peaceful field of browsing sheep troubled him with its unwelcome evocation of dreams from the night that was gone.

For the first time in their dealings of the morning she spoke unbidden, addressing her inquisitor directly rather than awaiting Tryton's questions.

"You look unwell, Lieutenant."

He was taken aback at this unexpected solicitude. His reply was weak and thoughtless: "Had a bad night. Didn't sleep."

Her lovely lip curled at this hint of self-pity: "Better than I did! I hated it in there. How could you do it - keep a woman in a cell? You limeys claim your English Police are the best in the world and then you keep me in conditions like that!"

"Look, Miss. I have a duty to the preservation of evidence. At the moment that includes you. As soon as possible, you will be released."

The good W.P.C. Horncastle had been responsible for the overnight comfort of their prisoner. She took this slur upon the honour and the hospitality of the Hull City Police force as a personal insult and was moved to intervene:

162

"The Inspector's right, Miss Macsen. Don't go whining about your conditions to us. You had a clean cell, extra blankets, and a fish supper - hot fish and chips straight from Whitefriargate and the North Sea. I'll tell you, young madam, that there are some folk who will deliberately get themselves arrested just to enjoy accommodation like that for the night."

Tryton was privately amused to see the American woman wrinkle her pretty nose in disgust on remembrance of those fish and chips, that Great British Delicacy. (After all, what do you expect to eat in Hull, if not fish?)

They continued their journey in frosty silence. The road now traversed a high wold side, like the great heaving flanks of a corpulent sea monster left ashore by a freak wave. At a place where a long tree-lined drive came up from a chalk valley to meet the public road on a ridge, the American woman cried out: "Stop! This is it!"

Pickering, who was at the wheel, turned off the road into the drive-opening where the trees began. They led from the large fields of the open wolds into the wooded valley. There was no sign of farm or dwelling down there, just the rough gravel track disappearing amongst the forestry. No plaque or notice to indicate what place this was or where the track might lead. Only two ornamental stone vases, each on a brick pillar either side of the drive entrance, to dignify the spot.

"Where are we?"

City dwellers all and one foreigner. Not one of them really knew. Tryton got out of the car and stood in the centre of the track, looking downhill. There was no-one about. This drive could be one hundred yards long or it could be one hundred miles long for all he knew. He looked back up at the police car, parked athwart the entrance. It was turning to rain, fine sharp drops spitting out of a sky which had turned from blue to grey within ten minutes in the entertaining way that English skies do.

No-one else was willing to leave the warmth of the vehicle. Tryton pulled his trilby down to protect his ears, and turned up the back of his raincoat collar over his neck to protect against the gathering mizzle.

All things come to he who waits and on this occasion Tryton was fortunate in early fulfilment of the proverb. A little red Post Office van with shiny black mudguards was struggling up the bumpy track out of the valley. As it crested the rise just before the public road, Tryton stepped out in front with his hand raised in friendly greeting. Seeing the prominent "POLICE" light box on the roof of the black Wolseley nearby, its postman driver thought it wise to comply:

"What can I do for you gents? Out chasing sheep rustlers are we?"

"Er, no" said Tryton, with feigned diffidence. "We seem to have got lost out here. Can you tell me where that track leads?"

"Just a big house: 'January House'. It's not a through road. A dead end. Private."

"Oh" said Tryton, compounding his pretence at diffidence with the intonation of the uninterested: "Sounds very grand. So who lives there then?"

"The Honourable Mister Roderick Baynard. Well-known local gent' and man-about-town. Surprised you've not heard of him."

"I see. Anyway, perhaps you could give us directions for the Brantingham road?"

Tryton heard the ensuing litany of lefts, rights, junctions and "you can't miss it" with little comprehension because the rest of his mind was working overtime on an entirely different route. He waved the postman off with cheery thanks and walked back up to the waiting Wolseley. Opening the rear passenger door he leaned in: "Miss Macsen. Have you ever seen the stolen pavement?"

"Yes. I've often stood and looked at it for a while, in the evenings after the excavators had gone home."

"Would you know it again?"

"I think so. Its pattern was simple but distinctive enough for all the fact it only used the three colours - red, black and white. So, yes, I'd know it again. But why?"

"Because we are going to look for it."

"What, now?"

"Yes, now! Because there's no time like the present. I need your assistance. I cannot express my request more politely or urgently than that. If the mosaic has been brought here then the sooner we look, the less chance there is of it disappearing again."

He knew she was reluctant and judged that here was a beauty whose relatively-short life had already taught her to offer the male sex the minimum in co-operation. Yet at the same time he detected in her such strong emotional attachment to the mouldy relic whose recovery was prime objective of his enquiry. If right about this, he judged it gave him more than enough lever to guarantee the help from her he needed, however she felt about him.

"Sergeant Pickering and Constable Horncastle! Miss Macsen and I will proceed down the lane and try to get into the house itself. I would like you two officers to move the car well away from here. It stands out like a sore thumb in this exposed terrain. Go up the road and hide it. Put it in a wood or a barn, somewhere like that, and then move on foot back up the public road near to this drive entrance. Find yourself a vantage point and wait for us here. If you hear three blasts on my whistle that means we need your assistance urgently. Constable Horncastle, you are the only one of us in uniform and I would be grateful if you would please cover it over, with a civvy raincoat or something. I do not want us to draw attention to ourselves."

Tryton and the American archaeologist set off down the lane with Sergeant Pickering's blessing ringing in their ears: "Be careful down there, sir!"

Tryton had a shrewd idea where his sergeant envisaged the greatest amount of care should be deployed but found himself in merry pin. The rain had passed over, the sun was out again and it was a fine spring day. It was a long time since he'd last enjoyed the simple pleasure of a walk in the country with a pretty girl beside him.

The track was badly-rutted, as if the sort of heavy vehicle to which she referred used it regularly, but beyond the Post Office van there had been no sign of anyone else in the lane during the ten to fifteen minutes they were parked there.

As they walked, the silence from his companion became increasingly-irksome and Tryton sought to break it: "What are you doing here in England, Miss Macsen?"

"Doing? I'm being dragged around the prairie by a crazy cop-lieutenant from some one-horse police department that gets his kicks out of locking up dames! That's what I'm doing in England, mister!"

Tryton was taken aback at the strength of her bitterness. He tried in a hopeless sort of way to make amends: "Look, I'm sorry! I'm sorry that I kept you in last night, but you're the only lead I had. You were our prime suspect at first but the more help you give me the less you are under suspicion, and by the same token the more chance there is of getting the mosaic back. I'm simply doing my duty."

"Only obeying orders" she said in sarcastic reference to last year's trials of prominent Nazis at Nuremberg – still a fresh memory for everyone.

They continued down the lane in a silence of disapproval which appeared to be a speciality of his companion. After a hundred yards or so, with little change in the monotony of the belt of trees and the bare fields above, Tryton tried again: "When I asked you about your studies you told me that that is not how you originally came to be over here. What brought you to England?"

Either his persistence or more likely the warmth of her recollections achieved some thaw in her icy manner. She looked up at the sky and sighed.

When she spoke quietly to him the trans-Atlantic accent was less pronounced: "You're looking at a nicely-brought-up girl from upstate New Jersey. Daddy was in shipping. Mom was golf club, country club and Ivy league. And I'm their only darling daughter who did everything right and is engaged to be married to Michael Christou, High School hero and son of local attorney Nicholas Christou, into whose law practice Michael is sure to follow. Except that this is 1943 and Michael volunteers for war service. And all I can do is wait"

"Go on...."

166

"Michael is allocated to the US Eighth Air Force and posted to England in Flying Fortresses. He's based in East Anglia, flight-engineer on a 'Fort' called "The Auburn Bombshell" flying daylight raids over Europe. He claimed they'd named the plane after me but to be honest I wasn't much flattered."

"I realise what you're going to tell me. I'm sorry. I didn't mean to pry."

"Yes. It's alright. I've come to terms with it. I realise Michael didn't stand a chance. Every mission was in broad daylight, flying in rigid formations over heavily-defended targets. Your Royal Air Force did most of its heavy bombing raids under the cover of darkness...."

"I know, but that was no picnic either" he said gently: "A seventh of all British casualties in the war occurred in those raids, amongst our aircrew. An elite generation. Something like a hundred thousand men and half the bombers we had."

Whether his point had registered was doubtful as she continued anyway: "Maybe so. All I know is that Michael only lasted five missions: Bremen; Essen; the 'U-Boat' pens at Kiel; the Augsburg diesel factory and then Kiel again."

"They were shot down?"

"Oh, no. Nothing like that. They were taking off from Mildenhall with a full bomb load and all the tanks full of fuel. Struggling into the air when one of the four engines failed. The engines which were Michael's babies as flight engineer. I know how he will have fought with the switches to bring them back to life, I can see it in my mind's eye even now. Their pilot tried to put it down on the main road instead but there was a farmer's tractor with turnip trailer in the way. The plane was unstable with one engine stopped and too heavily-laden for the others to provide enough power to get level and get airborne. A wingtip just caught the ground and that was it. The Fort' flipped over and came down close to the airfield perimeter, exploding and killing everyone on board, as well as the tractor driver and his grandson."

"I'm sorry."

"Thank you. It was a great shock at the time, even though in my heart of hearts I knew that one way or another something of the sort was bound to happen. He'd had his five missions and that was the average life-expectancy of a bomber crew at that time. Except that there was nothing average about Michael."

167

"And is that how you came to be in England?"

"Yes. Michael was killed in December 1944. I had to wait another twelve months before coming over, when the war was finished and Daddy was prepared to arrange safe passage with one of his shipping contacts. I went to Mildenhall and laid a wreath at the huge crater which was still there, out on the edge of the airfield. Their official war graves were a few miles away in a country church yard, as if to pretend there were enough pieces of them left to need a plot. But all I had left of Michael was out in the grassland on the edge of that airfield. By the main road."

Tryton said that he understood and of course it was true. He really did. He touched the arm of her jacket; brown leather with a large circular badge showing a white eagle with a bomb in its beak, sewn onto the back.

"Is that his jacket? Is that why you wear it?"

"Yes" she said, almost in a whisper.

"Everyone thinks I'm crazy. But when I wear it, I feel closer to him – as if he's still here. His friends parcelled up all his possessions left in the hut and posted them back to me in the U.S. He always wore this jacket in the air, in every one of his five missions. But for his sixth he wore another - I think because the weather had turned a lot colder and of course this would be worse at high altitude. I know this sounds silly but I've convinced myself that if he'd been wearing his usual jacket, this one, then they wouldn't have crashed that day."

Tryton understood the delusion well. Flying in fixed formation into a visible wall of shellfire was an unenviable experience. Once experienced, never forgotten, even if tomorrow you had to go back and do it again. No one could criticise the fliers whose lives dangled like cotton threads in a room full of shears if they clung to the most pathetic superstitious comforts or reassurances - whether lucky rabbits' feet or St. Christopher medallion.

He remembered his own charm, a miniature figure on a chain of his birthday's patron saint - 'Michael the Avenging Archangel' crafted out of Maltese silver and blessed by a priest. A little silver badge which he still wore inside his shirt to this day. The sacred token which - he could not deny - must have done its job.

After all, and unlike so many others, here he was.

Alive.

Now he knew the real reason why she'd flinched last night when he mentioned a Flying Fortress. Not the reason he'd first thought but, as he admitted to Pickering later, it just shows how you can never make assumptions about people.

They were down in the bottom of the valley now and dense woodland was all around them. The track went sharp right to follow the valley floor and they did likewise. Down here the route was less direct than the straight descent they had just made and it was still not possible to see where this unmade road led through the trees.

"Did you stay in England once you'd got here in late 1945? Is that how you came to be at Oxford?"

"Yes. Somehow, in a terrible way it kinda made sense, as if Michael's death had been meant to happen - to bring me onto the next stage of my life. You see I arrived at Mildenhall on the anniversary of his death, just before the first Christmas of a world at peace after the horrors of war. I don't know whether you know Suffolk but Mildenhall is actually a rather lovely village - not in the least overshadowed by the large air-base next door. It was a sad time for me as Christmas often is for people who have lost those they love, but I was not the only one. The villagers were really kind to me and I settled there into a wonderful little black-and-white rented cottage with a view of the River Lark.

It was while I was there that something rather special happened. That year, the year before last - that's 1946 of course - a farmer was ploughing his land at Thistley Green, which is near Mildenhall. I don't know whether you read about this in the papers at the time but, anyway, his plough was pulling the most amazing things out of the ground. Solid silver plates and goblets: The Mildenhall Treasure."

"The stolen contents of a Knightsbridge safe-deposit box" opined Tryton, his policeman's cynicism making unwelcome appearance. It had been meant as a joke but he should have realised that English irony would be lost on an American.

"No!" she almost spat, her eyes flashing with a passion that thrilled him: "It was Roman, from the fourth century - that's between the years three and four hundred A.D. to you. Sixteen hundred years old!"

"The same vintage as this pavement then?" said Tryton, anxious to restore an impression of serious attention.

"Yes, that's exactly right, Lieutenant! But you never saw anything like this. It must be worth millions of dollars. A friend took me in her automobile to see it while they were still pulling more out of the ground. I was actually allowed to handle one of the pieces before it was taken away - an enormous flat silver dish, the edges like rolled rope and in the centre the finest, liveliest, most lifelike reliefs of lightly-clad dancing figures; men and women. "The Triumph of Bacchus over Hercules". It was the most magnificent work of art I had ever seen and here I was in my gumboots standing in a farmers field wiping the loam of Old England off it, holding it, stroking it!"

"So what was it doing in a Suffolk wheatfield?" asked Tryton, with his detective's need for complete explanations, for leaving no stone unturned.

"The quality, the quantity and the value of this stuff, even in its own day, means that it must have belonged to someone wealthy and important. An Imperial official perhaps."

"Why would he want to bury it, then?"

"They were very unsettled times. As uncertain as wartime. Perhaps it was wartime. The hoard amounts to a complete dining service and it was either buried by its owner for safe-keeping, in the hope it could be recovered when things calmed down - you've got to remember there were no banks in those days - or else it was captured loot taken by brigands, robbers or sea-borne pirates which they buried for similar reasons, perhaps because they couldn't get back to their raiding boat fast enough when carrying it."

"And where does Oxford figure in all of this?"

"Well the treasure went straight to your British Museum in London, where it remains to this day, of course. But, for me, having such direct contact with it at the time was personally very profound. I suppose I couldn't come to terms with the idea of a society so accomplished, so sophisticated, so incredibly-civilised, I guess, being driven out of its very existence by the kind of brutal greedy people that did bring it crashing down."

"It's happening everyday," said Tryton bitterly. "But what sort of people do you have in mind?"

170

"Why, the Vandals and the Goths; the Marcomanni; the Huns and Alemanni. All those other tribes. "The barbarians". And even in your own sleepy English county of Suffolk, the Saxons. The people who became the South Folk. The people against whose cruelty and barbarism some frightened late-Roman official was burying his best dinner service in a field"

"But, if these distant events don't trouble the average modern Englishman, why should they bother a sassy New Jersey girl like you? Wasn't it your own countryman, Mister Henry Ford, who said that history is bunk?"

"Yes it was. And he was so very wrong! He knew a lot about automobiles but nothing at all about life. My Michael died to stop the same sort, the people who would sacrifice the world of decent values on the altars of modernism and production. The Nazis represented that threat, barbarians with fancy uniforms and clever aeroplanes but quite without humanity. There have always been people like that and there always will be, taking what they want. They don't just go away. History teaches you amongst other things the worth of making a stand: just as Michael did, even as your own country did against them".

"What was it Machiavelli said about the lessons of the past? Those lessons are important. And that's why I went to Oxford to learn them in a university outside my own country. And the reason why I'm studying the subject and the period I chose. Also, I suppose, the reason why I've ended up here - being dragged around the English countryside by a grubby cop!"

Parry-Jones had been quite right, of course. That was exactly what he'd first identified in her: A Woman of Passion and Belief ("...with the surname of a Hero of Wales").

Tryton found himself just as impressed as the Welshman with the strength of her feeling, her knowledge of points of history over which he'd very little understanding and even less interest - until now. If it was still the passion which excited him, not particularly where it was applied, one aspect fed upon another. His fascination grew but there was still one aspect of her reasoning that gave a small lingering doubt on which to question her further: "How can you know it was a society worth defending? How do you know they were any better than those who destroyed them?"

"I just know it was" she said, her eyes flashing again, "I just kinda feel it!" (And that was that).

Albeit limited to what little learning his schooldays had given him, Tryton always understood that the Roman world - for all its remarkably advanced features – was an ancient society often capable of the most ruthless and stunning cruelties. But if this American woman claimed the barbarity of modern Fascists made contrast, even he could remember how anxious both Hitler and Mussolini were to invest their sterile doctrines with the trappings and badges of Ancient Rome. As Napoleon Bonaparte did before them.

Still, who was he, a mere provincial policeman, to argue with the overwhelming force of feminine intuition?

They reached the end of the drive where varied woodland on the valley floor opened out into broad expanses of sheep-cropped sward. The few trees decorating these visions of Elysium were protected by encircling iron railings against the destructive attentions of livestock. Beyond them was the house, as old as the forestry which hid it. A Georgian mansion in the Palladian style with detailing to fix it as 'Greek Revival', here was unexpected find amongst the dreary scenery of the Wolds.

A decorated slab above the portico confirmed the completion of its construction in the first month of 1748. Hence its name: 'January House'. Its wealthy builder must have begun work at once on hearing of the Hanoverian victory at the Battle of Culloden, moved to express the establishment's new-found political and economic confidence following the savage sup-pression of the Jacobite Rebellion by 'Butcher Cumberland' in 1746.

As for so many Northern families, the likely destruction of their more prominent or decorative buildings by raiding Scots had, until then and for hundreds of years before, always inhibited investment in such projects.

"Wow!" gasped his American companion, as if she'd never seen it before. "What a pile!"

Tryton was forced to admit it was.

The warm red brick of old walls glowed russet in the sun where white facing stones, lintels and porticoes shone as contrast.

172

From here-on in the potholed track became a properly-gravelled drive, widening as it neared the house. Those who live in remote country locations are often keen for the initial approach to their hideaway to be as rough as possible, discouragement to uninvited or malicious visitors. Only in sight of the house did its surface improve.

By the west front of the house where the drive was bordered by some of the first daffodils of Spring, nodding yellow, a gunmetal-grey Bentley coupe had been parked with self-conscious carelessness.

Tryton was no tactician but he judged that any approach across open lawns to the front of the house was unlikely to prove wise.

To their left another track diverged from the main drive and dived back into the woods, lined with wrought iron estate fencing and almost overwhelmed by rhododendron bushes. He rightly guessed that this would be the service road and, like most tradesmen's entrances, could be relied on to bring them out at the back of the house. Policemen being classed with tradesmen by polite society in his experience; and polite society's facility for condescension, self-interest, swearing, avarice and adultery being part of that experience; the tradesmen's entrance would do him nicely.

"In here!" he hissed and pulled Miss Macsen by a slim arm into the dark tunnel that was the back drive. Holding her arm, he realised how much he enjoyed this contact and her closeness, keeping hold for a little longer than essential. Once they were in the shadow of the trees again she gently eased herself free, albeit without complaint.

As expected, this route did lead to the back of the house.
Closer to, the structure could be seen to be suffering degrees of neglect. Crumbling stonework, eroding mortar and peeling paint.

They were approaching a large courtyard at the rear where a gaggle of outbuildings and stables clustered around its northern prospect.

Here a succession of less-wealthy and more pragmatic owners had coped with the pressing problems of their day by short-term solutions unsympathetic to the fabric. A Victorian occupier had deformed the courtyard facade with cast iron pipework for the new-fangled sanitation he'd installed by screwing mock Gothic guttering the size of an aqueduct to its eaves. One of his successors, bemused by moisture penetrating through ageing porous bricks, had chosen to render the whole rear wall with a miserable grey cement soon marked with lichens, algae and the stamp of damp.

"Where now?" she asked and it was fair question. A solid wooden entrance gate, painted in that sickly pea-green so beloved of English land agents, yawned ambiguously open before them at the threshold of the courtyard. The way was half closed, half open to them, and Tryton hesitated.

This time he took her by the hand and led her to the gate. Together they carefully peeked around its edge into the stable yard paved with bricks. It was a scene of bustling activity which surprised in this remote valley and made contrast with the tranquility of their lonely approach to the house.

While several stable girls busied themselves around the horses whose well-bred heads extended in nervous equine curiosity from the upper doors of their stalls, on the other side of the walled square a group of men looking like builders unloaded tools and materials from a navy-blue van. The builders' was not the only vehicle. Parked beside it adjoining the back wall of the house were a large yellow tipper truck of the sort Miss Macsen had described and, secondly but most curious of all, a big, shiny, dark green, army lorry with a yellow gas disc on the back. Its wheel nuts were painted alternate red and white in that pointless fashion only peace-time armies think important.

Tryton pointed to the tipper truck and whispered: "Is that the lorry you followed here from Brantingham Quarry?"

"No" she said. "It's not the same lorry but it's definitely the same livery. Look at the door."

On the driver's door of the yellow cab was a stylised motif in the shape of a turretted castle tower in black. Below it the legend: "BAYNARD'S BRITISH GYPSUM WORKS."

There was no chance whatever of entering the yard with all this activity and all these people coming and going. Behind them they heard an engine and Tryton pulled Miss Macsen back amongst the rhododendron bushes at the side of the drive as a tatty old red tractor with steel tyres pulled a trailer loaded with logs into the courtyard. Instead, they worked their way around the outer wall of the enclosure whilst keeping to the shrubberies. Again she pulled her hand away once the necessary contact had established the next move. He was sorry because he'd enjoyed its tenure, surprisingly small and delicate in his palm.

On the eastern side of the house they again found a more formal facade presenting to open lawns, this time with a paved terrace and stone balustrading intervening. The windows on this frontage were all white and sightless with internal blinds pulled right down. This had the virtue of making a direct approach to the house on this side less exposed, with much less chance of detection.

After a sprint over a tennis court, they climbed a shallow flight of steps onto the terrace and crossed its disintegrating and subsiding Yorkstone flags. Large double French windows of small panes and apsidal tops were the only entrance. Tryton tried the handles and found them unlocked. He peered through the glass and saw an empty hallway.

"Come on!" he said. "This'll do."

"You're not going in there."

"Oh yes we are. You and me both. Come on, lady!"

They were and she did, finding themselves in a magnificent hall and stairwell supported on marble pillars and gilded column heads. Classical statues filled the niches with alabaster heads, limbs, and torsos, whilst enormous paintings of pasty-faced, long-nosed men in black armour riding overweight chargers occupied every wall.

Miss Macsen was transfixed by all this splendour and stood in careless fascination at the foot of the stairs, gazing upwards.

Tryton at least was more alert and in a whisper directed her view downwards, not upwards. On his request she looked at her feet.

175

The hallway had once been attractively floored with dark blue and brilliant white ceramic tiles in a contrasting diamond pattern. A traditional Edwardian motif in an English country house. But pickaxes and shovels rested against an elegant French nineteenth century mahogany sideboard because someone had recently been excavating a large area in the centre of the hall, exposing the ancient and original solid floor of beaten earth.

On the edge of these works an enormous cylinder rested upon scaffolding poles and large wooden blocks, like a huge spindle. This giant tube had been created by rolling up a laminate of various materials into a monstrous 'swiss roll', just as one might with a carpet wrapped for storage. Except that this was obviously not a carpet.

They approached together. She ran her hands across the top where some of the material was exposed between the textile and resin backing, then closed her eyes and gasped:

"This is it!"

"What do you mean? This is the…?"

"This is it. We've found it straightaway. This is the pavement! Can't you see?"

Tryton was as excited as she at their early success but struggled to equate this object with the horizontal rectangular envisaged for a pavement:

"Are you sure? It doesn't look very much like it. How can you tell?"

"This is how it was prepared for removal and just as it was stolen. It has been brought here as found and someone is obviously about to relay it in the hall!"

The pattern she had told him of was just visible at the top of the roll. The pavement had surely been stolen to order for the collector who owned this house, a person who apparently had plenty of everything but still wanted more. Presumably for this acquisitive mind the imposing mock classical interior of his house could only be adequately appreciated when complemented by the addition of an authentic classical floor, on the two hundredth anniversary of construction of the building.

The fact that the pavement was of such immediately local origin and almost exactly fourteen hundred years older than his house would probably offer a degree of serendipity such a selfish mind could not resist.

A birthday present for the house?

The next step was to be sure about the identity of the guilty party. Tryton found himself in a home of the patently wealthy and, by definition, influential. Another reason for ensuring one hundred and ten percent certainty in his evidence gathering.

"In here!"

They stepped left into a drawing room which was much more informal; clearly designed for living in, not for impressing.

Only from the big French windows looking out from here did you suddenly realise, for all its discreet, wooded setting, what an unexpectedly-clear and commanding view of the silver river the house had from this elevated site, over the Wold side and down the dale.

Behind a cluster of armchairs and sofas that faced the fire there was an inlaid card table that bore a brass lamp with a green baize shade and a collection of family photographs in various gilt frames. Amongst the wedding pictures of lantern-jawed young women and anxious young men with red faces and premature hair loss, the babies in coachbuilt prams and small boys in sailor suits with long noses (like the hall paintings), there was one that stood out. Tryton picked it up off the dusty surface of the table and wiped the glass of the frame with his sleeve.

"That's Sir Oswald Moseley!" he said.

"Who's Oswald Moseley? Does he live here?"

"No, I doubt it. He was the leader of the British Fascists in the years before the war. 'The Blackshirts'. The man who would have been the Hitler or Mussolini of this country, if we'd been daft enough to give him half the chance. He was interned during the war for everyone's safety, including his own. I wonder where he is now – up to mischief, I'll be bound."

Tryton studied the picture carefully. It had obviously been taken at some public meeting, which was why he assumed it taken before the war.

Moseley was shaking hands with a man in a dinner suit, someone much younger. Tryton didn't recognise him but there was another fellow standing behind, partly obscured by Mosley's shoulder in the handshake, someone he did remember. A man he'd last seen in the middle of the Humber estuary, standing over the body of a dead artilleryman but looking a little older. His friend from Bull Sand Fort: Colonel Sir Martin Baynard.

There was the sound of workmen's boots on the tiled floor of the adjacent hallway. Tryton and Miss Macsen ducked behind a sofa and found themselves sprawling amongst piles of newly-printed pamphlets which they sent sliding in confusion onto the threadbare carpet. Fortunately their accidental scattering of this political material was done silently and they heard the cheery whistling of a contented labourer in the hall, seeming unaware of the intruders within.

Tryton lay on his back behind the sofa and studied a pamphlet, published by an organisation calling itself the Union Movement and entitled "The Right Way Forward". It gave word-for-word report of a public speech given at some hall in Leeds by the Honourable Roderick Baynard J.P. (Tryton feared he was beginning to get the picture).

He sighed and looked directly at his assistant where she lay behind the sofa beside him, passing one of the pamphlets for her examination. Her flying jacket was zipped up to the neck and her woollen hat pulled well down but neither was enough to contain all those spectacularly-coloured locks. Tryton gave what he imagined was a cheery smile but probably looked like a grimace. All he got in return was a scowl. The momentary unburdening heard in their stroll down the long drive had passed. Now, with the pavement found, it seemed she felt any need for closer communication with him was gone already. Somehow, she was closing her mind to him once again.

Why was she so contrary; one minute up, the next minute down? Even Tryton was becoming conscious of his dawning infatuation - anxious to give it such expression as he might dare and she would allow, but almost as exasperated as entranced by her contrariness. She passed the pamphlet back as if she couldn't be bothered to read it and whispered crossly "What's this little lot about?"

"We're amongst extremists, Miss Macsen. Fascists! They kept a low profile during our war against their European brethren but perhaps now it's over they feel a little safer about trying a come-back. Dangerous people to cross!"

"Then the sooner you get me out of here the better. I've done what you asked of me. I've found the pavement for you. Now I want to go home."

It was unclear whether she meant just Beverley or right back to the United States of America but either way Tryton had to acknowledge it as a reasonable request. He gave a grunt of acquiescence. Crawling forward on his elbows he stuck his head round the upholstered side of the sofa which hid them and listened for the sound of anyone in the hall again. It seemed quiet.

"Come on!"

They tip-toed across the drawing room to the hall door and Tryton made another careful reconnaissance of what lay beyond. Again he judged it safe to cross from there to the next set of French windows.

"Out through the doors and run for the trees!"

She did as he asked. They scampered over the excavations in the hallway where the Roman mosaic was to be placed and fumbled at the handles of the outside doors. Still there came no challenge. Thus far, they'd managed to be lucky until, outside on the terrace, she tripped momentarily on an uneven slab and grimaced with pain. He caught her and dragged her firmly along:

"Come on!"

Over the tennis courts again, along the blank end wall of the stables and then back through the shrubberies and into the trees. Here they paused to get their breath and Miss Macsen was obviously limping.

"I think I might have done something to my ankle. Pulled it or something like that. It hurts."

"Here, let me have a look."

She lifted the hem of the long pleated skirt she was wearing and, whilst it was a pleasure to inspect, Tryton could not see anything obviously wrong.

"You'll be alright. It looks OK. You've just pulled it, that's all. It'll come right in a minute."

"I don't think so. I can't run. I don't know whether I can even walk."

"We've got to get moving, to get out of here. There, put your arm round my shoulder and I'll support you, then you can hop!"

"We can't get all the way back to the car like this, not all the way back up that hill."

179

"We've got to, lady. There's no other way out" said Tryton, taking her hand and putting it round his neck. She didn't weigh much at all really. Surprisingly light and delicate a frame for so combative a temperament, he thought, his arm brushing hidden curves hinting at a softness she seemed anxious to deny.

Supporting her in this way, they made some progress. Down the side of the service drive and past the yard gates again, then along the main drive proper - keeping to the trees. They reached the bend where the house disappeared from sight and began the ascent of the hill. It looked a long way up to the road.

Suddenly they heard the sound of footsteps behind them and Tryton feared the worst. Not daring to look at who might pursue them, he was at once conscious of the pressing need to justify their presence here on this private track leading to a house of secrets. He had an idea which at the time seemed inspired and whispered in the ear of the woman draped on his arm:

"We're being followed! Just do as I do. Don't argue."

Upon the moment he took her arm and spun her round so that she faced him, then pulled her strongly towards him. Putting his left hand behind her head he pressed her face to his, touching her lips with his own and gazing into almond-shaped brown eyes which positively arced with tiny white bolts of electric fury. The passion was real but it was founded in rage and not the attraction which Tryton wished their unseen pursuer to diagnose. He felt the resilience of those warm lips whose profile had tormented him but knew full well that his unsolicited assault upon her had gone much too far. Only the danger of their predicament protected him from the thunder of her inevitable rejection. Tryton heard a gruffly-accented East Yorkshire voice at their elbow:

"Hello! What's all this then?"

Tryton looked up from contemplating skin like velvet to find the oily sheen of a gun barrel placed not far from their heads.

Two gun barrels to be right, side by side and bolted to a wooden stock in the stumpy, broken-nailed grip of a barrel-shaped man in a camouflage jacket whose moleskin trousers, heavy boots and white, pudding basin-shaped motorcycle crash-helmet completed the ensemble. Ugly little motorcyclist's goggles with tinted yellow lenses had been pulled down to invest piggy eyes with even greater inscrutability. The gun didn't waver.

"I say! Steady on! There's no need for that. Put your gun down, there's a good fellow!"

Tryton could hardly believe himself. Even to his own ears he sounded like someone from a P.G. Wodehouse novel. If he did, then he was succeeding, because that was the plan – such as it was. His reedy protest must have had some effect for the double-barrelled shotgun was lowered, grudgingly.

"What are you two doing on the Baynard Estate, apart from the obvious? This is private land you know."

Tryton looked around for the motorcycle that surely went with this helmet and goggles but the gamekeeper had come upon them by the foot-borne stealth inherent in his calling.

"I'm most awfully sorry" said Tryton, feeling obliged to continue with his Woosterian characterisation. "My fiancee and I were merely out for a country stroll, when the poor gal turned her ankle. We were trying to make a short cut up to the road there when you found us."

"Where have you come from?" asked pudding-basin head, his hackles rising to the tones of this upper-class wastrel and emphasising the last word of his question.

"Over there, somewhere over there."

Tryton gestured vaguely to a high Wold, well away from the house. To his amazement, Miss Macsen had obviously devised a complementary role for herself which she presented with enthusiasm, leaning in angular fashion upon her companion whilst making enough fluttering and eye-rolling to confirm Tryton's account. Looking at her, the gamekeeper was no doubt persuaded that here indeed was a girl of sufficient breeding and no intellect likely to be foolish enough to attach herself uncritically to such a twit as he had at the end of his shotgun.

Their interceptor must have relented, for he broke his gun and took out two cartridges to confirm it had in fact been loaded.

They were grateful for this consideration at the least but he offered them little more:

"Well, get yourselves up the drive and out of the estate then. No doubt gentlefolk like you will have a nice motor car within call," he sneered.

"Yes, thanks awfully" said Tryton, more oleaginous than ever. "I think we left the Riley at the top of the next hill. So sorry to have troubled you."

181

He watched them go with the gun still broken across his knee and the brass ends of the two cartridges gripped in his teeth. The idiot in the mac and the big trilby supporting his girl in the long skirt and the woollen hat. (Obvious what they were hanging around in his woods for – pity he hadn't caught them at it).

It was only as they struggled away up the trackway that he noticed the female's jacket and the badge on her back. A white eagle's head with a bomb in its mouth. No adornment for a lady, that! It made him linger on the drive longer than the more commonplace trespassers might have merited and he watched their slow and painful progress away from him with renewed suspicion. Removing the cartridges out of his mouth, he put them back into the shotgun again with thoughtful deliberation.

Tryton and Miss Macsen were both well aware of the game-keeper's continuing scrutiny and stayed in type. Only when they were out through the brick pillars at the very top and finally onto the public road – well out of sight - did she push him disgustedly away with the heel of her hand and turn to confront the policeman:

"DON'T-YOU-EVER-DO-THAT-TO-ME-AGAIN-YOU-LIMEY-PIG!"

Tryton knew he had blown it. Hard to say whether the price of their escape was made too high by the cheap ruse which enabled it. He did not know what to say, yet could not apologise for an act which provided some outlet for the growing emotions which swamped him. He stood miserably alone on the Brantingham road as she limped off ahead again despite her injury, wanting to save her but unable to move.

He heard the noise of a motor vehicle coming up behind and instinctively stepped back onto the verge. There was the squeal of drum brakes and the black Wolseley pulled up next to him with Pickering in the driving seat.

Tryton got into the front passenger seat and they set off up the road after the American woman. When they caught her up she still would not get in and Pickering had to set the car into first gear to follow at a crawl. Tryton dropped the window and put his head and elbow out: "Come on, lady" he said gently. "Please get in. We'll take you home now."

"No!" she said. "Never!"

"But you've hurt your leg. You can't get anywhere in this state."

"I'd rather crawl on my hands and knees than get in a car with you, you creep!"

Pickering gave his Inspector a long slow look as if to say 'I told you so'.

Fortunately, this unseemly situation was resolved without prompting by the redoubtable W.P.C. Horncastle, whose queasily thick ankles belied a gazelle-like agility as she leapt smoothly from the rear door of the moving Wolseley. It was only travelling at about three miles per hour and she was able to take hold of Miss Macsen then safely drag her back into the car in one flowing motion. This forcible seizure was quite definitely the final indignity so far as the archaeologist was concerned, but at least it had the virtue of enabling Pickering to accelerate firmly away and at last to quit the sinister boundaries of the Baynard Estate.

In fulfilment of Tryton's undertaking, Sergeant Pickering drove them all in the Wolseley straight to Beverley, where Miss Macsen lodged in a Georgian terrace on North Bar Without. Here she was delivered up to her bewildered landlady without even a parting glance or word of thanks. Their promise to return the Dodge on the morrow met with total indifference. She stormed upstairs with much slamming of doors whilst the landlady folded her arms as Pickering and Tryton slunk away.

Apart from an inexplicable bout of amateur philosophising from Pickering on the way back about "hate is only the reverse side of love's coin" (I ask you – and this from a police sergeant!) all that Tryton was left with was tomorrow morning's miserable prospect of reporting these failures to Superintendent Maister.

"What the devil's it got to do with you, Pickering, anyway?"

"Sorry, sir, only trying to help!"

"Yes, well when I need moral guidance and advice from you, sergeant, rather than from the priesthood, I expect I'll ask for it! Until then ...."

To Tryton's shame, this bad-tempered and sarcastic response made an end to the matter he did nothing more to improve upon. Doubtless poor old Pickering went home that night to tell his wife what a difficult time he was having with his new boss these days. Even his own famously good-natured patience with the young Inspector must be wearing rather thin by now.

"Agricola had to deal with a people living in isolation and ignorance and therefore prone to fight. His objective was to accustom them to a life of peace and quietness through the provision of amenities. He therefore gave private encouragement and official assistance to the building of temples, public squares, and good houses......And so the population was gradually led into the demoralising temptations of arcades, baths and sumptuous banquets. The unsuspecting Britons spoke of such novelties as 'civilisation' when, in fact, they were only a feature of their enslavement"

Cornelius Tacitus, senator and historian 56 A.D. – c.120 A.D. writing in 'The Agricola', biography of his father-in-law, Gnaeus Julius Agricola; legionary commander then governor in Britain, c.70 – 84 A.D.

X

If the town and tribal capital at Petuaria illustrates no more than decline and decay, then the adjoining buildings and estates of the Villa Januarii speak of an energy and commercial prosperity in total contrast.

Arriving at dusk in the horse-litter of its owner, Flavius Candidus was at once impressed with industry and activity. Even at the curfew hour, landed slaves still tilled its fields, hewed its woodlands and drew its waters. Oxen dragged ploughs and pulled timber, even as the night watchmen lit the guttering flares which light its halls and mark its gates.

To us now, it has become notorious how those burdens of taxation and civic office; the implicit sense of threat from the urban poor and this realised menace of sea-borne raiding, can all conspire together to drive the wealthy and privileged into the relative safety of their walled and gated country estates. As our towns decline and disintegrate, so the villas flower.

Despite sunset, the extensive facilities of this example were apparent. Not lavish buildings overall and neither was their external architecture dramatic or decorative, but the solid accumulation of hundreds of years of steady, thoughtful development by one family. A villa rustica; a working farm house with comprehensive outbuildings. Stables, barns and threshing floors, kitchen gardens and fishponds. All these were glimpsed as they entered its darkening grounds through a tall brick archway, set in the enclosing boundary walls of stone.

In the extensive stockyard he heard before seeing a massive grey and white bull, tethered to an iron ring in the wall. As the light of day retreated and dusk crept in, it bellowed in muscle-bound frustration at the encroaching dark and all his cows away in their fields, in frantic need of a reunion. Candidus smiled at this, at what he took to be a good omen, this welcoming symbol of his religion and those deep mysteries by which our world was created when Mithras, Lord of all the Ages, slew the sacred bull. As the bull died, the world came into being and with it that continuing struggle between good and evil in which he, Candidus, was even now to play one small part.

The steward of Januarius waited on his master at the foot of the verandah steps, two slaves standing with this freedman to hold burning tapers to light the way, once the litter which brought them was set down and the magistrate with his honoured guest helped from it:

"Welcome to the Villa Januarii, house of my ancestors and inheritance of my sons."

If M. Ulpius Januarius was forced to suppress all his personal pride in that small, plain town wherein his political eminence lay, once upon his estate and in his own home a more ebullient self-satisfaction was on display. "Come with me, Flavius Candidus. My staff will show you to a hot bath and a comfortable room, and then I hope you will honour me by joining myself and some good company at dinner."

"It is better to murder a man's brother than refuse his invitation to dine!" joked Candidus. "I'd be happy to join you."

"Splendid! Any man who can quote from Tacitus promises us good after-dinner conversation! We will see you in the triclinium at the tenth hour. But in the meantime, there is the little matter of that undertaking I made to you in the town, standing on the eastern bastion. With your consent, I shall send down my personal physician, Nicomedes of Epidaurus, to treat that head-wound in the privacy of your own room."

Candidus could only repeat his genuine gratitude; as he'd already said. But grateful as he was, he understood enough about prevailing modern conventions of client and patron to wonder at the price of all this hospitality and care. When might he find his debt called in?

The villa was a long, linear building; suites of square rooms giving onto a linking corridor. The house slaves leading him to his allocated dormitory held lamps aloft to guide the way through dark passages, creating monstrous, moving shadows on painted walls. Candidus glimpsed spectacular designs and images underfoot in momentary pools of light cast onto the tessellated floors over which they passed.

His room was small, clean and simple in that country way, but comfortable enough. White-washed walls and a tiny wooden-framed window of opaque bottle glass, reinforced with a spiked metal grille, would make the most of what sunlight tomorrow's day might bring.

At this time of night, the only light came from an iron tripod holding a brace of round, red earthenware oil-lamps whose smoking wicks fizzed and flared in the draught from the opened door. Surprising how much warmth these small lights alone can give to a room like this.

The wooden bed was stronger and its bedding cleaner than that on offer last night from the 'Rose of Petuaria'. Candidus gave this structure an exploratory bounce and decided he was well-satisfied.

Having taken a brief but refreshing hot bath in a small, separate building just across the garden and then returned to his room, it was not long before the doctor was announced as promised. Nicomedes was indeed a Greek, just as his name and occupation expected. Candidus remembered the description of him given in the town: "Priest in the cult of Aesculapius". This was no mere metaphor from Januarius for his physician's commitment to the craft but literal statement. The thorough physical examination received from this pedantic fussy little man was prefaced with incidental ritual; the shaking of miniature silver bells as might be seen in a temple and the administration of sanctified oils. Was it medicine or magic? Candidus found it all rather tedious and unproductive. He began to wish his host hadn't noticed that mark on his head, as concerns grew that he would miss the promised dinner or else offend its giver through a late arrival.

To be fair, Nicomedes did a good job of tidying-up his most recent wound, even if the salve he applied to the scalp made Candidus wince at its sting for quite a while.

Whilst arguably useful for any man who is able to afford their fees to allow an occasional inspection by the doctors of one's bodily health, Candidus had already endured more of their attentions than most men still living. He was reluctant to suffer more. It followed that his own philosophy fell firmly into the non-interventionist school of thought. His next and final appointment with the medical profession was an occasion he expected to be confined to the death bed. There was no wish to allow them any other chance of practising their practices upon him - ever again or until then.

187

Which is why he was so inevitably irritated when livid scars engraved into his flesh at the military hospital in Vercovicium fort should once again prompt comment from a resident of Petuaria, even if, this time, someone holding medical qualification as their excuse for prurient enquiry.

"Dear me!" tut-tutted Nicomedes. "That's a nasty scar! How did you come by that?"

Of course Candidus was obliged out of courtesy to recount the whole weary story yet again, right up to his discharge from the army. This time it arguably proved worth it to discover that friend Nicomedes had studied long ago at Alexandria with the self-same military surgeon who'd treated Candidus. This Greek had more reason than most to scrutinise the handiwork of his old student friend with genuine interest.

Candidus made some platitudinous comment about the world being a small place, adding his concern about being late for dinner, but Nicomedes carried on, telling him there was absolutely no need for worry since he was invited to the same table. However, at least he got the message and started putting his bottles, bells and balms back into their little wicker case. Preparing to go, Nicomededes paused one last time:

"What you're here for is not my business, Candidus. My job is just to treat the consequences. But a word about how to avoid the condition recurring is definite part of a doctor's role. All I want to offer you is some friendly physician's advice. I'm nobody's messenger but be very careful in Petuaria, whatever the reason for your visit. There are some dangerous people around here, bad men who easily get the wrong impression. If they do, then those they get to do their dirty work will stop at nothing – believe me. What you've had so far would only be a taster. Right, that's it! I've said my piece, more than I ought perhaps. It's well-meant, whatever you choose to make of me or this tough little town. A promise - I won't mention it again or when we meet at dinner. May Fortune bless you, as I leave you in peace. That's it, I go!"

No sooner had he got rid of the surgeon and his disturbing warning than there was a flock of servants at the door, bearing formal clothes for dining presented with their master's compliments.

Candidus being blessed only with what rough, outdoor items survived his adventures of the last forty-eight hours, he had to concede that even a modest man of his own sober requirements, wary of display, should present properly-dressed for such an important dinner. Offered a choice between the more formal 'cenatoria' or the more comfortable 'synthesis', he naturally opted for the latter. Even then, this 'mixed dress' comprised a tunic and small cloak whose 'palliolum' of lightish material and loud scarlet ill-suited his quiet temperament.

Feeling self-conscious in this undoubtedly-fashionable but unsettlingly feminised outfit, Candidus made his cautious way down to the dining room along the corridor, hoping no-one would see him. Arriving, he was first struck by the size of this triclinium, the largest room he had so far seen in the house. Its lavish decoration in wall, floor and fittings was next observation and third was the number of diners.

He was at once in mind of that well-known saying: "septem convivium novem vero convicium". (Seven makes a dinner, nine makes a brawl). If he hoped the old saw didn't come true tonight, the personalities assembled meant he could not be sanguine. These nine, counting their esteemed host, Marcus Ulpius Januarius, were distributed across three large couches according to importance. With the householder at their head upon the 'summus lectus', Candidus was grateful to be sharing the 'medius' and so spared the humbler, 'imus' couch.

Introductions were rapidly made. If Candidus had a social fault, it was in his nervous tendency to forget people's names almost as soon as told them. At least this time he had a head start in remembering Januarius his host, the little Greek surgeon who'd just treated him and (surprise, surprise) Cicerius Felix who - together - made up a third of the party. With the addition of himself, that left only five other individuals to identify and observe.

Cicerius Felix, the mining engineer met on the Abus ferry yesterday (then supped with before that fateful encounter in the theatre) was from the outset cool to the point of hostility. No doubt considering himself deceived over identity by a man whose every word could not be trusted, he held aloof from the outset. Not a good start, but who could blame him?

189

Januarius for his part simply breezed over this little local difficulty with: "I believe you two gentlemen know each other, already" and left it at that.

Candidus thought it better to concentrate on the other diners. The meal began with house slaves bringing in a selection of dressed eggs and British shellfish as the starter course. It was obvious everyone-else already had a head start on the wine but Candidus allowed a slave to fill his cup just the once, on a mental resolution not to repeat his over-indulgence of the night before. Tonight, he would need his wits about him even more.

On their arrival at the villa, Januarius had passed some comment about the "inheritance of his sons" which is why Candidus guessed the two fine-looking young men sharing a place with him were with their parent. If so, then Januarius must be proud as any father could be of such healthy and well-made offspring. That was why it came as such a shock, later, when Candidus suddenly noticed the thumb missing from the right hand of the elder boy, a lad of about seventeen.

Any injury like this would be disastrous handicap for a young man with ambitions in public life. Particularly because it precludes service in the army through the simple inability to hold a sword. In the absence of this customary first step in public life, any further career advancement must seem highly unlikely without benefit of that primary foundation for military training. Besides, any practical supervision of his father's agricultural estates, too, must surely be just as inhibited, if their overseer cannot from time to time at least take an implement into his own hands to show the humblest labourer how and where he wished it wielded best.

His private sentiments turned to imagining the unspoken grief of the father, sorrowing that this rare blessing of a perfect-formed child surviving into the threshold of adulthood could by random accident become so marred. This sad thought still in his mind, Candidus looked across at the other younger boy, his father's compensation.

A new-made well of deep sympathy for Januarius froze on the moment and turned to solid horror. Now reaching out for a mussel, this younger scion of the Januarian line was identically-disfigured. A red and angry scar on his own right hand likewise glared where once a thumb belonged.

190

Candidus smelt a rat and its stench was deliberate self-mutilation on the altar of draft-dodging. A rich and influential father bending under the onerous and expensive strains of public duty was determined never to lose his precious sons to the Army; to those Legions that cross the pontoon bridges of the Rhine frontier and dash themselves to pieces on the numberless hairy hordes spewing out the endless forests and plains of Outer Germania. Or die of thirst in the Persian desert.

Disgusted, Candidus soon found another rat at his arm in the shape of one Trimalchio. Here was the foghorn of the party; a man who within minutes of the meal commencing must announce in detail the more-than-explicit implication of his uniform; namely high official status as 'Praefectus Reliquationis Classis'. Commander therefore of the Abus squadron from the decks of its two, first-rate triremes ("Defensor" and "Interceptor"), he launched into immediate boasting over recent successes for his flotilla of deep-sea camouflaged patrol craft. Dubbed "Pictae" by their sailors and artfully made sea-green from stem to stern in every sail, sheet and even sailor's shirt, this pun in their title made fair reflection for demonstrable naval efficiency wrung from these vessels. Successful not only against the Northmen but also against the tiny raiding canoes of the Painted People, rowing down from furthermost coasts of Caledonia; these 'Pictae' preyed upon their namesakes, the Picti, with ruthless satisfaction.

For all his undoubted naval achievements, Candidus obtained an intense dislike for this rotund fellow almost at once. This despite the undoubted efforts of his men. Here was another Greek, and none the worse for that, just like the physician. After all, the Greeks remained the premier maritime nation, the finest sea-goers in the world, enlisted in an expertise where the land-bound Roman could offer little.

But Trimalchio was a braggart and a bully who proclaimed the mastery of his command through indiscriminate flogging of both seamen proper and also the corps of marines who defended the decks and pulled the oars of his galleys. Merging with the patent cruelty of this officer were other mannerisms of speech and movement suggesting more deeper-rooted vices.

191

Respect, admiration and regard for Marcus Ulpius Januarius already fast-dissolving upon the condition of his grown-up children, Candidus found his esteem further reduced for any man who would allow a creature like this Prefect of the Fleet a place in his household or any proximity to his sons. The reasons for this tolerance were soon transparently-obvious, in a dining room where rank and status made sole arbiter for admitting entry.

Not since he'd left Londinium Caesariensis and the Court of the Vicarius had Flavius Candidus found himself at a table where politics, glory, and competitive aggrandisement of the self hung so strong in the air as here. There was not a man amongst them that was invited for the pleasure of their company or the wit of their speech. Candidus realised they'd all been chosen instead for some influence in their field, as part of a network of contacts Januarius was cultivating towards an as-yet inchoate purpose. Of that there could be no doubt.

The same held true for the balance of their party - another less senior officer of the fleet come along as 'minder' for his commander plus a tribune of irregulars soon established in conversation as o.i.c. Numerus Supervenientium Petuariensium. Yes, the self-same 'Petuaria Interceptors' so cruelly ridiculed by Rufinus in last-night's bath-house.

Yet this final fellow was just as good (or bad) a specimen of the new officer-class as one could reasonably hope to find. Hard campaign experience and the grit that comes from a rise through the ranks are all that matter nowadays, preferred over more traditional qualities of a gentleman; like family, education, manners or even basic literacy. Often technically-excellent soldiers, the sheer crudity of these men (increasing numbers of them barbarian-born) leaves us with decision-makers who hold no understanding of our state or its history; so risking the repetition of great military disasters from our past or their finding fresh humiliations to heap upon our people.

The barbarians press down upon the west yet priceless Legions are shamelessly wasted, marching east into the parched oblivion of endless desert wars. So why is it that politicians and rulers must always ignore the lessons of history, as if they were of no relevance to what they plan to do now? How many times have we invaded the east, yet why do we never learn from the last experience?

192

Arriving at these social assessments as a man of his own times, Flavius Candidus was not wittingly fired by the prejudices of snobbery. After all, his own origins were no less humble. However even as a one-time junior army officer himself, now enquiry agent on the staff of the civil governor, he felt he'd achieved enough experience of witnessing such occasions, stuffed with personalities on the make as they so often were, to justify his harsh conclusions.

Candidus made mental note of an underlying theme to his eventual inspection report: What dangers there are for the safety of the state and the public good when a conclave of self-regarding officers comes together, unsupervised and unaccountable. It was as if even their most basic administrative decisions were shaped by that underlying hunger for personal advancement and financial advantage; cloaked as always with their flowery and ostentatious protestations of selfless integrity and public service. A viper still writhes beneath but, like all well-practised hypocrisy, it will never fail to astonish and (at first) overpower – if only through its sheer effrontery.

How best to draw the poison inherent in such gatherings framed a question as old as the Fall of the Republic. To his mind, one good way was their counter-balance with a feminine presence - offering charm, lightness of touch and incisive wit to deflate pomposity or a ponderous male atmosphere. Whilst he could be perfectly happy with masculine company (and had very little else in the army) even an extravagantly-presented dinner like this must fall completely flat without the sparkle of the ladies.

After all, this was no matter of personal prejudice or mere chauvinist sentiment. Matching the conventional social outlooks of his day, Candidus well understood why this householder thought it important enough to deserve specific expression in the big mosaic decorating one of the reception rooms he and the other guests passed through on their way to dine. Even a rough-neck like himself could easily understand the intended imagery, recognising its abstract central design as one of those fans the ladies use, but opened-out. Its meaning was a social cliché of course – a deliberate allusion for the visitor of what calm and peace they would find within this happy home, distinct blessing bestowed from the lady of the house herself.

If that was the case, well, where was she?

There was no lady, no 'Domina', to be found anywhere. Yet this Januarius, as Candidus well knew from the commission-brief of the devoted father-in-law, was indeed a married man. So the very first of his questions must be along the lines of 'where's your wife?' Raising it gave him no problem, since 'Find the Lady' probably represented the only party game to which Flavius Candidus was never averse, whilst a strong personal conviction that no party was ever complete without its hostess provided another, as equal spurs to his professional diligence.

Fact was, the only woman so far seen was a pretty young serving-girl. She it was who'd brought the second course in with great ceremony and a willowy walk, holding it aloft on a silver platter as she sidled by. No complaint there about either - it was a large ham boiled in figs then rubbed with honey before baking, and her undulating delivery could only add to its pleasure. She might have done well rubbed with honey herself too but, there it was, good wholesome food and well-presented. Whilst the other guests cheered and shouted out to her with exclamations of approval, Candidus still thought it odd that (for all her dancer's figure) even so strikingly-attractive a domestic should receive plaudits more properly due the honoured wife and mistress of a great household. Whilst not left so distracted by this striking absence as to forget a mental note, privately to explore his chances with this serving girl later on, he still understood well enough where the dictates of duty required his professional efforts first to lie - with the wife.

Looking around him, Candidus took another gulp of wine and was pleased to find another beautiful woman upon whom to rest his tired eyes. Unfortunately this visual comfort was entirely two-dimensional because she was only painted on a wall. Distracted for a moment from her closer inspection by recurring requests to raise his beaker in yet another toast to the great victories of the Classis Britannica (he'd swear it was already the third they'd offered the fleet that night) he returned to pleasurable contemplation of a Painted Lady.

Here was a vision as arresting as life. The fresco artist had captured a living person using technical skills remarkable even by Italian standards; certainly for such a cultural wasteland as these northern provinces.

The features were drawn as small, delicate, and tending to the elfin but her brown eyes were so large and hypnotic the viewer became immediately locked into the portrait – wherever you stood. If these eyes also gave an effect of intensity which, together with a long face and a swan neck, might have denied her the entire approval of Flavius Candidus, according to clearly-specified ideals of feminine beauty held in his own head, there was still no doubt that – if she truly lived – then here was a woman to turn heads and attract attention. The longer he looked at her, the more fascinated he became.

The unknown painter placed her face and shoulders against a circle of aqua light so the vision was sanctified by its greenish glow. It wasn't clear whether this halo was just to suggest vivacity or offered deliberate statement of religious significance. Since religion and superstition were such inescapable features of everyday life, whatever your beliefs, he assumed it must do. Who was this woman and why was this portrait of her set so prominently on the dining room wall, amongst the painted dado panelling and the frieze-framed perspectives of fanciful seaside villas overlooking passing galleys crewed entirely by cherubim?

Across the room, Januarius must have spotted the abstracted fixation of his guest amongst the hubbub of conversation. He called out above the speech of others:

"Ah, Flavius Candidus, I see you deep in contemplation of the Tyche!"

Candidus looked up, embarrassed and surprised to realise his absorption was detected:

"The Tyche? Is that what you call her? So, who is she?"

"Why the face you see before you, Flavius! That of my own dear wife as a young girl - painted a few years ago when we first were married. Don't you see the family resemblance to her father, your employer the Vicarius? See the deep red hair? The full nose and mouth? But she is so much more than a wife; so much more than that to the citizens of Petuaria; to the voters of the proud Parisii tribe. You know well the list of public offices I am honoured to hold under the generous patronage of his Excellency, the Praeses, and his brother in duty, the Vicarius; all of us blessed in trust and authority by the Emperor Himself".

(Januarius paused for a moment, as if considering the effect of his words on his listener, before continuing.)

195

"But as well as these offices of duty, there's another to mention. A special rank held by both blood and inheritance - Clan Chief to the most loyal Parisii tribe! And the significance of that for any woman I take as my own is that she is made Queen to the tribe, their chieftain's consort. It follows for the Civitas of Petuaria that she is Goddess to their City - even as mighty 'Athena' is to the Hellenes - crowned with the Corona Muralis, the Crown Of Walls. My own wife - living personification of the tribe and deified embodiment of their town: The Tyche herself."

"I see. What powerful burdens of symbolism for just one woman to bear!"

Januarius frowned at the suggestion of inadequacy unintentionally implicit in his diner's remark: "Oh, no! Not for her! No, when you meet her, you will know. Hair like flames. It is a reflection of the spirit and essential to the Goddess, just as it was for my first wife…"

"What a pity she's not with us tonight," offered Candidus, inadvertently weak in riposte.

"She is with us all the time. You will see representations of the Tyche throughout the house. It is an idea and a feeling that is important to us here. The great pavement upon which we rest, for instance. It bears the same motif."

Candidus looked at the floor and thought for a moment about this new point of information; that the magistrate was already on his second wife. The wild but unworthy idea that the first might now be buried right under the floor beneath them as quickly flashed through his mind as it was dismissed. If so, where might the latest incumbent be found? He noted how Januarius had sidestepped his expression of regret over the absence of this significant lady from the dinner. If the magistrate had ambitions in politics, then avoiding direct answers to difficult questions would be an essential skill.

The room was so large that the nine diners on their three bronze couches around the well-stocked table hardly covered any of the ceramic glories in the spectacular mosaic supporting them. It was exactly as Januarius described.

The centrepiece of the large square panel was a bust of a female deity around which the rest of the room and the pavement were no more than decorative border.

196

The Tyche herself once again; set like the wall-painting inside a roundel which was itself held in an octagonal frame of stylised ropework. The blue-grey of slate; red terracotta; chalky-cream and the deeper brown of fired clay, together this sparse palette gave the few colours woven by an unknown mosaicist from thousands of tiny squares into masterly levels of detail and complex designs set for ever across the floor.

Eight compartments radiated around this centre, each one containing perhaps less-accomplished representations of a wine jar. To complete the square, six adjoining semi-circular panels enclosed in every one a reclining water nymph. Holding a branch and resting rather awkwardly against a large vase, her upper drapery conveniently fell away from one breast in that excitingly-careless fashion for which these mythic young ladies were justly notorious.

Did he or his contemporaries still take such ideas seriously? Or were they just stock images out of the mosaicist's catalogue? Asked on the right day and in a weak moment, someone as thoughtfully sympathetic to countryside as Flavius Candidus might admit he'd visited more than a few sylvan streams or sacred wells, if not in mild expectation at least on the off-chance. After all, what else had he been brought up to believe these mysterious green places were, but the secret abode of nymphs and suchlike? Or of someone-something even older - the Mother Goddesses, maybe? Peasant superstition, all of it? Perhaps, but the deeper into the dark woods you go and the more alone you get, the harder it becomes to scoff at the idea of such creatures or to deny the existence of beings you might never credit from the safe camaraderie of wine-shop or barrack-block. The sense of a presence that becomes so real it pounds in your head. Someone there, beside you or behind you.

Long, lonely combat patrols beyond the Emperor's Wall, deep into the heartlands of the Votadini people, the Maetae, Selgovae and Picti, had taught him how fearful these hidden places could so quickly become.

He'd never forget the first time he and his young comrades-in-arms had stumbled by chance out of the trees and into one of their woodland springheads. They'd found it decorated with human heads set onto sharp poles, bulging white spheres of chalk rammed into sightless sockets as if they could make the dead see. (Poor devils – how much did they suffer before being allowed to die?) A picture of terror and sacrificial agony to live with him always.

So whether our Candidus really believed in the Old Religion and those traditional stories given him from childhood, or by now was totally sold on that more personalised creed represented by Mithras, is a separate question for another day and perhaps better left unasked. Particularly by a Christian.

What is certain is that a primitive belief in the idea of a spirit of place - for every place – was still strong enough for most ordinary folk to concede the practical need for the odd nymph or river goddess to make the occasional appearance amongst we ordinary mortals. For whatever reason. Which means every lake, stream, wood and hill will have its own mischievous guardian spirit who must be appeased and treated with a careful respect. So much was obvious common sense.

What the ruling classes thought about all this was another matter, but anyone with their roots in the countryside understood the real sense of primeval mystery which cloaked these secret haunts. Which is why Candidus's whimsical admission to himself of private regret he'd never yet met a nymph in the flesh, so to speak, was coupled with a wry rejection of hoary legend's other requirement - that these flighty dwellers of the woods must be pursued in all the accoutrements of a satyr. To be as much goat as man, your human torso giving way to hairy legs and cloven hooves, seemed to him - at least - to be demanding too high a price for sylvan pleasure.

So Candidus's spiritual attitudes reflected the growing ambivalence of his age, but even his earliest military experiences had shown him how keen was greedy commerce to infest not only the licentious soldiery but even religion's lofty aims with its tawdry trade.

The holiest shrines of his day swarmed with crooks and chancers, pimps and tarts. If it was only his Mithraic code that framed a personal disapproval of arrangements notoriously available to the visitor at lesser, coarser shrines in the south-west of the province; their corps of prostitutes standing by to service pilgrims with the simulated classical encounter; this did not mean he would necessarily deny the liturgy or symbolism intended in such arrangements. If nymphs were real, it was only Mithras and his own preference for the genuine or more spontaneous experience that fuelled Candidus's moral disapproval of such alternatives.

Yet Candidus was no prude and neither did he lack a sense of humour. Only rueful cynicism and a private acknowledgement that he was not by nature 'felix' – lucky – would force the admission from him that he'd never to date surprised any bathing beauty; certainly none of quality. (Short of taking a living one out to the woods with him). Not unduly superstitious either, but second to no-one in his enthusiasm for the female form, Candidus might good-humouredly retain this faintest of faint hopes. One day, perhaps, when out walking under luckier stars.....

If others responded to the country a little differently, in ways where sex was nowhere to the fore but goats remained as prominent, then in his view that was a matter for them.

Unfortunately for modern Christian liking, there were too many old-fashioned thinkers still to go along with classical writers like Horace; a man for whom the most natural response to a pleasing landscape must always be the immediate sacrifice of a sheep or goat. No time to waste – cut its throat upon the very spot, to appease the spirit of place. For the true pagan, such blood sacrifice gave best and most natural expression of private approval for pastoral landscapes; even if - to Candidus's surprisingly fastidious mind - such bloody procedures were best kept indoors and confined to the necessary rituals of sacrifice. After all, if effected outdoors, they only meant a messier process, one likely to put right off any handy nymph nearby that was otherwise veering to the point of willing.

Reluctantly returning his thoughts from fantasies of rural seduction towards marshalling a favourable review of the new laid floor before him, if only out of courtesy to its hospitable proprietor, he realised how a mosaicist's portrait in tesserae must preclude the fine-line and telling detail that enables the fresco artist's representational successes on a wall. But there was still no denying how well the central Tyche figure illustrated across the floor succeeded in conveying more than a hint of serious majesty from such rare economy of line and colour.

Her steady gaze from prominently-emphasised eyes was just as arresting as that of the Painted Lady above her; just as appropriate to the confident bearing of a deity. A crown of city walls and towers confirmed the personification of their protector. Over the left shoulder, a cornucopia; indispensable accessory to the Tyche. Appropriately too, this particular horn of plenty was spilling out not only with the fruits of the land but also with its teeming shoals of silver fish; Petuaria's harvest of the sea. Curls held her face whilst a white tunic with red facings of the Dalmatian type covered the shoulders. As with many a deity, confirming the precise sex was the only controversy left in this otherwise dramatic final portrait, but convention already told him it must be a warrior queen.

"Yes, very impressive" agreed Candidus: "The workmanship is remarkable. How do these people do it?"

"Thank you," smiled Januarius, who always warmed to a man who praised his house. "Local craftsmen too. There's a long-established family firm in the town who've done most of the pavements around here. All the houses along the escarpment. And the great villa which manages the Imperial Estates on the south side of the river, the one you will have seen by the main road before you caught the Abus ferry. My fellow director in the lead-trade, honest Julius Protius."

Candidus remembered this colossal establishment well, as large as some he'd seen in Gaul or even Italia itself. Being this far north meant it always attracted extra comment from every passer-by. (Marching north on the road down to the river and ferry, straight from Lindum Coloniae, it appears in the middle of open, rolling wheat country on the left hand side of the road, at the point where you first see the river).

Two monumental corridor buildings, each one of them bigger than the civic basilica at Petuaria, flank a courtyard large enough for a whole Legion to parade upon in open order. Its furthermost prospect is filled by the house itself: all elegant verandahs and colonnades off a huge, aisled dwelling bisected by three wings and built on two floors, a tower at each corner.

As did every nosy passing traveller, Candidus found himself speculating as he went by on just what opulence and display might be found inside this 'E'-shaped domus. ("How the other half lives").

In the courtyard, he'd seen a row of massive grain wagons parked beside the imposing barns whilst their drivers lined up the queues of patient oxen that would drag them to the port. It all hinted at the immense scale of agricultural productivity which could justify such substantial investment. That its rooms would hold decorated floors to rival those in the dining hall at the Villa of the Januarii offered little surprise to anyone.

Candidus looked again at the floor by his feet. At each end of the central panel already described was an oblong frieze containing four round-arched panels shaped like windows. Inside each panel, the head and shoulders of a female similar in appearance to the Tyche, but for the absence of a crown of walls. A 'nimbus' or halo of projected light hung around each one, a veil of unearthly power to underline her sacred nature. Such symbolism was commonplace but its true significance was something even the godless ignored at their peril. That religion and superstition hung like a mist around every feature of Roman existence – even its most mundane – was unquestioned fact of life. A fact even more true here in the countryside. Death rode everywhere across a world where life was short and the spirit worlds beyond uncharted. Superstition's terrifying influence underlay the whole natural order and every human occupation, however every-day the activity. You could never take chances – deference to its ritualistic demands the only safe option, at least if you wanted to avoid death's early hand on your shoulder.

In Britannia itself, whatever new superstitions or beliefs the Roman had once brought to Britain, more deep-rooted and pervasive Celtic ways always endured beneath.

That was why understanding what local variations might underlie conventional beliefs approved by the state was integral part of his commission, a necessary precaution. Candidus needed to be sure he had the measure of every single influence that could affect his mission - divine or human. Careful as he always was, even he would come to be surprised by just how important and prophetic the abstract messages conveyed in this piece of provincial artwork below would prove to be in the practice of his brief out in the teeming streets.

"Who are the ladies with the haloes?" asked Candidus, careful to be respectful but curious, despite himself. Directing his question at the householder, the reply he got came from elsewhere: "The goddesses who symbolise the four towns and quarters of our canton" interjected Cicerius Felix from his left, on the mettle of his tribal pride and forced to put this ignorant but devious stranger right.

Proceeding next most tediously to list them all by rote, Candidus strained to hear him across the cross-cutting conversation of his fellow guests. He affected polite interest in the inordinate inventory following, if only to defuse whatever resentment Felix might still bear him for a false identity offered up last night.

After all, demonstrating a healthy respect for local customs and beliefs was not just about not offending the natives, not upsetting the Brittunculi, these 'Little Brits'. In an unquantifiable spirit world, who could really know or truly dare defy the untracked powers of local gods?

The key fact he'd soon absorbed and already knew: if Januarius was their chief of men then, amongst the Parisii, the status of his wife became akin to that of a goddess, an incarnation of the tribe. So far, so conventional. Need it matter to him? He knew it did if he had business amongst these people and if their religion became involved, as it surely must: "You can't be too careful. It's not just a case of not offending their Gods, either. Mortal men can be pretty vindictive on the subject, too".

Nor was it just about religion. Status was as much of an issue. Provincials like Januarius commissioned pictures like this for their houses because they wanted everyone out there to know that they were privileged beneficiaries of a classical education.

Even in a backwater like this, or possibly more so, it still seemed to matter. So if the reality was that the sophisticated elite to which men like Januarius belonged no longer really believed in the old gods anymore, they just clung to them anyway as reassuring concepts – traditional stories from a better age. Except that, with the Church Militant rapidly gaining ground under the patronage of Constantine, traditionalists like him must box clever with their explanations when the thought police came round, if they were not to become proscribed as religious renegades. After all, as a civil magistrate, supporting Church orthodoxy was by now added to the expected duties of such as Januarius, a duty he was caught resiling from at his peril.

Fact is, such restrictions on dissent only made Candidus feel more angry inside, an anger he kept to himself. He could well imagine how adroitly a smoothie like Januarius would deal with questioning like that, innocuous discussions of theology all too prone to lead on to later denunciation over some more secular matter: "That big mosaic of Orpheus and his lute? What, me, a pagan? Oh, no, you've got it all wrong there, my good fellow. Let me assure you! Symbolism, my dear fellow, utter symbolism. Nothing more and nothing less. Don't you see the different aspects of Our Lord – the charms of music victorious over death; the triumph of our civilisation over relentless barbarism; of education over ignorance; of Christ over the Devil! Surely an educated and sophisticated officer of the state like yourself can see there's nothing inappropriate going on in all of that?"

That was why the very best interior designers were not just craftsmen handy with the tesserae. They also needed to be masters of ambiguity, if their chosen floor designs were not to get wealthy clients into deeper water with the local frumentarii: with officials become so enthusiastic in their zeal that they would enforce a pattern of prescribed belief and approved vocabulary which not even the increasingly bitter edicts and legislation issuing from our un-baptised Emperor had yet demanded.

Felix was still going on. When he'd finished his ponderous explanations and Candidus given what nods of animated comprehension seemed enough to satisfy this tedious teacher, he was able to relax and pick up on a rather more interesting conversation going on to his right.

203

Easing back into his couch on the conclusion of this over-long lesson in local geography, Candidus found himself able to tune in to the general discussion for the first time. It was, as he soon realised, not just political talk but careless talk - of the very worst type.

Dangerous talk.

The theatrical Trimalchio was pontificating loudly on the supposed virtues of the Imperium Galliarum: Everyone in the room knew what he was referring to but no-one offered challenge. In a society where the willingness to denounce others had become a foremost social virtue, such silence must be significant. What Trimalchio was conjuring up out of the past were the supposed merits of that 'Gallic Empire' which, some eighty years ago, split off from the central authority of Rome in surely the darkest of years, as if through schism we could assure survival, not hasten our end.

That year when the noble Emperor Valerianus was humiliatingly defeated and then captured alive by the Sassanian King Shapur I at Edessa on the Persian frontier. So long ago but still - what inconceivable horror! The only Roman Emperor ever to fall into enemy hands – Valerian the Valiant reduced to crouching footstool for an Oriental despot, thanks to the treachery of his own bodyguard. When he died from all their misuse, Shapur had him stuffed and kept him on as furniture.

This bogeyman of Rome, this Shapur, he had previous for it. Sixteen years before that, he'd already killed Gordian III in battle and overrun much of the east. Taken together, the greatest disaster to Roman arms since the Republic; not since the third man in Caesar and Pompey's Triumvirate learnt how little men of business know of desert warfare. When the richest man in the world grew hungriest of all for a military success to match his fellow Triumvirs'; when Marcus Licinius Crassus so arrogantly crossed the Euphrates and straightway lost his life and seven legions on the parched sands of Carrhae. Another much earlier lesson for the superpower of the West at the hands of that recurring power in the East – the kingdoms of Persia.

But how could it have been possible? How many times do we need to break them?

Are these Persians like the German Marcomanni or the British Caledones? Needing to be taught ever sterner lessons yet through our fresh slaughter of each passing generation? Do not the bitter experiences of their forefathers give sufficient warning to their sons?

True, it was no Roman but Alexander of Macedon who first reduced Persepolis and all the realms of Xerxes, of Darius and their Persian heirs, into utter ruin; apportioning their provinces to his generals. Much later on, but still two hundred years and more gone by, it was our very own Trajan, best and greatest of Emperors, who himself stood victorious in the ruined capital of Parthia, on broken Ctesiphon near where they now call Baghdad. How dare those Sassanid hordes, these barbaric scaled horsemen claiming succession from Persia and Parthia, rise again to thwart us? Will they never learn from history; of how harsh defeat inflicted on Rome can only lead on to more terrible retributions yet?

Even in far-away Britannia and Gaul, these events of two generations ago mattered a great deal to our forebears. Their confidence faltered and seemed to fail them. Once again, the onslaught of barbarians on all sides threatened a tide of darkness to spread across the world, extinguishing Rome's light. If this was what was happening in the East, then Trimalchio's argument became that only through his seizure of power in the West did the Gallic Emperor, Postumus, save our end of Empire from complete collapse. (As if his motivation really was so selfless....)

Candidus and presumably every listener was perfectly well aware of how Trimalchio sought to draw modern parallels in recounting these tales, overtly insinuating what lessons we could take from the past. Even so, what precisely did he have in mind? Secession, yes, perhaps – Britannia ceding from the rest of Empire.

Or was this just a homily on the wisdom of resisting what for hundreds of years had always provided irresistible temptation to Rome's rulers – the vainglorious military expedition into the East to restore peace and teach them a lesson?

Except that the real lesson was one understood by any Roman child who'd ever played with toy soldiers upon the mat.

That, as every schoolboy knows, the Persian desert is much like the German forest, an insatiable graveyard for our armies. But if Candidus's first analysis was right and secession the real theme of this booming harangue, then Trimalchio must be talking-up the concept of Imperium Galliarum itself. In this excruciating discussion, loyal Candidus's private views soon became deeply unsympathetic, even if not formed from first-hand knowledge. As events of even before our grandparents' time, his understandings must naturally be only hazy - but it still seemed obvious to him that encouraging treachery and rebellion anywhere will only weaken Rome's Imperium everywhere.

In those days of our forefathers, these early Gothic invasions in the west had paralleled disastrous military adventures in the east. Even then, it was not as if the West was actually done for. Brave Gallienus, son and heir to the tragic Emperor Valerian, was still holding the line in the West on the Danubian frontier with some success - whilst his young son, Salonus, did the same along the Rhine. Or at least he did until one Marcus Cassianus Latinius Postumus, most trusted General of Gallienus and Trimalchio's vouchsafed hero, so coldly murdered Gallienus's son, poor Valerian's grandson. Simultaneously-slaughtered with Gallienus's teenage heir at Colonia (capital city and fortress of Lower Germania) was his military mentor Silvanus, Praefectus of the Praetorians. The intended result was chaos everywhere – deliberate destabilisation – and not just on the Rhine and Danube frontiers.

With his legitimacy founded solely on these ruthless acts of dreadful and destructive disloyalty, Postumus took advantage of all the chaos he had created to seize control of a decapitated Imperial establishment in the West. It was hardly an auspicious start to his regime but so typical of that dark age of internecine strife; a period which only such enlightened rulers as our Great Constantine have finally put behind us, once and for all.

When our Army is weak or distracted by civil war, the barbarians move in. When the Army is made so strong and numerous that the barbarians are driven back, then its officers will turn to that meddling in politics they've come to see as an even more natural peacetime occupation than hunting with hounds or gambling.

To the people of those times, and until the Army and its officers were cured of their flawed outlook, it must have seemed inevitable that this whole bloody and destructive cycle could and would repeat itself, over and over again.

It was the soldier-Emperor Aurelian who was first successfully to strike these vipers down, and their 'Gallic Empire' with it. All the more surprising then that such creatures as Trimalchio might even dream of mentioning it now; not when strong men like Diocletian and our beloved Constantine, the well-named 'Great', have so successfully held the Empire safe together ever since.

Another reason why, to a dutiful servant of the state like Candidus, there could be no nostalgia or approbation attaching to these treasonous ancient events. So he bit his lip and quietly kept his own counsel, as any right-thinking man would do. These were not histories best recalled by persons holding office under the authority of the Emperor, he thought, but there was worse to come:

"My father once gave me a coin...." intoned Trimalchio, waving a scented hand for emphasis.

Candidus comforted himself with a private doubt whether such a cruel and affected officer could ever have had a parent. Even if one could be found to own up to the responsibility, then his gift of coin must surely have been coupled with a round of bread on a staff and a lump of cheese in a handkerchief; together with a cuff round the ear and an instruction to make his own way in the world hereafter. Unfortunately the tale that was to follow was neither so concise nor convincing.

"It was a coin of Carausius and dedicated to the Genius Britanniae, to the personified spirit or protector of this island province, just as the Tyche is to the Parisii..."

Now this really was embarrassing, Trimalchio treading on much nearer times.

It was barely forty years since the British usurper, Marcus (Aurelius) Mausaeus Carausius, had been assassinated by his own chancellor, the accountant Allectus. Weakened by strife, their 'British Empire' was soon reclaimed by Roman expeditionary forces from the continent, led by Constantius Chlorus, the revered father of our Blessed Emperor.

207

That is why, for the older generation at least, these remain events within living memory. Which is also why they are best forgotten, too. Nevertheless, if positive lessons for the present can be found in their history, even Candidus himself was prepared to make an exception and review them.

The late Carausius in question was a senior naval officer who'd achieved considerable success against Saxon and Frankish raiders on the coasts of Northern Gaul. In an envious and competitive world, his achievements at sea only attracted jealousy and suspicion at home. The principal allegation made against him by his enemies within the state whose seaboard he'd so effectively defended was that the interceptions made by his galleys and armed freighters were not of incoming raiders but rather their outgoing colleagues, laden with booty from plundered towns and villas. The calumny lay in the contention that this was his deliberate policy and an alleged failure to ensure the recovered goods were returned: either to the rightful citizen or else to the Emperor. Either would have done, but more especially the latter.

True or not, imputations of this nature and in this operational context were as easily made as impossible to refute. The appointed 'Caesar' to the West, Marcus Aurelius Valerius Maximianus, exercised delegated powers he held at that time under the Emperor Diocletian. Indeed it was Maximianus himself who'd originally appointed this Carasius to command the British and Rhenus fleets together with their associated, coastal land forces. It was this same Maximian who so willingly ordered the execution of his Admiral upon what seemed such trumped-up charges.

The reply was predictable defiance. Carausius would not surrender to his fate but proclaimed himself Emperor and seized all the provinces of Britain with the support of their garrisons. Across the Channel in Gaul, another rogue Legion held the town and installations of Gesoriacum, the largest port and fleet base, in his outlawed name.

This independent regime hung on for ten years but, when it came, its inevitable overthrow was reputedly celebrated by loyal citizens everywhere.

Commemorative gold medallions were struck, showing Constantius Chlorus entering the grateful walled city of Londinium whilst appreciative citizens waited on one knee to applaud him, "The Restorer of the Eternal Light" approaching its towered gates in triumph. These same souvenirs depicted the troopships of the expeditionary force rowing energetically up the Tamesis river, confirming for the first time the key significance of Roman sea power - here in the rise and fall of this usurper.

Remembering how hairy, hoary old Rufinus - mere river pilot to the supply barges of the Sixth Victorious Legion - would hardly breathe the name of Carausius in an empty, provincial bathhouse some forty years after his death, then how could a senior naval commander like Trimalchio dare discuss the virtue of those disgraceful days with other military or naval officers; in the presence of a magistrate; before a beneficarius consularis from the staff of the civil governor himself? What in Mithras's name was going on, if not some plot for another break-away state?

In retrospect, Candidus for his own part began to feel compromised. He wondered whether this effect was deliberate; whether there was some sort of attempt being made to attach him even by unwilling association to a disaffected faction of which Januarius may well be head. A principal viper, if not the full Medusa. Linked with such a conspiracy, Candidus would be outlawed. The report to his master of which this type of information could be molten core could be stemmed and quenched by the simple expedient of completely discrediting its maker. Easier in a way and probably more effective than killing him.

His mind raced ahead whilst the pompous Trimalchio blundered on: "Now there was a man! A man who placed some value on these islands. A man who understood the future importance of the fleet to their survival and power. Control the seas and you control the destiny of these provinces....."

Candidus was in turmoil. The hypocrisy of those regular protestations of selfless loyalty and obedience to the Emperor littering the most ordinary conversation with Januarius was showing through. Even at his most concussed and hungry, Candidus recalled how he'd at once identified them as cant.

He waited now for some intervention from the magistrate, for him to show his hand one way or the other, but he said nothing and appeared detached from the conversation. What was the game?

Trimalchio thundered on regardless: "It is a long way from here to Byzantium, to the New Rome our Great Emperor is a-building, out there in Asia. We wish him well in his historic and expensive project, of course we do, but back here in these islands the pressures are different, our priorities more immediate. Our whole way of life is under threat but does he hear the groans of the Britons? Not always, I fear, not from so far away. No, what we need is a man on the spot. Someone who understands local conditions and the security situation we are facing here, day-in and day-out...."

It was a familiar but dangerous argument. The fact remained that the Northern Provinces of Germania, Gaul and Britannia could never make it on their own. The tax revenue they produced was never going to be enough to fund the disproportionate cost of the garrisons necessary to keep order and hold them safe. Only an Empire balanced by fiscal duties gathered from wealthy possessions in the prosperous East could finance the armies that protected the turbulent West. And that was why every usurper proclaimed in Britain was driven in the end to cross the Alps into Italy; in pursuit of the military success over there that would give them finance and legitimacy back home. Just as Constantine the Great himself had done, straight after his proclamation by the British armies at Eboracum, thirty-one years ago.

However, this was not an adventure in which Candidus wanted any part. He presumed Januarius did and that was why he cultivated the officers of the fleet and the goodwill of local army commanders. Here was a wealthy man of good-enough family whose role in the lead trade could give him equivalent quality contacts in Germany and Gaul, tipping his influence onto another level altogether. Was it enough?

This Januarius was no military man, as any candidate for the purple must surely be. Whatever influence he might wield in the region from here, his backwater-base, it could never be enough to take the entire Province or cement its secession.

Worse still, his sons had literally cut themselves off from the army and whatever footholds of power their ambitious father might need inside that dominant public institution.

Candidus was driven to conclude this magistrate was merely the front-man for someone even more notable; someone of wider standing yet. Whether inside the Army or the Classis Britannica he could not say, but there was someone bigger and more important out there, controlling all this, of that he was certain. For a fleeting moment Candidus wondered whether it might even be his own boss, before rejecting the possibility. Surrounded as he was on all sides by unprincipled servants of the state, obsessed with looking after 'Number One', Candidus would not believe it possible of his lord and master in far–away Londinium. Not the dignified and principled boss he so admired and respected, for all his remoteness; the man who'd given a broken-down old horse soldier a fresh chance and decent employment. Surely not. But if not him, then who?

While everyone else remained silent, Trimalchio continued to monopolise their attention with his flamboyant reduction of economic and military complexities of Empire into a handful of half-truth garnished with simplification; presented on a ringing platter of tendentious couplets. If the others were silent, it was only because they were essentially enthusiastic to the theme – but for Candidus it was more the pre-occupation with escape and report. His mind on other things, he no longer heard the booming tones of the Praefectus Reliquationis Classis, droning on.

Flavius Candidus had been ideal junior to middle-ranking officer material; a young man with old-fashioned ideals of duty and loyalty; someone who could be relied upon to eschew that murderous circle of entrepreneurial power-broking which more senior colleagues relied on to make or break their careers and fortunes.

Those who'd appointed him to his latest, particular and peculiar post in the civil administration knew an incorruptible like him could sear like a heated javelin through whatever strata of deceit, corruption, and treason they might send him into. It is a truism that those public institutions most requiring these qualities of integrity in their functionaries reward and value them the least.

211

So it was in the Office of the Vicarius, but Flavius Candidus would do his duty notwithstanding, even if it made him approaching priggish in some eyes.

His discomfiture was broken by the arrival of the third course - a choice of sweet dessert or apricot stew whose attractions sufficiently distracted Trimalchio to give everyone respite from his perorations. It was then that Januarius made his intervention, and it could not be random chance which made him present it as a question for the beneficarius consularis:

"Well then, Candidus, my dear fellow. What a debating club you've found yourself amongst, eh? Do you have anything to contribute for us?"

"I'm afraid your learned discussions are beyond a discharged veteran, an old horse-soldier like me! The past is gone and means nothing to such as me. My world view doesn't go much beyond fetlocks and harness-brasses, while ships just make me ill. So I'm the very last person you should ask for comment about the deeds of dead or famous men..."

If he'd tried to turn the interrogation of Januarius aside with humour, the irony-free Trimalchio was quick to counter-attack under the tutelage of his host and patron: "Ah yes. But you do live here, don't you? Here in this province, here in this island. Like any of us, a native-born Briton must care about our peace and security...?"

Everybody was looking at him. Candidus coloured, self-conscious at such scrutiny. Why was he focus of all their political proselytising? What is it about the corrupt and devious that they must see everyone else in their own terms, and cannot rest until they have a conversion? The pressure was tangible: "Now, that's where you're wrong, captain! I'm no native-born Briton but a son of Gallia Narbonnensis. Which is not to say that – like any citizen of Empire who bears belt and badge of minor office in the service of his Emperor – I'd ever be careless of the safety of His Possessions."

Candidus was confident to have outpointed the best of the party on their home ground – in weasel words and hypocrisy - even if unsure how long he could keep it up.

Fortunately, this barrage of doubt on the resilience of his duty was as suddenly lifted, with the unannounced entry into the room of the man who'd first greeted Januarius with his guest at the house steps. Shouts could be heard outside and this freedman bent to whisper in the ear of the magistrate, his master, and then afterwards to Trimalchio's. The face of Januarius crumpled with alarm and worry and he nodded emphatically before dismissing his servant:

"Gentlemen, there are troubling events on the estuary tonight. I hear that merciless, thieving pirates have penetrated our river once again, but rest hopeful we will witness their punishment at the efficient hands of Trimalchio's brave men. If you are agreeable to this unwelcome interruption to our meal, can I suggest we step outside to observe what we can of the action from the gardens. Do take your drinks out with you if you will..."

Trimalchio had been the first to rise and this wine-house fop showed an unexpected willingness to assume his res-ponsibilities: "If that's the case, I cannot stay here, I'm afraid, Marcus. I must get back to the harbour and my ships at once."

Januarius was dismayed at the disintegration of his plotters' conclave but retained enough grasp of essential courtesy to voice concerns for his guest: "My dear fellow, I realise you must resume your command at once, but you surely cannot go out alone; not into the dark between house and town. Particularly not tonight, not when sea-wolves prowl the creeks and inlets. If you cannot wait till daylight, perhaps I can send a body of my own men with you for protection?"

"Thank you, Marcus Ulpius Januarius. You are as ever the attentive host, but forget I always bring my own safety with me. A vexillatio of Marines waits in the entrance lobby and they will return me intact to the dock."

Of course! If Januarius had not, then Candidus could not fail to have noticed these ugly fellows on his way into the dining room; these seafaring louts wrapped in green mariners' cloaks that leant with studied insolence upon broad-shafted javelins. Across their broad backs, a diagonally-buckled strap held to each his diamond-shaped shield; its stretched blue leather cover painted in gold on black with the trident of Neptune and the stylised thunderbolts of Jupiter.

213

(Interesting to wonder how much longer those conventional Christian symbols of the modern army – the "In This Sign Conquer", the PX or "Chi-Ro" – could safely remain as notable omission from the fighting heraldry of the Emperor's most loyal Classis Britannica).

Flogged men they may be, if their commander's reputation was to be believed but, whatever they might do for the enemy, they certainly frightened Flavius Candidus. Even just loitering at the door. And as armed gentry of dubious loyalty, no sensible person's choice of company for a moonlit stroll in the country. Candidus thought in his position he would rather take his chance with the Saxonici but Trimalchio still made his farewells and left under their close protection regardless.

In addition to the marines, he also took back with him his medical countryman, Nicomedes of Epidaurus. Sorry at least to see the kindly doctor go, Candidus was surprised to note that, whatever Trimalchio of the Abus Squadron saw as duty, his brother officer - that land-lubber colleague from the Petuarian Interceptors - seemed keener than most to remain at the villa.

The armed party for town having departed already, the balance of his diners went out into the garden. After the heated room, the chill of the night air hit the face like a cold-water dive, reviving flagging attentions. Slaves were on hand with outdoor British cloaks for those more sensitive to changed temperatures but Candidus was glad of the cool. They made their way across the lawns, trying not to fall over low, ornamental box hedges bordering gravel paths and floral beds, but slaves bringing burning torches to illuminate the scene and prevent accident were sent packing by Januarius for the sake of preserving night-vision amongst his gathering of spectators.

They were not needed anyway. It was a still clear night where the Moon Goddess was magnified almost to her greatest extent as she turned the broad river into meandering sheets of beaten silver, leaving the villa gardens in near-complete darkness under the shadow of their overhanging woodland.

As already explained, this venerable house was sited by its long-gone founder on the last and gentlest of a series of sandy ridges leading down from the escarpment of the high ground to the shores of the Abus River.

Seen from up here, upon this final declivity, daylight will offer you the most absorbing panorama of all the acres of land and water which lie to the south. On a night aided only by the moon, it was surprising to see how much of this daytime detail could still be made out beneath its blue light and purpled shade.

In the deeper darkness of the gardens Candidus was aware of numerous people standing on the lawns around him: fellow diners no doubt; other members of the proprietor's family, his freedmen, house-slaves and farm labourers. All of them mingled together in this temporary equality of the night to observe what great and terrible events they might witness together.

Truth be told, Candidus could at first see little of note, even with the aid of an ample lunar orb. Above them all, the Goddess Epona and her wild horses rode the towering clouds. He took a generous swallow from his wine-glass and looked again.

On the other side of the river some small red embers glowed and grew. He thought he could make out one or two rectangular shapes on the water nearby – shapes which might well be ships. A shadowy figure in the gloom next to him took his arm and shouted "Look!" in that familiar way people in crowds do at public spectacles, momentarily abandoning the hostile inhibitions of daily society.

The distant ember flowered and soon became a raging pillar of fire, raining orange sparks from a dark cloud of combustion visible even against the night sky. There were collective sighs of wonder and fear from the assembled watchers in the garden. These were not domestic pyrotechnics on the festival of a goddess but the fiery signs of War. Raiders!

"Where is that?" asked Candidus of his invisible guide, unconsciously pointing with an un-seeable arm.

"May the Unconquered Sun God confound my judgement, but I fear that pyre can stand in only one place!"

"Then tell me, friend"

"Why, that lovely house at Vinovium! The home of Gaius Julius Protius, steward to the Imperial Estates, friend to our host."

"You mean the big one on the way down to the Abus ferry?"

"Yes, that's it." (The speaker's voice faltered with despair until he found a straw to clutch) "Unless I mistake the alignment and it's only that small temple to the River God, the one you see nearer the shore line...."

215

Mistaken he would not be. Pirates who'd risked their lives in an open boat on the German Ocean; penetrated the signal stations and naval patrols at the mouth of the Abus River; then laid low and hungry in the daytime cover of an innominate inlet; pirates with that determination would not be satisfied with the petty arson of some wayside shrine as such slight reward for their trouble.

That little temple with its hollow shell of white-washed stonework and leaky red pantiles would offer them nothing: its pagan treasure of processional silverware and liturgical implements looted long-ago by militant Christians taking perceived encouragement from their Emperor's role as Protector of the Church. No, these cruel parasites had more ambition than that.

From the curved prow of their black ship hidden amongst the reed beds, no leader of brigands would fail to notice the great house and its spreading farms, standing way beyond and well above the little temple that hugged the southern shore. If any innocent wayfarer on the road could note these suggestions of wealth, then to these raiders they were arrant promise; the outstanding attraction of massive gain from expendable others, waiting to be taken by themselves alone. Instant riches!

Candidus found something truly bizarre in this little group of well-behaved dinner guests standing quietly on the manicured lawns of another villa, with their mannerly host and his respectful household staff gathered around him; watching a not-so-distant fire that signalled bloody murder, rapine, robbery, destruction and misery even now being inflicted on their own kind a few short miles across the river.

In his travels across Gaul, a youthful Candidus more than once encountered the blackened ruins of once-prosperous, well-founded and strongly-fortified cities burning in the invading path of migratory German tribes. The Alemanni, Marcomanni, Franks and Goths: a roll-call of bestial cruelty crossing continents by wagon. Aside from their hideous atrocities committed against innocent man, woman and child alike; the feature of their passage hardest to reconcile was the sheer scale and social permanence of what physical destruction they would wreak for paltry gain; the mere baubles they would carry off for sake of mindless havoc wrought, leaving behind only poverty and bleak ruins to last a generation.

216

At least in Britain, he was happy to find, its sea-girt isolation had to date protected it from the worst of continental Europe's experience. The professional vigilance of both our army and navy had more than played their part in this success. In the current, stable military situation - welcome blessing from the long reign of the present Emperor - the British armies had till now shown themselves more than capable of controlling those who might pose an equivalent threat to their home Province. Indeed, there were still men of note crossing the northern sea to settle in the south of this island; escaping the insecurities of their native Gaul to reconstruct their fine estates in the more peaceful downlands of Britannia.

Unless quickly suppressed, any attack like this could cause much wider panic. Either way, Candidus found it depressing to become passive spectator at such familiar cruelties now re-occurring here in Britannia. If Candidus was depressed, then Januarius was beside himself with misery, physically tearing at his clothes with frantic hands: "This fire must be the house of Gaius, the home of my dear friend and colleague, Julius Protius! Why, the barbarians are amongst us and rage unchecked! Where is our fleet? Where are the warships? Where are Trimalchio's men?

In the absence of its departed commander, the vigilance or effectiveness of local units from the Classis Britannica was hard to judge. Certainly there were vague outlines of what might be ships on the river; shadows which seemed to come and go in the vicinity of the opposite ferry-landing, but friend or foe? It was hard to say.

Watching, they all saw a spurt of flame arcing up from one vessel in the river in a feeble curve till it fell upon another, which momentarily flared with spontaneous ignition from stem to stern. Candidus fancied he could almost hear the terrible shrieks of burnt or dying men wafted on the delicate wind.

"Greek fire!" exulted the man beside him. "The fleet are on them!"

It was a momentary compensation, only. The unforgiving column of incendiary products rising high into the night sky from the house of Julius Protius did not abate but rather fed upon itself to become a dark tower of fumes. Candidus turned away, sick at heart.

217

"Arm the men!" he heard Januarius tell his bailiff. "Have the hounds in the garden stood-to – that's if we can trust them against their own!" (This last made little sense to Candidus, but the servant clearly understood his lord's meaning and what was required because he immediately turned to go).

Januarius identified his guest in the gloom: "Ah, Flavius Candidus! There you are! These are sad events indeed. How I regret it should be at our house you come to witness them. A sorry reflection of the wicked times in which we live. But I would not have you fear for your own safety or for the house in which you stay. We are secure and well-protected here, I can promise you that. Would that dear old Protius had been so careful in his precautions!"

"Is there a place in the line for an old soldier who still knows how to wield the spatha?"

"My dear fellow, we are not come to that! There are men about here younger and fitter than two old veterans like ourselves, and plenty of them too. No, take to the quiet comfort of your bed and when the Unconquered Sun God brings us the safety of day we shall see then what melancholy works the Children of Darkness have wrought and just what fierce vengeance Rome has brought down upon them!"

Candidus took his host's advice and went, leaving the magistrate standing alone and apart from the crowd in his garden, looking out and across to the fires; his tall but stooped frame faintly silhouetted against the phosphorence of the river.

In the tranquility of his little white-washed cell, Candidus soon fell into a relentless and disturbed sleep. Whatever respite this might have brought him was ruined by fevered visions of a dark tower wreathed in smoke and flame, over and over. On its fighting top, a weapon or something else of terrifying potential was about to be unveiled from beneath canvas shrouds by a Warrior Queen with red hair....

He awoke screaming.

Daylight cool and green as a mint-leaf infusion filled the neat room. From the angle of the rays it was already well into the morning. Somebody outside on the verandah was whistling as they walked past his bottle-glass window.

218

The sense of natural calm struggled against his recollections of the night, its remembered actuality at first indistinguishable from tormented imaginings in a sleep just ended.

Wrapping himself in a blanket, he opened his door and peered out into the corridor. Nobody about.

An atmosphere of unreal peace pervaded the old house but his thoughts were full of the blackened ruins that would now be the great villa on the far shore. With his face dashed with water from a bedside ewer, he was soon dressed and making his way to the kitchens. One of the cooks gave him an apple and that was all Flavius Candidus ever needed to break his fast.

Strolling down the central corridor whilst polishing this item on the coarse weave of his usual russet tunic, he saw that the slaves and officers of the household were all about their daily duties, acting as if nothing had happened.

An open door gave out onto the colonnaded verandah and thence into the rose garden. He took his apple along a gravel path between those miniature hedges of slow-growing box which had brought down the more unwary of last night's spectators. In the corner of the garden, with its back to the house and adjacent to a tall boundary wall topped with tiles and pierced by a single, round-headed wooden door, was a stone seat. The heads of antique lions emerged from carved acanthus flowers, pitted with moss, to hold the sandstone bench in their ferocious frozen maws. Over this horticultural throne a timber arbour offered the perforated leafy shelter of climbing dog roses.

As good a spot for contemplation as mortal man might wish for. With the house behind and orchard wall to the right, ahead lay ordered formal gardens. They gave the impression of stretching all the way from himself to the river, but for the final intervention of several low-lying fields. To his far left, beyond a tall beech hedge, grew the great wood which blocks any better view of the nearby town.

Candidus bit firmly into his apple and looked again towards the river. A faint spiral of dirty grey smoke still rose sluggishly from the high ground near the ferry-landing on the opposite bank. (So he had not dreamed it then).

219

In the middle of the lawns, paved paths met at a small fountain. Its centrepiece, green bronze streaked with corrosion, was a pair of miniature figurines in well-known pose: 'Cupid Embracing Psyche". In common with many who have seen the crueller side of life, close-up, this Flavius Candidus retained a surprising susceptibility to the sentimental. If pressed he would have confessed it himself; the effect this affectionate couple of tiny winged lovers had upon him, their petrified devotion preserved for ever in the struggling gardens of this embattled northern enclave.

It was these peaceful surroundings which gave him chance to consider his position. In respect of Marcus Ulpius Januarius and the general situation in Petuaria, he was satisfied that he had more than enough to offer in report to the Vicarius. When and how was the question. However, the job was not yet done. His master had sent him on a twofold mission. If its second limb impinged upon the first, it was still driven first and foremost by the tender concern of a well-to-do father for his darling only daughter, a girl married off to an important man of wealth and prospects in a dynastic union from which the father wanted reliable returns. Reassurance of her well-being would be as anxiously awaited in Londinium Caesariensis as any news of irregularities in the local administration. So far, Candidus was yet to see her. Until he could find out where and how she was, he dared not leave for home and his master. These raids were just a complication or an interruption, not an excuse.

Suddenly he heard a crunch of movement on gravel, right behind the arbour seat. It gave him quite a start. Squirming round, he could at first see no-one; not until he peered over the back of the bench. Crouched and jammed in there, hiding between this stone couch and the prickly stalks of the hedge which backed it, was a small child. Leaning down, Candidus put hands which seemed by comparison enormous under the armpits of the tot and lifted it straight over to the other side like a dockside crane. Deposited to stand upon the garden path with short legs and little feet, square and bare and beaded with tiny filthy toes; adult and infant were able to inspect each other with equal frankness.

A little boy, only about two or three years old and dressed in a yellow tunic somebody obviously expected him to grow into, viewed his rescuer with open disapproval. Large and sombre blue eyes set behind heavy round cheeks studied him with that unselfconscious interest of the very young. A bump of a nose, no bigger than a button and dotted with the faintest sprinkling of freckles, served to prevent those huge orbs of vision from becoming so wide as to merge. His hair was as blonde as straw and shaped like the wooden bowl which no doubt provided stencil for whatever shears had crudely trimmed it.

Soon deciding that the shiny apple in the hand of the man on the seat was the most interesting thing about him, a tiny finger pointed away from its other four companions in a splayed palm to touch the polished skin.

"Yan-yan" remarked the little lad, conversationally.

Candidus relented at once and handed the fruit over. Immediately it was taken into the grasp of two miniature hands and delivered to a hungry mouth where small pearly teeth were recent arrivals newly-identified as useful. The donor watched this practical demonstration of gratitude with amusement and some pleasure. Having surrendered his breakfast without argument he had to make the best of it. It was one of those moments that occur to the childless, when they suffer a jolt of insight into the delights of children, cracking their usual condescension at the inherent burdens and responsibilities.

Fact was, Flavius Candidus had never knowingly participated in parenthood, being a full-time professional soldier who had never found the love of a good woman and so consoled himself with the occasional bad one. (Who knew what fatherless urchins still ran about the garrison towns, bearing his face and features?)

It was rare that he would ever trouble himself with any sort of regret but here was just such a moment. What were his chances of being a proper father now? Getting on a bit and rendered creaky by the spectacular scar that ended his Army career, he wondered what woman would have him - apart from one too charitable to be interesting.

Nevertheless, even he could acknowledge how much he would have liked to have had a son of his own, indeed sons. One thing was certain, even if he lived beside a fortress of the Danube frontier, in a vicus where the decurion and his recruiting party went house-to-house every week, he'd certainly not have let his own sons' thumbs be chopped off just to spare them a noble death with the Legion.

Distracted at this bitter recollection of an apparent atrocity detected only yesterday in another father who should have known better, he felt the bile rise in his throat at the very thought of it. Attention was only returned to the child in front of him by the beginnings of a yelp, prompted by the half-eaten apple having been allowed to fall onto the gravel path.

Anxious like any grown-up to prevent the implacable horror of a screaming infant, Candidus was quick to recover the apple and take the boy by the hand with a promise that a quick rinse in the nearby fountain would make it good again. 'Taken in hand' is not really the right term, because their progress to the fountain in the middle of the lawn was made by one broad brown forefinger of his being grasped for guidance and support by all five tiny and almost translucent fingers of the child. The trust and vulnerability implicit in this tenure was something Candidus found particularly touching, in his sentimental soldier's way, as he took the golden cherub to view his cast-bronze equivalents.

He wondered then whose child this was, roaming at will in the enclosed garden. From the colouring, he could not be of the Januarian line. Perhaps he was just the offspring of some farm labourer or house slave, allowed free run of the lawns. Anyway, whoever he belonged to, someone somewhere would soon be missing him. Candidus would take him back into the house and re-unite him with his parent.

In the meantime, with grit washed away and the apple refreshed by the bubbling spring that filled the lead tank below Cupid and Psyche, Candidus squatted on his heels beside his new ward. Large eyes where the blue iris seemed so much greater in proportion to the white than might be found in an adult continued to observe him intently while the apple was slowly finished off.

222

Eventually the remains of a core were held out to Candidus, its disposal clearly falling within his remit. His solution was to throw it as high and as far as he could. It went spinning into the heavens like the stone ball fired from a catapult, eventually falling to earth in an adjoining field against a backcloth of white clouds, blue water, a distant shore, and lazy grey smoke from a burnt-out villa decorated with the blackening bodies of its dead staff.

The little boy was particularly pleased at this piece of bowling and threw up his hands in delight, doing a wobbly jig beside the water tank. Very soon, however, his interest in the spring and its statues faltered and a fretful look passed over his face like a cloud over the sun: "Mamma...."

Candidus understood the problem well and tried to understand where such an important person might be found. Already equipped with precocious degrees of determination for so few years, his new friend seized him again by the same finger (the only effective way to navigate this hopeless grown-up) and pulled him back along the path. Candidus decided the best policy was co-operation but was surprised to find himself being dragged away from the house.

They soon found themselves at that old door in the tile-topped garden wall which led through into the orchard. It was fastened on a latch and the little fellow pushed against it without success: "Mamma..."

What his mother did in an orchard was at present unclear but it might explain the insatiable taste for apple.

Candidus undid the latch and pushed the door open. Its bleached and splitting planks swung outwards and away from him on squeaky iron hinges. He bent down to pick the little boy up and gently lifted him over the stone step of the threshold and onto his chest. The child rested a tired blonde head on his shoulder and patted him indulgently on the back as you might a docile horse or an old dog, before placing exploratory fingers into his porter's eyes, ears and mouth, just as small children always do.

Half-blinded as he was by this unwelcome invasion, Candidus struggled patiently through the archway, bent almost-double in his anxiety to make sure he didn't bang his young charge's head, folding him under his bearded chin as he did so.

It was only on the other side of the wall that he was finally able to stand upright and look about him, the child still clinging close to him like a little warm monkey.

His bowels turned to water.

The whole orchard was crawling with Saxonici. They rose like angry wasps, disturbed from putrid fallen apples. From behind every tree it seemed a hairy-faced sea-wolf in a black cloak jumped to their feet, as the rickety garden door swung loudly back on rusty pivots to slam and rattle against the high wall, its clatter his general announcement to the meeting.

Stricken by fear, his movements the slow-motion of waking nightmare, Flavius Candidus turned to flee with the whoops of the enemy in his ears and the child tight in his arms.

"WOLSELEY – A ONE & A HALF LITRE CAR OF UNUSUAL QUALITY"

(Cover of a post- war advertising brochure – c.1948)

XI

On their way back from delivering Miss Macsen to Beverley, their newly-repaired and re-equipped Wolseley 10 was beginning to demonstrate its own disapproval of what they'd been through – as if to match her own – through a chronic misfire and go-slow. By Ferensway, Pickering had to admit defeat. He stopped the car outside the city railway station and twiddled aimlessly with the spark plug leads, to little effect.

"I'd better take her back to the garage, in the morning."

This truculent transport did at least get them back to Alfred Gelder Street and the Central Police Station before finally expiring. So much for the 'comprehensive service' invoiced by the garage to the Chief Constable. There is nothing like the motor trade for making a sickly car much worse and here was another operational problem to lay before Superintendent Maister in the morning.

Tryton spent the night rehearsing his report but, on entering the front door of this architecturally over-decorated police station, still felt no better prepared for delivering the unwelcome information his to announce. Maister was waiting. How to introduce the matter was immediately revealed as item number one on his Superintendent's agenda:

"Ah, there you are Tryton. What the hell is this business over at Brantingham you've got yourself involved in?"

"Business at Brantingham, sir?"

Tryton stalled, trying to sound like a busy detective whose workload made remembering individual cases difficult.

"Yes, Tryton, Brantingham! A solicitor's letter. "Urgent. Delivered by Hand" if you please! I've had a formal complaint, Tryton. A complaint about police officers making a nuisance of themselves on private property. Very recently. Snooping around on land belonging to my client, a respected member of the community, land belonging to a magistrate. A Justice of the Peace. Here you are! What can you tell me about it?"

A formal-looking letter on ivory-coloured note-paper was thrust in front of him. Tryton received it dutifully and studied the contents quickly. It came from a lawyer in a local firm acting on behalf of the Baynard Estate.

Its indignant themes were fulmination about private property; the invasion of privacy; police malpractice and oppression. It was signed by and presented on the expensively embossed note-paper of Meredydd Parry-Jones, Solicitor and Commissioner for Oaths, his professional credentials and practice address highlighted in black wax.

Tryton's master-stroke in his choice of representation for the American archaeologist turned to ashes on the moment.

"Why can't lawyers use plain English? What is this long-winded git blathering about, Tryton? What have you got to tell me?"

So he told him.

Maister went redder and redder with suppressed rage, as if a brass gauge inside his brain was registering increasing pressure until some internal valve would blow and release it all in a cloud of steam and invective.

When Tryton had finished his story he looked steadily across at Detective Superintendent Maister like a becalmed man-o'-war: waiting with resignation for the broadside that would topple his yards; silence his guns; and rupture his hull before sending him to the bottom of the sea. Yet the response that came was so uncharacteristically calm, so wearily reasonable, so uncannily quiet in its delivery that Tryton was stricken with a dread more profound than any shouting match could bring:

"Now listen to me, Inspector!" Maister began, at first almost in a whisper:

"Listen to me, Tryton! The Honourable Roderick Baynard is a landowner and an industrialist of considerable local standing. He sits as a Justice of the Peace, often as Chairman of the Bench, in the Petty Sessional Division of South Hunsley Beacon at their little courthouse down in Brough-on-Humber. He is, in short, not a person even into whose grounds, let alone whose home, a police officer would go without at the very least holding a search warrant signed in blood by the Lord Chief Justice of England, supported by the Lord Chancellor as his chauffeur and the Household Cavalry as military escort."

"But the man is a receiver of stolen goods. And probably a Fascist!"

227

"Mister Tryton, the Honourable Roderick Baynard may be a Chinese Communist for all I care but his politics do not enter this equation, however objectionable they may prove to right-thinking 'Daily Express' readers like ourselves. He has the ear of the Chief Constable, the society of the judiciary, and the friendship of influential voices at Westminster - whatever the result of the last election. He is, in short, not a man ever to be crossed, Mr. Tryton. Not any of the Baynards. And yet, incredibly, you have succeeded in crossing the pair of them, both brothers, in a very short time indeed. Once is unfortunate, as they say, but twice is definitely careless!"

Superintendent Maister did not seem the type to be quoting "The Importance of Being Earnest" but, either way, Tryton had to agree he'd put himself in a difficult position. And not for the first time. A forthright tongue and indomitable nature had similar effect in his Air force career, where undoubted skills and courage as combat aviator counted as little for advancement when set against the fawning and lick-spittle of less-accomplished rivals.

"But what about the pavement? It's still sitting there - a priceless historical relic about to be cemented into the fabric of Baynard's house. It must be recovered!"

"You, Mister Tryton will do nothing! Nothing at all, do you hear me?" shouted Maister: "Yes, I will transmit the gist of your flimsy and pathetic report to the Chief Constable of the East Riding Constabulary at Beverley, within whose jurisdiction the entire matter begins and ends. But what he chooses to do about the pavement, the Baynards, or anything else to do with the whole damn business is a decision I am content to leave entirely within his operational discretion. That is after all exactly what he is paid for. And you, you will cease to have any further involvement in this 'foreign' enquiry whatsoever. Do I make myself clear? Nothing at all. Do you hear me?"

Tryton nodded silently.

Satisfied that his senior detective was now fully aware of the enormity of vested interest he'd dared confront alone and confident there would be no repetition, Maister continued in a suddenly mellow fatherly tone that dazzled Tryton with its unprecedented charm:

"By the way, did you know an urgent witness-warning had come through for you? For this afternoon's Quarter Sessions at Beverley - that timber-stealing case."

Tryton was unaware of this particular request for him to attend and testify, although he remembered these cases well. A local family made a traditional living in stealing bulk timber from commercial yards, a particularly devious craft handed down from father to son. ('Chip off the old block', as they said). Arrest and charge would always lead to 'Not Guilty' plea and full trial of evidence; the same police failure (to prove these were the actual pieces of wood lost from the yard) and the same flimsy excuse for its possession by the family ("We bought it in a farm sale") always accepted by an East Yorkshire jury. Their trials routinely ended in acquittal.

This harmless but pointless social ritual was on this occasion to be played out in the Quarter Sessions at Beverley, whose town police had carried out the latest doomed enquiry.

Tryton's only involvement had been to effect an amiable arrest of the culpable father of six in Hull on their behalf. Yet some idle barrister somewhere had decided that the best way to avoid having to read his brief any earlier than the night before trial was to require his instructing defence solicitor to demand the prosecution produce every one of their witnesses in person on the day. So Tryton's purely administrative evidence on behalf of the Crown about the routine detention and delivery to Beverley Police Station of this middle-aged patriarch (his clothing always covered in forensically non-attributable sawdust, even when presenting himself before the court) must be given in person.

"No sir, I didn't know that. But there's another problem! As well as every thing else, the Wolseley's packed up. Sergeant Pickering's had to take it back to the garage that serviced it. So I've got no transport. How am I going to get over there in time?"

This question would normally have guaranteed sarcastic reference to travel facilities available from the new-made 'British Railways Board', but Tryton sensed he was currently on a winner with Old Maister for some reason and should capitalise on it to the hilt while it lasted. He was not disappointed:

"What? No transport? Well, look here. I'll tell you what, Tryton. Special circumstances and all that, and only on condition you look after the old girl. Here you are. Take my car. Here are the keys. Just make sure you bring her back safe this evening."

Tryton could not believe his luck. He accepted the genially-offered car keys with alacrity and effusive thanks then saluted before leaving the room with a spring in his step. On his way down the corridor, and still reeling from Maister's unlikely display of generosity, he called into his own small office to check on the morning's post or other developments before going on to Beverley.

This conscientiousness was not rewarded and he was left wishing he hadn't.

There was a note resting on the seat of his chair; obviously placed to make sure he didn't miss it. It was dated and timed at six o'clock the previous evening in Sergeant Pickering's careful handwriting. Effectively, his attendance as witness before Beverley court was no longer required because the content of his evidence had suddenly been agreed by the defence barrister and could be read out instead. Tryton read this cancellation with the utter deflation of disappointment, until the idea for an alternative shape to the day grew in his head.

Conscientious to a fault as he normally was, if police and national service had taught him anything, it was about how to 'skive-off' if you really had to. Guile was not in his nature but sometimes had a place. He folded the note then tore it into four pieces which he crumpled up and stuffed into his sports jacket pocket. (He'd have to square this with Pickering later).

Tryton sprinted down the worn front steps of the Central Police Station into warm spring sunshine, still dangling a set of keys for a brand-new Jowett Javelin on his finger end. Life was looking good again and he even stopped at a florists en-route.

The drive to Beverley in this borrowed car, playing with its not-inconsiderable performance on straight roads crossing the flat landscape, was exhilaration itself.

Duly reporting to the police sergeant responsible for witness liaison at the courthouse, Tryton received this officer's rebuff with an affectation of hurt ignorance: "A waste of my time!" This charade of duty over and - now finding himself expected in neither place - the rest of the day was his to command.

230

The Javelin was reversed quickly from its rest beneath the ancient trees and pillared classical portico fronting the Sessions House then driven only a few hundred yards down New Walk to its junction with North Bar Without. Here, a parked Dodge Weapons Carrier in faded olive green was anachronism amongst the bank managers' cars and wood-framed shooting-brakes of local residents. Hull City Police had acted promptly on their promise of the previous day by ensuring Miss Macsen's unusual transport was returned to her at once, he was pleased to see. If that alone improved her mood, then it could only be helpful to his plan.

The vehicle's location confirmed that the address he had for her lodgings matched the pink-washed Georgian terrace they'd delivered her to last night. Tryton rapped confidently on the door using the brass dolphin provided. A middle-aged lady, careworn by lively children, answered the door immediately. She guessed at once the purpose of his visit and shouted to someone up the staircase behind her:

"It's for you!"

"Who is it, Mrs. Holtby?"

"A gentleman to see you, Zuleika."

He could see her standing at the head of the stairs, tightly wrapped in a white bathrobe. Caught unawares by a visitor as she crossed the landing. Her hair was still wet and the water made it darker. This redness of blood lay in rivulets on her neck to point at her breasts.

She came half-way down the stairs but was not pleased to recognise him: "You!"

"I'm sorry" he began. "I'm sorry for the way things turned out yesterday. At least you helped us to find the pavement."

Her eyes sparked. "Sorry? You're sorry! Sorry for behaving like a complete pig, you mean!

He took the crumpled bunch of conciliatory carnations wrapped in newspaper from behind his back and held them out, more like clumps of garlic against a vampire than the peace offering he'd intended. Unfortunately the red blooms had wilted in the glazed heat of the car's rear parcel shelf where he'd unwisely left them and she inspected them with scorn:

"Just leave me alone, you stupid policeman. Leave me alone, do you hear!"

231

It seemed there was nothing more he could do. He turned as if to go and then two words spilled from his mouth with an inspired recklessness he did not know he had:

"Cohors Equitata!"

She stopped, astonished.

"What did you just say...?"

"Cohors Equitata...."

"What the hell are you talking about, you stupid policeman?"

"I don't know what it means. I don't know where I got it from. It just comes into my head whenever I see you..." (He really was as genuinely taken aback as she was by this involuntary Latin tumbling out of his own mouth). She came right down the stairs now and stood directly in front of him, looking straight into his eyes. Furious, she took hold of his raincoat by the lapels:

"Listen to me, cop! No-one invents words like that. What are you playing at?"

"I'm not playing at anything. Sometimes I think someone up there is playing with me."

Her hands released him as if angry to be provoked into such proximity. As they did so they dragged the collar of his mackintosh away, exposing his best sports jacket and a little gold badge still kept in his button hole, more through habit than sentiment.

"R – A - F." she read out slowly. "Flyboy, eh?" (He just looked at her, trying not to shiver with excitement as she ran long fingers with painted nails down the weft of the lapel to come to rest on the badge). "You never told me you were a flyer...."

"You never asked."

Her attitude seemed to change.

"Alright, Spitfire Johnny! Go and sit in the front room. Mrs. Holtby will make you a cup of tea, if you ask her nicely. I'll be down to speak to you properly in a minute."

She was as good as her word, emerging in a floral sundress. The landlady withdrew. Over the cup of tea he offered her a sunny day, the use of a car and the pleasure of his company. He astonished himself with his daring and her acquiescence:

"Where shall we go?"

"Where would you like?"

"York!"

"Why not? It's only two o'clock. We can be there in an hour. Is that where you want me to take you? Or would you prefer the sea....?"

"Eboracum. That's where I want to go. To the Place of the Boar, the City of the Legion. I've always wanted to see it. Take me there this afternoon, flyboy!"

They got into the car and drove.

Detective Superintendent Maister's favour was in much more than just the loan of his brand-new black scarab, but in the gift of fuel – what they call 'Pool petrol'. Realising the impossible luxury represented by an automobile in post-war Britain hardly started with affording its purchase, unattainable as that remained for most people. More difficult yet was getting hold of enough fuel to run it on the road; beating those official restrictions still strangling its use under the icy grip of petrol rationing.

Doctors, midwives and police officers were amongst the tiny minority afforded special treatment – everyone else must go by bus or train. That was why public use of official cars was such a sensitive issue. In view of what by any standards was the major local scandal of last year - a secret Home Office report to the Police Committee of Hull City Council, culminating in the sudden retirement on ill-health grounds of their charismatic Chief Constable, Thomas 'Tosh' Wells, over alleged misuse of police cars and the fuel ration - someone like Tryton knew better than most what dangerous ground he now trod.

Yet if something inside made him reckless, the explanation must be simple enough. The question of his Superintendent's fuel allowance was being deliberately disregarded for the sake of opportunities he thought it offered him in the warmer attentions of Miss Macsen. No clearer illustration could be needed of how far she'd affected his professional judgement, but whether his passenger realised the personal and professional risks he was taking just for her was presently unclear:

"What's being done about recovering the pavement? Why aren't you there today, instead of taking your one-time prime suspect out for a motoring tour in a fancy automobile which quite obviously isn't yours?"

His reply was vague, long-winded and non-conclusive. It certainly didn't provide sufficient answer for her perfectly-reasonable question. She was cute enough to try another angle of attack:

"What makes a guy like you into a cop? What are you doing in a job like that?"

It was unclear to Tryton what type of 'guy' she thought him. Despite her surprising trust and willingness to step out with him again, pessimism told him that in her book he was already marked down as just another 'rotter' with transport, to be abandoned when their entertainment value receded. But – aside from this momentary aberration over Maister's car - Tryton was a man of honour and persistence. Despite the sordid realities with which his all-consuming working hours might sour him, he still retained what some would call a naive belief these qualities of character would see him safe through a hostile world. He was, after all, an essentially honest man. It was this outlook, coupled with a renewal of insight into the attitudes of this difficult lady, which gave him inspiration; an answer for his motivation.

"What am I doing? Why am I a policeman?"

"Yes", she said. "That's what I'm asking. What's it about, for you?"

"Holding back the barbarians. That is what it's all about. Yes, I really think so. Holding back the barbarians!"

He returned his attention to the road ahead, just in time to swerve around a struggling tractor and its trailer, dangerously overloaded with sugar-beet, before returning to the correct side of the carriageway. There was a long silence from his passenger as his answer sank in.

"There you go again!" she said. "You're doing it again!"

For all the note of irritation, a smile played around the edges of that sensual mouth as she toyed with the idea. Bull's-eye! He'd struck home.

There was a pause and then she came back to it:

"OK! So why have you and your gallant English 'bobbies' not got yourselves into a big blue van and driven down to January House; gone 'rat-a-tat-tat' on the shiny front door of the Honourable Roderick Baynard and said: "Excuse me, sir, but can we have our pavement back and, by the way, please step into our van, so we can take you back to our nice police station; keep you in a cold, cold cell overnight; and then charge you in the morning with theft." Why are you here with me, when you could have done that today?"

Now there was a question. One that troubled him as much as her. He looked across at his passenger and there was that glint in her eyes. He knew then that all his troopships were burning on the beautiful beach where he had just landed:

"Because the Honourable Roderick Baynard is not a barbarian. Or at least he is not identified as such, not by normal English conventions in social signalling. He is a patrician. And the thought that troubles me in the work I do is the thought that I am not here to hold the line against all cruelty and avarice, against any deceit or every act of violence. Sometimes I worry that – instead - it might only be about the suppression of one alienated under-class and that there are different rules for the Baynards of this world, rules which are not for ordinary coppers like me to get involved in."

"Who are the barbarians, then?"

"I sometimes wonder. It used to be so simple. The pilots and bomb-aimers of enemy aircraft; dropping high explosive and incendiaries onto rows of little houses. On the house where the wife of a working man was cooking tea for a husband who had just cycled into the other end of the street. A street where his children were playing hop-scotch outside his own front door when it blew out. And of course the men who sent those aircraft against us. I had friends in the army who were amongst the first to enter the death camps in Poland and eastern Germany – where the SS killed hundreds of thousands of Jews. They never got over the sight. Barbarism beyond belief! But it became less simple, even so".

"At the end of the war, in Yugoslavia and the north of Italy, I was flying an aircraft we called a 'Typhoon'. It easily lived up to its name, equipped with powerful rockets designed for destroying tanks. Using weapons like that on helpless German soldiers, hopelessly retreating and running away in pathetic horse-drawn wagons or open civilian cars, it ceased to be simple any longer. I couldn't hide behind the impersonal nature of air-warfare any longer. Flying at such a low level, I could see exactly what I was doing to them and - yes – I suppose it was barbaric."

He paused for a while to concentrate on passing another slow-moving vehicle, a sky-blue and cream passenger coach taking a party of school children on an educational trip. The girls waved white handkerchiefs out of open top windows as they overtook whilst the boys pressed their tongues and faces flat against the glass in expressions of insulting torment.

Tryton accelerated hard to overtake and the Jowett roared ahead with a satisfying willingness, its flat-four engine pulling away strongly.

"And after the war? What are the barbarians you and your kind hold back from us now. Is it back to being simpler again?"

"It seemed so. Until now. Lovers that murder their mistress. Husbands that batter their wives. Wayfarers' distraction burglaries on country-widows, sneaking out of their cottage with a life-time's saving for old-age hidden inside a shoebox. The drunken lorry-driver who runs down the child standing at a bus stop. The dockworker who steals distress flares he has no real use for from a Hull trawler that later founders under the creeping weight of frozen spray, in the awful dark off Iceland, invisible to assistance. The schoolmaster who abuses his pupils, the cleric who betrays his cloth."

"Are they your modern barbarians?"

"Oh, yes. Well, I suppose they are. Less obvious but each barbaric in their own way, of course. Brutish, destructive and selfish. Easy to identify. I think of the victim and do what I can, to mark their outrage and that of decent people as a whole. There is satisfaction in that. Or else there was."

"What's the problem - now?"

"The Honourable Roderick Baynard, whoever he is. The pavement... And you."

She looked out of the window at the countryside streaming by, and he marked the curve of her neck with longing: "And why should any of these cause you a problem?"

"Because Baynard holds the pavement, to which he has no right. And because I believe my report will be shelved and nothing done. All because Baynard belongs to a different class to the sort of people against whom the jurisdiction of the English courts is more commonly invoked."

She laughed: "Ha! You limeys! Still bound hand and foot by the decadence of your class system. You still can't free yourselves from it, can you, even after two World Wars? Are your English aristocracy any less criminally-driven than the lowest social elements – the poor dupes you usually concentrate your attentions on?"

"I suspect not. Probably worse: 'Mad, bad and dangerous to know'. Every one of them, I expect. Anyway Baynard is hardly an aristocrat, just on the strength of an 'Honourable'. Minor gentry. But still too influential to touch, it seems."

"You mentioned three things causing you a problem. What of the third?"

Her directness never ceased to surprise him, but his English diffidence prevented the reply he longed to give her. (Days later, he would still be kicking himself for his embarrassing slowness and how he skirted the real issue. Another missed opportunity).

"I had to see you. Professional self-respect. To explain why, despite everything you think you've been put through in the last two days, I'm just a cog in a machine which even to me seems unwilling to do anything about what's happened."

"I see. But it is still kind of you to take me to York....Inspector."

They entered the city through a mediaeval barbican gateway in its creamy stone walls, under a little clapperboard house serving as a bookshop perched high over the internal arch. Driving from Walmgate Bar into the busy streets you could see it was still an important garrison town, green and khaki army vehicles everywhere.

They parked near Lendal Bridge, where there was a good view of the river and of oarsmen practising in their flimsy boats before the slipways to the Rowing Club.

On the other side of the bridge, the rear walls of ancient buildings backed onto the steep riverside. Prize amongst them was the City Council's mediaeval Guildhall, bombed heavily during the war because so close to the nearby railway station but still surviving as another defiant statement of civic pride.

Here was another city yet to recover from wartime. Aside from old damage and the continuing prevalence of battledress to confirm large numbers of National Servicemen stationed nearby, there was a gloom that went with post-war austerity; with bombed buildings, bad food, leaky taps and little children crippled by polio. He would have liked to take the American woman into a cafe but was hard put to find one that was open or held enough provisions fit to build a menu of any quality.

Instead, they walked up to York Minster. The magnificent Cathedral dominated its city like a great grey ship but, as with most fine buildings here, stood in desperate need of a good clean. Its intricate carved stone-work was blackened by the smoke from a thousand chimneys and coal-burning fireplaces, still the main means of heating - whether domestic or commercial. Built on the ruins of the headquarters building of the old Roman legionary fortress, the Minster and its attentive Close of ecclesiastical buildings crouched around their green received their shelter from a private corner of York's ancient city walls, here still true to the alignment of their Roman predecessors.

They walked for a while in the neat rose gardens at the side of the Minster and he would have very much liked to take her hand, yet dare not. A gate took them into a cobbled lane where they stood together in silence, looking at the beautiful seventeenth-century facade of the Treasurer's House. He was within an ace of putting his arm round her but still he hesitated, like an inexperienced youth.

"I can feel it strongly here," she said thoughtfully.

"What do you mean?" said Tryton, alarmed and anxious at the same time upon the thought of an announcement from her concerning them both.

"The sense of the past."

Disappointed, he did not personally think that banal sentiment worth much further exploration. It hardly matched his current preoccupation, after all.

She was anxious to see the museum, so they retraced their steps back towards Lendal. Across the river the scene was lifted by the sight of enough daffodils to satisfy even Wordsworth, their yellow heads massed along the grassy rampart backings of the city walls. Uphill were the monumental offices of the late-lamented London and North Eastern Railway Company. On the Minster side of the river, the collections of the Yorkshire Philosophical Society were kept in another classical building, its temple-like portico supported by high pillars.

This, the Yorkshire Museum, was set in ornamental gardens running down to the River Ouse, only a high railing lucky to escape re-cycling into Spitfires during the war separating them from the riverine embankment and its promenade. Next to the Museum building were the ruins of the thirteenth century St. Mary's Abbey. Beside the path leading to the YPS and its mock Athenian repository for the society's relics was another instalment of the city walls. Its conclusion in a massive and unusually--shaped watch-tower right next to the museum seemed to excite his archaeological companion. (At least he'd identified the key to this strange young lady's passions).

"Look! The Multangular Tower."

He obediently looked, but could not have called himself much moved. Nevertheless, if he was to get anywhere in her affections this was the sort of thing in which he was going to have to show some real interest.

"Imagine it...." she said. (He did try).

"A line of eight enormous bastions, fronting the river. Mounted with catapults. The south-west prospect of the Roman fortress, built to impress. This was the corner one. A statement of military power and Imperial authority in the Late Empire. The Empire of Constantine the Great, who still favoured the distant northern city which had placed him on the road to Rome and becoming the most powerful man in the known world, master of the Empire and first protector to Mother Church."

Heady stuff. Tryton watched a peacock strut across the well-clipped lawns.

"So this was the Roman city wall?"

"Oh, no. Not the city. These were the south-western defences to the military camp. The barracks of the Legion and military headquarters to the whole northern region lay behind it, to the north. There would have been a bridge leading out of the Porta Praetoria right here and then the civil city is on the south side, the other side of the river, its streets teeming with a polyglot population from all over the Empire: the Colonia Eboracensis."

Even Tryton's ponderous policeman's imagination could produce a momentary glimmer of how it might have appeared. He turned and went with her into the museum, suitably impressed. Now museums were a different thing. Tryton had never got on with museums. Old rocks and ancient bones, broken pots and mouldy relics of the long-dead. All displayed in dark wood cases under dirty glass, only a small label in faded ink from the hand of some dessicated academic to offer tersely-condescending description: "a Funerary stele.." or "Outline of a Romano-British burial in gypsum". Grotty junk.

Zuleika Macsen by contrast was in her element, so immersed in these dusty cabinets that all conversation stopped. Unlike Tryton, she could see past the infelicity of display and isolate each find, as if communing with its era. Tryton for his part was rather lost, like a sheepdog at a beef-cattle sale. He made a superficial tour of various rooms and then picked desultorily at those few cases where an exhibit gleamed or colour stood out.

There was a life-size sandstone statue of a Roman soldier which he rather liked and spent some time squaring up to; staring directly into sightless, carved eyes. ("Figure of Mars" was all the attached plaque told him of the fellow). He carefully inspected the oval shield, the crested, Greek-style helmet and the detail of the sword hilt but considered himself - a modern man in raincoat and trilby - more than a match for this petrified dandy.

Bored with this sculpture, Tryton cast around 'till another show-case caught his eye. It took him a moment to understand what he was viewing. For once the caption was informative: "Burial found in 1875 on site of booking office for new railway station. Hair of young Roman woman, fastened in a bun with two pins of Whitby jet."

Looking at the glass canister, the centuries rolled back.

240

Whoever buried this unfortunate girl had lovingly dressed and arranged her beautiful hair for the last time, holding it with a pair of black pins crafted from a material not to resume its place in fashion until that era sixteen-hundred years later, when her body was accidentally exhumed by railway 'navvies'. A hair-style not to find favour again until the reign of Queen Victoria; not until the exact era of its re-discovery under the new railway.

Yet for all the miracle of its survival it retained that sordid mockery in any remnant of the dead, the strands of hair literally lifeless and lank. What troubled him most was the colour. My, what a beauty she must have been, tripping through the shops and colonnades of the Colonia on a spring day like this, with her dangling earrings of elephant ivory catching the sun and burnishing rich auburn tresses, as she sparkled and laughed with the barrow-boys and shop-keepers along the Via Principalis.

He looked up, alone in this dark hall. Along the corridor, he caught a glimpse of Zuleika Macsen in another room, passing the door frame on her way to another cabinet – wavy, beech-red locks shimmering on her shoulders. He ran after her, his big, black policeman's shoes skidding on lethally polished parquet floors. It was all too much. First the burials in gypsum (used by the Roman bereaved in misguided belief it preserved their relatives' remains) and now the unexpected shock from this unique remnant.

Someone like her. A rich man's daughter. Gypsum and auburn.

She looked up in irritated alarm as he clumsily bore down on her; she angry at his interruption to her fascinated studies. He took her elbow regardless and began to propel her forcibly away from the display case, heading towards the main doors.

"We've got to get out of here. I can't stand it any longer. It's here and now that matters - not all this old stuff!"

"Hey! Back off, Lieutenant! What's the hurry?"

He got her out of the museum. Together they swept between the colossal stone cylinders of the pillars that supported the entrance porch and down the steps. Little children played on the grass outside while an old man with one arm of his white jacket pinned-up empty sat astride a black bicycle with freezer box attached to sell 'Walls' ice creams to strollers. Youth and Age.

The wind took her hair and distributed fine auburn skeins of it across her face, tangling across brown eyes, a delicate nose and those curving lips. He reached out and brushed a piece away from her face. Dark as African copper; spun into wire but light as cobwebs. She in turn took his hand and held it, looking straight into his eyes. Now she had made first contact, he kept it:

"You said in the car that I was causing you a problem. What is it? And what's upset you so much in there?"

"I don't know!" he said. "I'm just a policeman. Just a man. A man who goes on facts. Evidence. Things I can see and hear for myself. Not feelings. But it's feelings that are bothering me now. Feelings I think I have for you. Feelings about what has been before; is happening now; is going to happen. Even a feeling somehow that what's happened before is continuous; it's still going on and likely to happen again. Full circle. Barbarians and fire. Auburn and gypsum!"

He hadn't held a real peach since the Italian Campaign but held sufficient memory of its soft texture for nearest comparison to her complexion, a complexion colouring with doubt and excitement at his words.

"I'm not sure I understand what you mean..."

He was sure she did. But he was not going to show her the russet hair set in gypsum, pinned inside its glass canister. Such a stark and morbid illustration of his point he point-blank refused to offer.

"It doesn't matter. It's here and now that matters. I realised as soon as I saw you how strongly I feel about you. If there is time, if you are given chance, if you will humour me in my attentions, then I hope you might come to feel some affection for me, too."

She laughed out loud at his 'Old World' wooing of any New World gal patient enough to wait around for its slow expression. She it was who pulled him to her for swift administration of a succulent kiss. It lasted twice as long as the rough and once-resented one he'd first given her, going down that muddy lane from January House.

He was still grinning stupidly as they strolled hand in hand through the Museum Gardens onto Lendal Bridge. The old ice-cream seller used his one good arm to doff a dairyman's peaked cap as they passed him by, in tatty courtesy and envious approval of Love's Young Dream.

242

("Gather ye rosebuds while ye may").

No doubt they were not the first pair of lovers to walk in these gardens holding hands, but it still felt like it. Tryton was in such a happy daze he hardly knew where they went. It seemed a long time since he'd experienced such depths of infatuation, something he'd never expected to encounter ever again.

With the wind off the River Ouse and a hint of rain, temperatures in the park had dropped. He put his coat around her shoulders, realising it was the first time he'd seen her without her late fiancee's flying jacket. She shivered and pulled it closer around herself.

The rest of the afternoon passed quickly in the way that such times do, even though their recollection oft-times proves more durable, until the point came when they found themselves back at the parked car. Tryton looked at his watch and realised there were two pressing duties left to be fulfilled that day and there was barely time for either. This young woman to whom his commitment and allegiance had now become absolute must be returned safe to the market town thirty-miles away where he'd collected her; then Superintendent Maister across in Hull must have his Jowett Javelin back before he left work that evening.

They set wheels to road at once and travelled quickly. Traffic on the way back was light and Tryton set a good average. Rolling down into Beverley along the York Road they passed the racecourse and crossed the Westwood, an area of open common land where cattle and sheep owned by the Freemen and Pasture Masters of Beverley graze at will.

In the middle of these commons Tryton had to brake sharply to a halt to avoid collision with a black and white heifer blundering onto the roadway with bovine complacency. Waiting for the animal to cross, a large lorry came up and stopped right behind them. Inside the car they could hear the loud tick-over of its engine and smell the diesel fumes.

It was a yellow lorry.

The road cleared of livestock, they set off again, laughing and joking, to run without further incident down off the Westwood and into the town.

At the junction of York Road and North Bar Without, Tryton had to stop again to give way to traffic coming from the right, out of the mediaeval archway of the North Bar itself. Waiting there at the traffic lights, next to the 'Rose and Crown' public house, he saw in his mirror the lorry catching him up again. He heard its brakes screeching as they brought the heavy vehicle to a halt. Fortunately, it did stop and Tryton returned his attention to traffic on North Bar Without, looking for a gap where he could pull out upon the authority of a green light.

Still waiting on a red, he heard the clunk of gears engaging from the truck behind. Checking his rear-view mirror he saw its enormous radiator grille move forward quite slowly and deliberately and almost at once felt his own car shudder as the lorry struck it. There was the sound of rending metal and the glass of the Jowett's twin, rear opera-windows immediately turned to fragments, green shards showering onto the empty back seat.

"What the hell is he playing at......?"

Tryton had barely turned round to look before the lorry disengaged, reversing slowly away with the Jowett's bumper still entangled in its own, violently dragged from its rightful attachments.

A few feet back from the now-less streamlined motor car, the negligent oaf at the wheel of this juggernaut stopped as if here was fit and proper place to await the righteous indignation of a motorist. However, Tryton had hardly opened his driver's door to offer it than the lorry moved forward again and, with renewed force, quite deliberately rammed the Jowett a second time, shunting the disintegrating car across the 'Give-Way' lines where it rested and right into the path of an equally-new Vauxhall Wyvern emerging from North Bar. This vehicle's lateral impact with the offside wing of the Jowett slewed the policeman's car around and partially onto the pavement in front of the 'Rose and Crown'.

"Get out, Get out!" Tryton yelled at his terrified passenger where she lay, half on the seat and half in the footwell. Upon his words she had the door open and was gone, the murderous intent of the lorry driver recognised in her mind as quickly as in his.

244

Tryton for all his warning was not so prompt in his own response and the yellow quarry truck slammed into the tortured sheet metal of Maisters' pride and joy for a third time, now entirely crushing the boot and rear passenger accommodation. Tryton was saved by his earlier half-opening of the drivers door. If he'd left this preparatory act any later, his escape hatch would have become jammed in the distorting bodyshell, denying release. He tumbled out onto the hard road at the momentary mercy of the truck driver, before getting up and sprinting for the pavement.

Disappointed in its aim of personal injury, the lorry executed a smart three-point turn in the roadway, faster than its bulk might have been expected to allow. The rear-mounted fuel tank of the Jowett ruptured in the impacts and spilt its rationed contents all over the carriageway. Petrol shimmered darkly in the sun, rainbow-coloured.

The lorry was now facing back up the York Road, set for escape into the country, but its still-hidden driver - from high in his cab - administered one last contemptuous coup de grace, flicking his burning cigarette down into the spreading pool of petroleum. The Jowett exploded at once, sending pedestrians hurrying for cover. As the yellow dump-truck stormed away through the smoke, an armoured car immune to the flames, Tryton marked the signwriting on its door: A black tower; beneath it, the lettering: "BAYNARDS BRITISH GYPSUM WORKS".

A workman in blue dungarees and a check shirt pulled Tryton through the front door of the pub for safety as the incineration of the Jowett reached its peak: "Are you all right mate? That bastard damn near killed you! Did you get his number?"

"No, but he nearly got mine!"

The landlord came up and wanted to offer him a brandy but Tryton was anxious to turn all this well-meant kindness aside and check on Miss Macsen, presumably fled to her lodgings adjacent.

"Do you have a telephone I can use?"

"Yes, of course. There's one right behind the bar. You must phone the police."

"Oh, don't worry! That's exactly what I'm going to do."

He went alone through the bar and into a corridor where the telephone was. The operator put him through to the switchboard at Central straightaway.

"Hullo, Hull City Police…"

"Hello …er…. can I speak to Superintendent Maister please, in C.I.D"

"One moment please, trying to connect you…." she said.

There was a pause and then a voice he did not recognise at first: "Hello. C.I.D. Superintendent Rivett speaking. Can I help you?"

"Er….yes. I was hoping to speak to Superintendent Maister. Is he in this afternoon?"

"No he's not. Superintendent Maister is unwell and has taken some leave. I think he's gone on a motoring holiday in Scotland. I am dealing with all his work now. To whom am I speaking...?"

Tryton dropped the receiver and let it dangle on its black curly cord against a brown row of "Bass" beer bottles behind the bar. He could hear a voice crackling from the speaker but did not pick it up again. With the name applied, the voice was recognised. He knew Rivett well enough - late ornament of the Special Branch department. Secretive and self-important. Not the sort of man to run a knockabout C.I.D. office. His usual location was the passenger terminal at Hull docks. All rubber heels and Primitive Methodism. Enough to make anyone want to take sick leave.

In a matter of minutes, what had been the happiest afternoon enjoyed for years had gone horribly sour. This business with the Baynards and the pavement was not going to go away, he realised. Someone had tried to kill him in a lorry belonging to the Baynards. Maister had suddenly been removed in suspicious circumstances and could hardly be touring the Trossachs in the burnt-out hulk now resting on the pavement right outside this pub. Special Branch had moved in. It all added up: suddenly things were getting really serious.

The driver of the damaged Vauxhall Wyvern, lucky not to have suffered total destruction of his dented machine from the exploding Jowett, was celebrating his relative good fortune in the front bar. Having just downed his second free brandy on the hospitality of the licensee, he saw Tryton making his way back to the front door.

"Did you get through to the police?"

"Yes, I did."

"What did they say?"

"They're sending someone down."

Leaving the pub, he turned left and walked calmly up North Bar Without, his departure covered by a crowd of excited sightseers gathering at the traffic lights to inspect the still-smouldering remains of Maister's car. As he got to Miss Macsen's lodgings, a fire engine went thundering by, bell ringing tinnily.

He knocked at the door and was let in by Mrs Holtby.

"Where is she?"

"Upstairs. What's going on out there? What have you been up to? She's come in upset, in a terrible state."

"There's been a bit of an accident by North Bar. Can I pop up and see her?"

The old-fashioned stairs were narrow and irregular, their edges rounded by a stiff carpet gripped tightly by brass stair rods. Halfway up there was a slight dog leg in the passageway as they changed direction. He slipped his raincoat off as he climbed, the shoulders of his jacket setting a row of be-ribboned war-medals, framed behind glass on the staircase wall, all a-swinging. On a tiny landing, a wooden door to his left was firmly shut.

"Next landing" shouted Mrs Holtby watching from below, before she returned to the lively children busy dismantling her front sitting-room.

The second stairs were even steeper than the first. Clearly designed for servants whose exertions and convenience were immaterial to the owners. At the top a low balcony overlooked the whole stairwell. Another door as agricultural as the first. Braced planking and gothic hinges. It was ajar and he pushed it open.

"Zuleika?"

It was a small garret with low ceilinqs, lit by a dormer window. Any claustrophobia from this lack of head-room was defrayed by cream walls, white lace, and the spring sunlight streaming through one of those horizontally-sliding sash windows peculiar to East Yorkshire. He closed the door behind him and set the latch securely on its 'sneck' then slid the raincoat and trilby hat he was carrying onto a bow-backed chair, upholstered with cream and maroon 'regency stripes'.

She lay upon her coverlet in an attitude suggestive of distress and despair.

247

For a moment endowed as idealised vision; lovely yet unrelated to the unconventional young American woman whose entrance into his life shook familiar certainties to their foundation. Facial bone structure, texture of skin and weft of hair; all conspired in spectacular but inexpressible fashion to create a living being he found irresistible. Perhaps more significant than these more definable aspects however, her colourings were manifestations of spirit, health and beauty. If their record here as written inventory seems ponderous, to eye and mind they were features pleasurably recorded in fractions of time.

If sheen of auburn and sculptured lips could escape the repressive envelope of old flying jacket, 'sensible' skirt and a shapeless woollen hat to entrance him with their message, then how was she in garb less tom-boyish, less work-a-day practical, more crafted to entice? The sun-dress she'd worn on this unseasonally-warm spring day had been a revelation in every sense. She was gorgeous.

Allowed only a moment in which to etch these clues of form and curve into his lifelong recollection, his entry into the room caused her to sit up with a start: "Oh, Michael, you made it! Are you alright?"

For an instant he wondered if she meant him, or whether some delusion seized her; so that it was another Michael who slid unseen into the room between them, his USAF flying jacket freshly-singed where he'd forced his way out through the shattered perspex canopy of a burning Fortress about to fall to earth.

"Yes, I'm fine. How about you?"

Those eyes were uncharacteristically red-rimmed. For all her beauty, he'd thought her a harder nut than this to crack. That brittleness of tone and sharpness of response which cinema-going taught him was American Woman seemed such a thin veneer in her case, after all that he'd seen.

At the age of twenty-eight, Tryton thought himself an old man prematurely aged in outlook and manner; first by a war which took his youth from him and then by a new occupation where cynicism became contagious disease. It was this self-realisation which made him so astonished she would embrace him, a gnarled tree reverential at her flower-like newness.

Yet the years between them were not that many, implacable as the gap between age and beauty can so often seem. For all his weary experience Tryton still retained a degree of innocence, if only in his limited understanding of what might sometimes drive a younger woman to older men.

There are some men that almost worship their women, that make of their small-town Helen some sort of a deity. Hardly a sound basis for two human beings to know and love one another, with all their failings, but perhaps this Michael Tryton could be forgiven his momentary aberration in that direction, here in that upper room filled with light and lace, fresh from a burning car. If the gold of late afternoon pouring through the transom made her his goddess, then he would soon know her as woman. (As he'd first said he would, if only he remembered).

"Michael! I didn't leave you ...I don't want you to think I was a coward or that I deserted you", she pleaded: "That driver was out to kill us. I thought that if I got back here O.K. you'd figure where I'd gone. If I'd hung around at the scene and there were others with him out on the sidewalk, then I'd be a sitting duck. I'm so glad you're O.K. Yes, I was terrified, but I did not leave you!"

He met her and held her as she rose up to implore his acceptance:

"It's alright. I know. It's exactly what I meant you to do."

Now supporting her, together they sank back into pillows and down. Here and now was the moment. Desire was absolute and would brook no damming. Seven years of widowed celibacy, imposed by already-outdated moral principle and his deliberate evasion of those few opportunities which might have unleashed the fires of temptation, fell away like blown ash. He tore at her clothing.

Her hunger was as great as his. Astonishment at her initiatives soon ceased to register. What she did to him, what she let him do to her.

Now confident of reciprocation for a suppressed passion which even until that afternoon her brittle scorn sought to defy, he now worked quickly but blindly on shoulder straps and fabric buttons running down her back.

Unabashed at his assault, she launched her own attack with nimble fingers that brooked no opposition from heavy fixings and durable clothing chosen in a time of austerity by a young widower who'd forgotten how to dress for the liking of women. With all obstacles to inhibition jettisoned; their collective impetus not diminished but inflamed, he drove into her with cathartic vigour.

Afterwards they lay in lace and studied the struts and coves of the low ceiling.

"Mrs. Holtby would have a fit" giggled Zuleika. He rolled over and stroked her face, the auburn threads falling over her forehead and down into her mouth.

"In my flat in Hull, there's a false panel in the ceiling where I keep an old Webley service revolver in a box along with some ammunition. After this afternoon, I think I'm going to have to retrieve it. We're both of us going to need its protection!"

"Then all the Councillors were so blinded that, as a protection to their country, they sealed its doom by inviting in amongst them, like wolves into the sheepfold, the fierce and impious Saxons, a race hateful both to God and to men, to repel the invasions of the Northern nations."

Gildas, son of Cau (Cleric and historian, sixth century AD): "De Excidio Britanniae" - The Destruction of Britain.

XII

There was a road that led straight up from the villa into the old hills, up onto the escarpment that looked out on its estates and over the slow, brown river.

Straight as a legionary javelin it ran to the foot of a steep bank where a few miserable Celtic huts huddled beside a stiff climb. Although many local roads offered no more surface than compacted gravel, this incline had at one time been carefully paved with cut blocks of local limestone, meant to retain a surface against the wash-away effect of those sacred water spouts which name the hill.

Pausing halfway-up to give respite to legs and lungs, Candidus turned away from the slope to look back at the countryside spread out like the embroidery in a worked quilt below him. Rich greens and golds in the cultivated fields of the Januarian lands gave way to the marshy margins edging the estuary. The great roaring wood made one shapeless black clump in the centre of the sandy plain; white villa walls and orange-tiled rooftops angular beside it.

In the orchards next to the house, smoke still rose from what they called 'grund hausen' in the native tongue of the foederati, primitive structures dug deep into the earth and crudely-roofed with bracken and branches. It still remained matter for disbelief that Januarius could happily contemplate the proximity to the house of these, his mercenaries. What the true Roman would prefer to call the laeti were salaried protectors, yet blood brother to the same mindless murderers who'd so cruelly destroyed the Imperial possession upon the farthermost bank.

Candidus had not shrunk from boldly arguing this ethical point with him during their visit to the haven that afternoon. Yet, whilst sincerely grieving for his friends across the river, if there was one risk over which the patrician landowner seemed least troubled, it was the little matter of his chosen gate-guardians.

Januarius the magistrate quite calmly relied on precedent, pointing out with justification how old and reliable a tradition it was in Roman military affairs to employ the defeated or captured enemy as low-grade expendable forces to fight their own kind:

"Why should not a rich man like me buy in some extra protection? You have seen for yourself - the navy can't save us!"

252

That they should camp by the house seemed obvious practical requirement if protection of the villa and its inhabitants was the main focus to their role and duties. Suddenly the words of Januarius last night in the garden came back to him: "Have the hounds stood to." So that was what he'd meant. The Frisians in the orchard.

'Hounds' he'd called them and so he surely treated them, like a farmer his guard dogs. Januarius laughed at little now but he did laugh at Candidus's fears. Even if 'Foederati' was a term he pointedly refused to employ; not when the loyalty of these "allies" was so dependant on the regular grant of Roman silver – the confiscated dinner services of those unfortunates whom Januarius had proscribed in his court, chopped into crude triangles of bullion that defiled the silversmith's craft which once had wrought them, then handed over to unthinking barbarians as worthless treasure.

Candidus was yet to recover from his embarrassment at this morning's flight into the garden and from there into the house; still clutching the blonde infant he'd meant to rescue but whose recovery was sole reason why the Germans of Januarius pursued him so angrily; straight into the flabby arms of the estate bailiff himself.

Protected from the anger of these warriors by the intervention of this portly freeman, a bunch of keys his only weapon, Candidus was left shamefaced to acknowledge their own side of the misunderstanding.

As the bailiff gently put it to him afterwards: "Even the Saxons love their children." Their son being returned to the father with much sign language of apology and good intent on both sides, the Saxons returned quietly to their camp amongst the apple trees and Candidus to his place in the house.

Chastened by his experience but still uneasy over the character of their protectors, that's why he tried so fruitlessly to air the same ethical point with Januarius when Candidus went by litter with the magistrate into the town that afternoon. (A trip he took as much to avoid the sniggers of the household staff as provide argumentative company for their master, a man of the people keen to get around his area for up-to-date reports on last night's shocking events).

253

At Petuaria there was an air of nervous excitement to permeate its mean streets. Down at the haven they relied on wooden walkways to negotiate the mud banks and reed beds bordering that serpentine, mud-lined trench to which their inlet channel is reduced once the tide is out. Here they found great military activity being displayed amongst the decrepit installations of the British Fleet.

Offshore, in Petuaria Roads, the whole complement of the Abus Squadron rode at anchor in a state of full readiness and high alert. A total of two triremes and five 'Pictae', the green deep-sea patrol craft, bobbed on a fast-turning tide with all flags of commission shown and catapults run out or ballistae unsheeted. A large jolly-boat was busy shipping groups of armed marines out to these vessels from the far landing. It was, of course, all far too late. That ancient Etruscan rhyme about stable doors and bolting horses came afresh into his mind.

They walked along and found themselves on a proper jetty, towering high above the filthy inlet. An excited crowd of dockers, fishermen, mariners, and casual labourers, with a sprinkling of townsfolk, was peering over its edge at something down in the channel below them. The sweaty, stinking mob parted slightly on the arrival of the magistrate, keen to let him through. It was obvious how willing they were to acknowledge and respect his authority, matter of note in itself from such a collection of hard-cases. From where they were standing, it was quite a way down from the top of the walkway to low water far below.

To their immediate right was a sixth patrol craft, its busy decks a mass of sheets, eyes and rigging. From this ship, one slack rope ran from its curved stem across to a blackened vessel, newly-towed into the haven. Its target was a long, low, alien ship of little draught with a tall curving prow and stern post to match.

There was no sail that Candidus could see and neither was there decking, only row upon row of benches. The whole ship was black; black not just with the bitumen in which it was painted from stem to stern (to caulk its joints and seal its timbers) but black from burning; black from fire. Every oar - bar one or two - was missing but all its crew lay rigid; tumbled in the twisted postures of death on the bottom planks of their ship, each one of them as dark and scorched as their transport.

254

As if 'twere needed, Januarius must point out these horribly charred and mangled corpses. He did so with such delicate distaste as befitted a gentleman but with absolutely no pity:

"Greek fire. The most terrifying weapon of our navies. A clever mixture of sulphur, nitre, naptha and black pitch. Very effective...but its technical superiority has gained us absolutely nothing at all. Science and engineering cannot save us from barbarism, Flavius. Killing a few rats won't rebuild the house of Julius Protius or resurrect my friend...."

They moved from this tawdry trophy of war and walked along the quayside to where marines were assembling under a limp standard. A stout figure in a cuirass and helmet type more appropriate to the Athenian Wars than any modern combat conditions came swaggering towards them, calling out loudly to the magistrate in ostentatious greeting. It had to be the Praefectus Trimalchio. Today, even Januarius could not hide his disdain for this spherical popinjay, whose departure into last night's darkness had prompted such overwrought affectations of concern at the time but now bred only coldness.

"Ah, Trimalchio! Got home alright then, last night, did we?"

"What? Oh, yes. No trouble at all, thank you. Have you seen the Frisians, here? Have you seen their ship?"

"Oh, that thing. Yes, we have," said Januarius flatly.

"Twelve dead, I counted" boasted Trimalchio, impervious self-confidence his natural protection against criticism. Since it did not register, it would not trouble him that Januarius was so much less than impressed. Skin like a rhinoceros.

"As many as that?" queried Januarius coldly.

"At least! Plenty more went overboard. Died like flies. They'll not be troubling us again. Word will get back to their own. My men have done well. We are about to begin a major sweep of the estuary. Hunt the rest of them down. No hiding place."

In the daylight and standing before them, Candidus realised how short and round this Trimalchio really was. A little, self-important sea-going barrel. In any other context he could have been an ideal figure of fun but Januarius was past being amused:

"And what of the House of Julius Protius, then? What's become of my dear friend and all his staff? Men, women and children. The painted house and the neat farms. The granaries and tanneries which supply the Legion. How are they all on this triumphant afternoon for our Great Fleet?"

Even a bumptious miniature admiral like Trimalchio had to acknowledge the scale of tragedy occurring under cover of last night's darkness. In a fleet where internal rivalries and faction-fighting gave insecure commanders the need to report the performance of all their officers as "excellent", Trimalchio's distant master in far-away Portus Dubris would only damn him with the faint praise of "above average"; implicit warning of his competence. The Praefectus Reliquationis Classis crumpled palpably. Even his conscience was pricked. He looked down at his pale blue, doe-skin boots, as if suddenly concerned about the black mud spattering their fronts:

"I'm sorry, Marcus Januarius! What can I say? There was nothing we could do. I just don't know how the sea-wolves do it. It's like they see in the dark. To survive a crossing of the German Ocean is surely achievement enough. Then they find their way into our estuary. They navigate the full length of the central channel, sandbars and all, without ever running aground. Their ships have such a shallow draught compared with ours, I think they just slide over the top of everything. When they get to where they want to be, they pull right up onto the shore and camouflage them with bushes and trees. Then.... a wait for nightfall. When set on shore, there's no stopping them... like wild beasts let loose! When they find the house of Julius Protius, they kill everything living then take what they want - mainly just gold and silver; jewellery, plates and cutlery. Next, they torch the main house which, by accident or design, spreads to all the outbuildings. Job done, they disappear. Hit and run. The usual thing – except this time, at least, we got them! On the homeward run, I know…"

Contrition could not save him now. They could both see the magistrate bridling already at this litany of excuses, as Trimalchio strained all the harder:

"Yes, I'm really sorry... Gods! I know, it's no compensation, but if only we'd caught them alive... precious Gods! Revenge might have been sweeter, even on brutal primitives like these; on creatures which value no-one's life, not even their own. I swear to you, Januarius, the very next lot we catch alive, I'll crucify them all myself, personally; everyone; one-by-one; so that their nailed bones are the first thing their cursed brothers see on making landfall at the farthermost point!"

"Crucifixion! What? Trimalchio, don't ever even mention that idea in front of the Bishop of Eboracum! With magisterial powers himself, he'll have us all proscribed! And what will it gain us, anyway? More rats will come! And never mind them, what of my honest friend? The Procurator for all those lands between the southern bank and Lindum Coloniae. What of Julius Protius?"

"Januarius, my dear fellow, how can I tell you? Murdered in his own home and cremated on the spot by his own killers in the ruins. A man of duty dying in the performance of his public office. An honourable death!"

"Don't give me that load of old Stoic rubbish. Bugger duty! He died alone in that wonderful old house, as it burned around his ears, because you and your men haven't got the wit or the balls to keep these murdering Frisian bastards off our shores! He died a miserable death but deserved so much better. He died serving a state which hasn't got the money, hasn't got the brains, and hasn't got the moral courage to stand up against these people. Something has got to be done!"

Januarius turned and stalked away, back to the town. As with last night, Candidus marked a new posture in him, even as he strode away, in the hint of a stoop which hadn't been there before. The stance of a man for whom worry, strain, and the whiff of defeat had become overpowering features of his life.

Their journey back to the villa together was an uncomfortable one. As the news spread, the atmosphere became that of a house in mourning. Candidus' original plan (to spend the rest of the afternoon hunting out the pretty young serving-girl noticed yesterday) had become acknowledged, even by his flexible standards, as inappropriate to the circumstances and risking tactless breach of hospitality received. Determined to escape all this gloom through other remedy, he instead went for a solitary stroll in the country, which is what brought him to Spout Hill.

257

Where the road crested the escarpment top, someone had set up a small altar, dedicated to the Spirit of the Place. To a water goddess, no doubt. Its formula wording was almost illegible, worn away by time, wind and weather and probably defaced with disapproval by some passing Christian, but you could still guess the sentiments. It was a good place to stop and think and, if you were the religious type, to pray. Whoever you prayed to. Candidus was not usually the religious type but he certainly did need time and space to think. He laid a nominal offertory coin amongst the fresh flowers laid by passers-by upon the altar top before becoming deliberately thoughtful and still.

Tomorrow, it was essential he moved on. The finding of his master's daughter, the wife of Januarius, had become an overriding priority. She was the key. With barbarian raids heating up the countryside there was suddenly an extra edge of urgency to the mission. He had little idea where to start, although the city of Eboracum originally seemed first and obvious choice. However, a chance comment overheard from one of the kitchen staff suggested Januarius had a sister at Derventio, a small town to the north-east but still within the Canton of Parisii.

This intuitive idea, that the wife might have gone off (as wives do) to her sister-in-law's, offered him a specific line of enquiry probably more worth pursuit than any speculative descent into the metropolitan fleshpots of Eboracum. Her notable absence coupled with the evasion of Januarius; his inability to offer even the most prosaic excuse for an absent wife; all hinted at domestic discord beyond the usual strain of marital strife. If that were right, then all the more reason to discover it, as the Vicarius in his paternal priorities would be bound to expect of any officer sent out under his commission.

His mind made up, Candidus descended from the hill and made one more visit to the town; the last (he hoped) before he came this way again one final time: en route south via Lindum Coloniae for the welcome first sight of Londinium's walls and home.

With a few pence he'd avoided losing, a goat's bladder tied with twine and filled with blood left over from the sacrifice was listed amongst his essential purchases for the journey.

Its vendor was identified in the ruinous priest from the crumbling temple to Mars Thincsus, sited for custom right outside the soldiers' compound, who offered him luck and health in a fulsome blessing marred only by the incoherence of drink, before pocketing the price and heading straight for the wine shop.

On his return to the villa that evening, Candidus loudly misinformed his host of how the promptings of duty led him. He laid a false trail in the shape of a voiced intention to head due north after first visiting Eboracum. Such conscientiousness in a civil servant Januarius could only applaud, but it did demand the offer of replacement money for the journey and a good horse to speed his errand. These were presents Candidus had frankly expected from his new patron and gifts which, once offered, he was more than ready to accept.

The night was peaceful, happily without repeating those bloody incidents of its predecessor. No doubt the whole fleet was beating up and down the moonlit river in fear of any repetition. In the morning Candidus woke thoroughly refreshed and ready to continue his mission, but for the customary ache in an old wound.

He walked down to the stables with Januarius and the bailiff to inspect a blue roan with a white star and a bottle-green ex-Army saddle cloth which was to be his mount. A blanket roll and a small bag slung onto the back amounted to his only preparations before it was time to leave, with repeated thanks and invocations to the goddess Fortuna given and received on both sides.

As he rode out of the yard and turned in the saddle for one last cheery wave to the magistrate and his servant, Candidus noted the distant figure of Cicerius Felix, the mining engineer, standing with the two gladiators away on the verandah steps beside an opposite wing of the Januarian villa.

He was glad to be out of its oppressive atmosphere, he realised, and the open road stretched invitingly ahead of him. Conforming to his publicly and repeatedly-voiced itinerary, he continued doggedly west until he reached the junction where another narrower road split off and headed north-east, up onto the west-facing edge of that same high ground to whose south Petuaria lay.

If followed for the next thirty one miles, then Derventio lay this way, but taking early diversion towards it from here would be just too obvious. He looked around him. Each direction was empty of travellers but he retained his suspicions and so returned to the Eboracum spur which he still followed for a while yet. Then, after only a mile or two of committing himself to this route, he once again left the surfaced way to take his horse into the uncultivated scrub increasingly encroaching onto the neglected ditches parallel to the road.

Beyond the scrub, wild woodland began, full of bears and wolves no doubt. It was into this cover that he nevertheless rode before finally dismounting. From here there was a good view of the main road without fear of himself being detected. Candidus was a patient man and he was happy to find his mare to be of similar character. He shared an apple with the beast much like one would do with a child and an hour passed pleasantly.

In that time there had been no other travellers on the road at all, but then there suddenly came the beat of hooves.

Two horses.

Candidus pressed a finger to the mouth of his own to impress upon the animal the need for quiet. It all reminded him of his younger days, out on cavalry patrol.

Two riders came thundering past. The two German gladiators. Tooled-up with leather jerkins and a long sword on each belt. Looking for him, of that Candidus had no doubt. The private certainty it was they who'd felled him in the old theatre on his first night at Petuaria had been with him for some time.

He let them go by and then took his bag off the back of the horse, leaving the blanket roll still in place for effect. From the bag he took the goats' bladder which, thankfully, had not leaked. The twine was unwound and its sanguinary contents emptied all over the saddle area.

This done, he shouted in the ear of the astonished animal and gave a stinging slap to its broad rump to send it galloping in terror all the way back to Petuaria. He was confident that instinct would guide this panic-stricken beast unerringly back to the Villa of the Januarii; its foam-flecked and rolling-eyed arrival in the yard coupled with convincing bloody evidence of his wished-for death (whether at the hands of gladiators, bandits, wolves or bears) sufficient to ensure no further pursuit.

To those who'd commissioned his death, he'd be as good as dead.

The only defect in this plan lay in the loss of the horse, which would turn one day's hard-riding into a full two days on foot. If it shook off the two Germans then even this inconvenience would be worthwhile, so Candidus began his walk back in good spirits. He still kept to the overgrown edges of the highway for fear the two horsemen might return and catch him on foot in the open. He still lacked any weapon and generally felt extremely vulnerable as a result. Wild animals were as much to be feared as robbers.

As a result, it took him another hour to get back to the Derventio turn-off but at least from hereon in he could be satisfied that every step was in the right direction: North.

By and large this was a sparsely-inhabited area, although he was aware that the first ten miles or so of this road would run through enclosed estates of comparable standing to the Villa Januarii. The magistrate's friends and neighbours. The 'country set' - any of them capable of denouncing or arresting him, if spotted. Sometimes even the houses themselves could be seen, set high above the route amongst huge fields for industrialised agriculture, but Candidus was determined not to be observed by anyone – not even the chain-gangs of slaves that worked these prairies or the scattered fieldworkers he saw from a distance. He continued to keep close to the scrub and woodland bordering the highway.

By midday, he felt he'd made enough progress to justify a rest halt, so found himself a fallen tree upon which to recline with a good view of the way he'd come. The lack of traffic was hardly surprising, in view of the route's increasing isolation, but there was now something else on the road, heading the same way as he. He heard it before he saw it - a large, oblong mass which rumbled, creaked and tinkled. An enormous four-wheeled wagon with a leather cover, drawn by one white ox and a heavy horse.

Obscured by the foliage of his tree, Candidus watched the lumbering approach of this juggernaut with fascination. Too big to be the usual pedlar's cart but too chaotically-hung with metal oddments, pennants, streamers and articles of cookware to pass muster as an army supply wagon, its function out here in the wilds was hard to guess.

Its driver sat high in the front upon a bench which raised him nearly to the roof of the wagon. A giant of a man with a polished brown head but a thick beard reaching square to his chest, he wore the leather apron of an artisan and the distinctive bronze plate of an army discharge certificate hung on cords from his tree-like neck. It was probably this latter detail which gave Candidus enough confidence to emerge from his vantage point in the trees and approach the roadway in time to greet the vehicle.

The great ox and the massive horse pulled up on the direction of their owner with that slow patience which went with their size. The man who held their reins was proportionate to these beasts in bulk and power - doubtless what made him confident enough to show no concern when a pedestrian suddenly appeared out of the trees in the middle of nowhere. Blunt but friendly in greeting, Candidus soon established Derventio as his destination and extracted the offer of a lift. Better to ride than to walk. (It might also give him cover and protection against two hired-killers seemingly sent after the Governors' enquiry agent by a Januarius until recently so anxious over his health).

Taranis was a travelling armourer and sword-smith, this overloaded cart his mobile workshop. Some clue as to the reason for his obviously-honourable discharge from the armed service of his Emperor might lie in the complete absence of a left leg. (In so far as Roman medicine differed from the Greek, it was in their particular enthusiasm for amputation as an efficient cure for most wounds). At least they had something in common for the journey, these two cast-offs from the military, although Candidus had once more reverted to a false identity in the interests of his mission and was not keen to reveal factual details of his own Army career.

The trade of this wayfaring smith lay at the gates of garrison towns where he earned a decent living from the repair or replacement of those weapons and military equipment which an increasingly-shaky commissariat were unable to deliver through official channels.

Most of the Imperial weapons factories – fabricae - lay in Gaul, Hispania and Italia, and their declining outputs of helmets, swords, and body armour were increasingly-diverted to the Rhine and Danube frontiers alone. That and the uncertainties of sea freight meant the handful of state-designated manufactories in Britain were left unable to meet the demands which combat, corrosion, and carelessness imposed upon the provincial army.

His solitary journeying made the sociable Taranis glad of company on the way and like many souls more interested in speaking of themselves than troubling their listener for personal contribution. This approach suited Candidus well. Comfortable on the bench beside the driver, Candidus rested his back on an enormous wooden and leather bellows which presumably ventilated the smith's fire, and listened to his tales. Twisting his head he could see back through the wagon and the racks of tools, swords and spearheads which, together with the insanitary jumble of itinerant bachelor living, completely filled it. It was then that he nearly choked on his tongue, struggling for an appropriate deity to justify such scared astonishment:

"May the Unknown God protect us! Taranis, there is a bear in close pursuit. Taller than a man. He's right behind the wagon!"

The smith was unmoved by this news and simply gave a flick of the reins to the unmatched pair that pulled them:

"Settle yourself, comrade. He's chained to the rear axle and you're quite safe. Consider him part of the crew. His name is 'Darius' and he's been with me for these two years gone, ever since the circus-master who imported him and owed me the price of ten short swords, two tridents, and a lot of sharpening work, finally went out of business along with all the local gladiators. Don't worry about him. Just don't go round the back of the wagon in the dark, that's all. Otherwise, he won't harm a fly, not unless it's threatening to land on me that is! A man in my occupation, a travelling arms dealer with one leg, he needs that sort of protection. I'll tell you, that bear's been a handy old thing to have around on more than one occasion, has good old Darius."

With this reassurance Candidus recovered his relaxation. The bear with a famous name was just a fellow traveller.

Study of the terrain through which they passed, together with amiable conversation, soon became their only pastime. (To step off the wagon and jog alongside was no longer appealing alternative).

Truth be told, he considered this countryside rather dreary. Too flat and lifeless for his taste, with too few trees. No running water to add movement. The streams in the grassy bottoms of the hollow chalk valleys mostly ran underground while the amorphous, rounded sides that rose around them were decorated with a mean black scrub ideal for ambush. Sinister, he found it.

Where it could, the road kept to the highest ground, engineered as it was by soldiers with tactical purpose in mind rather than the easy passage of civilians. Here the only virtue in the landscape was revealed in long-range views exciting in their distance and far-off detail. A patrol commander's dream. The drama of these high places had obviously commended them similarly to the ancients, for innumerable cairns and burial mounds of the chiefs and mighty amongst the Parisii and their precursors studded the skyline on this ridgeway. Dim, distant, and deceased ancestors to Marcus Ulpius Januarius crouched in their sleep of centuries.

The bear was growling now, its insistent but quiet statement of an undiagnosed irritation. Taranis stopped his wagon and slid down its side with a practised ease which belied his handicap. The man moved surprisingly well unsupported and either used a spear shaft or the cart itself when any adjustment to stability was required. Candidus noted how at all times he carried an old-fashioned short sword held in a scabbard pulled high on his chest.

First the black, shaggy beast whose complaint had caused the halt was fed and then it was the turn of the two hauliers in front. In the case of the bear, this was a messy business involving several hunks of not-so-fresh meat extracted from a blood-soaked bag and lobbed to a point as far away from the wagon as its long chain would safely extend.

Travelling at a carters' pace, they were not to see Derventio that day.

The night was spent with the wagon pulled into the rectangular turf enclosure of a soldiers' marching-camp, its grassy mounds constructed hundreds of years ago in some now-forgotten campaign yet still used from time to time for their original purpose by the odd passing detachment.

Even for a night, the military would in handbook-fashion erect a palisade of spears to crown these works, but the armourer and his fellow traveller were protected only by the height of walls and an unblocked gate within this green castra. All the more reason to appreciate a rack of swords and a bad-tempered bear for company. A fire might have provided traditional focus for their bivouac and its warmth for cooking but Taranis would not allow it. Rather he preferred a whiff of bear to keep the wild things off, whilst the unrent cloak of black night hid them from unwanted human attention.

Candidus slept surprisingly well sprawled in the wagon, his rest disturbed only by the snoring of the smith and the occasional prowling growlings of the chained bear outside. As the sun rose, they broke their encampment early and took to the road again. It was not till afternoon that they saw Derventio ahead, after a zig-zagged descent from the high ground to approach the town over a level plain of cultivated lands. The appearance of roadside tombs and stone memorials signalled the urban limits.

Any first view of Derventio when arriving from the south was never its most appealing prospect, the smoke and debris of manufacturing industry hanging wraith-like round the functional long-houses that are both home and workshop to the craftsmen occupying this area. Pottery and worked metal the principal output of these small factories, supplying an insatiable market extending as far as the northern frontier itself and beyond into debatable lands. As their wagon wheels sank into the hard-packed clinker surfacing its streets, Candidus wondered why a town like this should need the skills of yet another travelling metal-worker. Looking around him at the open-air foundries, short answer would seem to lie in the merely domestic creations of these artisans; the uncanny abilities of a wayfaring sword-smith falling into the category of practised magic by comparison.

Having passed through the grid of alleyways, single-storey houses, sheds, barns, sooty kilns and metal workings which mars the southern end of Derventio, their arrival at the river which gives its name to the town opened out more picturesque views. Founded on broad cut-waters of precise masonry, a strong bridge of massive timbers carries the road over the river to an unassuming collection of older dwellings that cling to the shelter of a steep hill, almost a cliff.

Above them all; bridge, river and town; were the stern grey curtain walls and towers of the garrison fort. Here was a rightness of plan, an architectural structure and scale, a balance of domesticity and temporal power, which together make the whole scene both interesting and comforting at the same time. A sense of the reassuring continuity of certain essentials in human existence; of tradition and duty, home and hearth, labour and nature all rolled up into one. Candidus realised with a jolt from his sense of approval that he must be getting old.

Trumpets rang in the fort and Taranis looked across at Candidus with an unspoken but shared recognition of once-sustaining routine. Two damaged men whose entire working lives had once been governed by such calls, now cast out into a shiftless world to find their own personal corners of order.

Their groaning wagon rolled across the uncomplaining bridge and onto the northern bank. A short drag up the hill found open land between the ditches protecting the southern gatehouse to the fort and the first buildings of the town where it could finally be parked. The ox and horse were tethered nearby with forage, showing an astounding placidity at such proximity to their brother, the bear, whilst Taranis assembled his camp and portable smithy before a fast-accumulating crowd of onlookers.

In the meantime, Candidus slipped back down the hill into the old town for his by-now customary reconnaissance. He soon came to the conclusion that he rather liked Derventio. A raffish, racey cavalry town where the horse was king and bright steels with polished alloys were forged and crafted to adorn the swaggering troopers of its resident garrison:

The Ala Picentiana. A famous regiment of distinguished history, not many years short from the four-hundredth anniversary of its formation and the legendary commander whose name it bore.

In the old town on the north bank below the fort there was, like Petuaria, little outward sign of urban pomp or civic display. Just the houses and shops of careful hard-working folk who could make a decent living from traditional trade with the soldiering or the farming classes. If their dwellings were simple in plan and externally plain, it soon became apparent from the fine commodities on shop counter or market stall that they would be tolerably well-furnished and adequately equipped inside, what with the quality pots, pans and the other little necessities of a civilised way of life.

If it lacked the salty interest of the swarming Petuarian docksides, then Derventio away from the metal workings was blessed instead with a rolling river and tree-dressed water meadows extending into an Elysian distance. The pleasant familiarity of these fine rural views did not deny enjoyment to the locals, whose evening custom from springtime on was to promenade along the river bank, whether as entwined lovers or lively families with children. It being at that hour, Candidus went down and mingled with these amiable crowds of strollers in what turned out to be a vain hope of finding out some useful information.

These citizens of the vicus were by no means hostile but they all knew each other. The only greetings he received from them were the minimal courtesies sufficient for an obvious stranger.

Unable to break through their reticent respectability for the purpose of conversation, Candidus returned to the town proper, whistling to give himself company, to a place where the mesmeric fascination of rushing water found him a good place to rest two elbows on the smooth timber of the bridge parapet.

Watching the river, his contemplative mood was broken only by a rotund farmer's wife, laden with produce in a brace of wicker baskets. Another dreamer, singing songs of the country softly to herself as she approached the ramp.

Candidus suddenly rotated to rest his back against the bridge and face her as she passed him by, wrapped in her thick cloak, offering her his most effusive greeting: "Good evening, madam. A successful trip to market today?"

Taken aback by this impertinence, she was rightly suspicious: "And what's it to you if t'were? I don't know you, do I?"

"Forgive my presumption, dear lady! Sextus Valens. 'Wanderer on the highway of life' just arrived in your lovely town. How favoured are the Parisii in the four cornerstones of their canton…"

"Well, we get by, you know…." she added, curious to encounter such extravagances of speech and chivalry on the dreary way home to rustic drudgery.

"Adorned with the presence of the Tyche, wife of Marcus Ulpius Januarius; magistratus and proud clan chief, I believe. Is she here then amongst us today, can you tell me, dear lady?"

At this, an expression of loathing and contempt clouded the broken-veined features of the good wife: "What? That painted whore! You'll have nowt but trouble there!" Without more, she was gone; hitching up her skirts and scooping up her baskets to sweep on and over the bridge with unexpected speed.

This wasn't exactly the reaction to his innocent enquiry Candidus had quite expected. Still puzzled, he turned to cross the bridge onto the south side, scratching his head as doubts grew.

He found a man upon a ladder leant against the eave wall of a house. He was securing a terracotta finial of fanciful design to the top of a chimney with iron nails, under the distant, stony oversight of his wife at the back door. Candidus tried a more direct approach: "Excuse me…sorry to trouble you, friend, but I am looking for the sister of Marcus Januarius. Could you tell me where she lives?"

The man looked at him with eyes of ice-blue intensity and put his hammer carefully into his belt: "Why?"

For a second time disconcerted by the bluntness of local manners, Candidus made allowance for a mouthful of nails limiting his speech:

"I'm told her sister-in-law, the wife of the magistrate, is staying with her. I need to see the lady on family business, that's all."

The man on the ladder spat the nails out of his mouth into his hand as if they were disgusting discoveries in a pie then slowly came down its rungs one-at-a-time, without saying a word. At the bottom, he turned to face his questioner square-on, staring at him directly with those glassy blue pupils.

He put his arm out so suddenly Candidus flinched as if a blow was to follow but all he did, this total stranger, was to seize him strongly on the upper arm.

"A gentleman to see the Tyche, eh?" he sneered. "A traveller from nowhere come to visit a fine lady. Let me give you some advice, young fellah. Keep away! Have nowt to do with all that lot, with all their goings-on. Let 'em get on with it. Don't involve yourself. Nowt but trouble the lot of 'em."

Candidus pulled his arm away and sniffed: "Look. I didn't ask for your advice. I have a message to deliver, that's all. Are you going to tell me where the house is?"

"Me? Na! I wouldn't have it on me conscience!"

The man returned to his ladder and Candidus to the roadway, heading further into the new town, more baffled than ever. In the Street of the Goldsmiths he found a shop open late and the young slave who ran it more forthcoming with the necessary information, probably because she was such a good customer to the business.

Those he sought would be found at the 'House of the Winged Victories', named after the carved goddesses of military success supporting its lintels and door frames all the way round. Ironically, this finely-decorated dwelling stood right back where he'd started, near where Taranis had parked his wagon, as one of the first buildings in the vicus just outside the south-east gate of the fort.

Dropping a silver-alloyed coin into the palm of the goldsmith's slave in appreciation for hard-won information, Candidus returned to the river-crossing and the old town on the other side. The slave, who valued only one metal, flicked the token onto the table and returned to his duties without a backward glance. Thanks are cheap, but not that cheap.

At the top of the paved street which led to the armour-plated gates of the fort there was an intersection of roads before the ditch crossings. Pursuing the slave's directions for the house, which meant an acute right-turn back on himself and down the hill away from the fort, gave him brief glimpse of the bridge again. Its wide planking was momentarily empty of travellers, but for two black horsemen thundering over, knee to knee. Their bull-necked, thick-set silhouettes were instantly distinctive; even at this distance and in the watery light of evening.

Candidus stopped whistling. His heart sank. Seeing the two ex-gladiators again frightened him, not just from the sense of personal threat but also from their sheer grim persistence. They were proving harder to shake off and more intelligent in his pursuit than he'd ever expected. Candidus shrank back against the building line, pressing himself against a house-wall. But the two horsemen didn't come up the hill to the fort and he breathed again. They must've taken some lower road leading out of town - or so he hoped. This was no time to be caught in the open streets by that pair.

The light was failing and he had two options: a standing offer from Taranis of accommodation in his wagon or else trying his luck at the 'House of the Winged Victories'? As night drew in, he made his way up there for a reconnaissance - to help him towards a decision.

A massive old door sheathed in green copper and fastened with heavy studs of the same material blocked his ready access. The crudely-carved frame to this shield of entrance was surmounted by two tall square-jawed females in stone, with assertive breasts and eagles' wings; their brawny arms held aloft to support the massive lintel. Somehow these emblematic figures hinted at what character of women he might find inside the premises; the widowed sister and symbolic mate to that most urbane clan chief of Parisi; Marcus Ulpius Januarius.

Probably the thought of confronting such formidable ladies at this hour persuaded him it was not the time. He turned reluctantly to go, mentally promising a return on the morrow. After all, it was only a short way up the street to the smith's encampment where the kindly Taranis had promised him space and a blanket.

It was nearly dark when he got to the wagon. Trumpets from the fort sounded the military's official confirmation of a sunset likely to have occurred regardless - the nearby sounds of friendly, familiar routine. For all their reassurance, even within a defended vicus protected by a resident garrison, the only beacon to location which an old soldier like Taranis would allow was one small cooking fire. By the time Candidus got there, it had all but collapsed into a faint heap of glowing ash. Without its light to guide him, Candidus must approach the van in the dark with an extreme care.

Uncertain whether simply to clamber in unannounced amongst the domestic chaos of the darkened wagon, or else offer to the sleeping smith some preliminary courtesy (like an introductory tap on the sides) Candidus paused beside a large wheel. In that same second he heard the rush of feet across the wasteland where this caravan had rested. Turning to face those who approached, he caught the flash of steel and the glint in the dark of an armoured, silvered, shoulder-piece; embossed in relief with the figure of Mars.

Alone and unarmed, he knew he stood no chance against the sheer surprise and obvious weapon-skill of the two Germans. Ducking at the first whip of a long slashing sword that cut the air above his head to tatters, Candidus crouched instinctively and rolled under the wagon. Jabbing sword-points probed and stabbed, looking for the satisfaction of flesh. He dragged himself along on one bleeding elbow beneath the planking where the oblivious Taranis snored, deep in his metal worker's dreams of rare alloy and streams of molten gold.

Beside him in the dark, Candidus could hear the two gladiators cursing and swearing in their guttural native tongue, hungry for a kill. Their weapons followed him, systematically searching the spaces under the cart as Candidus ran out of sanctuary. The two massive discs that were the rear wheels marked his end with a star of spokes that were as bars to his condemned cell.

First one sword from one side, then a second from the other side tested the obviously-soft resistance of his body. Trapped against the wheel that literally brought him to this conclusion, he awaited the agony of invasive steel for the second time in his life but now with no hope of survival.

There was a shriek of man in terminal agony and terror, a call of human extremity so final and penetrating he thought it his own - as the swords went in, sliding over bone and sinew. Except he realised this screech was not his own, heard and observed from the vantage of an ascending soul, but the final cry of at least one of his attackers.

There was an inhuman rasp to go with this fatal gargle which, at first, he could not identify, so alien was it to the ordered night-time streets and alleys of the walled canton.

He remembered then. The advice of Taranis in yesterday's leisurely wagon-drive through the chalk uplands and cattle-runs of the Parisii: "Just don't go round the back of the wagon in the dark!"

Darius!

He peered out from beneath the wagon's tailgate. The chained bear was drawn up to its full height on its rear legs, forged iron links strained to their maximum extension as the triumphant, wild-eyed, black beast exulted in its utter evisceration of the elder German.

His younger, quicker colleague had sidestepped those savage claws with the in-bred agility of the arena, for he was fled, leaving his slower senior spread-eagled behind, dead and disembowelled.

But not escaped scot-free.

Both gladiators' swords lay harmless by the cart. The burning brand which the now-dislodged Taranis soon produced as he rolled down from his bunk and out of the wagon lit a spatter of bloody drops leading away from the scene of this unlawful beast fight. In the confusion that followed there was neither chance nor inclination to pursue the second assassin, for all his tell-tale trail of blood.

Taranis struggled with the brake on the wagon. Once released it rolled only a few paces down the hill, just enough to drag the raving bear chained to its tailgate away from the ripped body of his victim. Although in normal circumstance both ox and horse could tolerate their travelling companion, Darius crazed from the taste of fresh blood was something else. Socially unacceptable in animal terms. Even his enforced removal from the scene as an attachment to their cart could not undo his draught companions' growing panic, each of these powerful animals pulling at ground tethers which looked increasingly likely to fail.

Short sword in one hand, a harassed Taranis rolled and hopped around, trying to pacify his ill-assorted menagerie.

Although it was dark now with most doors bolted and shutters drawn, many townsfolk were not yet abed and the electors of Derventio spilled out into their lanes while the part-time military pensioners of the night watch came creaking up the street in all their arthritic armour plate.

This tumult was of equal concern to the professional garrison, with cloak-wrapped cavalry troopers on sentry-go straining out the windows of their battlemented towers to decide what civil disorder it was that grew in the darkened vicus below.

The body of the first gladiator, recipient of the definitive wooden foil in this final discharge - death - lay in a glossy black pool of blood and light surrounded by a growing crowd of spectators bearing flaming torches. His chest ripped open. At the top of the hill, more light was released as the double doors of the fort's south east gate opened. A stand-by patrol was saddling-up and would be down in minutes, the annoyed garrison commander ordering their intervention to restore Pax Romana.

Candidus realised now was the time to go. Slipping into the easy concealment of the crowd, he was ashamed to be abandoning the charitable blacksmith to make what would inevitably be inadequate explanations to officialdom for a gutted corpse and a mad bear. Unfortunately, the peculiarly-secretive nature of his errand made assistance to the smith secondary to the priorities of his duty to the state.

Further down the street, he could watch all this coil and illuminated confusion from the safety of dark. His departure had been timely for the troop of cavalry disgorged from the fort were already circling the wagon, beating the excited townsfolk back from the scene of the crime with brass-bound edges of oval shields. His options had become single in number, reduced to one. He decided he would throw himself on the tender mercies of the Winged Victories, seeking sanctuary behind the high, blank and introspective walls of their mysterious town house.

There was a man who would kill him loose in the vicus and the only safety which might be found lay behind bricks and mortar. So Candidus hammered on the great, green verdigris door as hard as he could, constantly scanning the black well of the street behind for an attacker it could secrete without sign. A fillet of yellow light appeared down one side of the heavy door, announced by the creak of strained hinges. Aged red eyes studied him from this crack of observation.

Candidus showed his silver badge of office, holding it as near to the eyes as he could: "I'm an Imperial official in the service of the Governor. Open the door."

"What do you want with us?"

273

"I'm here to see the daughter of the Governor. Hurry man! Open the door, I beg you. My life's in danger!"

There was a woman's voice from within, interrogating the elderly door-keeper in harshly unsympathetic tones. When the door slid open to allow entry, it was at the hand of this chatelaine, a senior female domestic of wide girth encircled with enough belted keys for every palace door on the Palatine. The kingdom of women suggested by external carving was becoming reality.

Pausing only to dismiss the old man who returned grumbling to his porters' lodge, this formidable servant still barred his crossing of the enlarged threshold. The sounds of shouting and excitement continuing nearby drifted down the street and in through the open door, to further cloud the issue and discourage her.

"What's going on out there?" she asked with unconcealed suspicion. "What do you think you're doing, disturbing decent people in their own home at this time of night? What do you want?"

He showed her the silver badge. It meant nothing to her beyond the symbolic, because she had no notion of the government of her own country. Slave or freedwoman, the government of those who served this household was the only extent of temporal power she really understood. One thing she did know was that her mistress had a notable elder brother, a man who'd made significant, dynastic, second marriage with the daughter of the provincial governor.

Being of the Brigantian tribe herself (there are regional differences in style of dress), he guessed this servant would attach little credit to any man the Parisii selected as their chief. The authority of the Vicarius and his staff was something else; something even a simple soul like her would recognise and have to acknowledge.

It was these considerations which in less-reasoned but more instinctive fashion allowed Candidus into the house, once his employment and errand were understood. He lay back against it and sighed with relief as the enormous door finally slammed tight-shut behind him and its rattling bolts slid into place to bar the hostile tumult of the world. Once inside, he was glad to realise how quiet and still this dwelling became behind its protective walls.

274

The collapse into obsequious acquiescence of the house-keeper was completed by her anxious confirmation that the daughter of the governor, wife of Marcus Januarius, could indeed be found on the premises. He crossed quickly over a hallway guarded by the mosaic picture in black and white cubes of a savage dog pulling at a rope, just as the animal friends of Taranis were doubtless doing up the hill. ("Cave canem!") From the hall, he was promptly led away into the atrium, its traditional roof-opening up to the sky with water tank below, where several corridors set off in different directions.

Candidus had long ago learnt those who never ask never get. Nerve having brought him this far, he saw no reason to be diffident about pursuing his mission: "Where is the Tyche? May I see her now?" he asked.

"What! Now? It's ever so late, you know "

"Yes, I'm sorry. But it's most important I see her as soon as possible, that she knows I'm here...."

The housekeeper wrung her hands. Caught between the Scylla of domestic allegiance to an unforgiving mistress and the Charybdis of obedience to those holding office under the Emperor, her limited bucolic experience offered no safe decision either way. Her only hope lay in higher authority: "Wait here a minute" she said." I'll see what I can do."

Candidus sat down on a cool marble bench and looked through the rectangular aperture in the roof tiles, up to a clear night sky. The distinctive constellation of Ursus Major was prominent.

The Night of the Great Bear.

His chatelaine was returned to him sooner than he'd hoped, with a positive answer to his impertinent request to boot: "You'll get me into a lot of trouble, but I've spoken to my mistress. Her sister the Tyche is with her. They will see you."

"What, both of them?"

"Of course! What do you expect? This is a respectable house you know! You can't expect a married woman to receive a man off the streets, a stranger wandered in out of the night, on her own. We don't even know your name."

"I'm afraid that's not acceptable. My name is Flavius Candidus and I'm beneficarius consularis on the staff of the governor, father to your mistresses' sister-in-law. I'm here on matters of state and intend no discourtesy to your mistress or dishonour to her household. However, my instructions are explicit. I am to seek audience with the Tyche alone."

The housekeeper was near to tears as her dilemma worsened. Still wringing her hands, she bustled away again whilst Candidus sat back on his bench. Various slaves or servants came and went whilst he waited, some for no other purpose it seemed than a good look at the stranger. His tunic and cloak were white with the dust of the road and his hobnailed cavalry sandals thick with the mire of the streets. All-in-all he would make an unprepossessing sight to offer a lady, but she would have to take him as she found him.

It was a slightly longer delay this time but once more the housekeeper returned; homely features flushed with embarrassment and irritation at the further concession hers to announce:

"Very well, then. It's not for someone in my position to say anything against it. I've spoken with the mistress of the house and she's consulted with her sister-in-law. You're to be allowed a private interview with the wife of Marcus Ulpius Januarius. Just conduct yourself as a gentleman, that's all, or the house slaves will put you out on your ear..."

Candidus got to his feet and bowed in ironic appreciation like a courtroom plaintiff: "Lead on, my good woman. I appreciate your intercession in my cause." He passed her some coins she did not scruple to refuse.

As they left the atrium to enter the dark tunnel of a corridor, Candidus saw that the fountain he'd heard gurgling away was replica to a Cupid and Psyche bronze in the garden of a house on the banks of the Abus river. He suddenly remembered it then; that mental picture of the Saxonici crouching in their filthy bracken-roofed pits in the villa's orchard; biding their time waiting, waiting for he knew not what; and that sense of desperate need for a safe return to Londinium came flooding back to him afresh.

276

His passage through the halls and ante-rooms of painted plaster, over richly-inlaid floors themed with 'The Four Seasons', only confirmed that here was another fine house, if more femininely-decorative and formalised in display than the prosperous masculine farm-house of the Januarii. Its plan adhered more strictly to classical ideals of Mediterranean domestic architecture than most dwellings this far north of Empire. That in itself was a confident statement, the triumph of Latin culture and tradition over the practical realities of frequent rainfall, prevailing easterlies, bleak winters and chilly overcast summers.

They came to a room, its door frame blanked by curtains in deep red. There was the sound of someone playing pipes softly, accompanied by castanets. The housekeeper pulled back the curtain to douse herself and Candidus with the yellow flaming light from a brace of pottery oil lamps swinging in a pendant holder, on a bronze wheel hung in chains from the ceiling. Two young boys in light robes of an Egyptian style came out of the room carrying the instruments that had just been silenced. Candidus was ushered in.

At the other end of a floor freshly-strewn with rose petals, a single velvet couch was drawn up against the opposite wall under a suspended tent of rust-red drapery. The curtain flicked close behind him and Candidus was alone with the Tyche.

She was the wife of Januarius but he was their chief and so the Parisii had made of her a little goddess, doubtless with his encouragement, so she could receive honour beyond that of a nobles' mate. Someone fit to personify their canton and, yes, even their dreary declining capital at Petuaria Civitas Parisiorum. To Candidus something so exotic could never symbolise that decrepit little town.

Her face was quite oval and whited with those powders which young women use. Her grey eyes were unusually large and most expressive when she spoke to you directly, pressing some fervent view, so full of warmth and such degrees of animated personal interest as must be utterly sincere. By turns she was dazzling then ordinary.

Her hair at first seemed no more than brown, pulled back to the nape of the neck with a severity expressive of extreme virtue, but later he would see it set loose and incredibly fine, a veil of dark amber filaments which obscured the face. Pulling her head back it would slide away again in an auburn sheen and you could see her profile - a nose perhaps a little too rounded or too full to be aristocratic, and a cheek perhaps too puffy to be pretty.

But those lips! Carved for kissing and coloured precisely to their pretty margins with a purpled rouge darkened for drama, their suggestive curl was best viewed from the side. From there, his eyes soon descended quickly to the darkling cleft between her breasts, with all its enticing promise of sublime adventures.

He handed her his silver badge, which she turned over in her hands with little interest, examining it dismissively only for any (rejected) potential as costume jewellery. Then he passed across to her the general letter of introduction of him, which her own father had signed and sealed himself, still in its original leather document tube, which she studied rather more carefully and with much sighing and other signs of affection. He told her of his visit to Petuaria and expressed his mission in simple and misleading terms – framed purely around her own welfare. And all the time his head was spinning with the intoxication of immediate attraction and a sincere but hopeless wish that he had never, ever, come to Derventio.

Flavius Candidus was a man rarely troubled by the distractions of intuition but, in his overheated reaction to the beautiful woman now indicating the only spare seat in the room, the space on the couch close beside her, he knew at once that he was a lost soul. Something marvellously-terrible was going to happen. Irresistible and immutable, his uncomprehending insight registered - as if only to be glimpsed through her medium - the slow and measured tread of great and tragic events.

His mind unwittingly acknowledged in their ominous approach this additional quality of ceaseless recurrence – from generation to generation. That inescapable pattern of inherited and pre-ordained tragedy, varied only by the inconsequential detail of historical context and human personality. Events for which such as he can stand in no greater capacity than the mere expendable instrument of implacable Fate.

For all his veneer of modernist cynicism, this Flavius Candidus was at heart a dyed-in-the-wool old pagan, someone no more able to escape the essential fatalism of his Mithraic beliefs than Marcus Ulpius Januarius could, his powerful opponent.

She smiled up at him with an irresistible warmth and such immediate signals of sparking affection growing upon the spot, but behind all that encouragement there was some troubling reflection in her eyes which he could not place, like a dullness or an ache that looked long past him and so far away.

From hereon in, our Candidus was a drowning man. Unconsciously acknowledging these things in his heart, he surrendered himself willingly to the mysteries of the Goddess.

"One thing is on my mind to say and I must say it…. There are a number of men in this city, not by any means devoid of money or influence, who met periodically and conspired together to thwart all the forces which made for righteousness in the city…. I have not been afraid of these men, I have not been influenced by them, I have tried to do my duty and I thank the committee for their kindnesses."

Major Pulteney Malcolm, on his resignation as Chief Constable of Hull, 1910

XIII

They must have nodded off together. He woke with a start from those vivid but confusing dreams of towers and horsemen which regularly disturbed his night-time rest of recent days. At first, he did not know where he was in the low-ceilinged room, but then the glow from street lamps outside reminded him of Beverley and its North Bar Without. There was a brass alarm clock on a lace-covered wash-stand beside the bed. He studied its glowing digits with gummed eyes and remembered the bizarre events which ended what must now be yesterday.

The tousled auburn coils of hair that spilled out from beneath an adjacent pillow, like priceless coinage from a cut purse, were welcome reminders of sudden and unexpected victory in love. They also reminded of shared good fortune in surviving deliberate attempts to kill or at least to maim them both. The shocking audacity of an assassin who'd dare to show his hand in such a public place, in broad daylight, was further reason for fear. Whether that murderous self-confidence was in any way linked with some inexplicable 'career moves' currently going on within Hull City Police, he could not say.

Either way, he was becoming convinced that - in practical terms - he was now operating behind enemy lines . Hence the urgent need to arm himself with the service revolver somehow not handed in on discharge from the Royal Air Force, in 1946.

He broke the silence : "Wake up, sleepyhead ! "

"Uhhuh ! What time's it ? "

"Time we got away from here. Someone tried to kill us yesterday. We'd be daft to assume they've taken today off."

"Where are we going? "

"To the railway station. The early train into Hull. There's someone I want to try and make contact with. And I have a pistol hidden in my flat which I think we need, now. It may offer us the only real protection we can rely on."

"But you're a cop! What about the protection of your colleagues? Aren't you going straight to your buddies?"

He laughed:

"Forget it! In the game we've just joined, they're the ones who might be coming for us. There's only one man I can trust and that's my sergeant. Something's up. I don't know what. Someone's certainly got to my Superintendent before I could. At the least he's been suspended from duty while we were coming back from York yesterday, getting his car smashed up for him."

"What are you going to do, honey? And what's going to happen to the Roman mosaic?"

"Zuleika, that troublesome old relic is the least of our worries! The answer to everything lies with the Baynards, I'm sure of that much. They are behind all this. If that's right, then one way or another we're going to have to deal with them."

"Confront the Minotaur!"

He laughed at her classical analogy, typical of her but likely to prove apt in the pursuit of an aristocratic beast through the dark, mysterious corridors of an old mansion.

"If you like! However you see this nightmare we've suddenly landed in, the first step is to get out of here unseen. Number one reason being the protection of your reputation, and number two the likelihood someone may already be on watch at the front of this house."

(She'd tossed her head in amused indifference to that 'bubble' - reputation). "Do you mean we can't use the Dodge?"

"Not yet. Not this morning, no. It's such a distinctive vehicle. The only dodge we'll use today is hopping over a few back gardens on our way into town."

They were soon dressed and did as he'd suggested. He'd helped her to climb out of the bedroom window and they slid down onto the slippery, slate-tiled roof of a first-floor extension to Mrs. Holtby's terraced cottage. There was no light on in the back kitchen and they were able to slide down the adjacent drainpipe and into the yard without fear of being observed. The American woman scrambled easily over the leaning, bulging walls of miniature East Yorkshire brick which divided the long, strip gardens behind all these period properties.

Her lively, bubbly enthusiasm only suggested to Tryton's jaded outlook a failure fully to grasp the unfolding seriousness of what predicament her keen interest in Brantingham Quarry now threatened them with. Tryton was committed to doing everything in his power to shield her from a complete realisation, even if the only way to do so was by keeping her close by his side during whatever steps needed to be taken.

Garden-hopping brought them nearer to York Road where they found a house whose side alley allowed them onto the pavement, out of sight of Mrs. Holtby's frontage and any likely watchers. From there they crossed town via the cobblestones of Saturday Market and the lorry-choked narrows of Toll Gavel and Butcher Row, these strangulated streets still the main road between Hull and York. At the railway station, they caught a milk train from Scarborough which took them through to Hull, arriving at about eight-thirty in the morning to persistent drizzle. Leaving Paragon Station they crossed a soaking Ferensway by the South African War memorial and walked down Paragon Street to Queen Victoria Square.

Zuleika couldn't understand why English policemen didn't all carry guns (or 'sidearms' as she called them) like their American counterparts. Tryton became so deeply involved in this ethical argument with her that it was only when standing beside the City Hall that he realised his habitual and unfailing genuflection in memory of Jenny had been quite forgotten. Struck with shame, he glanced back across to the familiar bomb-site on King Edward Street where the Prudential buildings once had been. This morning it looked suddenly different. Most of its protective screen of hoardings had been pulled down and caterpillar-tracked excavators were busy at work, clawing their foundation trenches deep into sanctified earth.

For both himself and the city together, almost on the same day, the process of post-war rebuilding had really begun. He took hold of Zuleika strongly by one arm and pulled her to him, briefly explaining its significance. She hugged him close and they stood there silently in the fine rain for at least five minutes, not moving, whilst shop and office workers hurried past them with not so much as a sideways glance. Everyone knew this place.

Although this was the city-centre proper, large areas were left as empty and featureless as the Gobi Desert. Having been bombed flat during the war, the ruins had been cleared and levelled to await any post-war reconstruction programme. Here and there the odd survivor stood alone, monolithic memorial to the random whim of falling bombs. An office-block here, a department store there. The Yorkshire Penny Bank. Each one self-consciously separate and apart, like a six-foot girl at a High - School dance. Paragon Street, King Edward Street, and Albion Street were particular wastelands, acres of white dust which could be crossed directly without regard to the street plan.

After a joyless café-breakfast based on reconstituted eggs (Tryton ashamed of the shabbiness of his country and its general inability to put much onto anyone's table), they went into the City's Guildhall on Alfred Gelder Street where the Magistrates Courts would be in session. He was looking everywhere for Pickering, the one individual who could be relied on in the Constabulary to stand by him, so long as he could get through to him. If it was too risky to enter the police station and see him, he judged, Pickering might just have business in the Police Court opposite.

For her, the long corridor in the Guildhall came as something of a shock, what with its Dickensian gloom of tobacco smoke, dark wood panelling, and nicotine-tinted plaster. Hard-bitten, sharp looking men lined its walls, waiting for judgement. These were just the solicitors. Their clients, the defendants, were worse. Each had his own cloud of hangers-on and supporters, although what they found to admire in the forms of life attracting their allegiance was hard to say. Victims and witnesses, policemen and probation officers mingled with burglars and cheats, robbers and rapists; actors all in this theatre of guilt. The children of malefactors gambolled careless underfoot in their nursery of crime.

Tryton put his head around the door of what was usually the Stipendiary Magistrate's court. However, today, Mr. J.R. McDonald was absent or unwell, his place taken by a lay-bench of two men and one woman, ordinary members of the public sitting in a judicial capacity. Before them, a solicitor in a shiny suit was trying to mitigate the unforgivable, to save the irredeemable from their just desserts:

284

"Just look at his record" he said, waving a lengthy document at the Bench. "He's been inside almost continuously, since he was twenty-one. It's only weeks since he was released from His Majesty's Prison on Hedon Road, from serving a four-year sentence imposed while our gallant lads were still landing on the beaches of Normandy."

Warming to his bold theme of incorrigible recidivism as compelling argument against further confinement, the advocate continued: "Your Worships, what my client needs is a court that will give him a chance to break this pattern. Otherwise, as the record shows, he's simply serving a life sentence - in instalments!"

The Chairman of the Bench suppressed a snort. The defendant got six months.

At the end of the corridor, in court number one (the largest), judge and jury would soon sit at Quarter Sessions to try the more serious offences in the criminal calendar or those where a defendant specifically requested trial by his peers.

In its doorway, Tryton acknowledged a barrister he knew, bewigged and gowned but snatching an anxious cigarette before the morning's business. That prosecuting counsel was visibly under the influence of drink even at this hour was less disturbing than the thought that one day he might be a judge.

Having visited every courtroom with no sign of Pickering anywhere, it was unwise to linger, for fear of bumping into Rivett or his merry men. Elbowing a protective path through the crowd in the corridor, Tryton brought Zuleika out of the building.

She stood back for a moment on the pavement, inspecting its monumental scale and the massive group of classical statuary adorning its high rooftop: Britannia borne on a chariot drawn by lions. Idealised woman as personification of an island race; imperial pomp and circumstance captured in stone.

Wrinkling her nose, Zuleika pointed up to these dominating figures, arching her frame in a way which for all his worries he could still find physically diverting.

"Look up there!" she said.

(He dutifully did as requested).

285

"There she is - Britannia! Another Roman idea, you know! Propaganda to sustain an Empire. She's first seen on a sestertius of the Emperor Hadrian, second century after Christ. Apart from a few coins of Antoninus Pius and the late third-- century usurper, Carausius, she doesn't appear again until the time of your King Charles the Second. And even here in Hull you've got her statue, nostalgic reminder of another fast-declining Empire. I remember how Michael used to say how one day Great Britain would end up no more than America's aircraft carrier!"

Tryton had too much on his plate to worry about the ideological continuity of some mythical female, or else confront that curious mix of contempt and envy which our American colonists love to show for traditional British institutions. She was only being provocative.

"Look," he said. "We've got to get moving. This is the worst possible place to stand around. The police station's just across the road."

"Don't think I don't remember, Lieutenant," she said grimly, "let's go!"

Together, they traversed the bombed-out city. Safe beyond the range of even the largest enemy bomber, whether German or Japanese, no American city had ever experienced anything like this. It was inconceivable they ever would. To Zuleika and her fellow countrymen, the suffering of places like Hull was beyond their understanding. Three years after the Second World War had ended, she looked around at all this ruination with an innocent disbelief, appalled to see how a country bankrupted through a just war - and the debts her own as closest ally had imposed for the privilege of waging it - still lacked the resources to repair its worst effects.

Tryton's unease was for a different reason. Holding her small hand, he felt exposed and obvious to watching eyes as they hurried over desolate urban plains. His lodgings were in Kingston Square, near to the theatre, where the gutted frontage of the Co-operative Institute was still propped-up with girders like a skeleton, in the hope of better days.

"Wait here!"

She stood obediently, a small figure on the corner of Albion Street and Bond Street in a mizzle that showed no sign of abating.

286

Tryton had barely left her before a loitering 'spiv' with obligatory pencil moustache, in the 'demob' raincoat and stained trilby hat that was almost uniform of his trade, came along and tried to sell her a food ration card. Whether stolen or forged was neither here nor there, but Tryton had to return and drive the fellow away before he'd take 'no' for an answer.

"Will you be alright? I promise you, I'll only be five minutes."

"Don't worry, Lieutenant. I can handle it. Just get your ass over to that apartment and back here as fast as you can. Your blitzed city spooks me!"

Cheered by her confident self-reliance, he crossed the street again and walked along to the corner of Kingston Square, looking about him all the time. His lodgings were on the first floor of a terraced house belonging to a kindly Dutch widow, who'd been lucky to escape from Java after her English husband was lost on 'Force Z', the Royal Navy capital ships sunk by the Japanese in the Far East. It was easy to find as the only house in the street with a blue-and-white Delft wall plaque for its number. Tryton stopped dead on the corner and then stepped smartly back. There was a helmeted policeman in a rain-cape standing on guard at the front door of this house, another one climbing the steps. There was only one explanation - they were waiting for him. Nothing about his landlady would prompt police attention.

He turned and set off back down Albion Street to enable approach from the alley behind the house instead. Zuleika saw him returning from the corner in the shadow of the Hull Brewery building, where she was waiting. The rich hoppy smell from the output of these premises spiced the air as he went by at the width of the roadway.

She looked at him as he went by again across the street with obvious mystification, stabbing the gold ladies' watch on her wrist (present of a doting father) with an expressive but delicate forefinger. He loved her hands. Small and easily enfolded in his own palm yet, for all their porcelain elegance, practical tools not averse to creative skill.

Her pretty mouth shaped the question "five minutes?"

With a cheery wave, given as much to fend off his own growing sense of trouble as to reassure her, he turned right and struck out for the alleyway in mind.

Its exact ten feet of width was clouded by flags of laundry from the washing-lines criss-crossing its length, hiding one end from the other. In this narrow, secret world behind the expressionless walls of domestic backyards, each stumbling step of the journey revealed fresh obstacles beyond every sheet of linen. Picking his way through overturned rubbish bins and barking dogs, truant schoolboy footballers and the interrupted scandal of gossiping housewives, he found both cover and denunciation equally balanced: "Excuse me, madam; good morning, ladies..."

His meek greetings not even remotely thawing these icebergs who watched him go by with hostile curiosity, red arms folded in disapproval over angry bosoms tightly confined by floral overalls. If these gentlefolk were at all aware of the watch presently posted out on the street, then they would be first to announce his sighting to the constables. He could only hope their tete-a-tete in the ten-foot confirmed an ignorance of dark-blue serge accumulating in the square, and so he continued.

Bending-down to duck beneath yet another pegged bed-spread that flapped and dripped in the drizzle (why do people put washing out when it's raining?) he found the door to the Dutch woman's yard. Distinctive by fresh blue paint and the arc of regularly-scrubbed cobbles radiating around it, in contrast to all her neighbours', Tryton pressed against the latch. Peering around the door, he saw its small area of stone flags empty of children and the rear windows of the house free of observers.

Encouraged, he let himself in and approached the kitchen door. Trying the handle, he found it locked. This was rare event in that household and he knew it must mean she was out somewhere with her children. Unfortunately, the only key he held was for the front door - obviously unsuitable. A forced entry was going to be required, with apologies to Mrs. Neukirke. To be burgled when two uniformed policemen were guarding the premises would be particular annoyance to any ratepayer.

Nevertheless, he would try and achieve it as neatly and quietly as possible. Tryton quickly taped over a small pane of glass nearest the door handle with a roll of black-out tape from his pocket, having first checked that the key was still in the lock as usual. A good shove with his elbow punched the complete pane out of its beading, allowing his gloved hand and arm to follow, reaching in for the key he turned.

In the kitchen, he listened carefully for sounds of alarm and heard none, being able to creep into the hall and from there up the stairs. Like Zuleika Macsen, Michael Tryton was tumbleweed. Another one of those solitary beings without permanent roots that held, living out their lonely non-working hours in other peoples' spare bedrooms. This one was on the first floor, overlooking the yard, and the prize for which these risks were taken was soon in his hands. The service-issue 'Webley' long-barrelled revolver had been carried in all his aircraft in case of forced-landing behind enemy lines during the war. Tryton still struggled with his unwilling recognition that only here and now in peacetime England, even in the office of constable, was the paranoid actuality of hunted renegade become personal experience. Then as now, the contents of the brown box he was easing out of its hiding-place behind a panel in the ceiling became his only insurance policy.

Opening the box, he rolled the polished, rounded brass of live ammunition around his palm, before loading the weapon with their fatal potential. The rest of the bullets he carelessly emptied into an outside pocket of his raincoat. At the bottom of the cardboard shoe-box there was a knotted lanyard of petrol-blue cord which he looped around his neck and flapped under his tie, before attaching the other end to a hook on the revolver handle. The pistol was then hung out of sight in a large poachers' pocket sewn into the lining of his raincoat.

Despite the danger of his situation and the fear that two policemen outside might, at any moment, make their own forced-entry to search his room, Tryton remained cool and systematic. He restored the plaster panel to the ceiling and carefully folded-up the cardboard box which held the gun, before dropping its flattened remnant into the same pocket as the loose ammunition. He didn't want anyone alarmed by knowing he was armed. No need to get people over-excited, least of all the egregious Superintendent Rivett.

Slipping downstairs, he left by the same route, picking up the still-intact glass pane from its resting-place on a multicoloured floor mat made out of tied rags. He peeled off the tape which had prevented its cracking and pressed the complete item back into the splintered beading, re-arranging the whole to appear as original as possible.

289

Removing the key from its position inside the lock he went outside and used that to secure the door. A small gap at the bottom of the door meant he could carefully slide the key underneath and back onto the mat, to prevent suspicion over its loss.

Crossing the yard, he re-entered the alley. Rather than run the inquisitive gauntlet of the tricoteuses again, Tryton went right instead of left. Emerging from the alleys' other, opposite outlet presented him with a crossing of the far end of that street where the constables were, but he was confident he achieved it without detection. (It was a matter for professional disbelief that uniformed colleagues should be so obvious about guarding the front door yet so manifestly fail to guard the back door - 'Wooden-tops!')

He passed over the broad forecourt of Fire Brigade Headquarters in Worship Street, the guilty weight of the recovered gun hung from his neck now banging against his heart. A fireman in shirtsleeves gave him a cheery nod as he went by, his only worry in life the unravelling of a tangled hose attached to the brass pump at the back of a fire tender. Back in Jarratt Street again, he could see right down to its continuation as Albion Street beside the brewery, as far as that bomb-flattened waste where Tom Sheppards' museum once stood. By rights he should also have been able to see Zuleika where he'd left her on the junction with Bond Street. That he could not did not immediately concern him, what with knots of passing cyclists and pedestrians to shield her slender frame.

By the time he'd reached the gilded stucco facade of the Roman Catholic church, where Tryton could once more see his lodgings in Kingston Square, there were no obstacles to view but she was quite unquestionably gone. He broke into a run and arrived at the corner in seconds, to look up and down both streets for her distinctive jacket, jaunty hat, and auburn mane. In each direction there was no sign.

His imagination worked overtime, its heartless ingenuity constructing the worst possibilities as absolute certainty: That 'spiv'. The Baynards. The White Slave Trade. The inconstancy of the female spirit.

One minute he railed against her thoughtless irresponsibility, the next he damn-near wept at the thought of her being dragged into the back of an imaginary field-grey lorry and driven-off to unspeakable fate, recreating some Nazi atrocity. He looked down at the pavement in complete despair. There, almost at his feet, in her agreed place of station, was a gold watch lying on the wet sidewalk. A ladies' watch with loving dedication on the back from a wealthy ship's-broker to his darling only daughter. Watch glass lay in many pieces on the ground and the hands were stationary, their mechanism frozen barely four minutes earlier; a time beyond which its faithful motion would never recover from the loss of its mistress. He cursed himself for his slowness in returning to her. It had cost them both dear.

She'd not gone without a struggle, then. Theft or robbery meant nothing to those who'd taken her. Why, they'd even left a gold watch on the pavement, so keen to remove its wearer that her valuable timepiece meant nothing, whether as commodity or mere receipt for her going. He picked the debris up piece by piece, as if already all that's left him of his love. Four minutes since her abduction, but still no indignant bystander nor excited witness coming forward to denounce this outrage. Whoever achieved it was either so quick or inconspicuous, so discreet or authoritative, that any passer-by watching her detention did so without concern. That must narrow the odds:

Either the police or the Baynards.

Whichever it was, if they could spot her so promptly then they might be onto him already, a man with a pistol in his coat. Again, he cursed his stupidity and carelessness. Even the unguarded back yard of his lodgings might have been deliberate trap, allowing recovery of a gun that, combined with other events, must confirm his outlaw status; a maverick policeman beyond the pale whose account of artefact theft by a respected local family could never be believed.

Quite beside the passion he'd developed for the lady, he realised she also represented his only corroboration. As if it could, this must double the absolute certainties of affection. He needed her both ways and had to find her; whatever and wherever. On foot he stood no chance, although at least he had a gun, even if it was not one the Chief Constable had authorised him to be carrying.

The next priority was access to a vehicle and the only one he could think of was the old Dodge parked on North Bar Without. He had to get back to Beverley at once, on the next available train.

At the railway station he went into one of the cream-painted telephone boxes peculiar to Hull's municipal 'phone system. The exchange put him through to a woman's voice: "Hallo, Hull City Police. Can I help you…?"

"Yes, please. I'd like to speak to Sergeant Pickering in the Criminal Investigation Department, please."

"Yes, of course. Who shall I say is calling?"

He thought for a moment: "Oh….uh….right! Just tell him…. just tell him it's 'Magnus Maximus' calling. He'll know who it is. Just tell him that….!"

The telephone operator was doubtful but endured this sort of insanity everyday from the cranks, jokers, attention-seekers and anonymous informants who plagued her switchboard at police headquarters: "Putting you through now " she sighed wearily, without even bothering to challenge this pretentious identity.

"Sergeant Pickering speaking. Hello. Who's calling? Is it you, sir?"

"Yes, it's me! What's going on, Pickering?" he hissed.

"Mr. Tryton, sir! Where are you?"

"Never mind where I am, Pickering. Tell me what's going on. They've removed Maister. Suspended him, haven't they?"

"It's difficult for me, sir. Very difficult indeed, you must understand that."

"I'm sure it is. Just tell me what's going on, Pickering! Yesterday afternoon, somebody tried to kill me in a lorry belonging to the Baynards."

"Kill you? That's terrible. Look, I can't help you sir. They're keeping me out of it. It's Rivett. All they've said to me is that you're running with the enemy."

"What do they mean by that? 'Running with the enemy'. What the hell is that supposed to mean, Pickering?"

"I thought you might have better idea than me on that one, sir. All I've been told is to persuade you to come in. If you contact me, I'm supposed to persuade you to hand yourself in."

"Hand myself in? What are these people babbling about? What have I done to require a surrender?"

"I'm sorry, Mr. Tryton, sir. It's well above my head. There are powerful people involved in this. London's got an interest. We're out looking for you now."

"I know that, Pickering. They won't find me until I'm ready. What about the American woman? What part does she play in all this?"

"I'm sorry, sir - I don't know how to put this. The official line puts her with the bad guys. And you with her. I did warn you about that woman, didn't I, sir?"

"Cobblers! You know as well as I do, she's done nothing wrong. Someone wants to make a scapegoat out of her, but not if I can help it. Where is she now?"

"They're assuming she's with you."

"Negative. She's just been kidnapped! Is that by Rivett, or some of his cronies?"

"No. She's not been brought in here. Definitely not in police custody. What do you mean, kidnapped?"

"Lifted! Taken off the street in broad daylight and no-one turns a hair. Only uniformed police officers in an official police vehicle, exercising a legitimate power of arrest, only they could achieve that, surely. After all, this is England…"

"Not us. No-one's out looking for her, not yet. Just you. We haven't got her here, sir, so don't you think it would be better if you just came in and sorted it out? Rivett's not a bad bloke really, you know."

"Is he standing right beside you now, Pickering, my old mate? I'm being set up for something, you know. A flyer. One of the 'Brylcreem Boys'. Not a local either, so that definitely makes me expendable. It stinks and I'm not coming in till it's sorted."

"Look sir, I'll back you up. Just don't cut yourself off from your friends. Go too far out on your own and you'll lose touch, lose any grasp of reality, of right and wrong."

"Don't worry about me, Pickering. I'm O.K. Flying straight and level, my artificial horizon gyroscopically controlled. And when I'm not checking that, I'm looking straight through the gunsight above it…."

He placed the black bakelite receiver precisely back down on its chromium rests to leave his sergeant with the 'burrrrrrrh' of a cancelled call reverberating in his ear.

Even as Tryton stepped onto the Bridlington train, first stop Beverley, another black Wolseley with a firearms team on board was pulling out the yard at Central Police Station and into Alfred Gelder Street, its tyres squealing.

People had been listening in on his conversation with Pickering. A disturbing reference to the fighter pilot's fixation with the cross-hairs of his gunsight was being taken more literally than perhaps he'd intended. In the end, whether Tryton actually meant to provoke such a response is unclear but you would imagine he must have guessed what they were likely to do. Either way, they were still unable to find him quickly or to guess his destination. The train delivered him back to Beverley far more promptly than their black motor cars ever could, and a taxi brought him straight from the station to North Bar Without. He made the driver take him well past Mrs. Holtby's house first, so that he could study both sides of the road for surveillance, but detected none.

The Dodge was still there, parked on the cobbles in front of a neat row of white-painted, Georgian terraced houses. Paying off the taxi, Tryton walked carefully back down to Miss Macsen's lodgings from the Sessions House, alert for any hint of a trap. He had to have motorised transport, even if something as distinctive as this old Army truck was all he could get his hands on. Where Zuleika got the rationed petrol from which fuelled her comings-and-goings was an interesting question he really should have asked her earlier. That chance was gone now, but at least he knew its benefit could be applied to help him help her.

Mrs. Holtby received the disreputable young policeman who'd become something of a nuisance to both herself and (she thought) her lodger with obvious annoyance. (No, Miss Macsen was not at home). Grudgingly, the keys for the Dodge were recovered by the landlady from that upstairs room where Tryton so recently fulfilled a passion now transformed to fear. He received them from her with only mumbled thanks before fleeing the house and boarding the truck.

Mrs. Holtby stood in her front window, its net curtains pushed aside with brazen curiosity, but he didn't even register her scrutiny, so distracted was the detective by his quest.

Almost an automaton himself, it took several attempts before he successfully fired the engine of the Dodge in a cloud of blue smoke. She was still standing there watching him. Gears were engaged with little sign of mechanical sympathy and then, at last, he was off - heading for the York road initially and then the higher ground to its south-west, above the River Humber.

His mind was in turmoil: "Gypsum and auburn; Power and corruption; Barbarism and fire."

"COHORS EQUITATA"

The fact was, he didn't know where to start. Where to go next, what to do? The hint of panic. She could be absolutely anywhere. Then he remembered Superintendent Maister, whose sudden fall from grace was amongst the first indications of a world of reliable familiar faces and routine beginning to unravel. If his boss had been suspended, then it could only be because he had knowledge or involvement in these strange events. Things were beginning to look equally bleak for Tryton. He would start his search with Maister, in the hope that accurate inside information from a privileged source might avoid the desperate futility of a wild-goose chase. Anyway, he owed the miserable old duffer some sort of explanation for not returning his brand-new motor-car.

Tryton crossed the Wolds and dropped down onto the Hull to Leeds road at North Ferriby. The village lay on low ground which descended from the main road to confront the river at the Redcliff, mysterious pre-historic trading-post of the pre-Roman world. There was a church with a tall steeple and a lot of poplar trees. Opposite the church was a row of pebble-dashed, semi-detached houses with the usual Mock-Tudor accretions. He knew Maister's house at once from the large glass vase full of chrysanthemums prominent in the front bay window.

Maister lived a bachelor's life, his wife (according to that least-reliable of sources, the police canteen) having run off with a prison visitor some years previously. His eldest son had emigrated to Southern Rhodesia, presumably to escape his father's intemperate moods, after the youngest lad fell victim with his ship to a U-Boat on a Russian convoy, Archangel-bound.

Sadly, an intervening daughter gave little compensation but invoked his considerable displeasure instead by marrying an estate agent and remaining childless. If understanding these personal disappointments and family tragedies went some way towards explaining his Superintendent's temperament, they never made it more tolerable for the victim.

Apart from shouting at subordinates, the only pleasure left this irascible senior officer in his life was curious delicacy for a man of such harsh external outlook. The growing of prize-winning chrysanthemums was horticultural ability brought to the point of Art. Whatever terror he might inspire in the world of station sergeants, police cadets, pub informants and petty felons; in the narrow world of competitive chrysanthemum-growing, Ronald Maister bestrode it like a colossus.

Parking the Weapons Carrier outside the house, Tryton hopped out onto the pavement. An old man in horn-rimmed glasses and a button-up-the-front cardigan was digging in the garden next door. The spitting image of Stafford Cripps.

"Is he in?" Tryton asked, breezily.

"I think so. You'd better knock."

Tryton did as suggested. There was no response. He tried again and there was still no answer. He went down the path at the side and looked in the back garden. There was a large greenhouse next to the derelict air-raid shelter. Both were empty. He stood on an up-turned wheelbarrow and tried to look in at the kitchen window but it was too dark in there to see. Returning to the front porch, he knocked again. The old man in next door's garden stopped digging and leaned on his spade, watching. Tryton rested his hand against the ox-eye glass in the front door and the whole thing swung open on this gentle pressure. He put his head round the door frame:

"Hello. Anyone at home....?"

No answer came the stern reply.

Tryton stepped into the hall. On his right the living-room was ajar. Stepping in there, he found an overturned sofa whose every cushion had been cut open with a sharp instrument, and a broken lamp. A book-case had fallen forward and its volumes littered the carpet. The mirror over the fireplace was reduced to shards, promising years of bad luck, and ash from the grate had spilled over its tiled rim.

There had either been a fight in here or else a very untidy search. Possibly both.

The trail of destruction led into a small dining room, where an older man living on his own had tried to preserve those little conventions of domestic decoration which an unfaithful wife once taught him in happier days. Lace doilies and silver-plated napkin rings. There was a line of tiny blood-spots across the cream linen table cloth. Another opening led from the dining room into the kitchen. Smashed crockery crunched underfoot.

In the corner by the sink, Ronald Maister lay with his head in a pool of blood, arms and legs extended. Sightless eyes gazed at the white ceiling, uncomprehending. He'd been shot at close range in the side of the head, as Tryton soon saw when he dropped to his knees to examine the body. Burn marks around the entry wound confirmed the proximity of the firearm. It could not have been self-inflicted and there was no sign of the weapon in the kitchen. However, a glint of yellow metal under the gas-cooker caught his eye and he recovered the object. It proved to be a spent cartridge case of a type and calibre exactly matching those live rounds loose in Tryton's raincoat pocket. He took one out and compared the two. Identical.

Superintendent Maister had been shot in his own home after a struggle with someone carrying an Army 'Webley'. Tryton had been right. He must have known something of sufficient significance to require his elimination. An execution. No ordinary house burglar would carry out an attack like this. Carrying an almost identical weapon in his coat, Tryton realised that, once again, an unfortunate situation of coincidence might have been engineered to incriminate him. Yesterday, Maister's car had been destroyed on the road. Today he is executed at home. Or was it today? Could this atrocity have been simultaneous with yesterday's events? Difficult to say, but the body was quite cold and rigor mortis had passed over. There were signs of purpling to the flesh of arms and neck. It might well have been yesterday, but only a pathologist could tell.

Tryton followed the trail of devastation around the house in the hope of finding either some clue to the identity of the killer or else the information which had made Maister's silence so essential.

His usual experience of murder was of a drastic crime committed for the most straightforward and unsophisticated reasons: anger, avarice or adultery. Was this one any different?

Upstairs in a spare bedroom, a small roll-top bureau had been forced open. Numerous inconsequential pieces of correspondence were scattered over the floor around it. Bank statements and share certificates had been thrown about. Tryton went to this desk and rooted about in it himself, looking more for what might be missing than what remained. Just as the kidnappers of Zuleika Macsen had left a gold watch at the scene, so had the murderer of Ronald Maister left cheque books; what seemed to be a valuable, if small, collection of coins and stamps; and even some cash in a brown leather, folding wallet. Although the philatelist's album hadn't even been moved from its shelf in the desk, adjacent coin trays had all been pulled out and carefully placed on the bedroom carpet for an examination which seemed inappropriate to the slaughter downstairs.

Within the trays, half-a-dozen coins at a time were held tightly by holes punched through thick white cardboard. Above each metal disc, the collector had recorded monarch, type, and date of issue in a careful blue ink. The collection appeared complete, bar two. Their loss was attested by the presence of description over now-vacant recesses in the cellophane-backed cardboard: "Silver 'aureus' of Carausius: 'British' Empire c.287-293A.D. 'VICTORIA CARAVSI AVG'" and "Bronze coin of Magnus Maximus, the British Usurper: c.383-388A.D.(Trier Mint) c.f. the 'Mabinogian' (Welsh tales) & Kipling's 'Puck of Pook's Hill'."

Still wearing the police-issue leather gloves which had been his wise precaution against forensic cross-contamination or self-incrimination, Tryton slipped this card with its four remaining coins into the inside pocket of his raincoat. It joined the cartridge case from the kitchen as the beginnings of a body of evidence. Whatever the link, he could not believe that Ronald Maister had been killed for the sake of two tiny coins which anyone of modest means could buy in a York coin shop.

In a brief survey he recorded nothing else of note and went downstairs, pausing for one last look in the kitchen.

Tryton was a professional and had seen enough murder scenes and their victims to be consciously unaffected. (Their long-term effect on his subconscious was harder to assess).

298

In achieving this necessary dispassion, a sense of detachment from the victim was essential. (He'd never stood up well to cases involving small children). But this one was different. Ronald Maister was a man he'd known well, at least in the context of the workplace. He might not have liked him, but his Superintendent had inevitably been Sun and Moon to the orbit of his working day. Now he'd been brutally extinguished in the disarming refuge of his own home. Grief and anger rose in Tryton's throat to rout that cool restraint required of an investigator:

"Barbarians!"

Stomach beginning to revolve, he turned to go, needing the repair of fresh air. There was the shape of a man standing outside in the porch, his silhouette anonymous and threatening through the marbled glass. (The killer irresistibly drawn back to the scene of his crime?) Fury and revenge high in his mind, Tryton violently yanked the front door open to confront the figure. It was the gardener from next door, clutching his spade. Curiosity had got the better of him: "Is everything alright ?"

Tryton braced himself in the doorway, breathing in great gulps of air, before replying: "No, it isn't ! Has anyone else been here today?"

"Not today. But yours is the second Army lorry we've seen. There was one here yesterday evening, about six o'clock. Why, what's happened?"

"Your neighbour seems to have been shot. Don't go into the kitchen, it's not a pretty sight. Please can you telephone for the police immediately. I'm going to get help."

Leaving the old man goggling helplessly at him from the porch, Tryton strode down the garden, through the gate and slid into the driving seat of the Dodge. The engine fired promptly this time and he was away sharply. On the road, confused by worry, his concentration was poor and he took several wrong turnings. The formulation of purpose during this journey was slow in coming, his resolve still desperately shaken; first by the shock of Zuleika's abduction and now by the untimely death of Ronald Maister.

Inevitably and instinctively, it was towards January House that he drove.

The big house overlooking the river.

"Those who cannot remember the past are condemned to repeat it."

George Santayana (essayist, philosopher and poet 1863 -1952)

XIV

Inevitably and instinctively, it was towards January House that he drove. What was it she had said?

"Confront the Minotaur!"

So be it, then. All, or nothing at all! (He'd certainly be needing a gun on this job).

From the twin pillars of the entrance he sped down that long, sweeping track into the forested dip which hid the house and its grounds. Anger made him reckless but the armed camp set out on the front lawns still came as something of a shock. Seven white bell-tents surrounding a shiny green radio truck, its tall aerial tethered by guy-ropes. Khaki soldiers in black berets, some carrying artillery shells, moved between the circle of canvas and a short line of twenty-five pounder field guns facing up the wooded valley.

The 422nd (East Riding) Coast Regiment, Royal Artillery volunteers, on their Easter exercise, just happened to be guarding the house of their commanding officer's wayward brother. Whether that was out of their deliberate or unwitting inclusion in the Baynards' ruthless scheme remained to be seen.

Tryton spun the thin rim of the steering wheel in his hands as he passed a neat row of parked gun-tractors and ammunition limbers, adopting the same approach to the house he and Zuleika had made only the other day. The Dodge went up the back drive and disappeared amongst trees and rhododendron smartly enough, he hoped, to be noted by the casual observer as just another military run-about involved in the wargames on the front lawn.

Emerging from the trees again, the green gate of the rear stable yard was wide open and in he went. Empty of the horses and stable-girls which normally occupied this walled square, the only motor vehicle there today was an open Humber staff-car in matt green, bearing markings suggesting its temporary loan to these volunteers from the Regular Army.

Abandoning the Dodge at the kerbstone against which it harmlessly rolled to a halt, Tryton walked quickly across the courtyard towards a rear entrance leading into and through the kitchens.

Two women in white mop-caps and aprons were working bread-mix on wooden boards and showed little interest at the young man in a raincoat who stalked so purposefully down the servants corridor. ("There was all sorts coming and going at the moment").

Their trespassing visitor's recent reconnaissance helped him find his bearings 'below-stairs' more quickly than otherwise and brought him out into that magnificent hallway, beneath the chandelier-lit ornamental staircase supported on classical columns. Sunlight poured through the French windows from the terrace to leave the well of the stairs where Tryton stood in a deep darkness. From its shade he studied the scene.

Someone had been busy. The workmen must have been on overtime. Beneath the marble statues, French furniture, ormolu clocks and gilt-framed paintings, that hole in the diamond-tiled floor had been made good. But not with like.

A mosaic, composed of thousands of tiny red, white, grey and blue tesserae set in mortar, now filled the space cleared for it only the other day. That central, fluted medallion pattern, perhaps just an abstract to its long-gone maker but reminiscent to modern eyes of an opened umbrella or a ladies' fan, was still flanked by its panels of ropework and chequers. Tryton had never seen the complete Roman pavement before, but its description was so thoroughly drummed into him; first by some angry archaeologists in wind-torn Brantingham Quarry and then in more intimate circumstance by Miss Macsen; he could have no doubt that here was the item itself. Set in cement, it suddenly became permanent part of the whole fabric of January House, another valuable heirloom to be handed down to future generations as part of the Baynard Inheritance.

Except for one thing.

These were stolen goods. Possession might be nine points of the law, but the tenth part must surely still rest in the good title of Mr Reckitt of Brantinghamthorpe Hall, freeholder of the quarry-land from which this property was unlawfully-torn. Here was larceny on a grand scale for which not only the labourers of theft but also their masters, its counsellors or procurers, must surely answer.

That The Honourable Roderick Baynard J.P. - with probable connivance from his chinless military brother - was both arranger and beneficiary of this particular art-theft must be as certain a conclusion as any investigator could ever face. Except that now it wasn't just theft. In the space of only a few hours, abduction and murder were added as specific counts to the indictment.

Their precise links with the Baynards were still indistinct and incomplete, but no less insistent for all that. For the safety of Zuleika Macsen; for the memory of Ronald Maister; and for the preservation of his own life, honour and integrity, this Michael Tryton was not to be diverted from the target he had in his sights: Roderick Baynard.

It was as if just thinking the name was enough to conjure him up out of the air, like a malign presence. Heavy shooting shoes with metal cleats scraped on the floor as a man in tweed trousers with a Norfolk jacket, check shirt, and regimental tie, came in loudly. Adopting the sartorial conventions of middle-age some time before its actual onset was more compliance with the expectations of his landed-class than individual expression of personal style. Yet he was not so much older than Tryton. Ruddy in complexion, partly through heredity but also through that natural exposure to weather which those who only inspect land and merely direct labour nevertheless incur, there was a half-smile that played about his lips without hint of humour. Something in his manner left Tryton with an odd but immediate feeling that he'd met this man somewhere before; a long, long time ago, even if he couldn't place the exact occasion.

A second more familiar figure followed him into the hall. Like the first, there was prompt identification but this time without any problem remembering their last, brief encounter - at Bull Sand Fort. Colonel Sir Martin Baynard TD of the Coast Artillery could, in his khaki field-uniform and when indoors, look every inch the soldier. His diagonally-supported leather 'Sam Browne' belt gleamed with polishing. It took the weight of a green canvas holster, whose top flap did not trouble to disguise the distinctive black handle of a 'Webley' revolver.

Here was the hand and here was the weapon that took the life of Ronald Maister.

There was no evidence yet but Tryton was sure of it. Its proof and explanation must follow his prejudices. Tryton was determined - hot with hatred and anger as he was - and careless of his own safety in this keenness to confront. The Baynards must have already known he was there, because he got his chance rather sooner than expected, straight from the man he took to be Roderick Baynard.

"You can step forward now, Inspector. No point in skulking under the stairs is there, not when we've so much to talk about?"

More imperative than invitation, yet Tryton had no wish to quibble. Here he was at last, face-to-face with the Minotaur in its lair, at the stinking heart of its maze.

"How did you know I was here?"

"The Yank-tank pick-up with the Allied Star on the bonnet. What a lovely, battered old thing! Nearly as much character as one of my Bentleys! But hardly a discreet form of transport to run around in, not by any standards, eh? Especially when it's so well known to us, here, as Zuleika's. So, when we saw you drive into the yard just a few moments ago, we had to rush over and greet our visitor."

"Where is she? What have you done with her since this morning? What is she to you?"

The Honourable Baynard looked at his uniformed elder brother and they both laughed.

"My dear fellow, let's not stand here in this draughty hallway arguing like barrow-boys when we can retire to the comfort of my study and discuss this like gentlemen..." He opened his palm, as if in hospitable gesture, to direct him into the same room where Tryton and Zuleika had hid together behind a sofa, on their previous visit. Here was another gesture Tryton somehow remembered and recognised from somewhere else, from a man he'd never met in his life before.

"By the way, have you noticed anything new since you were last here?"

"Lovely floor" said Tryton, sarcastically, as if in a dance-hall.

"Yes, magnificent, isn't it?" said Roderick, quite unabashed. "We presume that was what drove you back here, to us. You wouldn't take good advice and leave us alone, would you, Inspector?" he sneered, taking his seat in a button-backed leather chair, behind a large desk fit to rival Maister's.

"Yesterday, you sent one of your drivers in a quarry truck to kill me and kill Zuleika, didn't you? And that crude attempt at a 'road accident' having failed; today you kidnap Zuleika in Hull because you know that will be certain, if nothing else, to bring me straight into your hands, self-delivered. It seems to me that you demand my attention, whatever I've been instructed to do, or not to do, about the pavement."

"My dear fellow, do please spare us all this talk of killing. You really do not understand the complexities of the situation, does he, Martin?"

Standing beside his seated brother, the Colonel smoothed back thinning hair with a gloved hand before shaking his head sadly, as if considering the irresponsibility of a juvenile relative:

"The thing is, Tryton," added this last, "there's a lot behind all this you don't know about."

"I'd guessed that much. And are you two gents about to enlighten me?"

"I think we owe you that, Inspector. As my brother says, there's a lot you don't understand."

"Try me."

"Please sit down, there's a good fellow. I can't run through it all with you standing over my desk like one of Martin's gunners on a charge."

Tryton did as requested and slid with studied insouciance into a chair that was twin to his opponent's behind the desk. Only the senior Baynard remained upright, still standing at his brother's elbow. (The canvas flap over his revolver holster was unbuttoned, Tryton noted).

"What does the British Empire mean to you, Inspector?"

"I beg your pardon...?"

"The Empire: British Colonies, Overseas Possessions and Protectorates. Are these things important to you?"

"Look here! I think we're all operating under some sort of cross-purpose. I came here to enquire about a kidnapped American woman and, yes, holding incidental interest in a stolen, historical artefact which, as I see you're both perfectly happy to point out to me, has just been cemented into your own hall-floor..."

305

"...so, never mind the Empire, these are the things I'd really like to chat to you two about. I certainly didn't come here to discuss matters more relevant to the Foreign and Commonwealth Office. I'm a policeman, remember, not a diplomat!"

"Yes, Inspector, we'd all noticed that! However, it's important to establish where your loyalties lie."

"I would have thought that's obvious! As a former member of His Majesty's Armed Forces, and in the office of constable, you know damn-fine-well what solemn oaths of loyalty and allegiance to the Crown have been given. And I, for one, still take them seriously - even if your brother clearly doesn't!"

Roderick coloured visibly, even behind his natural complexion: "Yes, alright Inspector. That's quite enough of a lecture, thank you. Keep your shirt on! There is some point to our reasoning, you know...."

"I thought you said you were going to explain things to me. So far all you've done is to ask me some damn-fool questions."

"Let's put our cards on the table. Tell me, are you aware of the League of Empire Loyalists?"

Tryton shook his head.

"No? Well, it's a discreet alliance of men like ourselves; men not without influence in our nation's affairs but unwilling to accept how the slavish policies of this present-day Labour government are leading to rapid disintegration of the British Empire. Look at what's happening out in India after Partition. Bloody chaos. Left unchecked, such bloodshed and chaos will follow the dismantling of all our colonial institutions, everywhere, believe me. Africa's going to be next."

"I see. So that's what you think. Fine. All well and good, it may not match my own views but I suppose we're all of us entitled to our opinions. I still don't see what any of this has got to do with me."

"Because it's essential that, before we go any further, we know where you stand, Inspector. For us or against us."

"Hey, look! Steady on. I only popped in for a social call. I didn't expect you to become my blood-brothers! It's not important to me. It's not important what I think. I'm not for or against anyone. But if you've really got to have an opinion from me, then it's on the futility of standing in the way of progress, against fundamental rights of national self-determination. The past is gone. Over and done with. The tide of human history moves on. The natural desire of people to govern their own countries. So, yes, last year we acceded to the inevitable by relinquishing India after at least fifty years of sustained political pressure to do so. All the time we held the country we never owned it, we never belonged to it, and nor could we ever be accepted as doing so, even after hundreds of years. How could we? You're wasting your time if you think that sort of human feeling can be resisted by a few reactionary backwoodsmen like yourselves, hiding out up here in Northern England, miles from London and the corridors of power."

"I think you would find us rather closer to the decision-makers than you're willing to give credit..." interrupted Roderick Baynard.

"Yes, well, no doubt you gents are the best judge of that. But please don't expect me to declare for your cause and help hold back the sea."

"What a pity. There are many amongst your colleagues who feel differently and whose support we can rely on. A lot of people are opposed to our surrendering sovereignty. We have many friends out there - loyal Indians too, genuinely sorry to see us go. Look what blessings we brought them – democracy and government; a system of laws; and the railways that spread its learning. History will judge us all but in barely a year we already have close Indian friends asking us: "When will the English come back?" Perhaps we never will. If so, then 'Never did the world have sweeter masters' is the epitaph we'd claim for British Rule.

On the other hand, if our League of Empire Loyalists has its way, then it need not be an epitaph but rather the continuing endorsement for a renewed British Empire! It was just as much our American allies' aim to bring down the British Empire as it was to destroy Hitler. OK, so President Roosevelt may have had his way and bankrupted us all, but the Empire still need not be lost.... "

"... Think about that for an idea, eh, Tryton? "Redditor Lucis Aeterna." And, as 'Restorers of the Eternal Light', perhaps we're following an ancient and traditional road down a well-worn path of duty? What do you think, Tryton?"

"Me? I know what you're saying. Don't think I don't. I've got the link you're making, don't worry, but I think you're both completely crackers! Mussolini tried the same arguments out in North Africa, back in the 30's. It didn't cut any ice out there, either. But at least I'm beginning to understand something. Weary as I am of asking you two, again and again, over and over, what all this has to do with Miss Macsen and the mosaic, I really do think I am starting to work it out for myself, anyway."

"Good, good! And if you are, then well done, Inspector!"

Condescension was so integral and unwitting a component to the speech and manners of either Baynard it hardly deserved protest. Yet as Roderick's continuing harangue proved, however lowly other folk's motives were rated, the Baynards took their own very seriously indeed:

"You must realise just how much this house means to my brother and I, not only as our home but as witness to the Baynard family's distinguished history of service to this country and its King-Emperors. I don't know whether you did know, but we recently celebrated the two-hundredth anniversary of the house itself being completed, in the first month of 1748. In the month of Janus himself, the two-faced Roman god who looks both to the future and the past, and so gives his name to the house. This sense of continuity certainly makes me - as an individual member of such a family – extremely conscious of the heavy responsibility placed upon each of us to maintain and be worthy of such traditions. Martin feels the same. The house and its contents are a permanent reminder of these ancestral achievements, which my brother and I will hold in trust for future generations."

"Bravo! A pretty speech. And is that the reason why you had to have the Roman floor? As fitting gift for the house on this, its biennial? A boost for your own vanity and misplaced sense of personal importance?"

Roderick scowled:

"If you like! Better here, than glued to a wall in a dusty museum, where no one bothers to come and see it apart from reluctant school parties or vagrants in out of the rain. Or sold to an American art collector. Perhaps it means more here, is worth more to us kept here?

"As symbol of another, older, British Empire - long ago....?"

"Exactly. Well done, Inspector! I hadn't thought a mere policeman capable of such sophisticated historical associations. Yes, it will represent just that; a symbol of national durability and local continuity in all our institutions; even in our houses and great families; which we Empire Loyalists all aspire to on a greater stage. Preserved here, it offers us a direct link with the past, as far back as the days of the great Magnus Maximus, or even the admiral Carausius."

"I was right! You really are crackers. Absolutely barking, the pair of you! Both as nutty as fruit cakes. But I did wonder just when those two names might make an appearance in our little chat. Funny that. Two names which for one reason or another seem to be constantly recurring on this enquiry, with frequency enough to make any police officer who knows his stuff want to put them at the top of his list of suspects. Except that these two have been dead some sixteen, seventeen hundred years! It's thanks to you two that even someone ordinary like me has learned a little bit about their background. The British Usurpers. Heroes? Maybe. Rogues? Probably. Selfish, greedy men who for the sake of vaunting ambition and self-aggrandisement stripped a province of its troops, a civilisation of its shield, and let in over a thousand years of barbarism. Men like you, Mr.Roderick, or perhaps like you, Sir Martin? Alright, alright! I see I've already offended you both with that last comment. No doubt you're both worthy men, and so are all your league of loyalists. O.K. I'm no historian. I know little of these things. But I do know that I knew even less of them until I ran across a ravishing beauty called Zuleika Macsen; a fascinating person whom even your own tame solicitor was good enough to explain to me bore the self-same family name as that ancient Maximus, preserved in Celtic form.... SO WHAT HAVE YOU TWO BASTARDS DONE WITH HER?"

This final, crucial question was almost shouted, but if Tryton had betrayed himself and his depth of feeling, the Baynards remained unruffled:

309

"I think you ought to brace yourself for disappointment, Inspector. Beautiful, charming and learned as Zuleika undoubtedly is, she is NOT what she seems. You and I might find some comradeship there, because I more than suspect we've both been her victims!"

"What the hell do you mean?"

"Exactly what I've said. The woman is an actress, a chameleon who adapts her camouflage to suit her background, to match the colours of her surroundings. A promiscuous adventuress who specialises in widowers. Listen to me, Tryton. She's deceived us both."

"I don't know what you're talking about!"

"Look, we all know you've been particularly attentive to her recently. What man could resist her? Funny, isn't it, what subtle, indefinable combinations of physical form and facial structure in a woman of character can do to us men, eh? What fools we are! The enduring fascination of the female form. We hopeless male creatures stand mesmerised! Families wrecked, fortunes lost, and empires destroyed. All for the sake of hair like flames, a pretty lip, and the seduction inherent in a voice which reduces grown men to blithering idiots! Don't argue with it, Mr. Tryton! We've all known it. And in Zuleika there's the finest of everything, the most overpowering of all these different scents and visual stimulants, neatly contained in one poor little rich girl from New Jersey. What a spell she casts! Am I not right? That's what we've got in common, you and I, haven't we? Comrades in arms.....her arms! We've both of us taken risks for her, both been tempted to step a little way beyond the strict confines of the law."

"How dare you! How dare you suggest a law-enforcement officer like myself has done any such thing. What are you talking about?"

"I can only speak for myself. I can only say that I am a man who has been more than lonely after the sudden disappearance of my first wife, two years ago. It made me feel very sad and alone. I still do not know where she went. Your people weren't interested either: "People have rows and deliberately choose to go missing all the time" said the policeman on the desk. Who knows? Your lot can't chase after every one of them, I suppose I must accept that…".

"Of course I have my compensations - the family businesses of chalk-quarrying and gypsum production. They give me the means to maintain this house and our ancestral traditions of public service in a modern world. I make myself busy. Keep myself occupied. I sit as Justice of the Peace at the Brough Magistrate's Court, in a small town where I'm told magistrates have probably sat since Roman times. Obviously that role makes me more vulnerable in my position, were there to be suggestions of malpractice. I'll readily admit that's a major part of what's making me so anxious to persuade you that this business about the Roman mosaic really should go no further. And I have the beginnings of a political career at Westminster, in which I sincerely believe I can achieve much for my country, much for my Empire, just as the Baynards have always done for generations. But amongst it all there are quiet moments of reflective leisure where a mind unoccupied has dwelt on a lack of female companionship."

"I hope you're not expecting me to feel sorry for you..."

"No, of course not, Inspector! But you might at least understand that this was the void into which a clever young American woman giving the name of Zuleika Macsen was to step. If that is her real name and not just another seductive concept to further bait the honey trap. Who knows? You might be able to tell me. What I do think is that a widower like you might identify with the kind of gap someone like her could fill for someone like me...."

"How the hell do you know that I'm a widower? I've never told anyone!"

"These people do their research. In my case, I thought I'd met her quite by chance, one day when I was out exercising my labradors in Brantingham Dale. She told me she was an archaeologist, field-walking as part of her research into the line of estates and country-houses the Romans once had in this part of England, along this river. And a war-widow, to boot. Personally, I found her a most fascinating young lady. Beauty and Tragedy together. The story she was telling me struck a particularly sympathetic chord, as a lonely local landowner stuck in a fairly-historic property of my own. With the benefit of hindsight, I realise she was just encouraging me and flattering me in this appealing idea of being an inheritor to their tradition."

311

"Their tradition…?"

"Then she told you about the mosaics…" put in the Colonel, anxious to nudge his brother's narrative along.

"Yes, that's right. Of course everyone around here knew there had been a Roman villa at Brantingham Quarry but what I didn't know, not until she told me, was that an operation was underway to lift and preserve these remarkable decorated floors off the site. I was spending more and more of my time with Zuleika, entertaining her here and taking her out socially. I'm not ashamed to say that I became quite frankly besotted with her and some might say - I do know that Martin here would probably be amongst the first - that I have made a bit of a fool of myself over her. After all, I am still supposed to be a married man…."

"Tell the Inspector exactly what you mean…."

"She took me several times to the quarry. We'd park the Bentley at the side of the wood, you know, quietly hidden in a little lane there, although I don't doubt that anyone who saw it, whether farm-worker or quarryman, would have recognised it as my car. You don't see that many Bentleys parked up in the byroads of East Yorkshire. I was getting careless you see, indiscreet. She has that effect on me and I shouldn't wonder if she's not had the same effect on you, too. A bit of kissing and cuddling would follow then we'd go for a walk before things went too far, I suppose. Hand in hand through the wood there, with the wind always roaring through the trees. What's that poem about Wenlock Edge? Yes, Housman, that's the fellow! I realise now that she was only leading me up there to look at the preserved mosaics, after the archaeologists had finished for the day. Leading me in every sense. She was worming a suggestion into my head that I should take one. Steal it, I suppose you'd say, but we stand by our feeling it isn't theft but rather a natural return to its own kind, to a country family which is backbone to the district, just as those people who built the villa must once have been. Their true inheritors. We feel entitled, you see. "

"You can't seriously expect me to accept that sort of half-baked sentiment as justification for theft?"

"Not in law. No. Not a justification, no. But an explanation."

"So you took it. How did you manage to do that so quickly and bring it over here?"

312

"It wasn't easy, I can tell you. It had to be organised like a military operation. Martin was the chap with the expertise there. We used lorries and equipment from our own chalk quarry, up the dale. The rolled-up mosaic needed a low-loader. And the help of a few of our own men – the Artillery are good at handling big objects like that. Zuleika gave the word, though. She told us exactly when the archaeologists had reached a state of preparation where it would be ready for us to lift out whole. We went in at night. 'In like Flint' and then out again. We were cock-a-hoop. Very proud of ourselves. Zuleika was thrilled. It was as if I'd proved myself to her."

"What happened then?"

"We made arrangements for the mosaic to be incorporated into the hallway. And I rather recklessly made Zuleika a proposal of marriage which I knew in my heart I wasn't really able to fulfil. I wanted her here in this house with me, you see, to enjoy and appreciate it all. She and the pavement seemed to belong together."

"Did she accept?"

"No, she disappeared the same day! The next I hear of her is when my own solicitor 'phones me about a fortnight later, to tell me she's in custody at the main police station in Hull. Which I presume is where you took her over."

"So your story is that she egged you on and that Zuleika was the mainspring behind your decision to remove the mosaic?"

"That's right. Exactly. But there's more to it than that. Let my brother explain that bit. It's more his field..."

"The point is, Inspector, there was a reason behind all this. A plan. She didn't fix on us just by accident. We've been targeted. This woman calling herself Zuleika Macsen has, we believe, been sent specifically with instructions to embroil us in this affair, to deliberately enmesh us in some disreputable transaction whose exposure would discredit and ruin us both."

"Oh, really? And who might have sent her on such a Machiavellian mission? The Russians? The Stern Gang? A Sunday Newspaper? Or perhaps the Boy Scouts?"

313

"You might jeer at the idea, Inspector, but the information we have received is reliable. This is political espionage. This woman is an intelligence officer of some kind. An American secret agent, we think. Where do you think she got that little truck from but off one of their airbases? Sent by a powerful nation with its own ruthless self-interest in the global decline of British power. Sent with a brief to engineer the collapse of what our enemies might label as a particularly extreme group, inside the British establishment, vociferously opposed to any such decline in our influence. The League of Empire Loyalists was her target and my brother and I as prominent members have been chosen as obvious pillars to bring down."

"What, here? Cloak and dagger in the wilds of East Yorkshire - from our wartime allies? Get away! I just don't believe it. Even if it were only partly true, you both seem to have been happy enough to step into the trap she was setting for you."

"My dear fellow, you really must believe us! My brother knows what he is talking about, especially with his connections in the military. This woman has betrayed us, just as she will betray you. Whether she had plans for the pavement to go elsewhere, I don't know, but that does not make the basic rightness of it being permanently lodged inside this venerable house of ours less inescapable."

"Where is she now?"

"Don't worry. She won't come to any harm. She's quite safe. She is being held to our order, in the manager's office at the gypsum works up the valley."

Tryton grimaced visibly. ("Oh, God! Not bloody gypsum again! The dreams. They were all coming true. Gypsum and auburn. Barbarism would bring fire. COHORS EQUITATA").

Yet it almost seemed a credible tale, for all that. Inside himself, he wrangled with knots of fear and doubt. Some of what they were saying could be true, or none of it. Tryton breathed in heavily then he remembered what she'd told him: "Confront the Minotaur!" Her words steadied him. This suavely-persuasive narrative was simply an essential aspect of the monster, he realised. The smooth gloss of its thick hide contrasting with the bloody shame of its deeds. The complexity of its tale-telling stood for the intellectual maze of its labyrinthine plots. To collaborate would be to surrender to the beast - as its next victim.

314

He had to concentrate on what mattered. What they had done.

"And what about Maister's car?"

"Ah, yes! That really was an unfortunate coincidence. Please believe me when I assure you that it was not directed at you personally. Not at all. Nor indeed at Zuleika. Indeed not."

"How was it then that one of your trucks had to shunt us off the road and damn-near kill us?"

"We have been frank with you, Inspector. I hope you will give us credit for that. There is one final confession we must make to you. I have already referred to the influence we enjoy in many quarters, including some of your own colleagues."

"Including Superintendent Maister ?"

"Exactly. He is a fine and honourable police officer of principle. He is also a man whom we have been happy to find so much at one with the aims and outlook of the League. There has been no conflict between that and the proper discharge of his duties."

"Until now?"

"My dear fellow, I'm afraid that your relentless pursuit of this little problem over the mosaic has put your boss into something of a moral dilemma. I don't expect it was intended, but you have been making his professional life rather difficult recently. There have also been some other people over to see him, recently. People whom we don't know, either. Agents of a foreign power? Perhaps. Or maybe our own ghastly government. Whoever they were, I suspect he has for the first time been confronted with the possibility of a conflict of interest, a conflict of loyalties, one he probably never expected to face...."

The Colonel intervened again: "You see Inspector, we just felt that your commander was in need of a little reminder, of a little push, just so he would remember what he owed us in terms of discretion and loyalty."

"What exactly did he owe you?"

"Well, the car for one thing! That had been a little present from us. A token of our thanks for his support; for good service in the past and a reminder or encouragement towards obedience in the future."

"A corrupt inducement. So then you had it smashed up."

315

"Inspector, please! I'm afraid that what happened was the man we'd sent was a little over-zealous, that's all. He has been disciplined. It really wasn't meant to go that far. And of course the fool did it when the wrong people were in the car."

"Why are you telling me all this?"

"Because you have asked us, Inspector! We want to share this with you. To be open with you. And because, as Roderick has said, we want to know where you stand. It is our sincere hope that, whatever misunderstandings we have all been through when working at a distance, you might now identify as your own those same patriotic goals which the League represents. Agree to support us. We think you could make a major contribution. Forget about the American woman. Forget about the mosaic. As if neither of them had ever happened. Stand by your country, instead."

"And if I don't?"

"My dear fellow! We had you marked down as a man of courage and conviction. Do not disappoint us!"

"But if I do disappoint you. What then? Shall I be killed in cold blood like Ronald Maister to preserve my silence? Because there is too much at stake?"

Their conversation ceased at once, lapsing into an electric pause. A cloud passed over the sun and the seated Baynard looked up at his elder brother before resuming: "Oh dear, oh dear! Oh, my dear fellow, I really do wish you had not made that last remark. Most unwise, most unwise….how did you know he was dead? "

"I went to his house this afternoon, just before I came here…I've seen him."

"I am most awfully sorry! That really is a terrible pity. You do understand that now we are left with no alternative. Just when I thought we were making some progress with you."

"You have been foolish, Inspector. We cannot allow men like yourself, not even good men like Maister, to stand in the way of the national interest."

"I would have thought the most essential interest our nation could have is in the pair of you being brought to justice. Whatever the future holds for this country, it has no need of cranks like you!"

"You will not bring us down with insults and abuse, Inspector. Go on, Roddy, put him right!"

"Yes. You haven't got a hope, Tryton. Be realistic. Have you? The essential requirement is evidence, isn't it? Let's be honest. You haven't got any; not a scrap, have you? We're not in the middle of a gangster movie. It's not some fictional police thriller. This is real life. Of course, it's unfair, isn't it? Life's like that. The popular, public perception of detective work is so different from the grim reality men like you must face every day, isn't it? In an Agatha Christie novella or a Dorothy Sayers story, all Hercule Poirot or Lord Peter Wimsey needs to do is extract oral information, verbal explanations from bystanders. To find out who did what to whom. Everybody is called into the library and an announcement is made. Case solved. End of story…".

"…but this is real life, Tryton, and finding out all alone who you think has done it – well, it's not going to help you now, is it? Not out here. So you've found out, or you think you have. Well done! Hoo-bloody-ray! It won't help you at all, of course, because you realise that in the real world your job is to gather real evidence. Hard facts. Knowing the answer simply isn't enough. You need witnesses; live people who will give written statements and whose health and resolve to testify will survive to a trial date. And you haven't got any, have you?

Those you've had have either disappeared or met a tragic end. And where does that leave you? I'll tell you, Tryton. Out on your own. Up the creek without a paddle. Why? Because whatever else you may think, my brother and I are not stupid. Whatever information there may have been which you might have gathered, the physical evidence all points to you, now. We have been to some pains in our arrangements to make sure of that. No, I'm sorry about this, Tryton, I really am. We genuinely had high hopes for you, but I'm afraid we've definitely come to the end of the road …deal with him, Martin!"

The Colonel reached for the flap over his holster, but the unconscious languor of an aristocrat slowed his movements, natural symptom of an arrogant self-confidence to which Life had never offered significant challenge. Besides, it never occurred to him that there might be any element of the 'Wild West' gunslinger in the man he faced opposite.

317

There was an unarmed civilian seated in front of him whom he was simply obliged to shoot, a dreary but necessary task he would carry out carefully and in soldierly fashion. He'd known that his own artillery volunteers outside in the grounds were about due to begin a scheduled bombardment of the far end of the valley with blank shells. They'd deliberately toyed with Tryton until that pre-ordained time, in the expectation that the noise of their practice barrage would cover any discharge of small-arms required inside the house, should that prove necessary.

Hardly had the Colonel's hand slid beneath the flap to his still-sheathed revolver than Tryton seized the blue lanyard around his own neck to yank the hidden Webley out of its raincoat pocket. The weight of its long barrel received perfect counterbalance from his grasp of its curved black handle. In that fractional moment he caught the frozen horrified faces of both Baynards, paralysed by astonishment at their helpless victim producing his own weapon, a weapon quickly levelled at the still-fumbling soldier as the trigger was squeezed. Its firing hammer sprang back and the gun leapt in his hand as its deafening report roared in the room.

Colonel Sir Martin Baynard suffered the fatal entry of its missile full in the forehead. Prompt, deserved, and equivalent retribution for the murder of Ronald Maister. His senseless body was blasted hard back against the Wedgwood blue and decorative white of the study wall, on which he left a scarlet smudge to mark his downward slide onto the floor. Dead before he hit it, it was this fall which brought his short-nosed Army Webley spinning out of its holster, too late to be of use, skittering under the desk.

At the same time, Roderick had launched himself sideways from his chair, even before that single shot which took his brother, and was hiding beneath the thick protection of the same desk, scrabbling for the loose weapon.

Tryton now lunged at him across the width of its embossed leather surface, scattering brass-edged family photographs, ink-bottles and letter racks, but he failed to grab this surviving Baynard.

The air in the room was clouded by blue gun-smoke and sharp with the whiff of expended cordite which caught in his throat.

318

There were shouts in the hall and, as Tryton turned to look, Roderick Baynard had crawled on hands and knees across the Axminster carpet with his brother's gun in one hand.

"Stop or I'll shoot !"

Tryton was sporting enough to give a warning but his consideration was exposed as the weakness of an appeaser when Baynard ignored its terms and rolled across into the doorway. A frightened maid stood there, framed in hysterical immobility by the bloody scene she'd found in the study, and Tryton dared not fire for fear she'd be victim. Like a writhing limbless lizard, Baynard had got himself into the hall where, now standing fully upright, he held this innocent as his hostage - one hand around her neck whilst the other pressed the revolver tight to her white forehead.

It was Tryton's turn to hide behind the desk and this proved wise precaution when the wall behind him became peppered with holes, where it was not already stained with the blood of a brother. Peering around the desk from his position next to the dead Colonel, Tryton looked to return these pot-shots but found it pointless because the hostage-taker and his prisoner were gone. Running to the door, he put his head out into the hallway to see these two dragging or being dragged into the shadows at the far end of a long corridor. The Minotaur was retreating into its maze.

A further shot came whizzing down its length to discourage any pursuit but Tryton would not be put off so easily. Baynard was heading for the front of the house. Whilst determined to follow, Tryton realised how easily a direct pursuit into the heart of the labyrinth could lead to extra harm, whether to the serving-maid or himself. Deciding on an outdoors outflanking manoeuvre as safer compromise, he crossed over the Roman floor itself to leave the house by the same French-windows he'd used as exit on his last visit.

Despite the sun, a chill north-easterly wind blowing took the edge off the heat of action and encouraged caution. Across the terrace and over those tennis courts again, round the side of the walled yard and onto the rear drive where the deep Stygian shade of its overgrown rhododendrons gave total cover. Here he recovered his breath.

Emerging from this hidden access at the intersection of front and rear drives, right on the corner of the house, he met the deafening blast of several twenty-five pounder field guns being simultaneously fired up the valley. The automaton gunners were totally absorbed in precision work, ministration by orchestrated numbers to recoiling ordnance. Unlike Tryton, they failed to note the surprising appearance of a dishevelled and highly-distressed Roderick Baynard on the front steps to January House, pistol in hand.

Tryton was relieved to see he had at least given up the hostage.

A silver-over-gunmetal Bentley coupe of recent manufacture was parked on the crushed chalk and gravel of the front drive. Roderick darted across to it, snake-like, still holding his revolver. Tryton dashed back into cover amongst the rhododendrons, crashing through their clinging foliage to get nearer to the corner of the house and a point where the Bentley might pass him. Twigs scratched his face. He heard the low rumble of its engine starting up and the crunch of big soft cross-ply tyres compressing gravel before a further salute from the guns wiped out any other sound in the valley. He took his own pistol and steadied its barrel on the thick, gnarled branch of some elderly shrub, carefully taking aim on the massive front offside wheel of the Bentley as it lumbered towards his hide.

The shot for which he was now sighting was not to prove necessary. In the awesome but impotent thunder of the guns, he could not have heard the straining gears and agricultural revolutions of an artillery tractor decorated with torn shrubs bouncing heedless down the main drive towards the house, loaded ammunition-limber in tow. Roderick's equal failure to detect this hefty on-comer might have been due to many things - preoccupation with what lay behind (an armed pursuer); the grief of sudden bereavement (his loss of a brother); or simply because this skilfully camouflaged gun-tractor merged exactly as intended with that blank wall of greenery wherein Tryton hid.

Whichever of these distractions explains his inattention, the consequences were for a few seconds avoidable but catastrophic when incurred.

The accelerating Bentley and the commercial-pattern Austin met head-on in an impact the sum of their velocities. Its violence - momentarily - stopped each leviathan dead in its tracks.

If each unbelted driver were not killed outright by the shock of intolerable deceleration, what then followed as the colliders bounced apart must surely have done for them. Lesser sparks, flashes, flames and combustions may have flared briefly after the accident and, if given time, more gradually grown to greater things. But their build-up was eclipsed by the detonation of all that racked ammunition in the jack-knifed trailer to the tow truck, whose strained hatches burst open to disgorge live shells that flew, brass-nose first, onto the hard and unforgiving ground. If only one of them went off, then that would have been enough. The explosions were incremental, building one upon the other, till they ripped across the mangled frames of the two wrecked vehicles and blew in every window of the house with searing thunderbolts of flame that penetrated deep into its rooms.

So close to the shock wave, Tryton himself must surely have been killed but for the cushioning effect of trees and bushes wherein he hid, which first absorbed some of its force and then caught him like a net when he was lifted off his feet and tossed bodily into the air. Even so, he must have lost consciousness for a moment or two and only came to after the remaining high-explosive in the ammunition limber was finally consumed in the very last of these apocalyptic blasts.

Untangling himself from clawing twigs and branches, lucky to have been missed by falling trees, he realised his coat was in tatters and his exposed face and hands bleeding from numerous superficial abrasions.

Stepping forward through foliage stripped of leaves in seconds, as if for instant winter, he returned to his vantage point of a few moments before. Resting at random angles only feet apart, both the Bentley and the Army Austin had been reduced by the fires to no more than deformed and blackened hulks, every flammable or consumable fitting melted and turned to ash or air in a fleeting furnace.

Roderick Baynard could not have survived this collision or the explosions but his death was not enough for the insatiable fires which now leapt across the lawns and clawed at his inheritance, invading his home.

Like an indiscriminate but greedy art-collector moving from room to room, the strolling flames touched a damask here, licked appreciatively at a wooden sideboard there, and resolved to take them all as their own. In no time at all, the house and its treasures were reduced to a ferocious inferno.

At the pinnacle of its mature magnificence, in the two-hundredth year of its age, the ancestral seat of the Baynards, their famous January House in the East Riding of Yorkshire, was utterly destroyed by fire. A tragedy to claim the lives of both the surviving sons of that distinguished family whose estate it always had been. Two brothers who were last of a line which had built and held the house throughout its history. That neither Baynard left issue may have been something of a blessing, since all that remained for their inheritors was a heap of ashes on the valley floor and a few broken walls, beneath whose ruins lay the charred bones of Martin Baynard – crumbled beyond what even the most able pathologist could diagnose as a shooting.

A pillar of smoke and fire rose up out of the dale, above the trees and high into the sky, till the winds took it and scattered its particles across the upper atmosphere. Far below and beneath, a motley collection of human survivors of this rural holocaust streamed away from the site and up the drive towards the nearest road. Trudging amongst shell-shocked artillerymen, weeping domestics, and bewildered estate workers was a white-faced man in urban clothes, a suit and the scorched shreds of a raincoat. Detective Inspector Michael Tryton of the Hull City C.I.D. He alone amongst the refugees retained a clear idea of what remained to be done.

Zuleika Macsen. He had to find her before anyone else got to her.

The whole kitchen facade of January House had collapsed onto all of the transport parked in the walled yard, burying them in rubble. Without her Dodge Weapons Carrier, he would just have to force-march to the gypsum works where the late Roderick Baynard told him she was lodged. However far it was. He had to find her.

Gypsum and auburn. Barbarians and fire. COHORS EQUITATA

By now, the pall of smoke and flying ash above him was marker to the tragedy for miles around. Amongst the first to respond was a shiny black Wolseley which came speeding up the unclassified road from South Cave. On the crest of a hill it paused, whilst those within stepped briefly out of the car to observe from a distance these obvious signs of major destruction. Two plain-clothes constables in the back, equipped with service rifles, and a Superintendent in the front with his dutiful sergeant-driver. He was the one who spoke first:

"Dear God, I fear we're too late!" gasped Pickering. "Come on, Mr Rivett, sir, let's get a move on. We've got to get down there and find out what's going on!"

"We'll have a job keeping this little lot out of the papers!" was all Rivett could say.

He needn't have worried. As the records don't show, the papers did him proud. A search of the archive reveals how they have never even mentioned the fire at January House or the death of the Baynard brothers, to this day, while Ronald Maister's tragic demise was put down to suicide. After all, and as everyone knows, we only ever hear about what they want us to hear, in the terms by which they want us to understand it.

**"Wondrous is this wallstone; broken by fate. The castles
have decayed, the work of giants is crumbling.
Roofs are fallen, ruinous are the towers, despoiled are the
towers with their gates; frost is on their mortar, broken are
the roofs, cut-away, fallen, undermined by age.
There are no Caesars now...."**

(A Saxon poet in the ruins of Aquae Sulis, the Roman city of
Bath).

XV

Reclining alone on a richly-upholstered velvet bolster in the 'House of the Winged Victories' in that small northern horse-coping town they call Derventio; the governor's officer, Flavius Candidus, reviewed his position - at first with an incredulous relish. Even in a life already full with experience, enlivened by the youthful extremes of Army service across the western half of the greatest and most-enduring military power the world has ever known, here was a first.

Never, even amongst the worst excesses into which a young subaltern might be led by his older, more worldly-wise comrades (those days in the wine-shop and nights in the brothel); never before, even amongst those exotic creatures lured to the frontier towns of Empire by Imperial coinage showered on licentious soldiery - whether the blond Batavian whores of Magnis or the silky Syrian girls of Aesica - had he found the startling anachronism of divine significance amongst the women whose comfort he'd sought and bought.

Here was a one-off, of that he was sure. Never before had he known connection with a real Goddess. Even if the urban cynic might decry her deification by the Parisii as just the workings of rural superstition, nothing more; the woman with whom he'd lain was undoubtedly the foremost being in their parochial pantheon. Her Divinity was irrefutable and only strengthened by his closer examination. Divinity made flesh, the living incarnation of their Parisii clan – its very genius.

Yet for all that, he could not claim a significantly-different experience from those serving-girls, slave girls, innkeepers-daughters, and occasional professionals which he (to some dawning shame) and all his military kind so traditionally use, abuse, and unerringly abandon. Candidus was glad to confirm that, for all her mesmerising other-worldliness, here was a deity retaining the compulsive physical attributes of a healthy and attractive young woman. A woman like her.

But there were complications, as there usually are. A price to be paid for overnight acts of reckless intimacy which, even if not fit to be met in coin, could never be ignored.

Its first instalment would come not from her status amongst the Parisii or whatever moral symbolism the stern tenets of the Christian might say attached to their loose actions, but from her other status as beloved only daughter of his lord and employer - a stern man of temporal power. Someone whose expectations of his good and faithful servant included establishing her welfare and confirming it to the anxious parent, not exploiting his enquiry as careering vehicle for her breathless seduction.

If the second instalment of consequence might come from her position as a married woman, it must be allowed (for all the good it might do him) that adultery itself was hardly unprecedented in the upper reaches of Roman society, riddled with hypocrisy as they surely still are. This does not make it any less dangerous an offence. The fact remained that – if discovered – their frenzied coupling made for the most dishonourable breach of her sacred vows imaginable – a capital offence in which he, Candidus, stood just as culpable as she. (Or lay).

These worrying thoughts of painful consequence were what re-introduced to his mind that person to whom she'd made those vows, her formidable husband, Marcus Ulpius Januarius: landowner, mine-owner and metal exporter; shipping-agent, sentencing judge and principal citizien; would-be politician and now, last but not least – and thanks only to Flavius Candidus – shamed cuckold.

A man who on two successive occasions of escalating violence had already sent paid thugs specifically to deal with Candidus. That was before any provocation. For all his shows of attentive kindness when face-to-face, friend Januarius seemed immediately to have identified him as serious threat to his prominent position – purely on the basis of his job. And that was even without finding-out what he'd been up to with his wife.

If news of Candidus' regular visits to the 'House of the Winged Victories' were to reach the ears of Januarius (as they surely must, all servants being indiscreet) any prejudice held against him must be utterly re-doubled.

The Magistrate's vengeful conclusion about the Vicarius's runner – that here was someone who seemed determined to cross him at every turn - would only make his final elimination into an absolute priority, his expendability beyond mere status and into strategic necessity.

326

Meanwhile, if Januarius and his henchmen did not do for him, then the Vicarius surely would, once he found out about his daughter. With this sober realisation, immature and almost boyish satisfactions over easy sexual conquest now gave way to a dawning sense of graver consequence. Candidus gnawed on his lip, a once-comfortable pose on the bolster unconsciously drawn into strained contortion.

With this reluctant understanding of what harvests he was as loath but equally-likely to reap came more troubled calculations yet for the wages likely from his sin. Suddenly, his mission had gone deeper yet into unimaginable territories – further than anyone (Candidus included) had ever imagined or intended. Never mind Rome, even Londinium itself seemed immeasurably far away. The further he went into the countryside and the more deeply he became involved with the Tyche, the more he was journeying into an alien world and a native culture he no longer understood.

All the same - what a mess, what a fool he'd been!

He'd asked her afterwards: "Why did you let me do that?"

"Do not delude yourself, my noble wounded soldier! Mine was the victory. I took you. Completely! It was always my intention. You are mere novitiate at the shrine of the Tyche. You will sleep in this house and dream of the mystery. The incubation."

"I love you."

"Of course you do. That is part of it, necessary for your devotion."

"What shall I say to your father? How can I look him in the eye? I must get back to Londinium at once..."

"Not now! Your report can wait. You are needed for me here. I seem to have been waiting for you - or someone very like you - for weeks."

"What are you doing up here at Derventio when your husband waits alone outside Petuaria, in his lonely villa, wanting for a wife to sit at table with him?"

"It is part of my role and duty to be obedient wife and an ornament to my husband. But I cannot escape my whole destiny and that of my tribe. And neither will I forego pleasure. Just as his first wife would not.... I often wonder how she died."

"What do you mean?"

"You have met him. A charming, charming man! No-one could imagine what he is like sometimes, when I am alone with him. Jealous. Vindictive. Violent. That is why I have had to come here. It is not the first time. He will beg me and implore me to come back with promises of a fresh start, a new beginning. For a few days it will be true as well. Then the mask will slip and it is back to his old ways."

"I can believe it - he sent men to kill me. Will I be safe here?"

"Here is the one sure place where you can have my protection and that of the whole tribe. The home of the Tyche is inviolable. I am the Protectress. Also, more practically, I have the personal guarantee of the local commander and with it his garrison. He holds my interests very close to his heart, as you shall find....."

"Really? Then, in that case, there might be something more you can do for me. You will know the main reason why I sought refuge in this house last night was an attack on me by a matched pair of assassins who work for your husband."

She shivered: "The two gladiators? They follow him everywhere, like a couple of evil shadows. Even separately, either of them frightens me! Their gods are different. I mean nothing to them. He only has to give the word...."

"Perhaps, but the good news is that there's only one gladiator left now. Theirs truly is a dying trade! That noise you heard in the Old Town last night was the attack they launched on me being driven off by a guard-animal belonging to a friend of mine, a travelling sword-smith with one leg; a man of rare skill with metals who keeps a bear to look after his wagon and to guard his stock. Unfortunately, one of your husband's men got stuck in its jaws. You will remember the German with the pony-tail and bad teeth? That's why my friend, Taranis the Smith, will tonight be studying the quality of welded ironwork holding him close to a damp wall under the headquarters building, inside Derventio fort. Unless I can help him out. Or if you can, instead. Is there anything you could do to get him released?"

"Their Prefect, Claudius Bassus, is a humane and merciful man - someone who reads Marcus Aurelius or Herodotus whilst seated on his horse, as he waits patiently to kill Saxon war bands under the eastern cliffs. If ever a garrison commander was sure to hear a well-presented application for your friend's release with sympathy, then he is that man."

"What! M. Claudius Bassus? Late decurio of Cohors I Equitata, up on the Wall?"

"I can't tell you his career history..."

"If it's the man I'm thinking of, then it is the history of a high-flier; a capable soldier whose most significant skill is the ability to talk the hind-leg off a baggage mule. They love him to death, up at headquarters."

"He's certainly a most charming and courteous officer.."

"Dark, curly hair and beard? Small in stature but built like a Rhenus wine-barge? He wears a gold signet ring on the middle finger of his sword hand; its black jet inset carved with an eagle"

"Oh yes! That's my Marcus Claudius alright."

"Ha! Who'd imagine It? My old mate, Bassus! We were junior officers in the same regiment together, you see. That's how I know him. Look at us now, eh? He got his Ala, while I got an unusual scar and a half-pension. The Wheel of Fortune turns, but M.Claudius Bassus was born lucky!"

This discussion and the activity which followed pretty much closing his audience with the Tyche, Candidus was later shown to a small cell-like room on the far side of the house, in which to see out the few hours remaining before resurgence of the Unconquered Sun God. A token arrangement to preserve outward conventions of chastity and decency in his hostess. (An arrangement which would achieve little, as he judged. The servants knew well enough, from all the noise she'd made). Alone in his cell, he lay on a cold bed, happily remembering her warmth, fighting sleep. The mysteries she had threatened would be revealed by incubation frankly scared him, so he clung to consciousness, resisting rest, but it was hopeless. The winged dream-carriers of sleep came for him as he lay there, using their sharp hooks to drag him into - not out of - their arena of nightmares:

A house which stood amongst trees was burning, a strange house not like any other but with several storeys, big like a palace on the Palatine. Out of the flames a man who could have been himself fled into the trees, their branches tearing at his clothes. He ran down the valley and at the far end was a tall white tower where the Tyche stood waiting for him, strands of auburn hair waving in the wind.

In the morning, Candidus rose late and outfaced the dumb insolence and knowing leers of the house slaves with a cheerful politeness. He freed his aching chest from its usual morning tightness by hot bathing, smartening himself up as well he could, before taking the leather document-tube from his bag and his silver badge of office out of the house and all of them up to the south-east gateway into the fort. His badge was what he believed would get him into the fort but he found otherwise.

The exceptional period of social stability and political security which the Empire has enjoyed under the Imperial Household of the Noblest and Most Blessed Emperor Constantine and his Five Heirs is truly something of a golden age. The price of these years of peace has lain in removing much of that civil authority and administrative responsibility which our military commanders traditionally enjoyed. Once it was these senior soldiers who governed Rome's provinces with a wit and economy only occasionally marred by those destructive bouts of ambition which grew in later times. When they did, it came to breed such a lust for glory and continuous bloody cycle of civil war that there never was an Emperor who was spared his violent death. Something had to be done. Which is why their powers came to be transferred and divided up amongst a massive and disabling bureaucracy of civil servants, a system whose first victims were decisiveness and efficiency and whose second was any co-operation with the army.

In the eyes of an Emperor who had come to power (as so many before him) through the declaration of himself as Caesar by his British legionaries at Eboracum on 25th July 306 A.D., this was a price worth paying - if it made sure no other soldier would ever follow him down that bloody road again.

The true cost of this weak guarantee against disloyal Generals ever again exploiting their day-to-day control of distant provinces as foundation for usurping the Purple would be paid on another day. When its fee was called in, the damage to the Empire's chances of survival resulting from that natural antipathy existing between soldier and civil administrator meant that, in times of invasion and crisis, this gulf would always prevent their co-operation against a common threat.

Which is why, when attending on the two sentries guarding the lower portals of the fort, he found it was not his introduction as beneficarius consularis but rather as former comrade-in-arms to their commander which finally persuaded the soldiers to allow him into their camp. Their crossed cavalry lances parted slowly and the two mail-clad troopers stepped smartly back, as much in deference to their supervisory N.C.O. now emerging from his flanking guard-chamber in the gatehouse as any courtesy meant for Candidus. It was this latter grumpy person who now escorted Candidus all the way up the paved Via Principalis and into the central headquarters building, without even the one attempt at conversation.

Looking around him and grateful to be spared idle chit-chat, it was good to see that Bassus ran a tight ship. After all the aimless amateurism of the Petuaria garrisons, it was a real pleasure to see the proper Army going about its duty in organised fashion. Ahead of him, he could see right up the road, straight through the arched entrance to the headquarters courtyard and into the Chapel of the Standards inside the Principia itself. Here were the venerated flags and glittering symbols of the Ala Picentiana resting under constant guard; votive emblems of loyalty and duty permanently visible to the soldiers of the regiment even as they went about their most routine task. Rows of stable blocks contained the high-quality mounts of the unit to whom conscientious farriers, stable-lads and their own affectionate riders were all devoted in that time-consuming cycle of attention; of feeding and grooming, which all horses demand. Cooking fires rose from the ovens set into the rampart backing, their appealing flavours mingling with the pungent odours of large scale horse-keeping in a powerful cocktail.

Some say the sense of smell is more powerful in the operation of memory than any visual prompt. Certainly the distinctive reek of a cavalry fort had always meant 'home' to Candidus - the only proper home or family he'd ever known - wherever he found it. Upon the instant, it took no more than this reminder for him to find himself re-living proud and happy days serving with Cohors I Equitata on the northern frontier, high on the Emperor's Wall.

Still in this relaxed and nostalgic frame of mind, he was presented to their commanding officer; a man who'd shared with him so many of those early and formative events. Meeting him again for the first time in years, inside a cramped and dark office beside the assembly hall of the principia, there was little more to add to his description given to the Tyche, the thumb-nail sketch of an old comrade. Perhaps there was the slightest leavening of grey hair in a strong beard once blacker than black. Perhaps our interminable grey skies had faded a leathery tan acquired in distinguished opening to his career, serving in North Africa amongst an irregular unit of Berbers deployed against their rebellious Arab brothers. Perhaps a slight heaviness around the eyes from that dulling, lonely weight of overwhelming responsibilities with no one to share them with.

"The Pocket Hercules" they used to call him then for his compact strength and the man seizing him so warmly and strongly by the forearm had not lost any of it: "Flavius Candidus, you wicked old reprobate! What in Mithras' name are you doing in Derventio, if there is not a woman behind it?"

Candidus paused, astonished but reluctant to make a full confession so soon, even to an old comrade. He remembered M. Claudius Bassus as a man who'd played the game of professional advancement with transparent commitment but consummate skill. Someone unlikely to be so indiscreet himself. Aside from a "Hail-Fellow-Well-Met" manner never failing to charm those folk considered useful enough to deploy it upon, his other successful method lay in open reliance on the principle you should be nice to everyone on the way up because you never knew who you might need on your way down. An outlook about which he made no bones and whose public advertisement within the officers' mess only endeared him further to the cynical minds of the High Command.

Yet for all the admitted history of calculation in his manner, Candidus would swear he detected some sincere signs of genuine pleasure from his former colleague on their meeting:

"So, Claudius, Fortune has endowed you with the deserved fulfilment of your dearest wish. At last you have got your Ala."

The Praefectus shrugged his shoulders, allowing himself one brief but happy smile of pride at this achievement, as if rediscovering a satisfaction in promotion which had by now almost slipped away under the grinding burden of its reality.

"Well, I was just lucky. In the right place at the right time, when my predecessor passed across to the other side. Fortuna be praised."

Candidus could well remember his old friend's systematic and remorseless pursuit of 'luck'. When and if the previous commander of this unit was still on his sick bed, Candidus would wager an amphora of Falernian to a quart of vinegar that M. Claudius Bassus would have been stalking the corridors of G.O.C. Northern Region; waiting for the 'off-chance' encounter with some senior influential officer emerging from those lengthy meetings where these things are decided; someone to "bump into" who could settle his candidature on the spot.

The Praefectus had been busy with guard rosters and shooed-out the two military clerks helping with this chore, on arrival of his unexpected visitor. Bassus gestured at the scattered wax tablets and unrolled papyrus on which his daily manpower-allocations and guard duties were recorded; the remorseless rhythms of military life upon which its discipline was founded.

"Just look at me, Candidus! Trapped behind a desk and wet-nursed by pen-pushers. Bogged down in the minutiae of stores and deliveries; weekly reports and bi-annual returns; unmanned by the endless demands for pointless figures and 'strategic' information from whey-faced weeds at Eboracum, who wear a fancy uniform amongst the colonnades of headquarters and dare to call themselves 'soldiers'! Ha! These are the true realities of command in our new-modelled army, Candidus. I sometimes think that these days they value the ability to write a report or settle the jealousies of the Duplicarii against the Sequiplicarii, the 'double-pay men' against the 'extra-rations men', more highly than any skill or experience in combat."

Candidus smiled wanly. These were problems which had troubled him but little, up there on the Wall in a unit where simpler issues of patrolling, concealment, forage and wilderness-survival had been the extent of his worries.

As a man newly-absorbed into the monolithic bureaucracy of the state, he could at least acknowledge how recently his understanding had grown under the frustrations of its counterproductive administration. The more complex and far-reaching the exactions of laws and taxes or the apparatus which supports them, the more sickly and declining seems the state or society which imposes them. He picked up one of the inked sheets of sliced bark which Bassus tossed across to him for inspection:

"April 12th in the twenty-fourth year of His Reign: this Three Hundred and Thirty Seventh Year of Our Lord:
- Total strength of the Ala Picentiana at Derventio, Marcus Claudius Bassus, Praefectus: - Net number of Equites: 412.
- Sent to procure barley from the headman of the village, as taxation in kind, 10 troopers; including 1 decurion from the turma of Victorinus.
- Sent to arrange for transportation from the Village of the Gulls at the white cliff and as escort for the barley-collectors above, 4 troopers from the turma of Martinus.
- Sent to procure wood for the bathhouse, 2 soldiers...." (and so on).

He handed it back: "Well, I see things have not changed that much over here, I'm almost as glad as sorry to say .....you're not up to strength, are you, Claudius?"

Bassus frowned: "No, but when were we ever? What with the marsh fever, all the agues, desertions, leave, abstractions and the odd casualty, we never will be I fear. The arrival of a new recruit these days is as rare as a pay chest....but my men are still sending out two separate patrols every single day. We have a long and difficult coastline of moorland and headlands to cover from here, as well as all the flat lands that lie between... but we do our share. This what we do, Candidus. We kill Saxons"

He paused, then realised he had been talking too much of matters operational to a visitor no longer of the military: "Is this what you have come here about? You have been announced to me as an official of the Vicarius. Perhaps I should be wary of what I tell you, now that you have gone over to the enemy! Is that why you're here?"

He laughed when he saw Candidus' pained look. "No, I jest, friend! You would not, I know it. By Mithras, it is good to see you, and looking so well, too! I remember when we first found you laid in the filthy straw of that hospital bed at Vercovicium fort. None of your comrades expected you to pull through, glad as we were when you did."

"No, of course not, Claudius. Everyone asks me that! But they would not send a man like me to check up on a man like you. My mission is concerned with others, with those who might betray the state, not its most courageous and dutiful servants, people like yourself. Even if the commander files his duty sheets in the name of the Christus but makes his most solemn oaths under Mithras....."

"You know the score, Candidus! We do as we're told. We talk the talk and walk the walk... but our thoughts are still our own, for the moment at least. So, if not me, then who are you hunting? "

"It's rather the other way around. At the moment, I am the hunted. When I was told who was commander to the garrison, I knew at once I'd be able to rely on your protection."

"In Mithras' name I'd swear it! You'll come to no harm in Derventio, not while I hold this commission. Who are your enemies?"

"One is the foremost citizen of Petuaria. A patron; a census officer; the Curator of Roads; the Priest for Life; an Aedile and the tribal chief to all these lands, perhaps even to some of your own troopers."

Bassus raised his head and looked directly at his visitor with a stern and certain gaze: "You mean Marcus Ulpius Januarius, don't you?"

"The very man."

Bassus whistled slowly through clenched teeth: "Flavius, you mad old rough-rider! You always were the one. Hot for action. Gallant and brave. Straight in, feet-first, sword-point leading. It's exactly why you nearly died that fine day in the territory of the Votadini. It's also why a coward like me has been spared, thus far and the Fates Willing. But this time I think you've excelled yourself. Do you know the scale of what you've taken on?"

"Thank you friend but I've no illusions. I know exactly who and what I'm dealing with. Unfortunately, I've got no choice in the matter. It's what I've been sent here to do. It's my job."

"Then you must be very careful. Very careful indeed, not a foot wrong! Make no mistake about it, Candidus. His power is considerable: Financial, with all the influence that comes from wealth. Political, in the cultivation and patronage of contacts and clients, some of them in the military. Tribal, too, in that allegiance which all the Parisii still bear him yet in ancient fashion. And don't forget the judicial, invested with the full authority of a magistrate."

"Oh, yes, I know all about that. I have sat in his court."

"Then you will know what they call him, hereabouts: 'The Chain'. They say there is no-one like him in all Britannia for adorning free-born men with manacles."

"Will you still help me?"

"Of course I will. So long as you understand the risks. Besides, there is something else that I should tell you, to make us equal partners in jeopardy."

"What is it?"

"You are a man. You were once a soldier. You know the solitary aloofness of their commanders. Though it was never borne by you or by any of us when we were rollicking juniors together, you'll remember that mix of fear, respect and pity we all had for the 'Old Man'. So it has become for me up here in the Commander's House, now that it is my turn to become what we ourselves called the 'Old Man'. I should not complain, I know. I am proud of what I have achieved. The height of my ambition. And after all, in a hard world, there is still every comfort to be had for the commander in his Praetorium. Save only one - the company of a wife. Unfortunately, I do not seem to have found one yet. Oh, yes, I know! I can be a difficult man to get on with sometimes, stinking of horses and oft-times riding back of a night with Saxon blood all up my arms.." he sighed, before continuing:

"Problem is, even if Derventio is not the isolated spot some people might think, its expectations of polite society too often limit my company to those gentry believing themselves suitable 'quality' fit to meet the Prafectus. And what a bunch of middle-aged snobs and wind-bags they all are…!"

"It goes with the job. The private obligations of public office...."

"Yes, it's all very well for a fellow like you, someone who can still wander into any old wine-shop or oyster-bar whenever he fancies...."

"Give over, you're not missing that much there! So what's the real problem?"

"Flavius, you should know the wife of this Januarius you speak of is lodged in this very town. In the house of his widowed sister right outside the gates of my own fort. A fine lady whose triclinium is the most-prized invitation for any socially-ambitious diner, in what passes for society hereabouts."

"I see..."

"Not yet, you don't! But meet the widowed sister and you soon will. I know you, Flavius Candidus! A looker in her own right, but play your dice well and she in turn will present you to her sister-- in-law, the wife of your enemy – the widow's brother. Now let me warn you very sternly indeed about that one, for fear you should ever meet her. The wife, I mean. Let the Gods witness it - the most exceptional beauty by any standards - and I for one have been very lonely up here. Phew! You should see her, Flavius...auburn hair, the face of a goddess and the body of a nymph....."

"And....?" Candidus feared the worst and could not look at his friend:

"You will understand, I know...I seem to remember you were a bit of a lad yourself, in your time. I'm afraid I've made rather a fool of myself over the wife of Januarius. Not that we've been indiscreet, you understand. Oh, no, far from it. We each have our reputations to maintain; mine in the dignity of command and hers in her various roles, not just as wife and consort but also as an emblem to the tribe. Either way and whatever she really is, I am too much in love with the lady and do not know where it will end..."

Candidus was aghast and struggled for platitudes: "I understand. Of course I understand! But this unwanted information could place me in a difficult position. You know who this lady's father is. My master! The Vicarius of Britain. The Army may not take its orders from him but it must at least acknowledge his supreme civil authority under the law...." (His voice trailed off).

337

"Yes, thanks a lot, I don't need you to remind me! But I swore on Mithras and the Bull that you could rely on my protection, Flavius Candidus, and I meant it. Despite my confession, I trust you to seal my oath to you with an equal promise from yourself, to safeguard me from denunciation to those instructing you. Better you should know from the outset than find out later. I would not have this gossip travel down the Great North Road to Londinium and the ears of her father, Longinus. You and I, we are both of us blood-brothers; sworn veterans of Cohors I Equitata and faithful servants of Mithras, after all!"

Candidus had known it. The warning omens were right. He should never have come to this place. The farmer's wife and the man on his ladder were both right. Dead right. (What was she? A witch, a native sorceress, to take such hold over him so quickly? It should be no surprise to discover he was hardly her first – Bassus had clearly fallen heavily, well before his friend's turn). Whatever she was, what had been his immediate intuition in the presence of the Tyche was already fulfilling itself - even if his obligations to M. Claudius Bassus under the Mithraic Code were fast becoming just as binding.

There was only one answer he could make: "Of course we are. On the same altar I swear it. But there is one more favour you can grant me, the one which brought me to your door…"

"Which is….?"

"The release of a prisoner, detained last night by the south gate."

"The Smith. What has he got to do with you?"

"He innocently gave me transport on the road from Petuaria. Out of simple kindness, he offered me the canvas shelter of his wagon overnight. But two hired-killers sent after me by Januarius came upon me in the dark. They would have succeeded too and cut me into slices if not prevented by intervention of the smith's tethered bear. It disembowelled the first and sent the second away with his life-blood pouring out from him as he ran. But Taranis is innocent. He has no part in my quarrel with Januarius and slept through most of the action. What's more, he holds the bronze certificate of honourable discharge - with wounds - from our army."

"I see. Well, that explains last night's carry-on, at least! Consider your friend released immediately! As for the victim, I'll send what's left of his servant straight back to Januarius in a pot. If my men can find the second, we'll deliver him to Petuaria, too, similarly-wrapped! In the meantime, I will hope for your valued company, as my honoured guest in the praetorium."

For the second time on his journey of enquiry, Candidus was fortunate to find luxurious quarters placed at his disposal. Despite the complexities of the situation, he could not turn down such a courteous invitation. Neither could he risk leaving the town. As it turned out, his friend Bassus had few spare moments left him from the preoccupations of his duty. Over the next few days, this meant Candidus was pleased to be left mainly to his own devices. Apart from mealtimes in the mess, their only shared activities were a spot of stag-hunting or attending with Bassus and an ever-diminishing cadre of his soldiers to worship at the local shrine to Mithras, a large cave hidden beside the river, one quarter-mile upstream. As for his dilemma over the woman, the God of Ages gave Candidus no clearer insight, leaving him to work it all out for himself...

For all the seventeen Roman miles of good road separating it from the cosmopolitan streets and attractions of Eboracum, Derventio was (as his first reconnaissance suggested) a lively-enough place in its own right. Self-confident enough not to feel overshadowed by the soft charms of the adjoining metropolis, its key atmosphere was that of the frontier post, a busy station from whose eastern and northern gatehouses regular cavalry patrols emerged to maintain the high standards of operational vigilance their commandant justifiably claimed.

The principal focus of all this military activity was the threat of Saxon longships trying to make landfall on a sparsely-populated coast of crumbling cliffs and infrequent beaches. Apart from them, only the occasional Pictish raiding-boat or curragh offered any variety in the type of visitor in want of warm greeting. This was important work. Left unattended, the broad and obvious vale whose mouth the fort at Derventio so sternly supervised would otherwise offer any coastal invader moving inland gratifyingly-prompt access to plunder - whether in Eboracum or its satellite towns.

The City's foremost guarantee of freedom from rapine and slaughter therefore rested on the confident efficiency of the Ala Picentiana and its enthusiastic commander. Whatever chinks may be appearing elsewhere in the armour of Empire, here at least was a regiment fit for its task and up to the job. No wonder M. Claudius Bassus had been such a favourite up at headquarters – he guarded their own back-door.

What of the regiment itself? First raised during his Gallic campaigns by Julius Caesar himself and mentioned in his famous book, "De Bello Gallico", its honourable title was acquired about a century later as permanent memorial to its illustrious performance in the Dalmatian Wars under the command of that legendary Prefect, Lucius Rustius Picens. The enduring pride in their unit of the current complement of soldiers was only intensified in its fervour by the imminent achievement of a significant anniversary. April 21st, the birthday of the personified Goddess of Rome itself, 'Romae Aeternae', was a doubly-auspicious anniversary which would mark the three hundred and ninety-fifth anniversary of the foundation of the Ala during offensive operations against Ambiorix, Chief of the Eburones. In "De Bello Gallico", the first-hand account of their founding General, the Divine Julius Caesar himself tells us how these legendary victories were crowned with the glorious achievements of this same cavalry unit. Nearly four centuries later, its faithful inheritors mounted as fierce a guard on the lordly strands of north-east Britannia.

Already there was an air of festival in the garrison town, with shops and houses decorated with woven wreaths of greenery and garlands of flowers. Horse-races were to be organised on the flatlands to the south of the river and the water meadows to the east of the fort. These events in particular attracted a steady stream of visitors to the town, hoping to find spare space amongst accommodation already at a premium. Outside the town walls, an impromptu fair grew up from hour to hour. Pedlars, craftsmen and travelling entertainers were arriving from all over the province, keen to set up the canvas booths they spread with whatever tawdry offerings might suck in coinage from the curious or ingenuous.

340

Only when drawn to the north could the eye detect one notable exception to all these folk converging on Derventio. Travelling alone in the opposite direction was the great encumbered wagon of Taranis the Smith, keen to escape the scene of his recent unjust imprisonment but glad to be free. Even at this distance, the sinister bulk of his devoted Darius could be seen faithfully trailing behind at the length of a chain, pleased to be re-united with his one true master and grumbling happily accordingly.

If only his friend Candidus could be as content. Finding himself loitering on a street-corner nearest the 'House of the Winged Victories'; buying from an adjacent stall a bag of freshwater oysters he could not bring himself to eat; even he realised he was acting like a lovesick youth. Surely his infatuation must now be tempered with the galling knowledge that he had shared (or else was still sharing?) this hypnotic lady with two other men - at least. If his own heated response to this appalling realisation was anything to go by, then the jealous discovery of his share in intimacy by either of the two rivals to her affections, his old friend Bassus or his new enemy Januarius, could bring on only catastrophe.

And yet Candidus lingered on in Derventio, like a moth at a flame, brushing the scorching margins of destruction. His natural human hope that things might get better only ignored the more obvious possibility they could so easily get worse.

He took the beautiful bay horse which an innocent Bassus had so generously lent him (imported at great expense from Africa, a fabulous gift from one of his Arab contacts) and went for long solitary rides in the country. This was rich farming land whose terraced fields supported an ancient pattern of agriculture unchanged in centuries. A way of life that seemed immune to irrelevant disruptions from the outside world, in a place where farmers were as much tied to the land by their own tradition as by any 'caste' edict of Diocletian or Constantine. Today he had ridden out of the strong east gate, onto a fine, well-maintained road of hard-packed stone which led him across lush, green meadows beside the river, up onto higher ground via an escarpment, and eventually to the sea.

Quite alone and unarmed, Candidus felt perfectly safe in the rural tranquility of these peaceful fields and rolling moorlands. Occasionally he would pass a solitary tied-ploughman working two oxen and a shard across their modest furrow. They'd exchange friendly greetings of goodwill where the blessing of some obscure Celtic deity would figure large, an alien conceit unknown outside the region but somehow fused officially with a suitable classical equivalent to suit Rome's purpose. Much like the Tyche herself, he supposed. One thing was sure, the name of the Christus had not much penetrated this inward-looking world of small native farms and steadings. Their traditional round-huts stood secure inside a bank and ditch, surviving next to their more-prosperous neighbours who'd upgraded to the Romanised rectangular dwelling-shape. Along the way there were even signs of those lucky few whose trade in cereals, leather, and meat with the Army had been enough (despite the ferocious levies of tax-gatherers) to finance development of their farm to a point where it could justly claim the epithet: "villa".

On the higher ground, these signs of cultivation and civilisation receded on the encroachment of wilderness but the road still forced its way eastwards regardless, driving hard for the sea. Giving purpose to today's idleness, his intention was to ride over and inspect some new road-works where he expected to meet the Praefectus, out on his rounds and overseeing the construction gangs. On an elevated straight route, this did not prove a difficult rendezvous to achieve.

He found Bassus sitting there at the roadside on a small, wire-haired, pot-bellied pony of the sort his Ala much preferred for the difficult terrain where most of their work-a-day riding occurred; so different a beast to this borrowed Arab racer. Candidus noticed a worn copy of (what he knew would be) Marcus Aurelius' 'Meditations' resting face-down and unrolled across his wooden saddle bow.

One of his own decurions sat to one side and an officer in the distinctive uniform of a legionary tribune on the other, both of them horsed. They were observing with relaxed cheerfulness the grim-faced sweated labours of a toiling gang whose knee-length shirts were rolled to the waist but did not obscure the familiar roundel badges of Legio VI Victrix dyed fast into the cream fabric.

342

Under the unfailing scrutiny of their mounted and helmeted officer, these twenty men dare not restrain the swinging rhythms of pickaxe and shovel, of metal singing on rock, but it remained obvious from their faces that they did not care much for the added supervision of cavalry.

Arriving on site, Candidus offered polite greeting to the introductions made by Bassus, to colleagues whose names unfortunately fled his memory no sooner than received. He turned to examine their project: "What's going on here, then, Claudius?"

"Road-widening."

"Oh, really. What's the point of doing that, out here?"

"Logistics. In the end, this widening will be done not just out here, and not just from the sea to Derventio, but all the way back to Eboracum."

"Where's the benefit in that?"

"Troop-delivery. The wider it is and the better the surface, the faster we can send larger groups of soldiers, whether it's cavalry or infantry, out to the seaside."

"And I take it this is not to collect sea-shells, like the Legions of Caligula at Gesoriacum."

"I think not. No, it is far more to the harvesting of Saxons that our efforts are directed."

"From what I hear, the Ala is already more than good enough at that game."

"I thank you. We hope so. I have made a simple rule for my men: the Saxonicii are always to be killed when still wet from the sea. They are a fast-growing threat but I will not have a single one of them set dry foot upon the sacred earth of our province."

"A good principle to work to. But is it a rule you have been able to keep up?" put in the Legionary tribune with all the natural cynicism of a professional rival.

"I'm confident we have. Our method is economical. Penny-packet patrols of light horse constantly ride the cliff-tops, watching for warnings from our signal towers. Our men catch the Saxonici as they come ashore; cold, wet, hungry and exhausted from rowing the German Ocean. We ride them down with lances in the surf as they drag themselves up the beach. Easy meat. They are too tired to fight and too tired to run away".

"Afterwards, their ships are pulled up onto the beach and loaded with the bodies of their crew, then set alight. The black pitch burns well. A good funeral pyre for them – let no-one say we do not do them justice. We leave the charred hulks set just above high-water mark as a warning for their brothers, their cousins and their sons; to whoever might be foolish enough to follow them. The wide sands of our eastern coasts are becoming lined with the blackened bones of their ships but they never seem to learn. Still the warlords and their criminal gangs come, no matter how many we kill."

"You will have seen many times what is painted in red, in foot-high letters across the main principia wall at Eboracum Garrison: "Our Eternal Vigilance is Shield to the Civilised World". What worries me most is the thought that one day raiding won't be enough for them anymore. One day, they may want to settle – to take our lands. If they do, they may well want our land and our silver and gold, but they certainly don't want our way of life. Our towns and cities are so alien to them, our civil society would not survive for long….of that I'm certain. We guard the light."

"I'm sure your methods are correct..." allowed the Tribune of the Sixth with unexpected magnanimity "...and operationally justified in the circumstances. But how do they square with all these reorganisations; with the new 'Mobile Field Armies' they're pulling back into the towns and cities, only able to intervene in the case of really large-scale invasion?"

"My fear is they don't square at all. That's the trouble. I don't detect any interest up at headquarters in doing the job properly. It's all about saving money. They are preoccupied with other, more political issues, rather than the tremendous mobility and efficiency which I believe this Ala can achieve, right across its commission area. Yet funding and resources is all they can ever talk about."

The other officer was as frank in his assessment: "Yes, reluctant as I am to agree – I'm afraid you're absolutely right, Claudius, even if it pains me to say so. Except that when you mention what it says up at headquarters, I'd say the writing's as much upon the wall for our famous Legion as for your own fine cavalry wing."

Later, Candidus rode back to Derventio alone, leaving them to their work and their soldiers' grumblings. As he got nearer to the town, he dropped down off the paved road and rode into water meadows nearer to the river. The boughs of ancient over-hanging trees budding under an early spring dipped to touch the waters. In more tranquil pools beside the oxbow bends, big fish idly took new-made flies. A timeless peaceful day where the idea of a whole way of life being under threat seemed impossible and far-away.

Following the meandering line of these river banks brought him to a secluded hollow in the land, ringed with willow trees. As he rode down into it, he was taken aback to be confronted by a tough-looking man in a white-bleached short-sleeve tunic, equipped with a wooden staff tipped with iron. And then another, similarly dressed and armed. The first took his bridle whilst the second came quickly around the other side of the horse. A third came up soon after, his face grimly threatening.

"Hey, what's going on?"

Down in the bottom of this natural bowl, at the waters-edge, was a tall and upright, four-wheeled coach drawn by two mules, such as the gentry use for travelling. Its body was trimmed with stretched leather the colour of oxblood and its single side-door embossed with a pair of contraposed J's; one facing forward and one facing back. The two-faced symbol of the Januarii and their patron deity – that duplicitous God, Janus himself.

He should have known it.

The two 'heavies' were heedless of his protest and, joined by a third colleague, together dragged him from the saddle of the Arab bay. His first attacker had already managed to give Candidus two quick but numbing blows to the side of the head before a woman's clear voice rang out in the clearing: "What do you fools think you are doing?"

The 'fools' were new to him but clearly not to her household.

They were not prompt to stop hitting him either but very reluctantly obeyed – eventually - and dragged him to the door of the coach, depositing him there for the attention of she-who-spoke before they withdrew to more distant, pre-determined guard posts set around the grassy arena.

Of course Candidus knew the voice of love and all his crowding misgivings of the week or this ringing in his ears evaporated on her husky invitation.

He clambered quickly in, aided by the anticipations of lust to fall headlong into the Carriage of Venus, as pleased by his unexpected rescue from the fists and staves of her unlikely cupids as the prospect of what finer pleasures awaited him next.

Here at last was his personal proof of all those ancient stories about bathing woodland nymphs and their wanton affections. The Goddess waiting to receive him warmly was fresh from the waters of the river; cleansed and reborn if still a little damp. She was effusive and tactile in apology, dabbing at the trickle of blood starting on his temple with a cream silk kerchief surely not brought by camel-train across all the deserts of Asia just to staunch a few cuts on the face of an oaf like himself.

"I have seen you standing on the corner at the top of the street, looking up at the house" she told him "and I watched you riding so boldly out for the coast this morning. I missed you when you were gone and feared for your return."

So that was how the whole reckless affair started all over again – with what seemed like a chance-meeting in a sylvan glade. Except that he wondered whether it really was chance. If his nymph was waiting for him, then it was a honey trap he entered without a moment's hesitation, keen as the apocryphal satyr he'd suddenly become, lacking only in its cloven hoofs.

There was a curtain on the carriage door which he felt he ought to pull across – he did not want some burly 'Cupid' standing outside watching. She pulled it back, much preferring to see what she was doing. The coach rocked on its wheels.

It became late.

Afterwards, on the way back, he rode at a respectful distance behind her carriage as if he - unarmed - could ever enhance the pathological protection she already enjoyed from three maniacs equipped with metal rods.

He must be mad. (He knew she was).

In the Praetorium, Bassus had already dined with the Tribune of the Sixth, who had left by the time Candidus got in. He sat, sociable with Candidus whilst a slave brought in a wooden platter of cold meat and a few cheeses left over, sharing another wine-jar with him. Candidus could hardly look at his friend but he made brave efforts at conversation: "You know, I do find it ironic how your brave soldiers are out in all weathers keeping the Saxons off our coasts and yet, not forty miles from here, Marcus Ulpius Januarius keeps a nest of them fed, housed and watered in his own orchard as "protection" for his estate."

"How I hate that man! A traitor to his own kind. A selfish insanely-ambitious viper in our midst. But there is nothing a mere local commander like me can do about it, Flavius. The only thing I can suggest is to raise the subject directly with the Legatus at Eboracum - delicately - in the context of public safety. A 'toe-in-the-water' job. Of course, I don't know what sort of reaction I'll get, but I can't believe he doesn't already know what private arrangements this Januarius has made for the security of his property. Sea-wolves! The very men I am charged with keeping off our shores - living in our woods, walking in our lanes. I ask you, it is like they want to flaunt their presence to provoke a reaction!"

M. Claudius Bassus was a determined but straightforward man, someone who believed there was a solution to be had for every problem. It was just a case of finding it. As a philosophy, it made him indefatigable in resolving difficulty.

Unfortunately, the other side of this same outlook could sometimes import a contrary defeatism, at the point when even a 'trier' like him eventually confronted those immovable obstacles we all must face. Like death and taxes, disease and vested interest. (Or the perversity of governments). Nevertheless, it was the positive side of his nature that was still to the fore when, the next day following, he set out early on a fast horse with two troopers on equivalent mounts as escort, riding hard for Eboracum and his friends at court. His mission – an alert to the High Command on a dangerous situation brewing in Peturia.

Since Bassus was to be gone for the whole day, Candidus thought it safe and possible (if not exactly prudent) to visit the 'House of the Winged Victories' again. Although she did allow him audience, he found her unexpectedly anxious and in no mood to replay their frolics of the previous day:

"We cannot go on like this. You know it is madness. One day Claudius and then, another day, you! What ever am I doing? We cannot risk being seen in proximity to each other again. The gossip in a small town like this is relentless. What they don't know, they will happily invent and my husband has spies everywhere. When he finds out, his rage will know no bounds. I have been a fool! My father has spies of his own, too, and they are paid for by the government ...including you, one of his own men! I must have been mad... yet some seem to expect it of me...Oh, I don't know! The more outrageously I behave, the more people see it as proof - the divine impulsiveness of the Goddess! It's like I'm not in control but only exist here to bring certain things about, the things that have got to happen..."

Despite everything, he still loved her. She would let him, too.

He left late, yet again.

In the evening it rained heavily, water coming down like waves of transparent arrows shimmering in the wind. April showers. The ash and clinker side streets of Derventio turned to black mud and even the paved roads held deep pools to soak the unwary traveller.

Announced by the trumpets of his alert sentries, M. Claudius Bassus rode white-faced and alone into the fort by the west gate just before dark, its damp gloom brought forward early by low cloud. The Praefectus had outrun his escort and his horse was completely blown, shivering in the wet and steaming in the stables under a green blanket. Its rider was in no better condition, his exhaustion deeper for the bleak weariness of spirit he'd brought back with him like a canker. Candidus sat with him in the hot room of the bathhouse as the commander tried to sweat right out of his body that spiritual chill given him by the cold corridors of Eboracum.

"How did you get on?"

348

"Candidus, my good and loyal friend, how I wish I'd never gone!"

"Why, what has happened? Did you speak to the Legatus or even get a message to the Dux Britannarium himself?"

"What, me? A mud-splashed lieutenant long-fallen out of favour. Why ever did we appoint him? Ridden-in unbidden from his relic of outmoded military practice to bother the High and Mighty, the General Officer Commanding, Northern Region? You must be joking! 'What, who's here? Claudius Bassus of the Derventio red-necks, you say? Oh, no! Not him! That damned pagan – bold adherent to the old religions – reactionary cultist of Mithras...Lord preserve us - send for the Bishop!"

"Would nobody listen to you?"

"Nobody of note. It was my own fault, of course. I should've realised. Stupid of me, going on a Sunday – Sol's own day! The whole general staff were at prayers, on their knees for the health and Christian well-being of the whole Imperial family."

"But you've been there all day...."

"Yes! Kicking my heels against those huge ashlar columns that hold up the Principia roof, on the promise that "someone would see me".

"And did they?"

"Oh yes. They did - in the end. A pretty-boy junior-tribune, wet behind the ears and weeks from his first shave, comes sidling up to me, stinking of scent, to explain that the Legatus Legionis has delegated the interviewing of less-senior commanders to the tribunician grade."

"The Legatus would not see you, rather than he could not see you?"

"Oh, yes! To be fair to the wee lad, he was offering me some important points of information."

"Good! And what were those?"

"Two in number, Flavius. The first of these is that they are very well aware, thank you, of the Saxon presence at the Villa Januarii: 'Not considered to represent any significant security risk, but we're keeping a watching brief'."

"I see. And the second?"

"A well-read man like you will remember, won't you, exactly what the writer Cassius Dio says the African Emperor, Septimius Severus, is supposed to have said to his two horrible sons, Caracalla and Geta, lying on his death bed up there in Eboracum over a hundred yeas ago? "Look after the soldiers!" he said. Wise advice but there's no-one up there who heeds it, not nowadays anyway. They say the donatives and gifts of gold to the Emperor have not been so lavish or forthcoming this year as they always were previously. Whether from the Senate and People of Rome, the grateful cities of Italia, or the provincials kneeling in tribute, the money supply to the army is simply drying up. While the endless calls on the Imperial Exchequer from the insatiable expenses of the Court or the incredible cost of constructing this new City of Constantine on the Hellespont, they seem to multiply from year to year."

"How is this any concern of ours, out here?"

"Well, I don't know about you, Candidus, but I want to be sure of being paid! You pensioners and civil servants might be different, but I certainly don't go through all of this everyday just for the pleasure of it, you know! We all have expenses to meet, even if it's just to maintain our contributions for the Burial Club or keep a woman in the Street of the Goldsmiths. I certainly know it matters a great deal to my men! And because the pressure to set up the new Mobile Field Army is as much driven by the parsimony of the Emperor's Treasury as by any real change in strategic thinking. Simple fact - combining units saves them money. That's the real reason for all these endless reorganisations, whatever tactical crap they feed us!

And because the G.O.C. in Britannia Inferior is just as much the unwilling victim of all these economies and changes in policy as any other little, local commander like me. At least his scented junior tribune was good enough to offer me this frank preamble as lame excuse for the likely decision of 'His Perfection', the Dux Britannarium, to disband the Ala Picentiana just five years short of its four-hundredth anniversary and then distribute its elite troopers amongst the Germanic mercenaries, ex-convicts and runaway slaves of the new formations. And, best news of all, the safety of Derventio and its rolling plain is shortly to be entrusted instead to those idiot amateurs in the 'Petuaria Interceptors'!"

Over the next few days the effect of this depressing discovery on the usually-energetic Praefectus' attentions to his beloved regiment became increasingly apparent. Moody and distant, there were more signs of resort to the illusory compensations of drink, while the twenty-first of April loomed ever larger. Candidus confronted his deflated successor to the famous Picens with its inescapable significance, one evening in the bathhouse:

"Come on, Claudius! Pull yourself together. You owe it to the Ala. There has been no definite decision yet. Why, they may come to their senses yet and acknowledge the vital role everyone knows you play in defending the coast. They might even change their minds, but they certainly won't if you let your regiment go to rack and ruin. Do your duty with your head held high. Offer all due honour and sacrifice to your military ancestors. Parade the Ala. Raise the annual altars to the Gods which have served Rome so well, to the Glory of the Emperor Himself, even if He's now adopted a contrary creed. Dip your standards and take their salute before an admiring population so that the name and reputation of the Ala Picentiana runs so high in public affection and esteem that, even up there in Eboracum, they might think twice before attempting to disband it."

To be fair to the man, here was one moral exhortation which hit the target. Claudius Bassus rose to the idea with immediate response.

The next morning he issued detailed orders concentrating for once on the regulation of drill, the spit-and-polish of ceremonial, rather than the grim timetables of combat patrol. It was his decree that, during the festivities, the flimsy gloss of parade armour should replace the dulled heavier plate of service wear, save for their continuing patrols.

Stone masons were commissioned in the sculpture and lettering of commemorative altars which would be dedicated on the day; whilst the one elderly priest left in the Temple of Hercules at Eboracum, a relic with a particular reputation in the traditional forms of worship proper to the State, was cajoled into making the long day's journey to Derventio over flooded roads.

So complete was the invigoration of Bassus that he even agreed to be invested with the authority and duties of 'Chief Starter' for the lively programme of horse-racing organised to coincide with the celebrations.

351

Horse breeders and dealers were added to the crowds attracted to the town, these temporary visitors thronging its muddy streets and unassuming alleys. Any sense of invasion suffered by the more-insular local residents was well balanced by a commercial boom for shopkeepers, tradesmen and victuallers of all description, who were quick to capitalise on what they realised was a flash-flood of customers unlikely to be repeated. There were minor fortunes to be made here if you were quick enough on the uptake.

Come the day, the rain whose repeated showers had punctuated their preparations dared not show itself. The morning announced with triumphant trumpets from the battlements of the fort was warm and jewel-clear. On the unfastening of the town gates, a stream of people was released to the east, heading excitedly along the sea-road to a point beyond the defensive banks and ditches of the fort where the regiment had by long usage flattened a parade ground for its drill and sports among the water-meadows.

Arriving at the site, the spectators staked their claim to chosen spots along three sides of the boundary to this square. The fourth was marked by the intervention of the rostra, a turf tribunal set up for the officers and their regimental standards.

As the sun rose higher into an unclouded sky, any dampness in this Field of Mars dispersed, although the better-prepared spectators were still reclining on chequered native blankets or piled-up shawls as protection against the ground. Others were busy unpacking from baskets their food supply for the day. For the more genteel, a temporary bank, fitted with planking, provided drier seating above the earth and a more lofty view to befit their social station. Here, the fine ladies of the Canton had assembled in all their haughty splendour, white parasols fluttering in the breeze to protect delicate complexions. Guarded from the sun by these shades and from the uncouth by fathers, husbands, brothers or other male companions of equally possessive outlook, the silken finery of these doves was matched with the formal white togas of the gentlemen; sober dignified men of principle and rank, self-consciously exuding Roman gravitas.

Now it was the eastern gate to the fort which opened to allow the exit of a tight-packed knot of officers, M. Claudius Bassus riding at their head. The hippika gymnasia were about to commence.

For Flavius Candidus, as a mere civil servant (even allowing for his veteran status from a frontier unit), his invitation to ride with and amongst the Praefectus and his officers on this auspicious occasion made for a most singular honour. As Candidus must allow, this was typical of the generosity and respect he'd received as their commander's former comrade, right from his very first arrival at Derventio. (How ashamed it made him).

Bassus had also insisted on his friend's retention of that glossy bay, even if it were amongst the best mounts in his stable. He seemed seated well enough himself on a lively chestnut mare, going out today without even a book on his saddle-bow. Riding at the head of his senior men, he cut a fine sight in his elaborately-decorated helmet of silvered iron. Its metal crest was fronted with an eagle's head and arrogantly-curving beak, the one-piece face mask almost covering his features to leave only 'T' shaped opening for eyes, nose and mouth. His cuirass of copper-alloy scales was hung over a white tunic of dazzling brightness, fresh from the fuller's vat and embroidered with imperial purple. A scarlet cloak flew in the slipstream of the gallop from magnificent, jewelled brooches holding it fast to his shoulders. Slung diagonally from the right shoulder, a broad baldric of white leather studded with enamelled strap fittings held the weight of the spatha; this slashing long-sword's hilt of bone carved as an eagle's head to complement his helm and further assert his Romanitas.

The tribunes of the Ala were accoutred in no less splendour, subject only to their proper badging and distinctions of rank. Amongst such heroic companions and obedient to their invitation, Candidus must accept their demand he armed himself in equivalent fashion.

In a full-face bronze 'sports' helmet bedecked with scarlet feathers, clad in a ring-mail shirt of full combat weight under a military cloak, only his Governor's belt and pendant silver badge of office could have identified the civil status of a beneficarius consularis to the sharper-eyed observer. He rode anonymous amongst the brotherhood of command, pleased beyond measure to find himself to all intents and purposes an officer in arms again.

Arriving at the Campus Martius, the unit commanders took up position by the rostra where they remained upon horseback, the eyes of the crowd turning again to the arched stone portals of the fort itself.

For Candidus too, excited as a schoolboy to be back in the practice of martial and equestrian skills once his main occupation (until so suddenly taken from him) but already flagging at the major effort involved, here was welcome chance to catch his breath behind metal lips sealed for ever.

He realised how quickly he'd forgotten the intensity of concentration needed to ride in armour in tight formation; the dragging weight of a chain-mail shirt on his own scarred frame or the heavy and asphyxiating claustrophobia of a metal face-mask worn to transform plebian features into the Olympian perfection of a deity. Hidden inside its frozen metallic inscrutability and limited vision, he studied the crowd anxiously through paired eye slits, seeking only one face. Scanning the rows of local peasants in chequered plaid and loud tartan or the lines of townsfolk in best tweed tunics, their wives and children enthroned on wicker chairs carried out from the houses, he could not find her.

Turning his armoured head with undue effort, so heartless soulless bronze eyes could look out and across the square, he saw the wooden grandstand constructed by the town council for the temporary elevation of its hereditary worthies. Even amongst its serried senatorial ranks of firm-jawed greybeards or fluttering feminine display, he still could not find her.

Had she left the town already?

The brassy trumpets blared again. Now the colours were paraded, the mounted bearers of vexillum flag and gilded imperial image following on from that principal emblem of the regiment, the Asiatic 'Draco'. An open-mouthed dragon's head, its sharp teeth and scaly face gleaming in gold leaf, allowing the wind to fill a tapering, tubular tail of coloured linen on which were sewn overlapping plates of metal. Held aloft on a spear pole, the dragon standard would hiss and rattle in convincing fashion.

Its bearer was no less impressive, his features also hidden behind the silvered mask of a parade helmet, a short cuirass of locked scales, and plated leg greaves embossed with Gods and Men, hinged to guard his knees. Even his armoured horse was hung with shiny metal work of high relief, from weighty chamfron over the eyes to roundel chest plate. Taking up their prominent position beside the rostra and a row of stone altars, both this year's and last's, the standard bearers saluted their officers with loud shouts and synchronised arms.

On the other side of the show field, Candidus saw at last a red carriage rolling across the grass to halt beside the bank of seats. The Tyche had arrived, late as always. He strained his vision through the constricted helmet for a mane of auburn but could not make her out. The eyes of the crowd were now on a cloud of cavalry charging from the battlemented castra towards them. Even an old hand like Flavius Candidus could feel a frisson of excitement through the thunder in the ground from their approach. The Ala, fully dressed for the Games, was a spectacular sight. Their participants were, in traditional fashion, split into two teams. Two hundred as 'Greeks' and two hundred as 'Amazons', each in masked helmets matching the gender of their role.

First the cavalcade passed the rostra, all silver faces 'eyes-right' to acknowledge their sanctified standards and offer obedience to their officers, before splitting into two opposing sides at opposite ends of the field. The crowd fell silent, overawed by the grandeur of apparently-divine beings and totally immersed in their irrefutable statement of military might.

In the spirited display which followed, the visible enthusiasm of the soldiers taking part showed just what a moral-raiser this event was for the troops themselves. What the ensuing two hours also proved was the sheer excellence of this historic regiment in their horsemanship, their discipline and proficiency with a wide variety of weapons. Relatively light as their parade armours were, they still had practical purpose in protecting both horse and man against the bruising showers of wooden javelins, short and long, which each side inflicted on the other as they rode by, opening the tournament.

These were followed by smaller groups separately engaging each other with swords, in close combats fierce enough to see many of the beautifully-painted wooden 'sports' shields, depicting legendary battles of manly 'Greeks' and statuesque 'Amazons', split or completely hacked to pieces.

Soon, three concussed riders had to be removed from the field by the capsarii, medical orderlies of the regiment.

Demonstrations of the Cantabrian Circle, a whirlwind of circling riders constantly hurling missiles at a shield wall of crouching 'Amazons' caught on foot, led on to a sudden counter-attack by their mounted 'sisters' whirling light hand-axes of a type once derided as the tool of barbarians but now become a fashionable cavalry weapon. (In the circumstances, some further minor casualties were inevitable).

Their mesmerising whirling; this to-and-fro of scarlet and gold, of silver and steel, continued at unrelenting pace. As one detachment of riders tired and withdrew, so another moved forward to take their place. Concluding in an individual competition for mounted lancers, trying to collect a tiny amphora on the tip of their weapon without breaking either their gallop or the vessel, the 'Greeks' and 'Amazons' at last reformed as one cohesive unit to parade en masse in front of the rostra, their stylised conflict over. Riding his own horse forward onto this ramp of earth, M. Claudius Bassus addressed his men with the dignified and restrained approval of a proud commander:

"Soldiers of the Ala Picentiana, you have done well today. You did everything in its proper order - you covered the whole parade ground with your manoeuvres. Your javelin-throwing was neat and accurate although you mainly used the shorter, more difficult weapon. But most of you were just as good with the long spear. Your riding and jumping was swift and lively, with good horse-control. We can all see that. If you had fallen short in anything, I would certainly have drawn your attention to it and, equally, if you had particularly shone in anything, I would have remarked on it too. In fact, while you undoubtedly have shone, for me it was the high level of consistency across your whole performance today which was the most pleasing. It is clear to me that my officers have spared no pains in fulfilling their duties and have omitted nothing from your training, while you have been as unremitting in your commitment to them. It is due to the outstanding care which they have taken that you are what you are today...."

He paused to clear his throat before continuing. Candidus wondered whether he was alone in detecting the deep emotion suppressed under the weight of all that armour and responsibility by this solitary horseman.

"Soldiers of Rome, we are gathered here today to honour the memory of an officer of long-ago. A man of virtue – of honestas – a man they called Lucius Rustius Picens. It is my belief that, were his shade to be here today, he would be as deeply proud of your performance as I am now. Truth be told, it does feel to me that he is here with us today. Our noble ancestor. But 'Picens's Horse' is older even than his venerated name. The record still shows its foundation by the Divine Julius Caesar himself during his conquest of Gaul".

Bassus waited whilst the significance of their direct link to the greatest Roman of them all sank slowly into the imagination of even the most unimaginative of his soldiers before continuing:

357

"Every year, we are gathered here in this place to celebrate that important fact but the auspicious day on which the standard of the Ala was first raised is one sacred to us all for another reason. Doubtless one that is no coincidence. Today is also the birthday of the spirit of that City which is mother to us all, the Goddess Roma Eternae. Whose light we maintain. That is surely why this day was first chosen for the Ala's foundation. So it is right and proper that we mark these happy anniversaries, as we do each year, with prayers, libations and sacrifice. The interment of old altars and our dedication of the new. However, there is this year an added importance for our celebrations. This year is the three hundred and ninety-fifth from the founding of the regiment. I am sure that you will agree with me what a significant milestone this is, one that takes us even closer to a much greater one. We must all now look forward to successful achievement of the unprecedented anniversary now in clear sight, the four-hundredth; the one whose safe attainment must surely place the Ala Picentiana up there amongst the most famous regiments in the whole history of Rome and all its great armies."

The Praefectus bowed his head in silent prayer. Through the side of his vision slit, Candidus saw one junior decurion cross himself quickly and anxiously. Beside him a yellow flame leapt up from the red sandstone block of an adjacent altar, bright against a sky of darkening blue, where the forces of the Rain-God re-grouped to renew their assaults of preceding days.

The old priest from Eboracum conducted the formalities of sacrifice with all that punctilious regard for proper observance upon which his professional reputation was based.

A goat was killed, and then a bull.

The white-faced junior decurion fidgeted ever-more increasingly with his Christian scruples and harness strap but blood was dutifully spilt and entrails examined notwithstanding, against an ever-darkling sky.

Nigh on five hundred horses chafed and stamped and snorted, tossing heads and harness under the patient control of their silver riders. Candidus felt one big fat drop of water hit his bare forearm, spread slowly out and roll gradually down from his wrist onto his hand where it gripped the reins. After a while, another followed then another but still the sky seemed unwilling to give on to proper downpour.

Dismounted troopers dug a deep pit with soldiers' entrenching tools silver-plated for the ceremony, into which altars dedicated these twelve months-gone were duly toppled for their new-made successors under suitable blessings from the priesthood. Every formality must be observed precisely for fear that, in a massively-superstitious age, any deviation from form could bring down upon them all the manifold curses of misfortune. Even the wording was pre-ordained by a rigid template. Year after year, the carved inscriptions (to one of which Candidus had this year been privileged to append his own name) would faithfully record their politically-correct devotion to the essentials of a military society; a traditional formula from which no-one dared depart - "To Jupiter Best and Greatest"; to "The Emperor"; "Eternal Rome"; to the personified "Discipline of the Army".

It either mattered not to them - or else they must wilfully disregard the fact - that even Great Jove Himself was now discarded by their reforming Emperor, a man only put there through those same British armies whose faithful sacrifices to the Old Religion he now declined. That same prince for whose health and safety their pagan imprecations were ever offered up, so that He, Unconquered, became intertwined and as one with the Sun God – CONSTANTINO INVICTO at one with SOL INVICTO. That same Emperor who, just eleven years ago, abandoned their Eternal City and all its Gods for the new city built over old Byzantium; that upstart metropolis where Jupiter's temples have no place and only Christian churches grow.

Neither, it seemed, did Constantinus Magnus care that the only reward for His loyal soldiers based out here on the crumbling lip of Empire - for soldiers to whom His Discipline was still upheld as Spiritual Virtue and a Good in its own right - would be the cruel dissolution of their precious Ala. For a man who could so easily jettison Old Rome for His New Rome out there in the east, such sentimental considerations would presumably not even have registered. He demanded their absolute loyalty yet seemingly valued it not at all, or so the mutterings grew.

Or as the Admiral Trimalchio would put it, four hundred years of military service and the ingrained traditions which sustain and nuture it, thrown away in a moment by an oriental despot.

These ceremonies of loyalty and military devotion were barely complete, their oaths of fealty and duty hardly out of their iron mouths, than a veinous bolt of white lightning went straight from sky to ground directly across the river. It was sharply followed by a monumental crack of thunder that sounded like an answer from the Gods and confirmed to them how very close this lightning strike had been. Hardly had the cowering civilians scooped up their shabby effects to flee than the rain came down in sheets, drenching everyone within minutes. The soaking rabble turned into a rout, driving each other into the town, followed by the carts and carriages of the gentry.

Only the Ala withdrew in good order; a strange ghostly-white luminescence playing around their lance points. It was not a pleasing omen.

The postscript to any important occasion in human affairs is so often anti-climax for its protagonists. So it was in Derventio for every inhabitant, whatever their calling. Their public holiday over, that cloak of smoke and fumes which marked the output of its industry quickly resumed its place over the worksheds of the new town. The farm labourers and slaves resumed their toil; the soldiers their onerous routines of daily duty. The visitors, pedlars, travellers, actors, tumblers, horse-thieves, hawkers, fortune-tellers and journey-men simply slipped away, with fresh fairs to conquer.

Memorable as the parade had been, its over-hasty conclusion on the lightning strike and the question mark over the future of his command all hung over M. Claudius Bassus like one great rain cloud, its symptom that continuing decline in determination which Candidus had by strong words only postponed before.

As the weeks passed by, its effects grew worse. Only hunting gave him pleasure now and the slaughtered pile of boar, deer and wolf which accumulated in the praetorium yard as outlet for his growing anger became ever higher. At least he brought them back, which is more than could be said of the mutilated Saxon corpses he left to rot beneath the crumbling sea-cliffs of the German Ocean, spread out as welcome for their late-arriving kin.

Candidus himself was riven by several obvious moral dilemmas. Most significantly, that fine sense of professional duty which first brought him to Derventio – as brief prelude to his planned return to Londinium Caesariensis and report to the Vicarius - seemed to have faded. There were two compelling reasons for this:

The first of these at least clung to legitimacy in his understandable desire to see what (if anything) was to be done about the Saxons at Petuaria, before his report to the Vicarius led on to more drastic action through Imperial channels.

By contrast, the second owed barely one shred of justification to his master's original errand and at best only mocked any parenthetical question about the welfare of a much-loved daughter which might make a footnote to his commission. Yet it was this latter issue which had somehow taken over to become the most assiduously-pursued aspect of the whole enquiry. If his answer had been obtained only through the most rigorous physical examination, the degree of thoroughness applied in its discovery must put in doubt not only the focus of his main report but also the amount of nerve needed ever to deliver it before the instructing father. Simple fact was, as he finally admitted to himself, he'd become so infatuated with the woman; this goddess, his nymph; that he never could leave town without her.

So he lingered on at Derventio, a moth whose wings had almost burnt away; once again finding himself in the position of continuing to accept hospitality from a man whose trust he'd already betrayed. The days went by with little to show for them, only tension, fear and the wild hunt.

Days became weeks and April became May.

With the better weather came better spirits for everyone, while Candidus's rationale for staying on further lay only in the random workings of Fate, the quixotic allocations of Fortuna, whose outcomes he was content to await with a deep fear for the worst and a fond hope for the best. He was playing a waiting game in the vain hope that, somehow, something would turn up.

Shortly, something did.

This first development occurred sooner than he might have expected. Candidus, finding himself excluded after another brief episode of intimacy, renewed once more his private siege of the 'House of the Victories'; attacking its copper door with bare fists, undermining its walls with tunnels of entreaty, bombarding its porter with a hail of coins. All to no avail. They would not give him entry but the increasingly-public nature of his thwarted visits was ever-more careless of scurrilous report and only enhanced the danger of the Praefectus up at the fort discovering the full extent of his lodger's emotional allegiance to the daughter of the Vicarius. If it was as well it did not come to that, there did come a day when he finally found the whole house, even the upstairs windows, shuttered and barred. There were no signs of life beyond his usual tormentor, her aged door-porter, exulting at this chance finally to dismiss his old sparring partner with victorious scorn: "Don't waste your time loitering here no more, young fella-me-lad! Your bird has flown!"

The melancholy Claudius Bassus separately announced a similar discovery to his friend, just as if it was news, over a cold dinner that night in the commander's house. In his honest and self-absorbed self-pity, it still never occurred to him for a moment that his friend might have other interest in this affair than supportive confidante. The Tyche had returned to Petuaria, for reasons obscure at present. Bassus took it badly while Candidus was forced to conceal his own desolation, deciding that the time was finally right for his own long-overdue departure. He began to gather money and effects together, looking secretly for suitable transport, even if determined that the house at Petuaria would still figure on his return itinerary to Londinium. By now it was late June.

The second thing came along somewhat later, now into July, and was much more serious. An exhausted messenger of the Imperial Post brought a whipped horse into the town with a message for the eyes of the Praefectus only.

Already old news in Thracia; well-known at The City of the Fish with The Pointed Face in the pro-consular province of Aegyptus; here in Britannia the garden town of Calleva Atrebatum was still digesting its significance. But up there in Derventio it fell as hard and fresh as hail, the worst of all possible news:

362

On the 22nd May in the three hundred and thirty seventh year of Our Lord, in the sixty-fourth year of his age and thirty-first of His Reign, at the height of his powers, Constantine the Great had succumbed after a short illness to that mortality which levels all men. From the white palace of Aquyrion, in the suburbs of Nicomedia, a city on the fulcrum of Asia and Europe, Imperial Messengers set out in all directions to distribute their grievous notice of the Emperor's death. If that were so, then Derventio and its near neighbours must have got the very last of them.

This news hit the Ship of State hard like a giant wave; as if an overloaded and under-maintained merchantman, wallowing in heavy seas, is struck by a freak surge whose shuddering impact stops it dead and threatens capsize for want of forward motion.

Demonstrations of grief engulfed the Empire. They exceeded in emotion and extent anything which had ever gone before. He had given the world an illusion of peace and prosperity for many years and, whatever view came to be put upon the reality of his achievements by future historians, that sense of a great light going out was keenly felt, the world over.

Eventually, just seventeen miles from that City where the Great Constantine had first begun his long march to power, news of His journey's end provided full circle. Finally, wearily and belatedly, it was a ripple of those sorrowing sentiments first to have riven the Imperial Court at Aquyrion which now reached a lonely garrison town in the north of the Island at the End of the World, to shake the bucolic complacency of its home-spun inhabitants and ever-loyal troops.

Having, in the twentieth year of His Christian Reign and the madness of the powerful, deliberately put to death his first and finest son, Crispus, upon the insane promptings of informants he himself had incited, this left the world's first Christian Emperor with three more sons. Too many for safety, as any student of succession law could have told him.

These issue of his second wife were those three over-indulged youths: Constantine, Constantius, and Constans. Each of them he'd designated as 'Caesar' and heir, but their father's triple division of the Empire at the same stroke further diluted their inheritance through an inexplicable but equal elevation of two nephews, Dalmatius and Hannibalinus, under the invented titles of 'Nobilissimus'.

Even an amateur observer could see that the succession question was getting really crowded and could only end in tears.

Of all these aspirants, only Constantius (perhaps because he, alone, was on the spot) could be entrusted by his late father's latest will with conduct of the funeral. By design not chance finding himself in possession not only of the body but also of the Imperial Palace at new-founded Constantinopolis, and possession being nine-tenths of the law, this Constantius de facto held one half the Empire. His first act from this admitted position of strength was one of admirable and magnanimous piety - a solemn oath before the church, as Constantius II, to safeguard the health and wellbeing of all his kinsmen. His immediate second was to devote all his energy to discovering sufficient excuse or trumped-up wrong in his brothers, his half-brothers' and his cousins' conduct which could avoid any obligation for care this fond promise might otherwise threaten. Perhaps unsurprisingly for the times, it did not take him long to find a most-willing confederate in this campaign of wickedness - the Christian Bishop of Nicomedia.

The blood-letting began.

Even in far-away Derventio, a bland reiteration of the Emperor's death and conventional expressions of Official Mourning, as given many times, did not prevent the messenger from supplementing his official account to the Praefectus in the fort with unofficial anecdotes of the massacres and arrests already in train.

Hardly a relative of their father had escaped the internecine contest of his sons. Inevitably the soldiers of Empire were the men employed to wage this bloody slaughter, under the feeble guise of legitimate vengeance or legal due process.

Even in the northernmost province of the island of Britain, in Flavia Caesariensis, M. Claudius Bassus was anxious to know which way the allegiances of his own commanders ran before the tidal wave of intrigue sank them all for good. Once again he rode out to Eboracum but this time could not feel properly safe without one hundred of his most trusted men to protect him, not from the ambushes of the enemy upon the way but rather the shameful potential for treachery from his own side. This time he was away for two complete days.

364

Candidus decided to postpone any departure until the result of the conference at Eboracum was known. Eventually Bassus came home again, unharmed but irritated by the dithering indecision which he found there.

Of all the Emperor's sons, it was his namesake and youngest who had been appointed longest to the administration, as "Caesar" of Gaul and Britain during his father's lifetime. There were other allocations to his various other heirs, while the strength of grip which the son called Constantius now held in the East has already been mentioned.

The only other son requiring reference here is Constans, who'd already taken Italy, Western Illyricum and Africa for himself. Perhaps this was just the effect the deceased Emperor had intended, because what Bassus found amongst those powerful soldiers at Eboracum who hold command across this frontier province was a crippling inability to commit their loyalties or declare their alignments to any of these 'Caesars'.

So uncertain were their influential generals in the outcome of the multiple murders now proceeding, or about the eventual division of provinces which might ensue, that they hopped from booted foot to booted foot in an agony of indecision that could as easily lead to execution as any ill-judged rallying call, whether made for Constans, Constantius or Constantine.

If the supreme commanders could not commit themselves, their subordinates inside that ancient warren of colonnades and headquarters offices built so long ago by the ill-fated Ninth 'Hispana' Legion were not so inhibited. Lively debates in the mess gave way to polarisation of views. Angry dissent gave rise to violent factions. Harsh words were exchanged, swords drawn, and old scores settled in the streets or alehouses of the Colonia. Controversy gave way to murder. A senior staff officer was stabbed to death in a brothel on the south side of the city. Already the discipline of the Sixth Victorious Legion and its associated units was fragmenting under the strain. Soon, factional groupings for and against the accession of Constantine were known to be forming amongst the younger officers who lined these corridors of power.

365

In terms of his appointment as 'Caesar' in Britain (predating the death of his Great Father) it was the considered opinion of Claudius Bassus that here in the second Constantine was the one son most entitled to claim true legitimacy. A view with some obvious merit, consistent with insular loyalties being expressed elsewhere amongst others of the British legions and up on the Wall by the limitanei.

Unfortunately, Bassus's visit to Eborac' soon established just how much a significant group already preferred the opposing claim of Constans. Those involved were increasingly open in stating their willingness – if necessary and only in the interests of the public peace you understand - to unsheath sword from scabbard in his direct support.

Prominent in this contrary faction were the senior officers of the Classis Britannica, the natural tendency of the fleet to look towards Gaul and the continent of Europe one consequence of their wider-ranging duties and contacts. Easily identifiable amongst the leaders of this 'Gallic' clique were one M. Ulpius Januarius and his important friends; whose notable involvement only made it the more certain that M. Claudius Bassus would ally himself with the opposite party. Everyone else was waiting to see which way the Sixth itself would jump.

After the decline of recent weeks that followed the questionable triumph of his regimental anniversary, this new state of insecurity and danger seemed to have galvanised Bassus back into action. He expounded on his latest analysis over yet another jug of Rhenus white whilst they lingered at table in the Praetorium:

"Candidus, my truest friend, I must place most trust in instinct! Its first promptings are so often vindicated by mature reflection. Only when I consciously shy away from the spontaneous and opt for different course on second opinion does failure attend my judgements. Before these great and weighty events of our times my instincts are very strong. They exhort me to action, to make a lightning blow against the nearest grouping of the Constans' candidature, as our own powerful statement for Constantinian legitimacy....

If we do, then where to make it? Why, at Petuaria!

"The benefits, if you will forgive me, are legion. Just one strike to preserve the Imperial succession will ensure all our futures. At the same time, we will destroy that nest of Saxons concealed at the Villa Januarii and arrest the treacherous and unworthy magistrate housing them there - because we are certain how his adherence to this 'Caesar' of the middle Empire must defy the express bequest of the late and Blessed Constantine. Our swift intervention will restore the Abus squadron of the British Fleet to its proper sense of duty, recover the strategic dockside installations of Petuaria to control of the proper authorities, shock Eboracum into sense and, above all else, render the Ala Picentiana so impeccable in its loyalties, so prompt and terrible in its obedient retribution, as will cover our standards with a fame and glory so recent that no-one will ever again consider its dis-bandment. The regiment will be saved and, you might think, the whole east coast with it!"

Buoyed-up by these comforting thoughts of glory, Bassus took another gulp of white before renewing his review with what appeared like an afterthought:

"And if these priorities of duty and military necessity are not compelling enough, the additional private gallantry in ridding a beautiful and noble lady, a living goddess, of the unforgivable cruelties imposed by a heartless husband, must surely so thoroughly cement the rescuer in her enduring affections as to give on to lasting happiness? If Eboracum hesitates, Derventio rides! What do you think, my old comrade? The die is cast. Everything points to action. Are you with us?"

Candidus did not at first know what to say.

Even if he found this chain of reasoning convincing in its order and logically-appealing in its component events, he feared this last parenthetical mention of the love and safety of a singular lady was the overriding consideration to which all others became mere supplementary.

Yet in this, as with all others, his own strong sense of Fate and innate instinct drove him to acknowledge the attraction of the arguments. He took his friend's hand and clasped it across the wooden table in the solidarity of a brotherhood already fatally-undermined:

"I am with you, Praefectus. I shall count it signal honour to ride with you, amongst the Companions of the Ala!"

367

Even as Candidus spoke, he knew in his heart what hypocrites they both were.

They rode not to save an Ala or an Empire but in a three-cornered fight over the one woman.

"A person with no sense of the past is a person who is a stranger both to his own roots and to the human condition more generally. For human beings are not creatures of nature; we are inheritors of the history that has made us what we are. Not to know our history is not to know ourselves."

Anthony O'Hear (contemporary commentator and academic, University of Buckingham)

XVI

As the official records show, it was on the eighth day of July, a fine summer's morning in the three-hundred-and-thirty-seventh year after the birth of the Christus, one thousand-and-ninety years 'Ab Urbe Condita' (if the traditional reckoning of the Romans is maintained, as all their punctilious officers would surely insist), that the Ala Picentiana filed out of its barracks at Derventio, ready to take up formation for the march.

Disturbed by the noise of its assembly, the people of the town poured out of their houses and into the streets to witness an entire cavalry wing gathering for war. What they saw must live on around the hearth-fires for generations, since they will never see its like again, not in these parts. No longer the gaudy insubstantial foils of parade armour, the flim-flam of practice show, but ever the dour and heavy weaponry of campaign. On their stocky broad-hoofed ponies, the four-horned saddle and its green woollen cloth are slung with cloak and blanket, grain bag and water bottle, leather satchel and bronze cooking-skillet. The overlapping bronze scales or iron ring-mail of body armour are fringed at the shoulder and kilted waist with red leather pteruges, decorative flaps edged with gold. Besides these devices, the only other concession to display is in the glittering 'millefiori' enamelling of belted-buckle and pendant strap-end.

Black-iron helmets of combat gauge, lightened only by the yellowed decoration of skimmed bronze on the peaked visor, flanged cheek-plates, and a broad neck guard; their peacock display of horsehair plume or dyed feather eschewed for the march. Full-length trousers and long-sleeved tunics in sober fawn acknowledge northern climes, as contrast with the slight tunics and vivid scarlets of last week's parade, whilst long sword and heavy lance provide the preferred weaponry for this expedition. Needing only their big leather-covered shields, round and bossed and edged in bronze, to be slung over the back to complete its inventory of equipment, the whole Ala is made ready for the march.

Those who tell the tale will say that Picens's Horse rode out of Derventio to such a cheering and mad applause from their population as would have served any incoming Consul well for a triumph.

The girls of the town offered kisses and their undying passion, decorating the plume holders and lance points of the soldiers with flowers of the hedgerow or more intimate memento, while retired army veterans wept to see a recreation by their sons of resurrected military glories they'd once known and never thought to see again.

Before them all, the prancing horses of the all-conquering Ala drove a flock of dogs, street urchins, and frightened chickens with an ease which everyone believed would soon be replicated on the treacherous levies of the Conspiracy and their craven mercenaries from Frisia, whilst proud but fearful mothers held spellbound children up at shoulder height to watch their own enlisted fathers ride away.

Outside the town, things soon looked different.

It was a lower, straighter and more arterial road they took to strike at Petuaria; not that remote, meandering backroute which once brought Candidus and Taranis to Derventio.

Out on the open highway, excitement from their leave-taking was quickly dissipated - replaced by that fixity of purpose which is true hallmark of the warlike Roman. This hardening of attitude was reflected by the achievements of a rising breeze, blowing off and away every last frivolous fragment of flower and blossom, every harlot's keepsake. Glory would replace them.

Relying on their unit strength and force to secure safe passage along the Emperor's Highway, and so dispensing with the conventional textbook requirements of prior reconnaissance, their Ala made rapid progress indeed. Lightning war.

Since no-one could possibly have had advance warning of their impulsive mission, as a gamble this tactic seemed vindicated by the complete absence of counter-attack. If there was one penalty to be had from such speed and disobedience to the theories of military writers like Vegetius or Frontinus, it lay in the hopeless failure of their baggage train to keep up with its Wing. Eventually, the one became completely lost to sight of the other and a small vexillatio of lancers had to be detailed to hang back on the roadside and provide escort for the supply wagons while they caught up.

There is one other aspect of their journey deserving mention at this point - the condition of the mean villages through which their route passed. Or rather their population.

371

Unlike the leaving of Derventio, and even if there were still one or two people willing to leave work or home to stand and watch this rippling column of horseflesh and armour riding through, these sullen rarities were - without exception - women or children only, or the elderly and infirm. Oddly enough - young or old - all their faces were uniformly daubed with streaks of ash, like mourners at some native funeral.

At the time, Candidus naturally took these marks as open signs of public respect for the Late Emperor and he did not register the consistent absence of men from the Tribe. After the euphoria of leaving Derventio, they provided disturbing encounters nonetheless. The unenthusiastic gaze of painted spectators, standing strangely still, was something they found repeated elsewhere – even in the tiny, wayside town of Delgovicia, its huts and sheep pens equally deserted. If dilution by inter-breeding and the strict laws of heredity had long ago turned the blood of a famous Ala founded in Gaul into local wine, it was only later that he remembered how it was those troopers from the Parisii who showed more agitation over these curious signs along the way, when compared to their Brigantian brothers. Either way, at least none of it prevented their safe arrival before the walled town of Petuaria Civitas Parisiorum at the end of a long day's hard riding.

If he had been cavalier in neglect of scouts on the march, Bassus correctly became pedantic in observing this essential once closer to the enemy.

Employing all that elaborate field-craft on which their operational success against Saxon or Pict was so soundly-based, Bassus chose to hide the majority of his troops in the deep woodland which clothed the escarpment above the town. This left only a few bare-headed riders to go out and explore the dispositions of the rebels. Posing as hunters after boar or mere innocent travellers dawdling along the Eboracum road, these various scouts were soon returned with consistently-alarming intelligence. The town was fast-closed against them well before the curfew hour. Its gates were sealed and barred, its walls bristling with spearmen; whilst all the galleys of the Fleet stood offshore in mutual safety, yet close enough to bring lethal ship-board artillery accurately to bear upon the land.

The Praefectus Alae was furious.

His fond expectation of triumphal, unopposed entry into a grateful Civitas, overcome purely by the advantage of surprise, was exposed as naive. Turning up in strength and asking the magistrates and councillors of the vicus for their civic keys was clearly not going to be enough. This town would not be taken so easily after all.

It was obvious their enemy must have been tipped-off in time to make some basic preparation for its defence. Who was responsible? Treachery without was one thing, the precise evil meant to be confronted by their expedition, but the thought of treachery emanating from within their own force was quite another. Suspicion secretly grew along tribal lines, Parisii troopers blaming their Brigantian comrades and vice versa.

Nothing could be done about it now. His men and horses were tired after a long ride and beginning offensive operations so late in the day would not commend itself to any prudent commander. Neither was the reduction of a fortified city by siege the best nor most natural task for mounted cavalry.

So far at least, Bassus held to the belief they had still concealed the actual arrival of the main force from their enemy within the town, even if some sort of attack was clearly expected. Time, and the work of establishing such a temporary camp as so many horse would soon need upon arrival of the supply train, must see their actual dispositions better known before too long anyway, even without an informant in the ranks.

So far as the enemy went, comprising only infantry as they did (in the shape of two Numerii of Tigris Boatmen and the Petuarensian Interceptors, together with such complement of Marines as remained onshore to guard the galley-pens), here was a force the Ala could so easily cut to pieces – given half the chance. If only they could be tempted out the safety of the town and onto open ground, the garrison would make short work for lancers.

Anxious therefore to test what level of provocation might achieve this tempting exposure, the Praefectus sent a complete turma out under the command of his newest and keenest tribune, young Julius Honoratus, to trail their scarlet coats before the walls.

It wasn't long before they had an answer.

From their distant safety hidden in the greenwood, it was now as 'Magister Draconum' to the Ala that Flavius Candidus sat to observe the outcome, still on the Arab bay. Beside him, M. Claudius Bassus, the Praefectus granting this honourable designation to his friend. Together they watched the red cloaks and fluttering standards of Honoratus' detachment riding fast and east down the public highway, past the extra-mural tombs and monuments of the lately-dead, ready to charge with futile aggression against the town's bolted and barricaded West Gate.

Far beyond the reach of human voice or even the recall of trumpets they watched it go, and only then did Flavius Candidus detect with horror the very first signs of people standing up and moving about ontop that western bastion where he and Januarius had once reviewed the security of his crumbling canton.

It was only then that the penny dropped: "Mithras protect them!" begged Candidus "The repeater catapult!"

"The what?"

Either the Magister Ballistae had made miraculous recovery from his typhus or else a knowledgeable replacement had been drafted-in to re-commission his baby. (No doubt an equivalent expertise could be traced among the sailors of the Fleet). Either way, it was undoubtedly the same contraption which these miniature figures upon the western tower were seen to unsheet.

Obviously repaired, it must already have been standing aimed, set, wound and loaded; tense and waiting for them; because within seconds a ceaseless cloud of flying catapult bolts shimmered down the Eboracum road and straight into the thirty-two tight-packed riders of Honoratus' turma. All unwitting, they'd formed themselves into the perfect target for this inflexible but pitiless weapon.

The metalled surface of the roadway was soon piled ten-deep with its writhing twitching victims; man and horse alike. Only five riders came back complete, every trooper blank with shock. One riderless horse followed them, galloping up rolling-eyed and frothing straight to an M.Claudius Bassus ashen with grief and disbelief at this unexpected setback for his beautiful Ala so soon after their confident arrival. His misery communicated itself rapidly down the shuddering line of horse soldiers and, for each and every rider, its only antidote must be bloody revenge.

Bassus caught the mood at once. He rode up and down the turmae, promising his men this was the prize they would have, if only they could give him the iron restraint of discipline, but their reward they must wait for as a dish best eaten cold. And cold they were already.

Where were the equipment wagons? The baggage train having failed to arrive, what every one of them most needed now was the respite of walled security and shelter for the night. Without the protective equipment needed for their encampment, they faced the dilemma of where and how to find it other than in a field bivouac. In the solution first identified instead, its capture and forfeiture would have offered the twin luxuries of shelter and immediate revenge in equal measure:

The Villa Januarii. (Bassus smiled once more).

But, no, not yet. Discipline would be reflected in restraint. Looting must be the last prize of victory, not its prelude. Fearful too of finding in the dusk yet another kind of ambush or clever trap hidden within the villa's dangerous confines, it was agreed that this first night would be spent out in the open, four hundred plus of men and horse hiding in the woods. Come daybreak, yes, this old house could become tomorrow morning's first objective and its evening's proper billet. But no, not yet.

So it was neither a cheerful nor a comfortable night that most of them spent on the ground, their minds preoccupied with thoughts of coming action or the fate of Honoratus and his men. In the end, it was as much their superstitious enemies' fear of the dark that kept them free from attack, out there in the woods, as any camouflage of leaves. Happily, no trumpeter's alarm or call for action came to test the vigilance of their picketed sentries or spoil a fitful rest beneath the dripping trees.

When these interminable watches of the night ended in a damp dawn, the troopers of the Ala were glad indeed to unwrap themselves from whatever rolled blanket or woollen cloak they'd passed it in and set themselves to the care of the shaggy mounts and oiled weapons who'd be their closest friends in action.

To the sleepy watchers opposite, leaning on their spears upon the western walls of Petuaria, this creeping light of dawn merely gave Virgilian views of cultivated fields and the gentle rise of hills, girdled with mist and distant woodland.

Only the unsightly unburied dead from Honoratus' turma, still lying there so grotesque and rigid on the roadside, only they remained to confound an illusion of rustic tranquility or give hint at danger. Whoever these few were that came against the town last night, to die so uselessly before the walls, no-one had dared follow them – at least 'til daybreak. What would today bring?

If those stiffly sprawled bodies laid upon the roadway jarred in this morning's Arcadian panorama, then what immediately served to shatter it completely and rouse the look-outs on the walls to frantic action was the sight of hundreds if not thousands of horsemen, streaming out the trees below the escarpment to form up in well-drilled divisions upon the sandy fields of the Januarian estate.

Iron becoming bronze and bronze becoming gold as every single standard and lance point came to reflect the ever-climbing sun, their helmets so gilded and their armoured fittings so shining through the morning mist as must convince any watcher upon the walls that here were deployed before them the very best. Troops of foremost quality and irresistible power.

It seemed that elite and special forces from the Imperial Household itself had taken ship direct for Britain, before making spectacular landfall upon the riverine sludge of Petuaria. As if Great Constantine's very own 'Domestici et Protectores' were even now deployed in all their shimmering glory upon the Elysian Fields of the Villa Januarii. His cavalry of the Household, those gold-masked peacocks of the battlefield, who take life with all the authority and decorative grace of angels but harvest souls like the very devil.

And if their opponent's sacred mission must really lie in the restoration of His Late Authority through the Imperial Succession, then not one of the mixed bag of rural reservists left to guard the circuit of Petuaria's mouldering defences could really believe what scale and grandeur now unrolled en masse before them, even as the cracked warning bell they rang so weakly from the basilica roof woke every sleeper in the town to harsher realities yet; its toll the announcement for many of the last day they'd ever know.

376

Such is the panicky exaggeration which bedevils the Theatre of War but – without official reports - whether those who held Petuaria ever understood what manner or quality of soldiers opposed them must remain uncertain.

Certainly they'd been tipped off about something, as their high state of readiness revealed. Either way, there would hardly be much compensation or cause for celebration in finding out it was indeed the Ala Picentiana, that regiment of formidable renown. Yet however hard the rebel sentries in the town strained their eye to confirm with more precision the exact numbers and type, they could not do so because this 'army' came no closer on to them, no further east.

Instead, the Ala filed as if on parade down a wooded defile beside the descending slope of Spout Hill, to ride in full battle array south along that sunken paved lane which leads directly from there through sleepy avenues of ancient oaks up to the wattle-walled stockyards of the Villa itself. Ahead of them, their Draco standard hissed and writhed and rattled to the affrightment of the enemy, as thirsty for revenge as its own men.

Shrouded as they still were in mist, the watchers on the town walls could only guess at their true numbers and intention, naturally falling into nervous over-estimation, an effect doubled through the device ordered by Bassus. Every second man had gathered brush-wood in the forest by the escarpment and tied it to their horse, trailing down from harness traces. The dust it kicked up as they galloped across the powdered alluvium of the Januarian lands raised a great cloud of uncertainty which hung behind the Ala and seemed to double its strength.

The arched entrance gate into the villa compound was closed and barricaded with a couple of hay wagons but it took only a dozen dismounted troopers to tear down and clear that feeble obstruction. Horsemen towed the two wagons out of the way, overturning them both in the process. Riding two-by-two into the large enclosure now opened-up, the first turma to go in met with an indecisive smattering of household staff, armed only with scythes and billhooks, who as promptly ran away.

Those soldiers of the detachment already dismounted for the clearance of an entry now set themselves to searching the barns and outbuildings within the yard.

There was a palpable sense of the Ala only just being held in check, their visible jitteriness increased by a growing suspicion that the reason why their plodding supply-train had not arrived was something terminally-unpleasant happening along the way.

Meanwhile, hearing the tactical advice of Candidus, the Prefect took most of his Wing on a sweep westwards and then southwards, around the house and towards the river. This reconnaissance of the unwalled side of the orchard field soon established its blooming apple and cherry trees were free of Saxonici today, even if their ugly thatched hovels and sordid pits with smouldering hearths confirmed they were not long-gone from the place.

Riding down a new-planted barley field towards the river put the house behind them. The Ala wheeled around in perfect order to return, to come back on itself, and then to address that subtle slope above whose modest crest the whitewashed walls and orange pantiles of the great house rose to sight. For a moment there was only the soothing jingling of swinging metal harness, horses chomping bits, their slow hooves flattening crops. But as their own spear-heads and helmet crests began to clear the undemanding fold of the ridge-top, there came such a roar - building from the garden of the house like a wild animal at bay in a circus beast show - that the soldiers' lance points all went down as one, even without the order being given.

If this were animal then its character was wolf, and not the type to suckle infant Romans.

Concealed within this enclosure, upon the close-cut camomile lawns of Marcus Ulpius Januarius; hidden amongst his pruned box-hedge and weed-less gravel; his carp-filled fishponds, his standing roses and his specimen trees; lined-up around the little bronze fountain of 'Cupid Embracing Psyche' that still bubbled happily away to itself; the Saxonici made their shield wall and their final stand.

The sea-wolves beat their rough shields with pointed swords or little axes and yelled their gap-toothed, coarse-voiced, foul-mouthed defiance at the advancing cavalry regardless. True to their master's last commission, defending his home to the end.

Above the din, the voice of M. Claudius Bassus boomed exultant at this peerless find, this sublimated focus for all the ingrained hatred which his coastal patrol bore their target raiders, cornered here within the immaculate grounds of his hated rival's house; no finer place to form a cockpit for all their darkest prejudice: "See how faithful are the hounds of Januarius! Ride down these curs like the dogs they are! Leave them dead on his lawn for the traitor to find in the morning!"

He held his sword high, its blade flat against the sky like a flag, and ordered his trumpeters to sound him the charge. They needed no encouragement. Tight-packed together, knee-to-knee, the entire formation charged as one, crashing over a flimsy wicket fence and funnelling into the square confinement of these pleasure gardens.

The interlocking shields of the Saxons went down at once under the sheer pressure of this moving mass of men and horse, their sword and axemen collapsing under the insatiable, questing lances of the riders. They never stood a chance.

Candidus had been proud of his place in the first rank, but it was from the mounted vantage of that bloody privilege where he saw what utter softness the disintegrating hardness of this outer shell of shields revealed. Huddled behind their dying menfolk were the cringing women and screaming children who'd shared their life in the mean holes they'd dug in the nearby orchard.

Here it was where the Discipline of the Ala finally broke, snapping like a rotten mildewed leather lead that can no longer hold a straining vicious dog. Men whose only métier in life was seeking out and executing the youth of Juteland, the sons of Frisia and Anglia, could never be counselled in restraint upon the field of battle. Not when last night they had seen a whole turma of their brothers go down a road leading towards the master of these Saxons and this house, with only five come back alive again. ("Murdering scum!")

Bred only for killing, they must resort to what they do best and the atrocious slaughter now dispensed could not be withheld. Candidus, a man who'd seen more than his share in his time, had thought himself well-hardened to Roman War - but even he wept amongst the maelstrom to see an infant swept away by its raging force, a child no more than two whose saffron shift and liking for apples he'd known so well.

He knew himself and his own sensibilities to be no more acute than those of anyone else his age. (How could they be otherwise; not with death so prominent in Roman life, even its chosen entertainment; not when child mortality is so commonplace that still-born infants lie buried under every domestic yard?) But please, in the Name of the Unknown God - not like this!

Now off the leash, the troopers ranged at will, some on foot and some still-mounted. Their blood-lust was up. They broke into the villa itself and drove more domestic staff out onto the lawn where their immediate murder could not be prevented, for all the powerless intervention of desperate officers.

Worse yet, another group of men found the grey and white bull still enclosed where he'd last seen it, inside the stockyard, and dragged the poor beast by its ring out and all the way around to the main doorway of the house.

At the foot of that same verandah where Januarius's kindly but just-now-murdered steward once greeted him into this venerable *domus* for the first time, all those months ago, Candidus saw a rowdy ring of laughing Brigantian troopers take turns to slash the great bull's throat with their military daggers – to him no sacrament but only blasphemous parody of his own Mithraic beliefs. The beast staggered to its knees, black blood pumping onto the greedy earth, before collapsing completely into the dust.

Shunning all this shameful bloody chaos going on around him, Flavius Candidus dismounted to find the unspeakable tragedy of a child's body buried under the tumbled remains of its father's shield wall. As he lifted the lolling straw head of the dead Saxon whelp over the horns of his saddle-bow, out the corner of his eye he caught a decurion of the Ala, flaming torch in hand, ducking nonchalantly under the trailing clematis of a colonnaded garden-walk and strolling calmly into the hall of this fine old house.

Within minutes, the whole of it was alight.

The prompt communication of these flames into the rafters and roof voids soon brought its rapid collapse, whilst military arsonists busied themselves everywhere, unchecked in their systematic destruction of every single remaining structure or artefact of value which might otherwise be claimed by the executors and inheritors of the Januarii or dare remind us of their hated line.

Climbing miserably back onto his horse, heavier now not only from its rider but also from the pitiful bundle across his saddle, resting silent on its mane, Flavius Candidus considered the appalling irony in these scenes.

A sophisticated society applying its most valuable and highly-trained resources towards its own destruction - Rome, the ultimate predator, turning in on itself.

The hopeless courage of the Saxon mercenaries - the futile loyalty of a people who lived in pits defending this beautiful old building against 'barbarians' dressed in Roman uniform. Awful irony on a truly tragic scale, degrees of devastation so much more dreadful and complete than the casual vandalism of random raiders, so cruelly imposed by those we'd claim for our sworn protectors. Child-killers!

Sick at heart, he rode off but found himself caught up once again in a group of swirling riders, representing some re-formation of the Ala, some return to order. He was with them, yet not of them. The men of Picens's Horse had recovered some sense of their duties - if not their honour - in an approximation to their ordained divisions.

In Candidus's eyes, their name and reputation was forever turned to ashes through their slaughter of the innocents and ignition of the house. Carried along with them, he found himself galloping amongst its re-constituted turmae before the bristling walls of Petuaria, the savage maw of their dragon standard gawping with gormless malice against their enemies.

Once again the smoke of a burning villa scarred the skies above the Abus River, but this time it was a self-inflicted wound. Still the wide-ranging depredations of the Ala continued remorseless, as yet more buildings outside the walls were torched. Now the fortified landing for the Fleet was put to fire and sword, a rearguard of Marines left by Trimalchio cut down by marauding cavalry, one by one, in and around their dockyard.

The ballistae mounted on the curtain towers of the town walls clattered and whirred, cracked and recoiled, whilst their toiling gunners kept up a steady rhythmn of fire, wind-back, reload with bolt; fire, wind-back, reload with bolt. The Ala, however, had learnt its painful lesson. Once bitten, twice shy, it now ran in looser formations and, if artillery bolts still found the occasional target, it was not often enough to be worthwhile.

Then he saw her.

On that same flat-roofed tower where the wicked mechanism rested which yesterday shot Honoratus and his men to pieces.

The warrior-queen, her auburn hair flying in the wind, dressed in a red shift tied at the waist with a golden girdle whose loose ends hung down, she was calling out encouragement to the men upon the walls, her words lost in the din of battle.

He realised then that the men about her were not soldiers, helmeted and mailed, but bare-chested native warriors with home-made swords, crude hunting spears and small bronze shields. Their hair was white as ghosts and stuck up in spikes where it was washed in chalk or lime. Now the empty villages and her sudden departure from Derventio made some sense. The Parisii had risen in loyal support to their Chief and obedience to their Goddess, doubling the amateur garrisons of Petuaria. No wonder the baggage and equipment wagons of the Ala had disappeared into thin air along with their escorts. No doubt their supply trucks were burning on the road somewhere, the decapitated heads of army drivers brandished aloft by bloodstained tribesmen, faces daubed in ash and minds deformed by an ancient frenzy fed with plants.

His heart leapt on this glimpse of her fatal beauty, as if it could scale the height of wall to be beside her, but at the same time he knew he'd lost her for ever. She was no longer the person he'd known but transformed into something different and barely human – a state of being from which she'd never return. The Celts were busy collecting heads now; the Parisii reverting to a stranger and an older world from long before Rome. Their Red Goddess exulted from her tower at all this bloody chaos unrolling below, the ultimate liturgy her faithful adherents could bestow on their Mother – Total War.

M. Claudius Bassus saw her too. An excess of blood and desire had made him mad for he stood aloft in his stirrup-less saddle and gestured to the troops with his sword - towards that same bastion wreathed in smoke on which her glowing redness shone: "There she is, my Greeks! There's our Helen, on the Trojan Walls. We alone will recover her beauty from wicked Priam and bring her safe home to Derventio. Poets shall sing of the Ala Picentiana as once they did of great Agamemnon's men!"

In any other context his vain conceits would have been fit for laughter - but not when men and women stood butchered in an inglorious bout of local strife which no Official History would ever deign to mention. Any humour in his madness vapourised on the moment. Still absorbed in his Homeric fantasy, Bassus could only acknowledge the reappearance of his closest friend momentarily, with a sideways: "What in Hades Name is that on your saddle bow...?"

"The Shame of the Ala!" Candidus shouted after his retreating figure, before the Prefect and his clique of officers swept on in pursuit of their Draco. Carrying the intolerable pain of this infant's rebuke with him, Candidus must still charge after them. With only moderate cohesion amongst the two besieged Numerii inside the town; weakened not strengthened by the crazed warriors of the tribe, the parade of devastation and assassination wrought by the Ala without the walls finally achieved provocation intended within.

At last the west gate burst open and a shouting mob of tribesmen and soldiers came running across the ditches; an unruly gang before whom the cavalry of the Constantinian side deliberately withdrew, making sure enough of the garrison left the protection of its walls before they could all be ridden-down on the plain.

Still feigning a retreat to draw out the Januarian faction, the Ala was regrouping about a mile from the town, almost back at the smoking villa they'd so recently torched. While Bassus conferred with his surviving tribunes and decurions, they heard the blare of many trumpets away to the west, out on the Eboracum road. Turning to look and shielding their eyes against the sun, all they could make out was the dust cloud attendant on a large body of marching men.

"Mithras be praised, reinforcements are here. The Legion is come to our help!" rejoiced the Prefect.

His men responded with cheers. They formed up in good order, with draco standards and their trumpeters to the fore, then set off at a steady jingling trot to meet their rescuers.

Bassus had been right. It was indeed Legio VI Victrix, marching out from Eborac' in full strength, but even from a distance it could be seen how this 'strength' did not even approach two thousand armed men. Their hearts sank.

Grumpy old Rufinus, the veteran river pilot, had been perfectly right - here was another one of Constantine's disastrous reforms. In an Empire where civil war and bids for the purple routinely took as essential foundation the martial power of those gigantic Legions whose might combined both the Empire's security and its very danger, Constantine resolved this conundrum through the simple expedient of reducing their strength to such pitiful numbers.

In ordinances originating from a risk-averse Imperial Court, its administration symbolised by the spiteful impotence of eunuchs, no wonder the obedience of the feeble and unmanned became preferred to those whose service came from duty, or that any more considered delegation of real power to the courageous or principled was always rejected in preference to the openly-weak.

The Legions held justifiable pride in their histories and their roster of victories but their encampments were too often the breeding-grounds for rebellion and revolution. Hence the Imperial solution found lay in their military castration, so that they could no longer present a threat to anyone - friend or foe - unless brigaded with others of their equally-belittled peers, or with that new-fangled urban shambles they call the Mobile Field Army.

How sad then that, even in his paranoid timidity, the Emperor could still deceive himself; wilfully-ignoring how much diminished these famous units were become when compared to their legendary predecessors. Emasculated as he himself had made them, still would he savour from his throne the hollow vanity of hearing that same roll-call of mighty names; that litany of thirty-three legions of proud history and great battle honours; his to deploy at will across the whole world just as an Augustus had; his to command like Trajanus or Marcus Aurelius once did.

This then was the real quality of the 'Fighting Sixth' so ill-met by daylight, down there on the Eboracum road. All its glittering standards, titles and insignia standing quite unchanged in splendour from their forebears, with only its manipular establishment left visibly wanting. This is not to say that those who marched towards them were not well-officered and drilled or were not (in Britain, at least) still properly-armoured and equipped; unlike their lightly-clad brothers of the Eastern Legions, so regularly sent out for slaughter before the Persian horsemen of Shapur.

That their commander still styled himself 'Legatus' was another dangerous indulgence, given the Emperor Septimius Severus's express proscription of this very title over a hundred years ago, fruit of his deep distrust for the senatorial class. If, even in those far-off days, Severus the African thought it important enough to use statute to outlaw a military rank (preferring the invented 'Praefectus Legionis' under a rule still current) then not even the most jealous modern ruler could find this particular Legatus much cause for worry.

He reclined feebly in a horse-drawn litter upon piled cushions whose soft comfort could not prevent the piercing claws of a venereal infection pursuing its slowly-fatal course through his nervous system. They saw at first glance how its pain had consumed him and made him cruel.

"Hail to the Sixth! We of Picens's Horse salute you! We welcome our brothers-in-arms' aid in suppressing a rebel force standing against the lawful succession."

"Is that Claudius Bassus who speaks, Praefectus Alae?" he croaked.

"Yes, I am the man privileged to hold that commission."

"And is there one Flavius Candidus with you, Beneficarius Consularis in the office of the Vicarius?"

"Yes, there surely is. Here he is with me, Legatus, in the vanguard of the Ala!"

"Good. Then will you both lay aside your weapons and step forward unarmed, since I hold signed warrants for your arrest on charges of treason against the State!"

If they had not ridden up so close, the Ala might have made-off and even regrouped, then returned to make a successful charge. But at this proximity they could achieve no momentum. In seconds, the Legionaries were in upon them and amongst them after only a preliminary shower of spears and throwing darts. Taken by surprise and surrounded, the Ala started to find itself being ground to pieces on the rock of the legion. To finish them off, the mixed garrison of Petuaria were soon on hand, swarming across from the town like jackals keen to pick off stragglers on the margins of the fight. Three hundred and ninety five years of mainly-honourable service about to be rubbed out forever, as quickly as that, without even a second thought.

The fighting spread out and fragmented as the Ala began to disintegrate. A gang of tribal spearmen with faces clouded by swirling blue tattoos tried to force their way into its centre, where Bassus and his officers rallied under their snarling draco.

Suddenly, from the town's west gate, a fresh knot of riders made a reckless dash - straight for this core and obvious group.

They were a motley crew equipped with every form of arms and armour; from almost naked (save for a two-handed axe) to a lancer whose complete suit of greenish-bronze scales covered both horse and rider in the manner of a Sarmatian cataphract. Beneath the pointed helmet of this exotic rig, Candidus glimpsed the familiar patrician features of Januarius distended by hatred and fury as he spurred his horse right at Bassus. This was the very last time Candidus saw either man, before they were both lost amongst the fighting.

He almost turned to follow them then pulled his horse up hard, shocked by the horrible realisation of how fast and large his resentments had grown. If fresh battle were joined, he could not say which of his rivals he'd most wish to kill first – M. Claudius Bassus or the Green Knight.

Enough was enough. He'd done his bit. The game had run its course and now he only wanted out of it.

The first attempt at escape from this murderous melee which Flavius Candidus made was directed away from the town, towards those rounded hills and green woods from which they'd emerged only this morning. However, he soon found the fields this way swarming with the local force, who barred the way with angry spears. As the Legion pushed the disintegrating Ala back along the road towards the town, to press it against the walls, he realised how those already-narrow avenues of escape were being squeezed even tighter yet. There was only one path left him.

It was when he rode desperately for the sea that he first realised how the dead child slung across his horse's shoulders as macabre spur to his conscience was actually sobbing, every jolt of the gallop jerking it into new and convulsive breaths.

Somehow, this unexpected positive sign of life amongst all the bloody chaos of the battlefield spurred him on to one last, desperate effort.

Taking the tiny boy by the scruff of the neck, he draped him over his shoulder just as he'd done that day in the garden, hearing his gasps and snuffles in his ear even in the clang of combat. The child would live, he'd swear it!

Within sight of the river he found its tributary streams creating a maze of banks and dykes. Even if he couldn't see them, any watcher on the town walls or the adjacent fleet-landing (assuming anyone left alive in there to know) would be able to see him. It was there and then, amongst all the hurrying-and-scurrying, that he became aware of a group of four mounted cuirassiers following him. He did not know their unit or their allegiance but feared that both were hostile. He dug his heels into his horse's flanks for more speed and saw them do the same.

He went down one muddy bank, splashing through a stream of dirty brackish-looking water, then struggled up onto the other side. His horse was fading fast. Anxious not to be silhouetted on the drain bank, he drove it down into another little creek. Preferring the safety of concealment rather than the diminishing chance of outrunning his pursuers on a blown horse, Candidus slid out of the saddle while still clutching his young charge.

Once again abandoning equestrian transport with an ungrateful smack to a broad rump, just like that day on the Eboracum road, Candidus slipped and slithered through the mud into a tall reed bed.

Now on foot and with this dead weight on his shoulder, it became obvious what a handicap his military equipment was becoming. An iron helmet and a chain mail shirt slowed his every step, making escape less likely but drowning in mud a repulsive possibility. Resting the still-sobbing Saxon pup on a mat of reeds, Candidus undid his helmet and lobbed it into the water before dragging the chain mail over his head and letting it fall with a metallic 'sigh' onto the bank. Scooping up the child again, Candidus resumed his flight, keeping close to the stream-bottom in water sometimes up to his knees. His plan, if plan he had, was to hide somewhere on the river bank until the hunt died down.

Unfortunately, no sooner was this simplistic strategy formed than one of the cuirassiers seen earlier appeared high on the bank at his side of the creek. Seeing the fugitive cowering below him, dressed only in a long tunic and carrying a child, the trooper gave a 'whoop' of triumph and dismounted.

Running down the bank with sword drawn, ready for the despatch of man and child together, his speed and over-confidence wrong-footed him on the treacherous slime so that he tipped forwards and slid head-first, gurgling, into the water. Candidus pinned him there firmly with a booted foot, bubbles boiling up out of the water, as he carefully slid the sharp tip of the spatha he'd wisely kept hold-of ever so gently under the leather-bound edging of his opponent's chain mail - then in hard between the shoulder blades before the usual 'twist' on extraction. Giving barely a moan the trooper was gone, brown waters turning to red as his legs slipped under. Candidus, taking fleeting moral comfort from a professionally-administered disposal quicker than any drowning in chain mail, turned to go.

Staggering on towards the river, down another filthy trench, his heavy cavalry boots were gathering so much mud he could hardly walk, let alone run. Kicking them off, his toes descended into cloying yellow sludge. Now it was the bloody scabbarded sword whose keeping had saved them which became his latest impossible handicap. Slung from the neck on a wide leather baldric, its sheath hung down and dragged in the water, tangling his legs. It had to go.

The creek he followed joined with another and then another, these intersecting waterways surely leading to the estuary. Lost and alone in this narrow world of deep silt and high reeds, under an empty sky, he could only guess the way. Suddenly, he heard splashing behind him. Turning his head against the slumped body of the child, he saw three bold cavalrymen who'd just lost a brother. They were riding hard and grim-faced towards him in a cloud of spray, straight down the ditch.

To them, the man they pursued had lost every sign and dignity of a Roman; his thin tunic soaking wet and smeared with yellow clay; his arms, legs and face filthy and caked with estuary slime. He looked like a barbarian and they would very shortly dispose of him at no higher valuation, as he did their fellow.

Breaking into a despairing run (as if man slowed by the weight of a child could outrun horses), Candidus at last emerged from the claustrophobic mouth of the creek to feel a fair wind off the river cool on his face. He understood its meaning. That minor passing comfort and reason to stay which the world offers the dying before extracting their end. Shafts of spring sunlight across a death bed. As if the Fates want to make your leaving of it all the less willing, he reasoned coldly.

The troopers were almost on him now, he could hear their vengeful oaths and cruel obscenities; their harness jangling and horses' hot snorting loud in his ears, but still he ran. At every step his bare feet sank and slid into the treacherous riverine mud - as if it would suck him under to escape the blades of the horsemen. Once, he looked around to see they had taken up their lancea, preferring to stick him like a pig rather than hack him to pieces with swords. The next ditch was bigger and deeper than the rest, the water up to his waist.

A big sky rolled around him and a stronger wind blew from shore to sea. He could see right across the river from here to the far bank and wished himself there, which somehow gave an unexpected sense of peace.

At the point where he gave up all hope and knew he must turn to face his hunters' terminal violence, a long, low, sleek, black ship came silently-skimming unobserved out the reed-beds within inches of his nose, forty oars rising and falling in perfect rhythmn.

He found himself face-to-face with one of its astonished crew, who reached out instinctively to grab the struggling wader. The vessel paused only for a moment, as first the child he held above his head and then its rescuer were dragged roughly over the side and safely aboard.

As its angry crew pinned every last trooper stone dead into the slime under a falling thicket of spearshafts and throwing-axes, Candidus fell comatose and exhausted under and between the rowing benches, on the very bottom of their onward-gliding ship.

"How goes the world with you? Are you hunting, building something, or playing the country gentleman? I was on the point of ending this letter when who should come along but the courier. I spent some time chatting to him about you and he was positive you'd weighed anchor and gone off on these amphibious military operations of yours, patrolling the western shores for curved ships, the vessels of the Saxons, whose every rower is a total pirate.

Captains and crew alike, they are teachers or pupils in the arts of banditry.... I beg you to be vigilant! The Saxon is the most ferocious of all foes, coming on you without warning but making off if you are ready and waiting for him. Resistance does not earn his respect and if you are reckless in it he will soon have you. Shipwrecks do not worry him, either – to him they are just an occupational hazard offering useful practice. Knowing the sea like his own soul, he will risk its every danger just for the chance of making one surprise attack. Setting sail, their custom when homeward-bound is to hurl one prisoner from every ten into a watery grave - chosen with heartless fairness by the drawing of lots, they consider it no more than a religious observance, this disgusting sacrifice their ritual of absolution.

Anxious as I am about these risks, it is the positive factors which reassure me: Firstly, the standards under which you sail are those of an ever-victorious nation. Secondly, a sensible man like you will never leave anything to chance. And thirdly..."

(Fragment surviving from a letter sent by the writer Sidonius to his friend Namatius, commander of the late-Roman navy in Gaul, 5th century AD)

XVII

Another shore. Far away.

The man walks up from the wide beach where the waves never stop pounding and 'The Old Grey Widowmaker' stretches limitless to the far horizon. He climbs up through the tall sand-dunes which roll along the margins of this coast, like a great wall built against the sea, and up to the boat landing.

There is a ship here in the course of construction and he runs his hand up the planed smoothness of its planking, then checks the curved spine of the keel by eye, just as he has done so many times before. The sets of ash oars are nearly all finished and lie neatly stacked inside the hull. It is his ship and it will not be long before its keel first kisses the sea.

Two small boys run down to meet him there. Each one takes him by a hand to drag him up through the drying fish nets then on, up through some more dunes, to a place where there is a cluster of houses.

The elder is his adopted son according to their laws, the one with a liking for apples whom he rescued from a battlefield on the death of his father, but the younger lad is proof of his own loins. He is careful to treat them both just the same. This is easier because they are both so much alike, each one with fair hair, blue eyes and a freckled snub nose. He is happy neither of them look like him, because it is better they should be framed in the image of their mother, so that they feel like full brothers.

Besides, there is not a man anywhere along the coast or in these villages with hair or eye so dark as he, for all the grey that invades it now.

He goes to the simple house where they all live together, a round pit dug into the ground and roofed with branches. Stooping his head to get in through the low door, he enters a dark world of familiar, homely smells, pitch-black until your eyes become used to it, the one central shaft of sunlight coiling with cooking smoke up from the hearth.

His wife is there and he fondly kisses her, because he is a man married later in life than many; a man who has had time to choose and who appreciates what a blessing the love of a good woman can be in an uncertain world. He toys with her carefully plaited hair, which is long, and fair; the colour of his sons'.

She is sad today because she knows that soon his ship will be ready and he will go a-raiding, taking risks with his life on the high seas in the hope of riches beyond the dreams of desperate people like themselves - the people forced to live in these barren lands, in their overcrowded villages amongst the dunes where the crops will not grow from wind-blown sand and salt.

She knows or almost believes without knowing that there are other peoples out there beyond the dunes who drive them to the sea; distant peoples far beyond Frisia, beyond even the cruel Scythians and those in turn who must press upon them; a mythical people who will merit nary a whisper in far-way Rome for generations yet, but whose awful horsemen already have a name to frighten children with; an unknown kind whose name is Hun.

But, for all their troubles, she is still so proud of him. Proud and loyal, because he is hers and a famous man on this coast, famous in all Frisia; what with his dark black hair and his peerless knowledge of the Red Crest's country; a man who can slip up their eastern estuaries and down their northern rivers, past their burghs filled with soldiers, without ever being detected.

So she kisses him back and plays with the jewellery hung around his neck, a rough gold pendant in the shape of Thor's Hammer and the little silver badge of office of a Governor's Beneficarius Consularis.

"All things from eternity are of like forms and come around in a circle"

(Marcus Aurelius, soldier, philosopher and Emperor of Rome 161– 80 A.D.)

XVIII

In the black car, they soon caught up with him, out there on the top road. Half-running, half-walking, half staggering down the lane along the chalky ridge-top, its route parallel to that densely-wooded dale from which the smoke of the burning house still came funnelling-up.

His coat was in tatters, his skin scorched and blackened, and his shoes had been lost in the blast. Only an obvious fixity of purpose and the anaesthesia of medical shock were keeping him going, suppressing the otherwise-disabling pain of red-raw and bleeding feet abraded on hard roads and the stony trackway.

"Stop the car, Pickering!"

They got out and held him upright, but his eyes were glassy and his speech vague. It was as if they were not there, as if he could not really see them.

"Where are you going, Tryton? What's happened down there?"

"Barbarians and fire. Gypsum and auburn..." he mumbled, lips parched and swollen from the fires.

"Get him a drink and sit him down in the car. He's talking utter gibberish!" ordered Superintendent Rivett impatiently. They doused his face in water and then Sergeant Pickering produced a small hip flask from his pocket. Their Superintendent, who had signed 'The Pledge', could not control his muttered disapproval of the demon drink, even as first aid, but they could see its contents revive the patient – at least for a while.

"Where are you going, Tryton? What's happened?"

"The Hall, the mansion in the woods...home of the Baynards. Explosion, big explosion....destroyed by fire... gone, all gone!" he gasped in hoarse tones.

Just then, as if to emphasise this fact, two straining fire engines came labouring up the hill from South Cave, their bells ringing and crews peering quizically at the idly-parked police car. Then they were gone.

The loyal Pickering was more sympathetic in his questioning: "What are you doing on the road, sir? Where are you heading for? Where's Miss Macsen?"

394

"The gypsum works at the end of the valley...the Baynards have kidnapped her ...the American woman... they took her this morning... she's being held somewhere...it must be there. The works. You've all got to help me! I've got to get there before something happens to her..."

"You've been with her all the time, or at least since yesterday morning, haven't you Tryton?" said Rivett slowly and gravely, making it sound like an accusation.

"Yes, I have! What does it matter?"

"For God's Sake, what is she to you, man? What's this hold she has over everyone? It's almost as if she's put a spell on you. Why, you've abandoned everything – your post, your duty...!" pressed Rivett, his cold lips pursed in thin disapproval. "Do you even know what she is; who or what you're dealing with?"

"What are you talking about? I think so, yes, of course I do...she's a historian.... dammit, she's a woman.... Look, what the hell else matters... what she is, or what you think she is? Or what she means to me. What matters is where she is now! Help me get there! I've got to get to her... before she comes to any harm!"

Even the puritanical Rivett must bow to the force of Tryton's pleading - his Constable's Oath gave precedence to the saving of life, just like everyone else's. He meekly agreed to pursue the rescue, instead of that firey column which all the other emergency services closing in from Hull and Brough seemed to be taking as priority.

It only took them a few minutes in the car to arrive at the enormous chalk quarry, lined with trees, in a corner of whose great white bowl the gypsum works were set. "BAYNARDS BRITISH GYPSUM" announced a painted sign, mounted beside the gap in the earthworks and spoil heaps they drove through.

"Stay here!" said Tryton and, still unshod, left them standing by the car with their firearms resting on the back seat, ready for use but unused. Astonishingly, even Rivett accepted the order without a word. This was something different. Yes, it was his enquiry but it was more than that. It was as if he was going somewhere they could not go. They were those who can only stand and wait.

Even on an overcast day, the reflected light off the brilliant white quarry walls and floor was blinding, making him screw-up his eyes against the glare. Crossing the rocky, exposed flatness of these abandoned chalk workings, Tryton began for the first time to be aware of pain in his feet and arms.

The gypsum works was a chaotic industrial assembly of girders, gantries, boilers, conveyor-belts and rock-crushers; some of these installations clad with flapping sheets of corrugated iron. A gigantic hopper hung over two mighty lorries; one of whose brethren had destroyed Maister's car, the yellow livery and black tower motif of the Baynards still visible under layers of chalk dust.

Tryton turned for a moment and squinted across the quarry floor to satisfy himself that Rivett and his men were remaining by the distant car, as he'd requested. They waved back. Tryton brought his arm across his chest instead.

Smoke from the massive fire in the dale was being blown down towards the quarry and starting to drift over its rim. Tryton was now in discernible discomfort from his blast wounds, which combined with the glare and smoke to cloud his vision. Trying to focus on the police car he found two vehicles parked side by side and only when he blinked did these reinforcements disappear.

"I must get on....I must find her."

He searched the buildings, the equipment sheds and workmen's huts, but there was not a soul to be seen. He checked the two lorries but their cabs were empty. Above them towered the hopper, a lofty structure sheathed in rusting tin. A white tower wreathed in smoke from the fire up the valley. He remembered, then....of course!

COHORS EQUITATA

Dragging himself along with growing difficulty, he found a metal staircase at the back which zig-zagged to the top. Putting his feet to the agony of its slatted slicing steps, he hauled himself painfully upwards.

As he got further up, the black Wolseley could be seen far below like a child's toy. Its fuzzy replication came and went with increasing frequency. Roderick Baynard had mentioned something about a Manager's Office and it looked as if there was a ramshackle structure of that description plonked on top of the hopper, to which these stairs led.

At every landing he reached, the pause for breath needed before resuming the ascent seemed to take longer. As he climbed higher, the smoke became thicker and got into his lungs.

Looking down through it, he could just make out what seemed to be the figures of wild horses galloping below the tower. He was sure some had riders. Funny that.... If his disorientation grew at these curious images, his determination did not diminish at all. He continued plodding steadily upwards, faithfully looking for Zuleika.

Suddenly he saw the shape of another person coming down the staircase towards him. Tryton froze. This figure did not pause and continued a brisk descent, almost ignoring him. It pushed past him by the handrail side, with sharp elbows hardly bothered to retract.

A man with dark hair and a neat beard yet somehow looking not so different to himself. He was dressed in a simple, open-necked, short sleeved tunic reaching down to his knees, carrying a small child whose tired blond head rested under his bristly chin. Tryton was going to say something but then the fog of smoke around him yellowed and became the nicotine-glossed emulsion of solid walls.

Tryton recognised the Casualty Information Bureau at 3, Ferensway Arcade and was aware of the miserable queue of which he was part shuffling forwards and upwards on the stair, to read the list of killed in last night's raid.

"Hallo, Spitfire Johnny!" He heard a woman's voice close to him but when he turned to face her there was no-one there.

As he got nearer the counter he could see lists were pinned to the yellow walls, their paper flapping in the strong wind which blew through them and down the valley, laden with particles of ash.

He felt sick and faint, thinking he was going to lose his balance, when someone took him by the arm and he heard a man's voice, gruff in his ear: "There's a Roman woman in the Infirmary!"

Tryton, irritated and confused, shrugged him off and pushed forward unsteadily to the information desk.

Here, waiting for him behind the counter, was a lovely girl with dark hair and sparkling brown eyes dressed in the navy-blue uniform of the Women's Royal Naval Service, her uniform cap pinned at jaunty angle to wavy locks.

"Jenny!" he said. "Gosh, am I glad to see you! You're looking absolutely gorgeous tonight but I was bloody worried, I'll tell you, after last night's raid. Look, now you're here, you've really got to help me! I'm looking out for an American woman called Zuleika Macsen. Do you know the name? Have you any idea where she might be?"

Jenny just smiled at him in that vivacious winning way she had and turned to gesture to a place behind the counter.

Here, some sort of Z-bed or couch was provided for staff to rest, where Zuleika Macsen reclined full-length, seemingly asleep. She was dressed in an elegant red shift of foreign style which came right to her ankles, belted in gold with knotted straps whose solid ends hung down off the bronze frame of the couch.

Over her heavy eyelids had been placed two coins. He knew straightaway exactly what issue they would be, of course; a silver aureus of that usurper Admiral, Carausius, and a bronze penny minted at Trier in Germany by Magnus Maximus himself, the Welsh usurper. Ronald Maister would have approved.

Back at the car, the four policemen had watched their shoeless colleague's progress with growing concern, but it was his loyal Sergeant who was the first to move.

"Good God!" said Pickering, as he began to run fast across the quarry towards the hopper tower, "He's going to fall!"

398

"We can only live in the present, the past is gone and the glorious future of dreams never comes"

(from a 'Powerpoint' presentation by Her Majesty's Inspector of Constabulary, Mr Vic Towell; Leeds, November 2006)

XIX

They were sitting at a metal table in the window of the wine bar with a good view of the Old High Street and people going by.

"You've been very helpful" he said.

"A pleasure" she replied. "Least I could do. Thank you for the drink. So what have you discovered as a result?"

"That the villa was completely destroyed by the quarry and there's no trace left of it today. That nobody ever wrote up a proper report of the site, even if all the finds – well, nearly all the finds – are in the museum over the road. And, of course, that one of the mosaics was stolen, shortly after the war."

"Yes", she said, "the locals still think the Americans took it."

"What do you think?"

"I don't know. How do you move something so big and so heavy? What made you so interested in the site, anyway?"

He smiled: "The villa. It's an interesting story. And there's a link. My grandfather was a policeman in Hull, just after the war."

"Oh, really", she said, "and what was he like?"

"I don't know. I never knew him. I think he was an Inspector."

"Well, you've obviously had a good day. Do you think you found what you were looking for?"

He rolled the last of the red wine around in his glass, refracting its colour across the aluminium table top, then looked directly across at her and smiled:

"Yes", he said, "I really think I have."

They were walking across the car park by the Marina, the wind from the sea on their faces.

"It's the red one" he said.

"Nice car."

"It's an Alfa Romeo. I'm trading it up next year for the new model. More power."

"Mmm, leather seats" she said, sliding in and stretching out her legs.

They were travelling fast on the dual carriageway out of town, the ruinous fish docks and beyond them the estuary flashing by on the left. He was trying to impress her with the car's acceleration.

"Where are we going?" she asked.

"I know a nice little hotel in the centre of York. It's Georgian."

"Now why should I like the sound of that so much?"

She smiled happily and reclined her seat slightly, strands and filaments of auburn hair spilling out over the back of the headrest to catch the sun.

Mosaic floor from Brantingham Roman villa: "The Tyche"
(Hull & East Riding Museums)

Photograph - the author: January 2007
(by kind permission, Hull Museums)

Author's note

The events described in this book are closely-based on known people, real places, partially-recorded events and incomplete physical evidence, much of which is still visible or discoverable today by the visitor. The rest of it is made up. You might want to decide which is which – or you might not. Either way, you might be surprised.

As described in most dictionaries, a mosaic is a picture made up of thousands of pieces of different-coloured stone or dried clay set in cement together to create a durable image. In the Mediterranean ancient world, mosaic was a popular type of flooring frequently found in the richer and more prestigious households. Not confined to such famous sites as the Pompeian or Italian cities of the period, even the villas of Roman Britain displayed these mosaic floors or pavements, many of them spectacular works of art of great size put there by house owners showing off their good taste and wealth to visitors. By their style, some modern experts claim a discernible 'school' or team of professional mosaicists was operating across East Yorkshire and North Lincolnshire in the early fourth century A.D. Were they based in Petuaria?

This book uses hundreds of known facts and then adds speculation to cement together a mosaic picture of the unknown, a possible explanation for one of the most puzzling, unsolved mysteries in Romano-British archaeology. The pavement that walked.

Like many provincial British museums (perhaps surprising to jaded metropolitans) the Hull & East Riding Museum in the High Street of Kingston-upon-Hull's historic old town presents its artefacts to a very high standard indeed. It is home to probably the finest collection of Roman mosaic art or frescoed wall-painting to be seen anywhere in Britain; rescued from great Roman houses of East Yorkshire and North Lincolnshire that once ran along and overlooked what we now call the Humber Estuary. In those days (according to the 1st century geographer Ptolemy) it was the Abvs or Arbus river. The surviving villas known along its banks held the most northerly examples of domestic art so far found within the Roman Empire. The wall-painting from Brantingham of the Tyche is undoubtedly the most mesmerising relic of them all. Her eyes bore into you.

One 1990s lunchtime in the Hull museum, I'd been standing there looking back at her for quite a while before I turned and idly read the caption to an old black and white photograph not noticed before, propped in the corner of a display cabinet since removed in more recent refurbishments. This was where I first read of the theft in 1948 of a Roman pavement previously discovered at Brantingham during the war. This footnote to an unsolved and forgotten outrage has intrigued me ever since. Unlike the other mosaics, this became the only one never to make it into the museum's permanent collection for display. Who on earth took it, why did they do it and how did they manage it? What happened to it and where is it now?

In offering one possible answer, I drew on local sources, archived newspapers and journalistic reports, as well as the opinions of professional archaeologists, to suggest a fictionalised solution to an astonishing crime. Two eyewitnesses who might still be alive are Peter Slack, who identified the body of the gladiator wearing silver-plated shoulder armour found at Brough (and then wrote up the villa site in 1951) and Sydney Coverdale, the young RAF airman who took aerial photographs of the villa at Brantingham in 1941. I'd love to meet them both. Unfortunately, not for want of trying, I've not found either, even if they could put me right over a few things. (If they do, then look out for a second edition). Till then, 'Tryton's notebook' must suffice and I hope some artistic licence over their roles or the precise dates can be forgiven. Choice and style of language is another difficult choice – modern tabloid vernacular lacks a dignity which came more naturally to people in other ages. Today, Latin is frowned-on.

Interesting as the real-life events of 60 years ago were; and even if the Baynards and their gypsum business are admitted as made-up; they don't answer the question of what really happened to the original Roman house or to those who lived there in 337 AD? (We do know fire was involved). So this part of the book provides us with a parallel narrative, itself closely based on fact, for which Marcus Ulpius Januarius and the Roman town are equally real. His ancestor's important inscription and memorial in stone can still seen in the Hull Museum. Dated to around 140 AD, it records the gift of a proscenium arch to a theatre in Petuaria - still the only recorded mention anywhere in Roman Britain of a known person occupying the position of magistrate (aedile). There is no reason to believe his inheritors and successors did not adopt the same family name nor at some point re-use his eminent forenames, too. Don't forget – a sophisticated and cultured elite of people who ethnically may originally have been Celts lived here according to classical Roman values for hundreds of years. Certainly his original gift provides a strong clue to civic works once to be seen in or near to Roman Brough-on-Humber; a tiny town whose magistrates court (where I once had the privilege of appearances) was only recently closed to save four-pence; so ending nearly two thousand years of locally-recorded justice unprecedented anywhere else in the British Isles. (Civic decay is nothing new). Similarly, the young Roman woman's auburn hair, with her jet hairpins and elephant ivory earrings testimony to her family's wealth, can still be seen in the Yorkshire Museum at York. They have always given me the shivers, just like they did for Michael Tryton in 1948.

The official status of Petuaria as a fleet base for a detachment of the British fleet, as well as a centre for Imperial officials travelling to the continent, is well evidenced in late-Roman documents later copied by monks. All in all, Petuaria seems genuine precursor to that strategic importance which the city of Hull, founded in the Middle Ages, still holds today. For anyone travelling by boats of shallow draught, the Humber is still a gateway into half of all England this side of the Pennines. Eight major rivers can be accessed from the North Sea over its threshold – the Ouse, Hull, Derwent, Wharfe, Aire, Don, Trent and Ancholme. That is why eight river goddesses shown reclining on the great mosaic from Brantingham are believed by many to represent the practical importance of these great English rivers in Roman times.

Whichever settlement guards the Humber is the pinch-point for all those wanting to attack or trade – whether Roman, Saxon, Viking, Dutch or German. From mediaeval times to the Civil War, Hull's Royal Arsenal provided a safe dropping-off and collection point for supplies and weapons needed for the English kings' endless campaigns in Scotland – hence the anxiety of Charles I to access it. Long before him, its safe distance from Scottish raids meant the base at Petuaria performed the same strategic functions of supply-base and jumping–off point for punitive campaigns in Caledonia by generals like Julius Agricola or later Emperors like Septimius Severus (based in and dying at York over a century afterwards).

Over the centuries, Hull has paid a high price for this key strategic role. Its sufferings during the Second World War were extreme even by the standards of London's 'Blitz'. As a port it made an obvious target that was easy to find from the air and in some ways the City is the real heroine of this book. The terrible fates of the Prudential Tower and the lovely Wrens immolated beneath it in May 1941 are accurately described. We owe them and everyone else who died in these raids a very great debt indeed, for whatever freedoms are left us today.

Out in the Humber, Bull Sand Fort, part of the anti-aircraft defences meant to prevent this sort of thing, is best seen today from the decks of a North Sea ferry en route for Holland, an incredible structure in its own right and home to some incredible tales. Even the football-mad gunner whose reluctant centre-forward chum dies there from insecticide is closely based on an authentic wartime event personally recounted to me by my good old friend, Joe Backus, who was that honest artilleryman and to whose fond memory (and his tragic friend) that chapter is respectfully dedicated.

What about Malton in North Yorkshire? Marcus Claudius Bassus was a known commander of the Ala Picentiana there, whilst Candidus himself and his links with that particular Ala at Derventio receive permanent record in a beautifully-lettered fragmentary dedication stone (see back cover). The original is still on view today in the Malton museum in the market square, not far from where it was first set up by the officers and men who garrisoned the place and perhaps first made it a racehorse town.

Nearby is a surviving carving of a big woman who helped hold up the door lintel of the House of the Winged Victories. (They were all real too, you see). As for the glorious Ala traceable back to Julius Caesar's Gallic Wars, it is an inevitable truth that hundreds of years later there came one final day when its men rode jingling out of Derventio fort, never to be seen there again.

And just one final thing: Even today, somewhere in the East Riding of Yorkshire, I know of another fine house that - quite

406

legitimately - holds part of yet another pavement from the Brantingham Villa, hidden inside its walls. Their fragment shows a wanton nymph. Unlike this book and sixty years later, the real story continues.....

Clive Ashman   **Cumbria, January 2008**

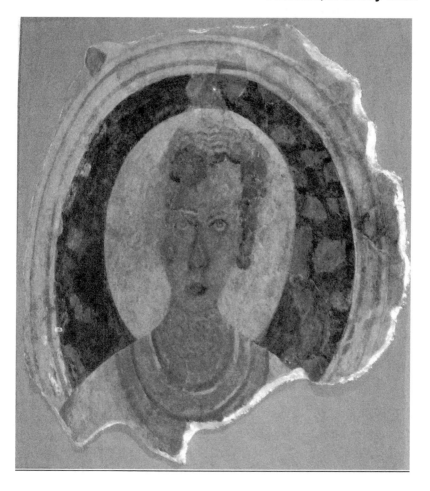

Wall-painting from Brantingham Roman villa: "The Tyche"
(Hull & East Riding Museums)

Photograph - the author; January 2007
(by kind permission, Hull Museums)

407

GLOSSARY of LATIN TERMS, PROPER NAMES and PLACE NAMES referred to in the text:

- **'Ab Urbe Condita':** 'From the Founding of the City' (of Rome). The calculation for the reckoning of years in Pre-Christian, Roman History.
- **Aedile:** A Magistrate in Roman times. The only surviving reference anywhere in Roman Britain to the named holder of such a civic office was found at Brough in East Yorkshire and can be seen today in the Hull Museums – in the dedication of a proscenium arch for a theatre at Petuaria by one Marcus Ulpus Januarius, aedile. (See below).
- **Ala:** Literally, a 'wing' - a regiment of cavalry, by definition serving on the 'wing' of an army. Usually 500 men (with the sole exception in Britain of the double-strength, or 'milliary', Ala Petriana, an elite regiment of 1,000 based at Stanwix, Carlisle).
- **Ala Picentiana:** Identified by archaeological discoveries as the resident cavalry garrison of Derventio (Malton) from the second century A.D. onwards. An earlier (first century A.D.) inscription from Dalmatia (modern Croatia) reports Lucius Rustius Picens as its commander. Although the regiment is recorded as having been raised even earlier, serving under Julius Caesar in the conquest of Gaul (France), Lucius Picens may well have given his name to the unit later on. Their fate or any withdrawal from Britain is not recorded, but they were certainly replaced by the Numerus Supervenientum Petuariensium from Brough by the 4th century A.D.
- **Abus Fluvinis:** The Humber Estuary.
- **Arcani:** Irregular native frontier scouts employed by the Roman Army who, for hundreds of years, assisted the garrison of Hadrian's Wall by acting as a form of 'Early Warning System' in the Border Country. (They were later blamed for treacherous assistance to the Barbarian Conspiracy in the 'Great Overwhelming' of Saxons and Picts combined, in 367 A.D.).
- **Aquae Arnemetiae:** The Roman spa town at Buxton, Derbyshire, still famous for its waters today. Good lead-mining country, too. The Romans saw no harm in lead water pipes, either, a practice some claim as principal reason for Rome's fall.
- **Ballista:** A bolt-firing single shot mechanical cross-bow of

varying size, whose chain-driven repeater design of Dionysius represented the most complex technology of ancient times and the Maxim gun of its day. (see 'Scientific American': March 1979)

• **Bassus** (M. Claudius): Officer recorded as commanding the Derventio garrison.

• **Beneficarius Consularis:** An officer on detached special duties - military or civil service.

• **Brigantes:** The major Celtic tribe whose area covered much of Northern England, on both sides of the Pennines.

• **Caldarium:** The hot room in a Roman baths.

• **Calleva Atrebatum:** The Roman city of Silchester, cantonal capital to the Atrebates tribe.

• **Carausius** (M. Mauseus): Admiral of the British Fleet, turned usurper 287 - 294 A.D. His successful use of sea-power attracted criticism, leading to U.D.I. for Britain. Murdered by his accountant, Allectus, who didn't last long himself.

• **Castra:** A military earthwork, camp or more permanent fortification, including some that later became solely civil settlements when the army moved out. Survives as a constituent place name all over Britain – usually as '...chester' (e.g. Manchester).

• **Cicerius Felix:** A mining engineer with poor personal hygiene. His popular style of hat is from Phyrgia (Asia Minor).

• **Classis Britannica:** The British Fleet (of the Roman Navy).

• **Cohors:** A cohort, being a military formation of 500 men at most, infantry or cavalry.

• **Cohors Equitata:** A mixed regiment of infantry and cavalry operating together.

• **Comes Litus Saxonicus:** The Count of the Saxon Shore. A military commander of the late-Roman forces and system of large forts which defended the east Coast of England from Saxon raids. Their need for this rank and system illustrates the problem.

• **Constans:** The third (surviving) son of Constantine the Great. Co-emperor with his brothers from 337 to 340 A.D.

• **Constantine I: ('The Great').** Sole Emperor of the entire Roman world from 324 to 337 A.D. First declared 'Augustus' by his late father's British legions (see Constantius Chlorus) at York in 306 A.D., he gradually developed his power thereafter by eliminating all his rivals, many of them close relatives by blood or marriage. Attributing his victory over his rival Maxentius in October 312 A.D. to the adoption by his soldiers of Christian flags and symbols after his vision of a fiery cross and the words "In This Sign Conquer", shortly before the Battle of Milvian Bridge outside Rome. His consistent support effectively elevated Christianity to the official religion of the Roman state, even if (for sound religious reasons) he was not himself baptised until his death-bed and allowed traditional pagan ceremonies of the Roman state to continue in parallel. A (seated) modern statue outside York Minster celebrates his life and contribution to the modern church. It also captures the arrogance of this pivotal but arguably deeply-flawed figure in the history of the Western world. Founder of Constantinople at Byzantium, modern Istanbul.

• **Constantine II:** The second (surviving) son of Constantine the Great (Constantinus). Co-emperor with his brothers from 337 to 340A.D. as a likewise-designated 'Caesar'.

• **Constantius Chlorus:** Roman general and father of Constantine the Great. He reigned for one year as a co-emperor with Galerius before dying at York after campaigning in Scotland. His earlier and perhaps most famous achievement had been the suppression of the usurper Allectus, the successor (by assassination) to the Admiral Caurasius. This was celebrated in commemorative gold medallions issued at the time (See the Arras Treasure) as representing the return of Britain to 'The Eternal Light' (of Rome).

• **Constantius:** The first (surviving) son of Constantine the Great. Co-emperor 337-340 A.D.

• **Corinium:** The Roman town at Cirencester, Gloucestershire.

• **Crispus:** The first-born son of Constantine the Great, by his first wife. Later murdered at least as a direct result of his father's orders if not necessarily his direct requirement.

• **Decurio:** (Military) A commander of ten men. (Civil) An official of a town council.

• **Delgovicia:** The small wayside settlement at Millington Pastures, near Pocklington, East Yorkshire.

• **Derventio:** The Roman town and cavalry fort at Old Malton, North Yorkshire.

• **Diocletian:** Roman Emperor from 284 to 305A.D. A

410

reformer and organiser who founded the Tetrarchy of senior and junior co-Emperors which Constantine later destroyed after not being selected himself.

- **Domestici et Protectores:** The personal bodyguard of the later Imperial Household, successors to the traditional Praetorian Guard destroyed by Constantine at the Milvian Bridge.
- **Draco:** The 'dragon' standard of later-Roman cavalry was copied from the Sarmatians of eastern Europe; a people first drafted to serve in the Roman army as foederati and hostages by Marcus Aurelius in the late 2nd century A.D. Their scale-armour-clad heavy cavalry or cataphracti set a fashion the Romans adopted widely and is often thought to represent the likely appearance of those Romano-British 'knights', under the command of one Arthur or Artos, who successfully fought off the Saxons in the late 5th and early 6th centuries A.D. under a similar standard. (The red dragon of Wales?) As a military standard, itself seen by many historians as symbolising an increasing barbarism and decline in effectiveness of the later Roman army.
- **Dux Britannarium:** The Duke of Britain, a military commander of all late-Roman land forces in Britain, with the exception of the Saxon Shore. (No cushy number either, because the particular incumbent holding office in 367 A.D., one Fullofaudes who sounds like a barbarian, was killed in action in an ambush somewhere up in the Pennines).
- **Eboracum:** The Roman city and legionary fortress at York. "Place of the Boar". Also a Colonia for veterans.
- **Flavia Caesariensis:** When late Roman Britain was divided into four separate provinces following its recovery by the junior Caesar, Constantius Chlorus, from the usurpers Carausius and Allectus, this was the name given to the northern frontier region governed from Eboracum and extending right up to Hadrian's Wall.
- **Flavius Candidus:** A military veteran employed as a special enquiry agent in the service of the Vicarius, as beneficarius consularis. The name of Candidus is recorded on an undated, fragmentary dedicatory inscription made by the Prefect of the Ala Pincentiana and found at Malton. (See illustration). Could this be the only surviving relic of the Ala's anniversary parade?
- **Frumentarii:** The secret police of the late Roman state.

(The name is derived from their original job of civil servants overseeing the distribution of grain, which gave them widespread contacts across the Empire and a 'cover').

• **Foederati:** Allies. In this case, the Saxon mercenaries brought over to defend Britain against other Saxon raiders. A short-sighted, short-term remedy with long-term consequences

• **Gubernator:** A river pilot working for the army, typical of the trade-based Roman soldiery and their varied skills.

• **Gesoriacum:** The Roman port and naval base at Boulogne in Northern France (Gaul).

• **Gladius:** A short sword, used for stabbing. The classic Roman weapon of the Republic and earlier Empire. (See spatha).

• **Hippika Gymnasia:** Ritual parade 'sports' for Roman cavalry, used to develop technical skills and unit discipline.

• **Honoratus:** Name of a junior officer of the Ala Picentiana at Derventio, commanding a doomed turma.

• **Januarius** (Marcus Ulpius): A prominent citizien of Petuaria. The proscenium stage of a theatre there was shown as the gift of a magistrate of this name in an inscription found at Brough-on-Humber, but dated to c.140 A.D. (Predecessor to a later magistrate of the same family, bearing his ancestor's name in this story? Such human continuity is hardly inconceivable.)

• **Laeti:** The laity. Low-grade militia or mercenaries. (See foederati). In later periods, relied on increasingly for defence.

• **Legatus Legionis:** Traditional title for the commander of a Legion, pre-Severus, who outlawed it.

• **Legio VI Victrix:** The Sixth Victorious Legion, based at York (Eboracum - the Colonia).

• **Limitanei:** Frontier troops.

• **Lindum Coloniae:** The Roman city at Lincoln, also honoured with the title of 'Colonia' because it was an official settlement of army veterans from early times.

• **Londinium Caesariensis:** The Roman city of London, capital of the Province. (The secondary honorific title was a later period addition under Chlorus, post the Carausian secession).

• **Longinus:** A known Vicarius of Britain, and identified in this account as father-in-law to M. Ulpius Januarius as well as the employer of the Flavius Candidus described above.

- **Luguvallium:** the Roman city of Carlisle.
- **Magister Ballistae:** Master of the Catapults. A specialist technical adviser and military appointment in defence work.
- **Magnus Maximus:** Not the last of the British Usurpers, but the last one of real significance. He stripped the Province bare of troops in order to cross the Channel and pursue his claim to the Purple. Still remembered in surviving Welsh folklore as 'Macsen Wledig'. Killed 388 A.D. in southern Gaul (France) or possibly Italy. Having fatally weakened its garrison, the last chance of Roman Britain's survival probably died with him.
- **Maximianus:** Co-emperor in the West with Diocletian 286-305 A.D. under the tetrarchic system of two senior emperors (Augustii) assisted by two junior emperors (Caesarii) set up by Diocletian, a system faithfully served by Constantius Chlorus and finally destroyed by Constantine the Great in 324 A.D.
- **Mithras:** A Persian Sun God who fought against dark and evil. Much favoured by soldiers and a serious rival to Christianity.
- **Navio:** Roman fort guarding lead mines and the Hope Valley in Derbyshire's Peak District.
- **Nicomedes of Epidaurus:** A Greek physician and adherent to the cult of Aesculapius who treats Candidus at Petuaria. A client of his usual patron, M. Ulpius Januarius.
- **Notitia Dignitatum tam Civilium quam Militarium In Partibus Orientis et In Partibus Occidentis:** The Army and Civil List. An official record of all officers and their places of station with Itineraries or routes in between, covering both the Eastern and Western (late) Roman Empires. If the edition we have is from 395 A.D., it must have had predecessors.
- **Numerus Barcariorum Tigrisiensium:** The specialist military unit of Tigris Boatmen based at Brough. Previously based at Lancaster but originally raised in Iraq.
- **Numerus Supervenientium Petuariensium:** The Unit of Petuaria Interceptors. Low-grade troops for low-grade work (and, later on, posted up to Derventio sometime after the Ala Picentiana had finally left).
- **Opportunum Sinus:** "The Gulf of Oppportunity/Advantage": the name given in Ptolemy's Geography (early 2nd century AD) to the land north of the Humber that lies between present-day Goole and Bridlington: i.e

modern East Yorkshire. ("Rich lands occupied by shadowy beings").

• **Parisii:** The Celtic tribe whose area covered all of what is now East Yorkshire and whose blood relatives in France (Gaul) gave their name to Paris. Inhabitants of the Opportunum Sinus and therefore, in Ptolemy's view, presumably the shadowy beings he describes. Seem more cultured than the Brigantes.

• **Petuaria Civitas Parisiorum:** (NB: suggested spellings vary: e.g. *'Parisorum'*) The Roman town and naval base at Brough-on-Humber. Cantonal capital to the Parisii tribe, one fourth of their territory or 'ridings'. (See above and also *'Tyche'*).

• **Pictae:** Green-painted patrol vessels of the Roman Navy. Even the sails and the sailor's uniforms were green. First recorded example of marine camouflage, their title was probably meant as something of a pun, since Pictish raiders trying to outflank the Wall were also their primary targets, after Saxons. Construction style unknown – probably looked more like merchant ships. To operate regularly in the North Sea or the Irish sea, even within sight of land as Roman sailors usually preferred, these scout ships must have been rather more rounded and substantial than the usual Mediterranean galley-type.

• **Picti:** 'The Painted People'. A mysterious Celtic race from Northern Scotland of which little is known apart from their warlike nature. Fierce enemies both of Rome and their southern upland Celtic neighbours alike, by land and sea, for hundreds of years.

• **Portus Dubris:** The Roman port at Dover in Kent - H.Q. to Classis Britannica – whose Roman lighthouse survives to this day on the cliffs only because the Saxons later thought it would make a handy belfry.

• **Praefectus:** Prefect. Commander of a larger military unit of 500-1000 men.

• **Praefectus Legionis:** Commander of a Legion in the later period, reflecting their reduced size and status (i.e. no longer a Legatus Legionis, see above).

• **Praefectus Reliquationis Classis:** An example of this rank is recorded in the Bristol Channel. Literally, the commander of the rest of the fleet (i.e. a detachment from the main fleet, as based at Petuaria).

• **Praeses:** A very senior civil administrator of equestrian rank, the civil governor of a late Roman sub-province such as

414

Flavia Caesariensis.

- **Praetorium:** The commander's house inside the standardised layout of a Roman fort.
- **Principia:** The headquarters and administration building at the centre of a Roman fort, also doubling as the main weapons store and housing the chapel of the standards.
- **Protius** (Gaius Julius): Imperial Procurator, proprietor of the large villa at Vinovium (Winteringham) on the Abus river, known director of the Lutudarum mining company.
- **Rostra:** A platform or tribunal from which a Roman general or civic leader would address his followers and troops. (Original in the Forum at Rome). Visible as a mound in many surviving Roman forts in Britain today, usually inside the main hall of the Principia or on the parade ground (e.g. Hardknott).
- **Rufinus** (M.): An Abus river pilot, serving on army supply boats working the Eboracum routes.
- **Senilis** (M.): A Petuarian magistrate of declining intellect and advancing years.
- **Sabinus** (Claudius): The military commander of the Tigris Boatmen at Petuaria, a specialist amphibious unit originally raised in Iraq, the Special Boat Section of its day.
- **Societas Argentorum Lutudarensis:** 'SOC LUT BRIT EX ARG': A privately-owned silver/lead mining and exporting company based in the Derbyshire hills near Matlock, whose operations are known from their official stamp on lead ingots ('*pigs*') found both in Britain & Gaul – including some near Brough stamped with the name of Gaius Julius Protius.
- **Sol Invicto:** The Unconquered Sun God, a single deity religion to which Constantine the Great also maintained some ambiguous and politicised adherence during his lifetime.
- **Spatha:** A long sword, for slashing at a distance. More typical of barbarians or suitable for mounted cavalry but, in the Later-Roman army, became a standard infantry weapon replacing the legendary short sword and close-in stabbing. (Another symptom of declining standards?)
- **Tepidarium:** The warm room in a Roman baths.
- **Taranis:** A wayfaring blacksmith, honourably discharged from army service after an amputation typical of Roman combat medicine. Appropriately, his name is shared with a bearded

Celtic god of wheels and smiths (Corbridge). Like many Celtic Gods, Taranis was considered by the Romans to be transferable to equivalents in their superior hierarchy of deities – here, both Zeus/Jupiter and Sol would apply.

• **Triclinium:** The formal dining room in a traditional Roman house, where meals were eaten lying-down, naturally.

• **Turma:** A cavalry squadron, as a sub-unit of an Ala.

• **Trimalchio:** A Praefectus Reliquationis Classis or sub-admiral commanding the Abus Squadron, prone to dabbling in politics.

• **Tyche:** In Greek mythology, a Tyche was the principal female deity governing the fortune and prosperity of a city. She symbolised its destiny. This was not an abstract idea but a literal belief. Literally, the word meant "luck", so equating to the later Roman goddess 'Fortuna'. During the Hellenistic period, most Greek settlements came to have their own specific version, customised to be identifiable with their own city (e.g. Athena) usually wearing a mural crown resembling the walls of their city.

In classical literature, she might be identified as traceable through different genealogies, for instance as a daughter of Hermes and Aphrodite, or considered to be one of the Oceanids, daughters of Oceanus and Tethys or Zeus. She was also considered to be connected with Nemesis, the god of fates and death worshipped by gladiators before entering the arena (e.g. as found at Chester). In a world where life expectancy was still very short compared to modern expectations (an average of 25 years for ordinary folk in Roman Britain), the peoples of the classical and Celtic worlds were intensely superstitious, even about the most mundane aspects of life. It is hard to understate this outlook - e.g. it was strongly believed that every place and creature had its own genius or attendant spirit(s) as reflected in countless dedications and sacrifices.

As a result, versions of Tyche appear on many coins of both the Greek and Roman period. In Roman Britain, it appears the cities of this period followed the Hellenistic convention, Londinium providing examples both in artefacts and coinage. Later, in medieval art, she continued as an idea, being shown carrying a cornucopia or an emblematic ship's rudder. Her depiction beside the wheel of fortune or standing on the wheel, illustrated the continuation of the classical idea of the Tyche into later, Christian periods as a figure still thought central to the circle of fate.

The famous figure of **Britannia** herself is a notable version of Tyche. She first appears on a coin of the Emperor Hadrian as a representation of the island province and continued to do so throughout the Roman period. She was later taken up as an emblem by King Charles II after the Restoration, with his mistress Nell Gwynne as the apocryphal model for coinage, but continues as a potent emblem of this country and its luck into modern times. In both mosaics and wall-paintings recovered from the Roman villa at Brantingham, East Yorks, and now displayed in Hull, the presentation of head and shoulder female portraits strongly suggest this type of symbolic being, rather than any ordinary portraiture. These figures or perhaps even this one figure can be realistically be expected to be associated with the closely-adjoining civitas or town at Brough-on-Humber (see Petuaria Civitas Parisiorum) or other settlements of the period which are associated with the local Parisii tribe. Another similar example was found in the remains of painted wall-plaster from a house at Derventio (Malton).

- **Uricon:** An abbreviated form of the correct name 'Viriconium'; used by A.E. Housman in his poem "On Wenlock Edge" for the important Roman city at Wroexeter in Shropshire. (Its site subsequently abandoned after the Roman period in favour of what became Shrewsbury).
- **Vercovicium:** An infantry cohort fort on Hadrian's Wall at Housesteads, Northumberland, where the hospital building has been identified by archaeologists and Candidus first received emergency treatment.
- **Vexillatio:** A detachment of soldiers, split off from their main unit or place of garrison.
- **Vexillum:** A unit flag of such a detachment, mounted horizontally on a transverse cross-pole and usually embroidered with the name of the unit or painted with a figure of Victory.
- **Vinovium:** Speculative but credible place-name for the large villa of Gaius Julius Protius and the ferry haven at Winteringham, Lincolnshire, known to have been situated on the south bank of the Humber where the Roman road from London and Lincoln, now known as Ermine Street, ends.
- **Vicarius:** The senior civil and administrative authority in

417

late-Roman Britain, to whom the civil governors of the four sub-provinces into which the Island had by then been divided were subordinate. The boss of Flavius Candidus. He had no direct control over the Army while the Army itself ran under two commanders - the Dux Britannarium and the Comes Litus Saxonicus – who equally had no control over his administration. (An obvious recipe for trouble and confusion, itself specifically-designed to avoid other types of trouble – i.e. usurpers. Kept the Emperor safe but the provinces in chaos, since the military and civil powers would rarely co-operate).

- **Vicus:** A small town or village of legally-acknowledged civic status; usually adjoining a permanent military fort. Its population typically comprised soldiers' families, traders and retired veterans and may be governed by a town council.
- **Votadini:** One of the 'client' tribes of Southern Scotland, north of Hadrian's Wall, generally kept loyal to Rome by regular payments of silver scrap and other booty. In later periods known as the Goddodin. (An epic poem told by their great harpist Aneurin tells the story of how 300 of their chosen warriors marched south in about 625 A.D. to confront the Saxon army in a suicidal battle fought in the ruins of "Cattraeth" - modern Catterick, Roman "Cataractonium", by northern Celts who still thought themselves the true defenders of a Roman heritage).

- Final footnote on two areas of artistic licence:
- (i) Strictly, **'Greek fire'** as a molten projectile fired from ships was probably not fully-perfected until Byzantine times (c.7th century A.D.) and
- (ii) Even if **gladiatorial combat** was opposed by Christian Emperors, it survived as a popular entertainment until first its suspension by Honorius and then its final abolition by Valentinian in 438 A.D, by which time most other recognisable features of Roman life had disintegrated anyway. However, in the circumstances, I'd still claim the idea of local moralists and zealots outlawing it in Britain – perhaps in deference to Constantine and just a little sooner than elsewhere - as more than likely and perfectly possible.....

BIBLIOGRAPHY

(Hull) Daily Mail, Saturday, 27th September 1941 edition: article: "New Roman pavements found at Brough" and Yorkshire Post, Monday, 29th September 1941.

"Roman Yorkshire 1941" - Yorkshire Archaeological Journal

"Roman Yorkshire" (Ed. D.Greene F.S.A): "Report on a Roman Villa at Brantingham, E. Yorks." Yorkshire Archaeological Journal 1951 - P.E. Slack

C.I.B.A. Technical notes on the use of 'Araldite' in the restoration of Roman mosaics – excavations at Brantingham - July 1965

"Excavations at Brough on Humber 1958-1961" J. Wacher 1964

"Brantingham Roman Villa: discoveries in 1962" - J. Liversedge; D.J. Smith and I.M. Stead. "Britannia - A Journal of Romano-British and kindred studies" Volume 4, 1973.

"Derventio/Malton: Roman Fort & Civilian Settlement" L.P.Wenham 1974.

"Roman Mosaics in Britain: An Introduction to their schemes and a catalogue of paintings" - D.S. Neal 1981.

"New Light on the Parisi: recent discoveries in Iron Age and Roman East Yorkshire" E. Riding Archaeological Society with University of Hull – editor P. Halkon 1989 (and subsequent editions).

"Brading, Brantingham and York: a new look at some fourth-century mosaics" - R. Ling "Britannia - A Journal of Romano-British and kindred studies" Volume 22, 1991.

"Roman Humberside" (2nd edn.) Humberside County Council Archaeology Unit: B. Sitch and A. Williams 1992.

"Roman Mosaics of Britain: Volume I: Northern Britain incorporating the Midlands & East Anglia": - D.S. Neal & S.R. Cosh 'Society of Antiquaries of London' 2002 Illuminata Publishers.

"The Roman Mosaics at Hull" D.S. Smith (3rd edition) 2005, M. Foreman and D. Crowther Hull & East Riding Museums & Art Gallery.

Partial dedication slab in the Malton Museum:

CAN….(DIDVS)   Candidus….. (*and*?)
PRAE…(FECTVS)   The Prefect
PICENT…(IANAE)   Of the Ala Picentiana
D….(ONVM)   Gave (*this*).
(Illustration by the author)